THE GIFT

A Love in O'Leary Novel

MAY ARCHER

Cover Art: Shanoff Designs
Editing: Sandra, One Love Editing
Professional Beta Reader: Leslie Copeland
Beta Reader: Eden Finley

All the good bits are theirs, and any mistakes are my own!

For every reader who's unapologetically enthusiastic in their love for the books they read, and for every author whose finger shakes when they click publish.

The Love in O'Leary Series

*DENOTES NOVELLA

The Date* *(Ash & Cal)*
The Fall *(Silas & Everett)*
The Gift *(Daniel & Julian)*
The Note* *(Tyler & Gus)*
The Secret *(Micah & Constantine)*
The World* *(Taika & Ethan)*
The Fire *(Jamie & Parker)*
The Night *(Liam & Gideon)*
The Castle* *(Brian & Dare)*
The Light* *(Mark & Fran)*

The Gift

Daniel

I suck at relationships and don't trust anyone, but there are reasons for that. For one thing, every person I've ever cared about has let me down. The only recent exception: O'Leary's town veterinarian...my new best friend.

I came to O'Leary for a fresh start. To pare things down to essentials. To forget about the failures in my past. The last thing I need is complications, and most definitely
Not.
A.
Boyfriend.

Julian

I've lived in O'Leary my entire life and learned to fly under the radar a long time ago. I do what's expected, say what's expected, and keep to myself as much as possible. It's a hell of a lot simpler spending my time working with animals than trying to interact with actual people. The one unlikely exception: the gorgeous guy who moved to a cabin just outside of town and somehow became my best friend.

But friendships are complicated, and one morning I find myself accidentally telling the whole town the biggest lie of my life. Which is how Daniel Michaelson, my very straight, very hot best friend becomes my fake boyfriend, even though he's most definitely
Not.
My.
Lover.

Success is never final and failure never fatal. It's courage that counts.

George F. Tilton

Chapter One

DANIEL

Last May

"Good morning, Daniel."

Three innocuous words, but somehow my father managed to pack those suckers with enough censure, impatience, and foreboding to make me regret picking up the phone. He was magic like that. And me? I was an idiot. Fool me once, Dad, shame on you. Fool me seven hundred and forty-three times, and I should really know better than to answer the damn call.

"Dad. Everything okay with you and Mom?"

"Yes, of course," he said, and just like that, the pleasantries were over. There would be no *How the heck are you, Daniel? What have you been doing with yourself since the shit show last Christmas? Where are you living, how are you handling the total implosion of your career and friendships, can I help?*

No, if I wanted those lines written, I'd need to write them myself, but for some other character. Someone who hadn't fucked himself over like I had.

"I was simply calling to see what time you and Ingrid

would be arriving at the house, since you haven't bothered to email and let us know."

I was stunned into silence for a second because *wow*. There was a lot to unpack there.

I took the phone into the living room and plopped down on the ancient sofa that had come with the little cabin I'd purchased on the outskirts of Nowheresville, New York, already feeling a headache forming behind my eyes. I hadn't had a migraine since January, when I'd left the city, and all it took was five seconds of conversation with the man who'd spawned me to bring one back.

Like I said, he was magic.

"Dad, I'm not coming this weekend."

I would have thought that would be obvious. Our last conversation, sometime after the eggnog martinis but before the caterers had brought out the lavish Christmas feast, had hardly been the kind to inspire filial devotion, unless there was a son out there who *enjoyed* being told he was a disappointment.

"You're a Michaelson, Daniel. You've been quick to accept the privileges that come with being a member of this family, but you refuse to live up to our expectations. Is it any wonder your marriage failed? Is it any wonder your friends don't want any part of you anymore?"

My gut twisted painfully, remembering.

"Find a new career," he'd said. *"Your last endeavor was lucrative, but not stable. Do something that will allow you to support a family and put that college degree your grandfather paid for to use for once."*

Basically the old "get a job and stop being a freeloader" conversation, but with a Michaelsons-of-Madison-Avenue twist: get a job we can brag about at the country club, preferably one that brings as much prestige as your writing career did, but that won't crash down around your ears and taint us by association. Again.

There was a reason I'd put that life behind me. There was a reason, a very good reason, why I'd kept my cell phone in a drawer since moving to this cabin, and had avoided any interaction beyond an exchange of pleasantries when buying groceries or getting quarters for the laundromat. There was a reason why sometimes, these days, I got startled when I heard another human voice because I'd spent most of the winter and all of the spring as a virtual hermit.

People were awful. When you were successful, they flocked to you like pigeons at the park, greedily pecking at the crumbs of your happiness. But when you had nothing left to give them, every one of them would fly away, and one or two would shit on your head as they fled.

I wouldn't forget again. I'd get it tattooed on me if necessary.

"Don't be ridiculous, Daniel, *please*," my father said. He made it sound like I was a toddler who wouldn't put on his shoes, and I swear when he talked to me that way, I felt like one.

"Dad, Ingrid and I are divorced—it was finalized over a year ago. What in the world made you think I'd be bringing my ex-wife to your house in the Hamptons for Memorial Day? And since I haven't spoken to you or Mom in months, what made you think I'd be coming in the first place?"

He sighed. "Because it's tradition, Daniel. Everyone is expecting you."

Expectation was literally the worst word in the human language. To expect something was to basically set yourself up for disappointment, and to have someone expect something from *you*? Even worse. So much worse.

"You're going to have to get over it," I said brightly. "I've already got plans here."

My father sighed. "Where is *here*? And what's more important than being with your family?"

I chuckled to myself. If I could tell him I was sunning myself on the Riviera or communing with Buddhist monks, he could work with that. Sigh about my temperamental artist's nature and collect sympathy from his friends.

"Tiny little cabin in the middle of nowhere. I bought myself an old pickup, and I might try my hand at writing country music lyrics. What rhymes with 'I'm way too old to justify my life to my father'?"

A sharp inhale. A pause. I could see his jaw twitching in my mind's eye since God knew I'd seen it enough in person.

"Fine. I'll tell your mother not to bother having your room made up. And from now on, we'll assume you don't wish to be included in our family gatherings. Goodbye, Daniel."

The silence in my ear was as loud as the slamming of a door.

Why did I always come off as the bad guy in these conversations? Was it so wrong to just want to live my life in peace? To let my accountants handle my money while I took a sabbatical for a year, or a decade, or the rest of my life? Seriously, was it selfish to just want to *be*?

I wished there was someone I could ask, but there wasn't another soul around for miles.

I threw the phone against the sofa cushion and rubbed a hand through my hair. It was getting long now. Maybe one of these days, I'd stop shaving, too, and go full-on mountain man. I had only myself to please, after all.

I grabbed a book from the stack on the floor and tried to read, but I couldn't. I'd done all the little chores around the cabin, and my fridge was stocked. I had nothing to do, and no one was expecting me, which was exactly the way I wanted it, but after that phone call I couldn't enjoy it. I was too aware of the solitude, too aware of myself. There wasn't a single ticking clock, or honk, or gurgle of water from someone else's pipes. Even the refrigerator was silent. The sound of my own heartbeat was making my headache worse.

I grabbed a sweatshirt and my hiking boots—one of the few things from my old life I hadn't boxed up and donated before coming here—and set out on the trail I'd discovered behind my house that led into the woods.

No one ever came out this way. The cabin I'd purchased sight-unseen last winter was located about a quarter of a mile down an unpaved driveway from Route 222—which O'Learians called the Camden Road since it led from Camden to O'Leary and no one in this place had any imagination, as far as I could tell. The other side of the highway was state park land and occasionally got hikers. I'd met one or two when I ventured over that way to tramp around Lake Loughton or climb Jane's Peak. But this side of the road was all mine. Sixty acres of forested land, purchased for a song… or, more accurately, for a sizable chunk of my remaining inheritance from Grandfather Michaelson, a man who'd died when I was an infant, but had nevertheless been the single best and most influential member of my family.

I wondered if *he'd* have been disappointed too, if he were still alive… and then I stopped myself. I hated all kinds of parties, but pity parties were the worst.

"You are here because *you* chose this," I reminded myself firmly. "Forget everything that came before, everything that wants to drag you down. Do not give one more ounce of headspace to a bunch of assholes who pretended to be your friends, or the woman who claimed to love you, or your goddamn parents, Daniel Michaelson. The past is in the past. Move the fuck *on*."

I nodded to myself, like I was accepting my own advice, and I rolled my eyes. Talking to myself was one thing. Having a conversation with myself was another.

I got maybe a hundred yards up the trail, not very far at all, when I spotted a big bunch of crows all huddled together in a natural clearing just off the path. A couple were startled by my arrival, but the others didn't seem to care. They were too busy pecking at something on the ground—a little brown mass huddled there, unmoving. An animal of some kind. And the fucking crows had killed it.

Now, you could say whatever you wanted about the circle of life or whatever. You could tell me that nature is nature and I should stay out of its business when it wasn't actively attacking me. I would have agreed with you on any other day. But on this particular day, at this particular time, I felt an instant, earnest kinship with that little animal that I knew would mortify me when I remembered it later. The animal was all alone, with no one to protect it, and had been set upon by a hundred beady-eyed assholes who chose to spend their lives picking at someone else. The poor thing needed to be buried. To be shown a little care and respect that it hadn't gotten while it was alive.

I rushed forward, flapping my arms, and the crows flew away, leaving me to kneel down by the animal. It was a bird. A little owl, I was pretty sure. It was covered in blood.

I crouched there, feeling more miserable than ever, and I wondered if there was a shovel in the shed full of junk the last owner of the cabin had left behind. Then the sweet baby twitched. It was barely a movement—a quick ruffle of feathers on its wing—but it looked like she might be breathing.

I didn't even think before I whipped my sweatshirt off

and wrapped it around the bird, carrying it back to the cabin only long enough to grab my keys, and then cradling it on my lap as I drove through the warm summer air to O'Leary.

I didn't have the first clue about animals. My mother was the type who donated huge sums to the humane society but wouldn't allow a pet to spoil the pristine sterility of the modern condo where I'd grown up, and my interest in hiking had begun at precisely the moment I realized that having no cable or internet at the cabin meant not only freedom from social media but also no access to any form of entertainment. I had no clue if it was possible to save a bird like this, or whether any old veterinarian could do it. Were there owl specialists? Was it likely there were any around O'Leary?

"I'm going to find you an expert," I told it, like it spoke English or I spoke Owlish. "We're going to get you fixed up, okay? You'll be hunting all the mice, soon as possible." Owls did eat mice, right? I was pretty sure.

I pulled into a spot outside Lyon's Imperial, the town grocery store, since that was the place I was most familiar with. An older man I'd never met before was setting up a display of charcoal and other grilling supplies out front, festooning everything with red, white, and blue bunting, and as soon as I slammed the truck into Park, I hopped out of the truck, cradling this bloody creature to my chest.

"Do you have a vet?" I demanded. "An animal doctor?" I elaborated when he looked at me like I had three heads. "Please, I found an injured bird."

The man—Abe, according to his name tag—frowned down at my sweatshirt. "What kind?"

"An owl. It's pretty bad off," I said. "It needs medical help *now*."

The old man's face twisted with a kind of resigned pity.

"Wild animal," he said. "Better to just leave them be, son. That's how nature works."

He had a point. I knew he did. But I was *not* his son, and I was tired of old men who tried to tell me how the fucking world worked. I felt like this little owl's fate and mine were intertwined in some weird way. Like giving up on her would be like giving in.

"But do you have a vet?" I repeated. I wasn't going to argue with this guy about whether some animals were more deserving of saving than others. "I can pay whatever he charges."

"Well, we got our Doc Ross, o'course." He pointed at a building a fair distance down and across the street. "Clinic's next to the bright red door. Can't miss it."

I nodded and ran off without even thanking him.

Doc Ross, I thought to myself. The name did not inspire confidence. It brought to mind either a man more ancient than the one who'd given me the directions—and with the same attitudes about wild creatures—or the mad scientist dude from *Back to the Future*. But I had enough money to bribe the guy, if it came to that, and I wouldn't hesitate.

I jogged down the street while the residents of O'Leary watched in fascination. *Nothing to see here, folks. Just the serial killer from the cabin in the woods, trotting a bloody corpse through your town.* From the little bits of town life I'd overheard at the grocery store, I could imagine this would be gossiped over for weeks, but I didn't care.

Let them call me strange. I'd been called far worse.

I pulled open the glass door to the clinic, making the bells jangle, and stepped inside. The waiting room was dark and the reception desk was empty. A quick check at the clock on the wall showed that it was five minutes before five. On a Friday. Before a holiday weekend.

Shit.

"Whadja forget, Kath?"

A man in a white lab coat emerged from the back room. He was short and slight, with dark hair and enormous blue eyes, like an angel, or one of those creepy little figurines a grandma might collect—though I couldn't say for sure, since my grandmother had preferred collecting husbands, at least after my grandfather died.

He'd stared at me for a second in silence, no doubt taking in the fact that I was several inches taller than him, half again as heavy, and covered in blood, but I'd give the kid this much, he didn't hesitate to walk forward, his eyes on the bundle in my arms.

"What's going on?" he demanded.

"Abe at the Imperial said you're the vet?" I was desperately hoping that he wasn't, that he was some vet trainee and there was an older, more competent person who'd come out and save the day.

"Yes," he said, killing that hope. "I'm Julian Ross. Is that a Saw-whet owl?"

I blinked. "I have no idea what kind of owl it is. I found it in the woods. Is it… can you…"

The man—Julian—looked up at me, and those blue eyes were absolutely resolute. "Bring it into the exam room."

He didn't hesitate. While I brought the bird in and laid it on the exam table, he'd gathered a bunch of equipment and gotten to work, talking to me the whole time.

"It's called a saw-whet owl because apparently it sounds like a saw being whetted," he said. "Which is amusing, really, because I'm way more familiar with the sound this bird makes than I am with the sound of someone sharpening a saw, but things keep their names long after the names are useful, huh?"

"I… yes, I guess."

"Hmm. It's a female. Poor thing. Any idea what happened to it?"

"A bunch of birds, crows I think, were pecking her to death." I sounded outraged because I was. Still. Ridiculously so.

He shook his head sadly. "Did you know a group of crows is called a murder? Another name that people don't understand much anymore. Crows can be a bunch of thugs. They'll gang up on another bird, like this owl, even though owls don't usually prey on them."

"They do it for no reason?" I asked. "I thought everything in nature had a reason."

"Eh. You watch too much television," Julian said, giving me a smile that softened his teasing words. "Or maybe there *is* a reason, but scientists don't know it yet. I could come up with some theories…"

I was distracted, completely. I'd never met a human like Julian Ross before. He had no idea who I was—not my name, or the balance in my bank account, not what I'd done for a living, or any part of my ridiculous history. He didn't even know whether I could fucking *pay him*. And yet he was working on this bird—this wild animal—like it was the most important thing he'd ever done in his life.

He kept up the soothing patter of conversation for what felt like hours. It was fascinating shit—like if an episode of Keeping Up with the Kardashians and Nature Planet had a baby—and I learned a lot, though I didn't really retain much, but I don't think he expected me to. It was his presence I found soothing.

I fell asleep in the hard plastic chair in the exam room, and only woke when he shook my shoulder.

"Hey! Everything's fine. She's okay," he said when I blinked at him blearily. "It's a little after eleven, and she's resting right now." He winked. "No visitors yet. You can bring her flowers tomorrow."

"She's okay?" I repeated, focusing on the essentials.

His eyes softened. "Yeah, she's gonna be fine… Uh." He tilted his head to the side. "You know, I don't even know your name."

"Daniel," I said. "Michaelson."

"Nice to meet you, Daniel Michaelson." He smiled, and… shit, he was handsome. Like a sunrise at eleven o'clock at night, his smile was that warm, that bright, that unexpected.

If I were into guys, I mean. Which I wasn't. At all.

"Listen, I'm going upstairs to my apartment to change my clothes and make some coffee. Come up and have a cup before you drive home? Driving while half asleep isn't a great idea."

I frowned. "But what about… the bird?"

"I've got her," he said simply. "I'll check on her. I'm used to it."

"Okay." I nodded and pushed to my feet.

"I think you need a better name for her than *bird*," he said, leading the way through the back room of the clinic to a small staircase, and then upstairs. "Something badass."

"Really?" I trudged up the stairs tiredly. "I'm planning to release her back into the woods, not keep her as a pet."

"I should hope so." He reached the top landing and turned around. He was taller than me now, and he'd taken off his oversized lab coat at some point so he was only wearing a pair of surgical scrubs and a t-shirt that showed off his lean strength. I wasn't sure why I'd thought he was slight before. The man was slender but fit. "I've found that giving an animal a name is… I dunno. Life-affirming." In the dim light from the lamp over the stairs, it looked like he might be blushing. "It could be superstition. I mean, there's no scientific reason why it works…"

"Or maybe there *is* a reason it works, and scientists don't know it yet?" I said, quoting his words from earlier.

His eyes widened and he stared at me like I was some kind of animal he'd never encountered, but he was clearly pleased. *So* pleased. And I hadn't even had to try.

He unlocked the door and led me inside. The living room was small and decorated with approximately the same style as my cabin—hand-me-down chic. But it was cozy and tidy, with particleboard shelves full of books covering every wall.

He pointed at a blue futon. "Make yourself comfortable. I need to shower, but it literally takes me thirty seconds." He whipped off his shirt as he walked away, and I averted my eyes, though I wasn't sure why I felt the need. It wasn't weird for another guy to take his shirt off.

A second later, I heard the water running.

I wandered over to one of his bookcases and ran my finger along the spines. Mystery, thriller, mystery, mystery, spy thriller, urban fiction, mystery… I sensed a theme. And then my finger coasted over one familiar spine, and I retracted it quickly, like it had burned me.

It kinda had.

"So, badass names?" he prompted, stepping back into the room. His wet hair curled slightly around his ears. He wore a pair of lounge pants and a dark t-shirt that made his eyes look even bluer.

"Wow. That was super fast. You weren't lying."

"I never do," he said. He looked down at my shirt and frowned. My eyes followed his gaze, and I saw that I was still wearing the bloody t-shirt from earlier.

"My brother Con's about your size. Let me see if he left something here." He rummaged through a closet and emerged with a shirt a minute later. "Here, you can put this on."

I took it and quickly changed shirts while he went into the kitchen to make coffee.

"I was thinking Trixie," he called.

"What?"

"For the owl. Trixie."

"No!" I protested. "That's a name for a…" I coughed, not finishing the sentence. "Just, no."

"You were going to say porn star, weren't you?" He handed me a cup of coffee and took a sip of his own.

"I… maybe."

"Hmm. Well, not the kind of porn I watch."

"Really?"

He gave me a small smile. "I can't think of a single guy on CockyBoys named Trixie."

"Oh." I cleared my throat. "That… would make sense."

He smiled again, more fully this time. "I was going for Trixie Belden, Girl…"

"Detective?" I said. "Right. Should've guessed." I pointed to his shelves full of mysteries. "It's not a terrible name. But I was thinking something more warrior-esque. Like Boudica."

He blinked, then scowled. "The what now?"

"Boudica was badass. When the Romans—"

He held up a hand. "I'm familiar with the whole sordid story. Ugh. *No.* Happy endings only, Daniel, for the love of God."

I ducked my head and laughed.

"Trixie it is, then," I agreed. I figured he deserved the honor of naming her, since he'd worked not one but two miracles that night.

Julian Ross had saved the owl's life.

He'd also made me think that there were *some* humans worth knowing and maybe, possibly, trusting.

———

Want more O'Leary?

Julian's brother Con finds love in *The Secret*, the third book in the Love in O'Leary series. Grab your copy here → https://readerlinks.com/l/1570171

And don't miss *The Note*, a Love in O'Leary novella, available here → https://readerlinks.com/l/1570176

Chapter Two

JULIAN

Present

HEY, Julian. It's Curtis. You around tonight?

The text alert flashed on my phone while I was sitting in Goode's Diner, watching my brother Constantine inhale an entire platter of scrambled eggs and insert himself into conversations at all the tables around us, as was the O'Leary way. I dismissed the notification immediately and set the phone face-down on the table before Con could see it and give me shit.

Curtis, I thought to myself, staring at the wall beyond Con's head. *Who the hell was Curtis?* There wasn't a soul in O'Leary with that name.

He could have been the blond from Albany who'd been in town for a wedding last winter. Or he might have been the sweet, younger guy I'd slept with a couple of times last April, when I'd been lonely enough to ignore the fact that I was being blown by a guy who couldn't legally buy me a drink. There were a couple before that, too—not a lot, by any stretch, and none at all in months—but enough that I couldn't say for sure who the hell Curtis was, sadly.

Sadder still, I didn't care. There had been only one guy occupying all my brain cells for months and months, and Daniel Michaelson wasn't a guy who'd ever send me a hookup text.

Sorry, Curtis.

"Earth to Jules! You gonna eat that bacon?" Con leaned across the table and waved his hand in front of my face like he was four, not twenty-four.

I snapped out of my cross-eyed daze and slapped his hand away. "Hey! Don't be rude, Constantine!"

"Rude? You're the one ignoring my pitiful requests for sustenance." He looked down at his own empty breakfast plate and then at the pancakes I'd barely touched. "And you're ignoring our friend Jamie, who walked all the way out from the kitchen to chat. What would Mom say?"

"Oh, don't bring me into it. I'm just enjoying my coffee before I get back to work." Jamie looked at Con's pouting face and laughed. "If you want more bacon, I can go grab you some in the back, you know."

"Nah. Bacon stolen from someone else's plate tastes better. Proven fact."

"I'd like to know the science behind that proven fact." I shoved my plate toward him. "Sorry, I'm not great company," I told Jamie. "I'm half-asleep still." I sipped at my coffee. "Late night."

"It's fine," Jamie said easily. "You're *restful* company, and sometimes that's better."

"He means you're boring, bro." Con drowned the poor, innocent pancakes in syrup. "Anyway, I thought you said you didn't have any animals staying at the clinic, Dr. Ross. Did you get an emergency vet call?" He paused, distracted by his own thought, while the syrup continued to pour from the jug. "Hey, why are there no dog ambulances?"

"Because they'd be expensive, and people don't always put their money toward the important things. Con, you're making maple *soup*."

"I know. I like it this way. What were you up late for, then?" he asked. "Let me guess. Reading?"

"That's the detective work that makes you such an invaluable member of the police force," I said, deadpan. "What gave it away? The bleary eyes?"

He nodded. "And the messed up 'do, like you went to bed with your hair wet. And the way you're wearing a sweater that's three sizes too big for you. Makes you look like a midget, and it's made of more holes than yarn."

"It is not!" I looked down at the heavy gray cable-knit. "I love this sweater. I wear it all the time when it's chilly. It was Dad's!"

"Julian, he died ten years ago."

"I'm aware of that. And yet this sweater's still perfectly comfortable." I pulled the sleeves of it more firmly around me. "Besides, the gray makes my eyes look nice."

"Who told you *that*?" Con demanded, smirking. "Whoever it was, I hope you put out after."

Jamie grimaced. "Dude. Seriously?"

I felt my cheeks flush. "Ignore him," I said. "Poor Constantine was born without a filter. He does the best he can."

"What? Just sayin'!" Con shoved more pancakes into his already full mouth and motioned toward his own eyes —Ross blue, like mine—with his syrupy fork. "I've got the same eyes Jules has, and nobody I hooked up with ever said that to me, girl *or* guy."

"Maybe that says more about the people you hook up with," Jamie suggested.

I rolled my eyes. "Or that the back hallway at The Hive needs better lighting."

"Hey!" Con's eyes widened and he choked slightly. He pointed the fork at me accusingly. "Unkind."

I shrugged again. "*Just sayin'*," I quoted sweetly.

The truth was, there were times when I envied Con. He was unabashedly about the flash and the bang… no pun intended. He went out to bars and scrutinized the available goodies the way I perused the sweets at the bakery across the street, and he didn't expect more than the simple pleasure I got from a chocolate cupcake, either. He'd never been hung up on anyone in particular, or not that I knew of, and he'd sure as hell never committed the most stupid, cliched, ridiculous, fatal sin of all: he'd never fallen for his straight best friend.

Jamie lifted his chin toward the front window of the diner, where the wind was whipping bright October leaves across the bleak sky. "It's definitely sweater weather," he said. "Barely October, too. Definitely a day to curl up and read."

He gave me a friendly wink that made his brown eyes crinkle beneath his shock of bright red hair, and I wished, not for the first time, that I could have fallen for a guy like Jamie—a guy whose life was an open book, who'd never had a conversation with me about anything more thought-provoking than the weather, and who was, you know, actually *gay*.

"Maybe I will," I agreed. But the truth was, I didn't plan to spend the day at home. I'd decided last night, when I finally finished my book, that I would drive out to Daniel's cabin today and drop it off. He preferred reading paperbacks, like I did, and we had an exchange going on. A kind of informal book club with only two participants. "What about you?"

"Jamie has a *date* this afternoon," Con informed me, cackling when Jamie turned an alarming shade of red.

"It's not a date. It's a… friend thing. Anyway, I'm working tonight."

"Sure," Con said. "Anything you say. You guys gonna come watch football tomorrow?"

"At Hoff's bar? I dunno. Maybe." Football was not my favorite sport—no sport was my favorite sport—but it reminded me of my dad, and I enjoyed hanging out with Jamie, Con, and some of the other guys. It was familiar. "Jamie?"

Jamie's face stretched into something that was half smile, half grimace. "Yeah, I don't think so. You might have noticed I'm persona non grata at Hoff's."

"Parker said he didn't want you there?" I frowned. "What the hell is going on with you two? I remember you used to be friends back in the day."

Jamie grunted. "Ten years is a long time," he said, and it occurred to me that maybe his life wasn't as much of an open book as I'd thought. Maybe no one's was.

"Doc Ross!"

I turned at the sound of my name and looked around the restaurant, past the two- and four-person set-ups in the middle of the room, and the individual booths that ran along each side, to the long banquette that lined the back wall. Lina Davenport stood up from one of those tables and waved enthusiastically, like she'd only just now noticed me. She came rushing over, high-heels clacking on the linoleum, eyeglass chain swaying.

"I thought that was you! Oh, Doctor, thank goodness you're here. I've been so worried about Macarena! He's *shedding*, and it looks awful, and I swear he's sick."

Jamie's eyes widened. "Macarena?"

"My baby bird," Lina explained, as though Jamie should have known this already.

"He's not shedding, Lina, he's molting. Remember we talked about this? Macarena is a cockatoo, and cockatoos molt every year. It's a totally normal process that—"

"Thank you for watching this episode of Animal Facts," Con said, not quite under his breath. "I'm your host, *Julian Ross*!"

I shot him a dirty look.

Lina gripped the strap of her enormous purse more tightly. "I know what you said about molding."

"Molting."

"That's what I said! I even looked it up on the internet, and it looked disgusting, but not a *thing* like what Macarena has. Can I bring him by?"

I blinked. There was not a doubt in my mind that she'd googled mold. But what the heck could I say? "I… yes. Of course. I'm happy to take a look at him if it'll ease your mind. Monday morning, call Kathy and she'll…"

"Oh, no," Lina said darkly. "Last time, Kathy insisted you couldn't see Macarena for days. I was a nervous *wreck*. But I'm free today. Any time today. I'll fit you in whenever."

How nice of her.

"I'm not open on Saturdays except in emergencies, Lina."

I knew exactly where this was going, though. A quick check of Con's amused face said he did, too. She'd push and I'd cave.

Lina's frown deepened. Her eyes narrowed. "Well, this *is* an emergency. So what time works?"

The muscle between my eyebrows started to twitch, so I rubbed it with my finger. "Eleven," I said weakly.

She beamed. "Perfect. Thank you, Doctor. I know I can always count on you."

"*I know I can always count on you, Doctor*," Con tittered after Lena had walked away. He snorted. "You're such a pushover, Jules."

"He's dedicated to his work," Jamie said, although his smile suggested he didn't totally disagree with Con. For that matter, neither did I. But Jesus, I hated feeling like I was letting anyone down.

I blew out a breath. Dr. Julian Ross, dedicated, professional pushover. I wasn't proud of it. Sometimes I wondered when the hell I was going to push things down too much and finally snap, tell the world to fuck off and take a stand for what *I* wanted.

Clearly, today was not gonna be that day. Tomorrow didn't look promising either.

"I know something that'll cheer you up." Shane Goode was standing near Jamie's shoulder, wiping his hands on his apron and chatting to Silas Sloane, one of O'Leary's three police officers; Si's boyfriend Everett Maior; Ev's grandfather Henry Lattimer; Dare Turner, a local ranger; and a bunch of others at the table next to us. His voice was too loud for anyone in the diner to pretend they couldn't overhear. "Karen Mitchener-Martin, Angela Ross, and Ms. Dorian were in here earlier, and they said there's been a break in Elliot Marks's disappearance. You don't have to be afraid anymore."

Con and I exchanged a look as our mother's name was mentioned. For the past couple weeks, the entire town had been buzzing about the disappearance of a camper visiting the area, followed by the disappearance of Elliot Marks, one of the ranger-types who worked with Dare at the state park bordering O'Leary. The suspicions whispered across the frozen food aisles at the Imperial and under the dryer bonnets at Marybeth's salon, involving everything from alien abductions to drug smuggling cartels, were terrifyingly ridiculous, but with one common theme—there was no *way* anyone local could have been involved.

To be honest, I had trouble believing it, myself.

"Ms. Dorian said there was a camera outside a store near Elliot's apartment building," Shane was saying. "Showed a tall, blond guy walking in, and that's the suspect. She said it was obviously that new guy, Daniel Whatshisname."

"Wait, what?" I whispered, the words punched from my gut. "Daniel Michaelson?"

"Eh. Just more speculation," Con reminded me, licking the tines of his fork like he hadn't consumed enough syrup. "Hardly surprising. You know Mama and her ladies got all offended that the guy brushed them off when they tried to send out the welcome wagons. She doesn't like him."

"She doesn't *know* him," I said hotly.

"Oh, and you do?" Con smirked.

I opened my mouth, then closed it.

"Wait." Con's eyes narrowed. "*Do* you?"

I felt my cheeks get hot. For a few months now, I'd considered Daniel not only a friend but my *best* friend.

"Jesus, Jules, you're a dark horse." Con's grin expanded. "Tell me all about him!"

I shook my head, my heart beating hard. This—*this*—was exactly why I hadn't told anyone that Daniel and I were friends. This was why I let my mother and brothers believe that I spent every evening alone, and my weekends hiking by myself. If I mentioned him, they'd want to know *everything.* They'd want to meet him and pelt him with questions about everything from his shoe size to his thoughts on global warming. And when he didn't answer—because he wouldn't—they'd start questioning *me* about why I bothered hanging around with him. I had no desire to defend my friendship.

"He's not a criminal," I whispered. "That much I can tell you for *sure*." There was no way the man I'd spent so many hours of quiet conversation with, the man who'd brought me injured animals to save and books to read, was involved in anything criminal. "Unless wanting to be left alone is a crime."

Con tilted his head. "You remember we're in O'Leary, right? I wouldn't be surprised if there *was* some town bylaw against solitude." He smiled, but I couldn't. "Chill, Jules. Nobody's got pitchforks out yet. But if he makes zero effort to get to know anyone, don't be surprised that no one is automatically thinking the best of him."

Con wasn't wrong.

Jess Siegel at Lyon's Imperial had asked Daniel where he was from, and he'd answered tersely, "The city." Coach Simms had asked him what he did for a living, and Daniel had said, "I work from home." Henry Lattimer had asked him if he had a family, and Daniel had replied, "Everyone's from someplace," which was obscure enough that Henry's girlfriend, Diane, somehow became convinced that Daniel was literally from a town called Someplace and asked him what state that was in.

Yes, seriously.

Even *I* had gotten politely but unequivocally shut down when I tried to pry the basic facts of his life from him, and unless he and Jenny at the Laundromat were having a torrid affair that I didn't know about, I was the one person he was close to in this town, though he'd been here since last winter.

"Excuse me," I asked, leaning around Jamie. "Did you say they're accusing Daniel Michaelson of being involved in the disappearances?"

"No." Si shook his head vigorously.

"Nobody's accusing anyone of anything," Dare said, holding up his hands. "Karen Mitchener-Martin's spreading rumors. Again."

I nodded, but my heart wouldn't resume its normal rhythm.

"I heard he lives in the woods because he's not right in the head!" someone behind me yelled.

"What?" I demanded, horrified.

"Julian, seriously, don't get your panties in a bunch," Con whispered fiercely. "It's just the usual bullshit."

"I heard he came here because he got into trouble with the law and he was on the run," Myrna Lucano said, frowning. "But he seems real sweet."

"I think that's a load of horseshit," Rena Cobb said. "He's a good man."

I didn't hear much of anything after that. There was a fire in my stomach, overriding all my common sense, a need to take action that burned through my passivity. I wanted to bitch-slap Shane Goode. I wanted to scream at the top of my lungs.

It might be the usual bullshit, as Con said, but this time they were talking about someone I cared about. Someone who wasn't here to defend himself.

I pushed to my feet, sliding my chair back over the floor with a screech.

"Listen to me, everyone," I said. "Daniel Michaelson didn't have anything to do with this."

"We know, Jules," Jamie said. He reached for my hand, like maybe he wanted to pull me down and shake some sense into me. "It's alright."

"I wanna know how he knows that!" someone yelled.

"Yeah, how do you know that, Doc Ross?" someone else asked.

"I know, because… I know because…"

I wanted to vomit. I wanted to disappear. I felt like I was poised at the peak of a rollercoaster, full to the brim with potential energy, and it scared the shit out of me.

"I know because Daniel was with me the night Elliot Marks went missing."

"What?" Con's eyebrows were near his hairline. "*With you?*"

It felt like Con was giving me an out. Was Daniel *with* me, like we happened to be strolling the same street at the same time? Or *with me*, in a total, claiming, I'm-vouching-for-this-guy kind of way?

The oddest moments define your life. It's not just about the occasions Hallmark sells greeting cards for—the graduations, the weddings, the birthdays, the funerals. It's also about the moment when you're ten, and your mom says you can't have a dog, so you decide right then and there that you're going to be a veterinarian. It's about the moment when your asshole teenage self goes off on a rant and says shit to your father that you'll never get the chance to take back. It's about the moment you keep your mouth shut and don't say what you really feel. And it's about the moment when you find yourself standing in the middle of Goode's Diner, in front of your entire town, speaking the greatest wish of your heart like it's actual truth.

My brain went quiet for a second; all the noise and the worry stilled to nothing. The words felt inevitable.

"Yeah," I said. "We're together."

"Damn," Con breathed. His eyes were like saucers and his hand was resting on his plate—my plate—in a puddle of syrup. "Mom is going to *freak out*."

All conversation stopped. Someone was making a choking noise. I could feel the tidal wave of curiosity gathering, ready to break over my head like a tsunami and drown me.

Oh, fuck. All the things I hadn't considered before my impulsive decision came flooding back, and I clutched the back of the chair unsteadily.

"I'm… I've gotta go." I threw some money on the table and shoved past Constantine toward the door.

I heard someone, Si maybe, calling after me, "Julian! He's not in trouble!"

Daniel might not be in trouble, but I sure as fuck was.

My mother would be livid and worse, worried.

I'd basically just invited O'Leary to gossip about me… and my *love life*. Oh, Christ.

And… and Daniel. I'd lied about him, when I knew exactly how much he valued honesty and privacy.

I was so fucked.

"Jules!"

I heard Con rushing after me as I pushed open the diner door with a jangle of bells and emerged into the chilly air, but I didn't slow down. I passed between a couple of parked cars and darted across the street to the building that housed my clinic and my little apartment above. I thought about going upstairs—God, I needed to be alone in the worst way—but Con had an emergency key. He'd follow me and make himself comfortable. I headed for the clinic instead.

"Julian! I'm talking to you!" Constantine put his hand on my shoulder just as I pulled my keys from my pocket with shaking hands and managed to unlock the glass door. I pushed it open and flipped on the light as I went inside.

"Con, I can't talk now," I said. "I've got to get ready for Lina Davenport, and…"

Con closed the door behind himself and locked the deadbolt.

"And first, you have to explain what the hell is going on."

"Do I?" I scrubbed both hands over my eyes. "I really think it's self-explanatory."

"You're dating the man in the woods."

I dropped my hands. "Could you make him sound slightly less like a killer from some 80s slasher film? His name is *Daniel*."

Con raised one eyebrow. "Fine, then. Daniel."

"Is it really so hard to believe?" I demanded, then I paused. "No, you know what? Don't answer that."

Quiet Dr. Julian Ross and *Daniel Michaelson*, the guy who's fleeing a criminal past *and* dodging child support *and* a Russian agent *and* looks just like the guy from America's Most Wanted?

Blond Adonis Daniel Michaelson, and *Julian Ross*, the mousy guy who can't reach the high shelves in his own kitchen and has never before expressed an original thought in public?

I could imagine exactly how that looked, and it wasn't pretty.

"Since when do you keep secrets, big brother?" Con demanded. He sounded almost hurt, and I sighed.

"Constantine, really. If I told you or Theo that Daniel and I were hanging out, you'd tell Mama. No, don't make that face, you totally would. Not intentionally, maybe, but it would have slipped out. And you *know* the next time she was pissed at Theo and telling him to be more like me, he'd totally have thrown it out there."

Con pursed his lips, which was as good as an admission. Our little brother, Theo, was a hothead, and Con was absentminded at the best of times.

"I wanted something to be… *mine*." The words came out and startled me with their truth. Daniel was *mine*. I was the only person in O'Leary he was friends with. And I had no clue what made me so special, or if it was just dumb luck that made his path collide with mine last May, but I liked having this special, secret part of my life. I liked having someone who didn't see me as old, reliable Doc Ross, when I was only twenty-fucking-nine.

Con scratched his chin. "Not gonna be *just yours* anymore," he said sadly.

I exhaled softly. "Daniel's going to be *pissed*."

Con's lips twitched. "You don't think he's gonna enjoy having folks speculate about when you two will get married or what you'll name your kids?"

I wasn't sure what expression showed on my face, but it was probably something close to terror because Con continued quickly, "I'm kidding. People aren't likely to talk to him. I know Si and Everett like him, but he's not exactly friendly."

"You've got to tell people to stay quiet," I begged, dropping into one of the hard plastic chairs in the waiting area. "Just for now."

"I can try," he said dubiously, sinking into the chair opposite me. "But they're gonna be more eager than ever to know what makes him so special *the* Doctor Julian Ross is dating him when no one even knew the dude was gay."

Heh. Yeah. Funny thing, Con. That's because he's not.

"They're gonna want to know how you got together," Con continued, "and whether it's serious. And that's just the people in town. Mama is... God. She's gonna birth kittens when she hears."

"I know."

"Like, she's not gonna know whether to give you her pissed off face or her disappointed face or her you-made-me-cry face." Con stared into middle distance, like he was seeing it all unfold in his mind's eye. "She's gonna tell you

Dad would be rolling in his grave." He shuddered. "It's gonna be *biblical*."

"Thank you, Constantine," I snapped. "I'm aware." My roiling stomach was proof of that.

The look he gave me was positively condescending. "Nah, bro. You *think* you know, but you've always been her favorite. Hell, you've always been this *town's* favorite. The responsible Ross brother, right?" He smirked a little. "Well, take it from Constantine-the-Hellion, the higher you are, the harder you fall. People are still talking about shit I did in high school."

I rubbed at the headache forming behind my eyes. "I haven't done anything wrong." Not that anyone knew of, anyway.

"Yeah, I doubt Mama will see it that way. But listen to me." He grabbed my wrist, forcing my hand away from my head, and I looked up at him. Like most other adult men in O'Leary, he was several inches taller than me. "When she gives you shit, and she will, push back. Hear me?"

"Yeah. Okay." He might as well tell me to flap my arms and fly.

"I'm serious, Jules. You know how much I love her, but Mama will smother you if you let her."

I shook my head. "Easy for you to say. You've done your own thing all your life, but I…"

"Had to switch colleges and move home after Dad died. Had to be a surrogate father for Theo and me." His lips twitched. "Had to sit through a billion of my high school football games even though you barely understood what was going on. Had to put that convertible of yours up on blocks and never drove it again. But you don't have to give this up, too. Take a stand, Jules."

Yeah, right. I'd taken a stand in the diner, and now I felt like I'd pushed something into motion that I couldn't stop or take back.

I forced a smile. "Hey. Which of us is the older brother?"

"There's never been any doubt about that, Jules. But there are a couple of things I do better than you. Knowing how to be happy is one of them." He sighed and pushed to his feet. "Okay, I've gotta get home. Mama's got me doing a couple landscaping jobs this afternoon."

Working at Ross Landscaping was an unavoidable part of life in our family—until the last year or two, it was how I'd spend my weekends, and I knew whenever Con wasn't on duty, he was helping out.

"That's odd," I said, distracted momentarily. "It's too late in the season for mowing and too early for leaf cleanup."

"Gotta keep up with Micah's Blooms," Con said, rolling his eyes. "How dare someone else start a business that competes with ours, right? Now we work twice as hard for half the money."

I shook my head and stood. "Such a hellion, you are. Tell me again about the joys of irresponsible living?"

Con shoved at my shoulder. "I blame you for being a good role model."

I snorted.

"Listen, I'll do what I can to get people to shut up. I'll tell them *it's complicated.*" He grinned. "Theo said even old Hen Lattimer from the hardware store is on 'The Facebooks' now, so he'll get it."

Oh, dear God. "Thanks. I appreciate it. Now I've gotta talk to Daniel. After I take a look at Macarena, of course."

Con frowned. "It's gonna be okay, Jules. If he's a decent guy, he's not gonna be nearly as upset as you think he will just because you spilled the beans while trying to save his reputation."

I smiled, for Con's sake, but I knew better. Daniel didn't give a shit about his reputation. No, Daniel was going to be pissed because I'd made him an object of speculation.

He was going to be pissed because I'd lied, when I'd promised him honesty.

Last June

"CAN WE PAUSE? I'M HUNGRY." I glanced over at Daniel, who was hiking up the path beside me. "And I'm sweating."

It was barely summer, and still cool thanks to the little bit of elevation and the shade from the trees, but I could feel the little rivulets sliding down the back of my neck and catching on the collar of my t-shirt, which was exactly as uncomfortable as it sounds.

Daniel wrinkled his forehead. "Sweating? Seriously?" He looked around us at the trees, mud, and ferns like he was searching for the source of the heat. *He* was fresh as a fucking daisy, naturally.

Of course he was.

"Some of us don't hike a million miles a day like it's our job, Bear Grylls. Some of us get a tiny bit winded walking up a mountain."

"More like a hill," he pointed out. "And not a very big one. Who or what's a bear grill?"

I stopped walking and turned to stare at him. "Wow. Okay, we definitely need to stop so I can catch my breath, to better express my outrage over your stunning lack of pop culture knowledge."

He grinned at me, and it did absolutely nothing to help me catch my breath. His blond hair was gilded gold by a stray beam of light filtering through the trees, his high cheekbones were like something sculpted of marble, his broad shoulders carried his backpack like it weighed nothing at all....

And he was straight.

Straight, *Julian. No lusty-lusty.*

"Bear Grylls is a national treasure," I said. "Well. I mean, not of *this* nation. Pretty sure he's from the UK. But still. A fucking *delight.*"

"Okay. Is he on that British baking show you keep wanting me to watch? Because I'm not watching that."

"Your loss." I took off my backpack and settled my ass down on a fallen log just off the path. "But no, he's a survivalist. A gorgeous one, with the best accent. He has a show where he gets dropped out in the wild with no food or water and has to figure out how to survive. It's hardcore."

Daniel dropped his backpack, too, and straddled the log maybe a foot away. "I bet I could do it."

I looked him up and down dubiously. "Maybe. There's a lot of urine involved."

A little laugh burst out of him, like he couldn't believe I'd said that. I kind of couldn't either. But I was a different kind of Julian when I was with Daniel. One who worried less over every syllable that came out of my mouth and how it might be perceived. It was a little like being with Con and Theo, except my feelings for Daniel were one hundred percent *not* brotherly.

I wasn't sure why things were different with him. Maybe it was because he hadn't known me my whole life, so he wasn't surprised and horrified when I actually *spoke* the snarky remarks I usually just kept in my head, or rambled on and on (and on) about animal trivia or pop culture. Maybe he just hadn't been around me long enough to get fed up.

Fresh meat, so to speak.

Whatever the reason, Daniel Michaelson, the man my mother referred to as *"that wackadoodle loner who lives in the woods,"* had somehow chosen *me* as the only person in town he wanted to be friends with three weeks ago, and it was hard to not feel like I'd won the friendship Hunger Games.

I opened my pack and took out my water bottle along with a granola bar. "Want half?"

"Sure."

We chewed in silence for a minute, just enjoying the air and the solitude.

Then my stomach grumbled, and Daniel laughed. "Granola not cutting it?"

"Not really. Pizza delivery sucks out here though."

"Do they even have pizza delivery in O'Leary?" Daniel stretched out his long legs.

"Of course. Papa Giordino's in Rushton. Delivers Fridays and Saturdays only, and last order's at seven because they close at eight."

"Oh my God."

"Not what you're used to, from before?" I asked, carefully not looking at him. I'd been hoping for a while now that he'd open up and tell me about himself. I mean, we talked about the most random shit, and I felt like I *knew* him, but basic facts were thin on the ground.

"Not what most people in the western world are used to," he said. "What kind of toppings do you like on your pizza?"

Daniel Michaelson, master of deflection. But okay, I could play.

"Broccoli, cheese, and tomato sauce."

He grimaced. "Are you… is that a joke? Are you making a joke right now?"

"No!" I laughed. "Who the fuck jokes about pizza toppings, Daniel?"

"But… that's like, a salad. Not a pizza."

"The addition of a green vegetable to a thing does not make it a salad. Sorry to burst your bubble. Why, what do you like? All the manly meats to make sure everyone knows you're the testosteroniest? *Rawr*!" I gave my most convincing growl.

"No! I mean, yes. But not because I'm the… whatever the fuck you just said. Because they're tasty." He closed his eyes and smacked his lips together in a way that should have been criminal. "Mmm. Meat."

"Just to be clear, you're saying you like manly meat. M'kay."

He rolled his eyes. "I'm comfortable enough in my sexuality to tell you that I like hard salami *and* spicy sausage, but only on my pizza. So there."

"Ah, well," I said easily. "Too bad for me. First Shawn Mendes is definitely straight, now you are. Somehow, I'll learn to cope."

He snorted. "Yes, I'm sure you cry yourself to sleep at night over the loss. So brave."

Oh, Daniel. Honey, if you only knew.

"What about mushrooms?" he asked suddenly. "They're like a cross between meat and vegetables."

"Mushrooms," I said flatly. "You mean, devil fungus?"

He laughed again and stretched out his legs, situating himself more comfortably on the log—at least, he somehow made the dirty, hard surface look comfortable. It simply wasn't fair for someone to trudge up a fucking mountain and still look like they'd stepped out of a photoshoot.

"So I see that mushrooms will not be our common ground," he said sadly. "Why the hate?"

His eyes danced at me and if this were a book, now would be the time when he'd lean forward and kiss me. Sadly, he merely reached for his water bottle and waited for me to speak.

Which, honestly, was pretty freakin' okay, too. I'd never met anyone who asked me so many questions or seemed to be honestly curious about the answers.

What the fuck were we talking about?

Oh, mushrooms. Right.

"They're little slimy… things," I said intelligently. "Every time we got pizza when I was a kid, I'd spend my time trying to pick the damn things out of my slice while my brothers scarfed down the rest of the pie, but it was no use. They infect everything they touch with their… you know." I waved my hand, unable to fully articulate the thought.

"Slime?" he guessed.

"Yes! Exactly."

"Uh-huh. So why do you get mushrooms on your pizza if you're only going to pick them out?"

"I don't when I'm by myself, obviously. But my family *loves* them." I shrugged. "You know how it is with families."

He nodded slowly, like maybe he didn't actually know.

"Do you have brothers?" I asked, folding my granola bar wrapper into a very precise triangle.

"Ah, no. Only child."

"So you get only the pizza toppings you want!" I crowed. "Lucky."

"That's me," he said. "Lucky." Only it sounded like maybe he didn't know that, either.

He fell quiet after that, but this silence felt charged, and I didn't like it, but I wasn't sure how to fix it. I cleared my throat.

"Do you see many bears out at your place? People forget that there are bears in these woods sometimes, especially close to the campgrounds. You should arm yourself with bear spray, especially if you're going out hiking alone, and especially-especially when there are young bears around. Sometimes they're really curious and get closer to humans than they should and…" I reached for my water bottle and took a deep drink, mostly to cut off my verbal diarrhea.

But Daniel didn't seem annoyed or even mocking. He nodded seriously.

"I haven't seen any bears. Coyotes, though."

I nodded. "Well, coyotes are everywhere now. Humans push into their territory and they try to take it back. Did you know coyotes even follow train tracks into the city?" I nodded. "True fact."

"I did *not* know that," he said. "That's interesting."

It was pathetic, more like. My brothers would give me sixteen helpings of shit if they were here. "Welcome to Animal Facts with Julian," I said, feeling my face flame. "I tend to go off on tangents and not shut up." *Especially when I'm nervous*, I thought but didn't say.

Improbably, he grinned. "If I had as many interesting things to say as you do, I wouldn't shut up. I like it." I felt my belly warm in a way that was totally inappropriate and more than a little dangerous.

"You're extremely interesting. You're a meat fetishist who likes slimy fungi and weird animal trivia. It's fascinating."

He laughed again. "I suppose when you put it like that…"

"Okay, favorite place you've ever traveled?"

"Arizona," he said promptly. "No trees. You can see the sunset for miles."

"And yet here you are." I motioned at the abundance of forest around us. "*Fascinating*. Favorite band?"

"Uh… I don't know. Do thirty-three-year-olds have favorite bands? I like a lot of things."

"Favorite band I've never heard of, then," I countered.

He studied a nearby tree, frowning, then looked back at me, like he wanted to judge whether I was serious.

I nodded encouragingly.

"Okay, um. Drever, McCusker, and Woomble."

"Who?"

"They're a folk act. Scottish. They haven't recorded in years, but they're what I listened to most."

"Listened? Past tense?"

He looked surprised. "I guess I haven't listened to them for a while. My laptop is still packed up in a box, and I basically put my phone in a drawer when I moved up here." He smiled wryly. "Fascinating?"

"Yes, kind of. Why cut yourself off from things you enjoy?"

He looked away. "We should keep walking, I think."

"Yeah, okay." I stood up and dusted off my shorts, putting my wrapper in my pocket. "Lead on."

We walked in silence for a few minutes while I puzzled over Daniel Michaelson. He *was* fascinating—both in the things he revealed and the things he wouldn't. I didn't want to pry into his history, but… okay, no, I *really* wanted to pry, but I didn't want to make him uncomfortable.

"Favorite author?" I asked after a minute, thinking this was neutral territory, at least.

He shot me an amused glance and I rolled my eyes.

"Fine, then, *one* favorite. And make it a real one, not something you think you should say. I don't want to hear about how *Heart of Darkness* changed your life, or I might vomit on this path."

He laughed again, loud and strong, and once again he almost seemed surprised by the sound of his own laughter. "Tell me yours, then, if it's such an easy question."

"It is easy. JD Pritchard. He's a mystery writer. Contemporary."

Daniel stopped and turned to look at me like I'd grown three heads.

I shrugged. "I told you! I'm not gonna sit here and talk about magical realism or whatever. I like a good, solid mystery, preferably with a romantic subplot. But Pritchard's more than that. He's insightful. That guy knows more about the human condition than… well, anyone."

"If you say so." Daniel shook his head. "I've never found him particularly insightful. He's kind of an idiot in person."

My jaw dropped. "No way. You've *met* him?"

Daniel hesitated, then shrugged. "We ran in some of the same circles, once upon a time."

"Well, if he's a jerk in real life, don't tell me," I insisted. "I prefer to believe that if I ever met him, he'd somehow find me cool and we'd become best friends."

Daniel snorted. "You're way cooler than he is."

"Oh, right. Of course I am," I agreed. "No one knows animal trivia like I do." I hesitated for a second, then asked, "So you lived in the city? I only ask because you said you knew Pritchard, and I'm pretty sure that's where he lives."

Daniel was silent for a long moment.

"I mean, not that it matters," I said as we passed out of

the thick forest and into the rockier terrain near the top of Jane's Peak. "I just wondered how you came to be here, you know? A guy who's met my favorite author, but somehow prefers living on the outskirts of this tiny little town, hiking up a mountain and eating my imaginary non-mushroom pizza."

He turned to face me, licked his lips, and took a deep breath like he was about to finally tell me something important. "It's a hill," he said. "Not even a big one."

I exhaled and forced a laugh. "Right." I walked past him, hoping he couldn't see the disappointment on my face.

A second later, he spoke. "People in O'Leary think I'm a serial killer or a mafia hit man."

Right or wrong, I was too put out to give him a bunch of platitudes about how that couldn't possibly be true when we both knew it was. "Well, they wouldn't if you'd just give them a simple answer. Provide a vacuum of information, and they're gonna fill it." I gripped the straps of my backpack tightly. "Someone tried to find you on Facebook but got overwhelmed by the number of people with your name."

"Do you think I'm a secret criminal?"

I snorted. "You're fascinating, but not that fascinating." I bit my lip. "But given that you're *not* a criminal, and presumably not in the witness protection program, why the mystery?"

He walked a bit faster until he was alongside me again, and we climbed in silence until we reached the peak. The air was warmer here, the silence more profound. The sky was bright blue and full of puffy clouds, and all of Herriman-Sizemore State Park lay in green-fringed glory at our feet. Bob Ross couldn't have painted happier trees than these.

I imagined Daniel would be in a hurry to get down the mountain again, if only to get away from my curiosity, but he surprised me by sprawling out flat on the rocks and scrub grass, using his backpack for a pillow. He stared up at the sky, not moving or talking.

After a second, I sighed and copied him, my head at a forty-five-degree angle to his. We couldn't see each other at all this way, but there was no way I could forget he was there.

It was restful, but then being with Daniel the past few weeks generally had been. I could talk as much as I wanted and he didn't mind, but we could be silent, too, and I didn't feel the same compulsion to fill it.

"You see that cloud?" he said suddenly. "It looks like a frog."

I twisted my head, trying to see what he saw. "I think it's more like a teddy bear? Look, the bumps are ears."

"The bumps are *eyes*," he corrected. "Or maybe we're both right and we can just enjoy them as clouds without reading too much into them."

I snorted. "If that's your attempt at metaphor…"

"Not particularly insightful? Not Pritchard-worthy?"

"A little heavy-handed," I said. "Eight out of ten."

He chuckled, but I kept my eyes on the sky until they watered at the brightness.

"I went to the woods because I wished to live deliberately," Daniel quoted.

I turned my head on my backpack, even though I still couldn't see his face. "Thoreau?"

"And also me. I left my old life because there was nothing true in it anymore. No crimes, no running from the mafia. No missed child support—no children *at all*, no broken hearts left behind. Okay?"

"Okay," I agreed. "But…"

I wanted to tell him that I didn't want or need him to confirm his innocence to me. I'd already pretty much decided that he was a good person the night he appeared with Trixie the owl. I just wanted to know more about him. I felt like I shared so much about myself, mostly because my fucking mouth wouldn't stop running, and I wanted to have some piece of *him* so it wasn't all one-sided.

Instead, I finished simply, "I wanted to get to know you better. I wanted us to be friends."

He inhaled so sharply I could hear it, and then I swear he held his breath for a minute. When he let it out, he said, "What does it mean to know someone, Julian? What are the essential truths about a person? You know I love pepperoni and sunsets and reading and a random Scottish folk band. You know how I take my tea, and how I feel about injustice. We've talked about books and plays and politics. You know I like scrambled eggs, and that I keep my cabin tidy while my truck is a mess."

"That's a random assortment of trivia," I said. "That's not *knowing* someone."

"Those are my truths," he argued, his voice almost pleading. "Those are the things that make me *me*, way more than anything you could find on the internet. Right now, you literally know me better than one hundred percent of the planet. Congratulations."

I huffed out a laugh. But as I looked at the clouds, I realized that maybe he was right. Here in O'Leary, people knew my history, so they assumed they knew me—quiet, reliable, passive old Doc Ross, middle-aged before my time. With Daniel, I could be myself—the Julian I wished everyone could see. A little more confident, a little more sarcastic, a little weirder, but happier too. And if I could be that for Daniel… well, why wouldn't I?

"I'm tired of lies, Julian," Daniel continued. "I don't

want to pretend to be someone ever again. And that's why I'm not making up some story about my life just to assuage the curiosity of the guy at the hardware store or the lady at the Gas n' Sip. But there are things I don't want to talk about. Can you be okay with that? Can we just be friends who are honest with each other about everything, but *not* spill our guts all the time? Can we just be Daniel and Julian, and have that be good enough?"

I could tell from the tone of his voice, half persuasive and half defiant, that he wasn't really offering me a choice —not if I wanted to keep this friendship. I could respect his boundaries or walk away. And I really couldn't stand to walk away.

"Yeah," I said softly. "Yeah, Daniel and Julian is plenty good enough."

———

Present

THE RIDE to Daniel's house was the longest of my fucking life.

He lived in a tiny log cabin in the woods across the Camden Road from the Herriman-Sizemore State Park, maybe twenty minutes from town, and usually, I savored the trip. The driveway to Daniel's cabin was the wardrobe that led to Narnia; what existed there didn't exist in my day-to-day, and vice versa. I could feel the demands of my family, my job, my *reality* sort of fall away as I got closer, because those were some of the few topics Daniel and I never discussed, so I was free to not think about them again until I was on my way home.

But now the two worlds had collided, thanks to me.

Now, every mile was one I had to *force* myself to travel, and I'd rather have been anywhere else.

I'd taken my time examining Macarena—so much time that even Lina had finally suggested that maybe his molting was, indeed, just a normal condition and we could keep an eye on it—but it was still only mid-afternoon by the time I got in the car and headed east. Early. Early enough that I could reach Boston if I kept driving. Or was the Foreign Legion still a thing? Did they have need of a nearly thirty-year-old veterinarian with poor social skills and a questionable relationship with the truth? The desire to simply disappear was *strong*.

My phone rang with my mother's distinctive ringtone, almost like she'd read my mind from a distance, and although talking to her was the last thing I wanted to do, I hit accept anyway.

"Julian Ross!" The accusation in her voice made me almost regret my decision, but after my dad's death I'd always worried that any call I dismissed from someone would be the last call I'd ever get from them.

"Mama," I said, trying to stay calm. I gripped the steering wheel tightly. "I heard you were out at the diner this morning. How was it?"

"Don't you try to distract me. Explain yourself."

"I'm doing fine," I said brightly. "It's chilly today, but I had some yummy pancakes. Saw a patient a little while ago. Thought I might make chili for dinner."

"I *heard* from Karen and Myrna," she interrupted, "that you made a spectacle of yourself in the diner today!"

I wanted to reject the description, but I was uncomfortably sure it was accurate.

"I *heard*," she continued, "that you're in love with that wackadoodle criminal who lives in the woods! I *heard* that you are moving in with him!"

Jesus Christ. Trust the O'Leary gossip line to take an already ridiculous situation and make it exponentially worse.

"You heard wrong," I told her.

She inhaled sharply. "Thank God."

"I never said we were moving in together. And I never said I was in love with Daniel."

I wasn't. I cared about him. A lot. Like, *very* a lot. And I wanted him so badly I'd need to jerk off *and* take a cold shower after going home tonight. But I wasn't *in love.* In lust. In friendship. In over my head. But thank sweet baby Jesus for small mercies, not in love.

Yet, my mind whispered helpfully.

"Are you dating him?" she demanded.

I sighed.

For a second, I debated telling her the truth—just blurting out the whole sorry mess. She'd take great joy in calling Karen and Myrna and all the other town gossips with some excuse. "*You know Julian,*" she'd say, "*Always trying to protect someone he thinks is innocent.*" And everyone would chuckle knowingly and agree that of course kind, *naïve* Doc Ross would do a thing like that. My problem would be solved in the blink of an eye. My reputation would be safe.

But that no longer seemed so important.

"Mama, I'm sorry that this has upset you. But I decide who I date. I always have."

Which was true. Although, admittedly, it wasn't so much that I'd ever taken a stand, and more that I simply never told her. My Grindr hookups had never progressed to the point where parental introductions were necessary. I'd certainly never dated someone she'd taken a massive and altogether irrational dislike to.

"I wish you'd keep an open mind about people," I said

when I could no longer stand her silence. "Try to remember what you went through when you came here."

Interesting fact: my mother, Angela Ross, née Betinelli, was *not* originally from O'Leary herself. She and my father had met in college, spending a semester abroad in Palermo. Legend had it that my Grandma Ross had given birth to a litter of kittens when my dad had brought my mom home for the first time. Funny how history repeated itself.

"It's not remotely the same situation. He has never attempted to be friendly or fit in, like I did. He wants nothing to do with us."

"He wants something to do with *me*," I reminded her. "And I like him. A *lot*."

She huffed. "It sounds like you've made up your mind, Julian. It sounds like it doesn't matter to you what I think."

I swallowed. I hated that she was hurt, *hated* it. And even as a part of me knew logically that I wasn't doing anything wrong, I couldn't stand to leave things the way they were.

"I do care what you think, Mama. I just think you're being overprotective, the way you always are with Theo, Con, and me." I hoped my voice was soothing enough to take the sting out of the words.

"I hate that you couldn't tell me that you were dating this… this…"

"Daniel?" I supplied.

"Yes! You're my boys. You're all I have," she said sadly.

Another pang.

The wind blew hard against the car and leaves hit the windshield only to scatter off, lost among the millions of other leaves that littered the ground.

"You still have me. Nothing has changed." Literally, nothing. I hesitated. "But I'd appreciate it if you'd stop spreading gossip about him. He's not a criminal, for goodness sake."

She huffed again and changed tacks. "I expect you at dinner tomorrow."

I could imagine how that would go.

"I'll come," I agreed. "But Daniel is a very private person. I won't discuss our relationship. I won't discuss him at all."

"Oh, for heaven's sake, Julian. Be an adult."

I felt like I was eleven and she'd caught me feeding a squirrel in our shed again.

"Believe it or not, I'm trying." I took the turn down Daniel's driveway. "I've got to go. I'll see you tomorrow." But because I'd learned when my young, perfectly healthy dad had died of a heart attack that I might not get another chance to say it, I told her, "I love you."

I pulled my car the rest of the way down the driveway and parked in my customary spot on the side of the house. For a second, I rested my head on the steering wheel.

Nothing like having to defend a relationship I wasn't actually *in*.

And now I got to go tell my best friend that we were dating.

I mean, who *wouldn't* wanna be with me? Ten pounds of fun in a five-pound bag, right here.

I opened my door, and a black-and-white blob jumped off the porch and attacked me.

"Hey, Honoria!" I said kneeling down to rub the head of the sheepdog Daniel had rescued after Joe Cross brought her to me a few months back. She wobbled unsteadily on her three legs and licked at my hand.

I grabbed a bag of treats from the back seat and turned toward the house.

The cabin was something out of a fairy tale. The logs

practically glowed in the sunlight beneath a steeply slanted green metal roof, a plume of wood smoke curled out of the rock-and-mortar chimney, and sitting on one of the hand-carved rockers on the front porch sat an incredibly hand-some giant carving something from a block of wood with his enormous, strong hands.

Let me repeat: Carving. Something. From. Wood. With. His. Hands.

Gah.

If life were fair, I would have been given a medal of valor for the restraint required to remain standing despite the tidal wave of *want* that swamped me. I wanted to get on my knees and *crawl* for this man.

But life wasn't generally fair, and that was nothing new.

"I think your girlfriend here likes me best."

Daniel's hazel eyes were warm and steady on my face.

"Poor thing doesn't know you don't play for her team."

I felt a blush climb my cheeks as I settled into the chair next to Daniel's.

Daniel didn't play for my team either, but that didn't seem to stop me from wanting him. In fact, I wanted more from him than I knew he could give, both as a friend *and* as a lover. He wasn't gay. He didn't talk about his past. And yet every time I saw him, I mentally jumped around like Honoria, practically panting with giddy excitement.

"Come inside," he said, setting down the thing he was carving and standing up. "I lit a fire earlier."

And of course, I followed.

No more sense than the dog.

Chapter Three

DANIEL

IT WAS crazy how happy I was when Julian stopped by. We'd been friends for months, I saw him all the damn time, and it seemed like logically it shouldn't be a special thing anymore. But my heart always kicked up a notch when I heard his car coming down the driveway, like an ingrained Pavlovian response. Something inside me settled when his boots thumped up the porch steps, and it was a little easier to take a deep breath when he was standing in front of me.

I tried to simply accept that happiness for the gift it was. But my mind was an old-school magician with only one trick: transforming good, simple things into sharp, pointy weapons, by reminding me that anything I bothered to care about was something that could be taken away.

I liked him. Julian was a good person. We were friends. As long as we didn't get too close, as long as I didn't—God forbid—start to *expect* anything from the man, we'd be okay.

I put aside the block of wood I'd been carving into something resembling a rounded blob and led Julian into the house. He settled into the spot on the sofa that I'd started thinking of as *his* seat, even when he wasn't here. It had long ago stopped feeling weird to have someone else in my space. Now it felt lonely when he wasn't.

"I didn't know if you'd be by today," I told him, perching on the arm of the couch near him and petting Honoria's head.

"I come most Saturdays, don't I?" His smile was warm. "I hate to feel like I'm imposing."

I snorted. "Because I have so much to do."

"Well. You might. Maybe you have raucous parties when I'm not here."

"Yes. Me, Honoria, and She-Ra the cat. It gets really wild."

"You eat all the food in the pantry?"

"Mmm. Chase after chew toys and then fall asleep, yes. I don't tell *you* how to party, Julian."

I loved the way he laughed, shameless and unreserved.

"That's fair," he agreed, his eyes dancing. "My idea of a party usually involves falling asleep with a book, so clearly I'm pretty hardcore myself." He made a face. "Ah, shit. I meant to bring you a book, but I got distracted."

"Distracted? You mean hungover from an evening of bad choices?"

He bit his lip and looked up at me. "Something like that. Um… Where's She-Ra?"

"Sleeping on my bed," I said. "Pretending to ignore me. Playing hard to get."

The little gray kitten I'd adopted a week ago was still getting used to the house and to Honoria, but she was pretty much running the place already.

"She can't be playing hard to get if she's already in your bed." His lips quirked and it made the simple tease into something else. Something hotter. Something dangerous.

I stood, needing to put some physical space between us, and stretched my arms to the ceiling. Julian's eyes darted to my stomach, where my shirt had ridden up a couple of inches above the waistband of my pants. He stared for a second and licked his lips before quickly glancing away.

It wasn't flirtation, I knew that. It was no different than me noticing and admiring the way a female friend looked in an outfit, with no creeper agenda whatsoever. What was weird was *my* reaction to his simple glance.

Stop it, I told myself firmly. *Julian's a buddy. A pal.*

But I felt a tug in my gut that called me a liar.

"How about a sandwich?" I said, already heading for the kitchen before he could answer either way. "You look like you could use a sandwich."

"Actually, I need to tell you something," he said, following me as far as the archway between the rooms. "You're not going to like it."

I opened the refrigerator and paused, frowning back at him. "Are you okay? Is your family…"

"No, no." He shook his head, leaning against the doorframe. "Nothing like that. It's more about me. Being an impulsive idiot."

"Oh." I stuck my head in the fridge again, wishing I could put my whole body inside. Julian was wearing that sweater again, the baggy gray one that highlighted his slender build and made his blue eyes look so fucking *blue*. It was hard to look at him. "Tell me, then."

"I, um. I went to the diner today."

"And they were out of pancakes?" I removed a loaf of bread and some bacon. "Or, no, worse. Out of coffee?"

"Stop," he said, chuckling. "I'm being serious."

"So am I," I said, turning my head to glance at him. "Lack of coffee would be horrific."

"This asshole, Shane Goode… Do you remember him?"

I grabbed a frying pan from the cabinet and set it on the burner to heat. "I don't think so."

"He's about my age. We went to school together. But he's never outgrown his emo phase."

I shook my head. "Not ringing any bells."

"He's still obsessed with his high school girlfriend."

I looked at him again. "In a stalker kind of way?"

"Yes. But no. She died years ago." He shook his head in frustration. "I'm not telling this well."

"You're really not," I agreed, putting the bacon in the pan. "Take a deep breath and start over."

He took my suggestion literally, closing his eyes and leaning against the wall while he inhaled deeply and then exhaled in a rush.

"Okay," he said. "Okay."

He crossed the room to the counter near the stove and pulled himself up to sit there, the way he'd done countless times while I prepped dinner. Every time he did it, I imagined what my mother would say about asses not belonging on counters, but I loved it. I loved him being at home here.

"Here's the backstory, you ready?"

"Hit me."

"Once upon a time, Shane Goode dated Molly Burke. She died in an accident. Shane never got over it. He talks about her like she's still alive, like they're still together. He's never dated anyone else."

"That sounds kind of sappy sweet?"

"No," he corrected. "Not in this case. He's gross."

I grinned. "Ah."

"And Molly was my friend Jamie's sister."

"Jamie who works at the diner?" I guessed, grabbing a fork to turn the bacon. "I met him."

"Yes. And I swear, Shane talking about Molly all the fucking time makes Jamie mental, but whatever. Jamie's an adult. It's none of my business."

I narrowed my eyes, trying to understand. I really couldn't care less about O'Leary and it's weird and wonderful history, but I could listen to Julian talk about it —or anything else—all day.

"So, you're upset because he was talking about Molly?"

"No. I'm upset because he was talking about *you*."

I dropped the fork in the pan with a clatter. "Me?"

For a second, my heart stopped before I managed to start it again. It wasn't like I was in the witness protection program here. I'd left Manhattan voluntarily, needing to put some physical distance between myself and all the fucked-up shit I wanted to forget—my career, my family, my ex-wife, the friends who'd mostly forgotten my existence once everything else imploded. My life wasn't actually in danger, even if someone in town connected the dots between Daniel Michaelson, O'Leary's hermit, and the bestselling author and heir to the Michaelson fortune I'd once been.

But I'd carefully constructed this life from bare earth, almost literally, and I liked it. I liked the rhythm of my days, and my weird menagerie of pets, and the fact that no one expected anything from me. I liked the Daniel I was when I was with Julian, and I liked that Julian had no idea who I'd been before.

"A couple of people have gone missing," he said. "A camper—"

"I remember you telling me that," I said, carefully not looking at him as I fished the fork from the bubbling pan. "What does that have to do with me?"

"Another guy went missing. And people—not the *police*

or anyone official, just a bunch of gossips—were saying maybe you were involved."

"What?" I snorted. "Oh my God, I'm a serial killer?" I laughed out loud.

"Shut up!" Julian slapped my shoulder. "It's not funny!"

I sobered, or tried to. But honestly, having someone think I was a killer was almost preferable to having them find out about my past because at least the killer thing wasn't *true*.

"I'm sorry," I said. "Sorry. Continue."

He folded his arms across his chest and glared at me.

"If you're not taking this seriously, I can't tell the rest of the story."

"I promise I am!" I shut off the flame under the bacon and stood back against the refrigerator, folding my arms across my chest, my face as blank as I could make it. "I'm very serious. Deadly serious. Tell me."

Julian huffed. "I didn't… I didn't *like* it. That they were talking about you."

He sounded so put out, so *petulant*, that it was very hard to keep my serious face, and the idea that he was upset because someone had been talking shit about me was… well. I rubbed a palm over my chest to ease the sudden warmth there.

"Julian, I promise you, it doesn't bother me what Gross Shane and a bunch of gossips—"

"Including my mother."

"Damn. Okay. What a bunch of gossips, *including your mother*, had to say about me. I had nothing to do with the disappearances—"

"I know you didn't!"

Fuck, didn't I wish I'd had that kind of unconditional support a year ago?

"So it's fine," I told him. "It's honestly, not a big—"

"So I told them we were together," Julian said miserably. He covered his eyes with one hand. "At the time of the disappearance. I said we were together."

"You gave me an alibi?" I moved toward him, prying his hand away from his face. "Are you kidding?"

"Yes. No." He took a deep breath, but kept his eyes shut so he wasn't looking at me as he explained. "Yes, I gave you an alibi. No, I'm not kidding."

"That's… that's…"

The nicest thing anyone had ever done for me. Misguided and possibly going to backfire, but still.

"You don't understand," he said. "I told them we were *together*."

"Yeah, I—"

"*Together*-together. As in, boyfriends or something. As in, that you were gay. As in, that we were most likely fucking like bunnies while these things were happening."

"Oh." I stared at him for a second, stunned. Then I repeated, "You told them we were fucking like bunnies?"

"No!" He scrubbed a hand through his hair. "No. I think it was implied, though."

"Oh," I said again, staring at him stupidly. "I, um… I have to." I took a step backward and jerked a thumb over my shoulder toward the living room. "I need to check a… thing."

Julian's eyes widened and he jumped down, like he wanted to come after me. "Daniel, I'm so sorry. It just came out of my mouth, and I didn't stop to consider…"

"No," I blurted, still backing away. "Stay." I motioned toward the pan. "Have some bacon. In fact, have all the bacon. And I'll be right back. Okay?"

"*Fuck*," I heard him breathe, followed by the sound of a

palm slapping the hard wooden countertop. I wanted to reassure him, but I needed a minute to process first.

I all but sprinted into the bedroom, closed the door behind me, and then rested my forehead against it with a *thunk*, staring down at my jeans, which had started getting tighter the second Julian's lips had said *fucking like bunnies.*

I knew Julian probably thought I was having some kind of heterosexual freakout because people thought I was gay or that we were together. In truth, I couldn't even think about any of that. I was too busy freaking out at my own body's reactions.

What the hell was I doing? This was getting ridiculous and unignorable.

Julian Ross was a guy.

A dude.

My friend.

And let me reiterate, every inch a leanly muscled, facial-hair-sporting *man.*

And I was *straight.* Always had been and therefore always would be.

"Straight as an arrow. Straight as a line. Straight as… a very straight thing." I slapped my palm against the wall. "Fucking metaphors. Whatever. Straight guys don't spring wood for other guys. This is a *fact.*"

But Jesus, it was getting harder and harder—no pun intended—to believe it.

A pair of judgmental green eyes met mine, and I felt myself blush.

"What?" I demanded of the cat currently cleaning herself on my bed. "I was having a private conversation here."

She-Ra, whose "badass" name I had not picked and would never admit I sort of enjoyed, was more hair than body. She gave no indication that she took me or anyone else seriously, which was sort of comforting in its own way.

"Look, it's not that I don't believe people can be bisexual," I whispered to her. "Of course they can. It's just that I don't… *didn't*… believe *I* could be. Like, surely it should have come up by now? I lived in Manhattan, for fuck's sake. I was *married.* I'm not sexually repressed. I'm an open-minded individual!"

And I was trying to rationalize my sexual orientation to a cat. Who was busy licking her own genitals.

"You're a shit therapist," I said, throwing myself down beside her and scratching behind her ears, willing my dick to deflate. "Should've named you Boudica."

My life in the city hadn't been simple—there wasn't a goddamn thing I missed about the place or the people I'd known, including my blonde, model-pretty wife—but at least I'd never had reason to question my basic biological responses to stimuli. Hot girls like Ingrid were supposed to get my dick hard. Guys were not. That was the lesson I'd learned when I was young, and I'd never once had a reason to question it.

Until July, when the fucking heatwave hit.

Last July

"I'M DYING. ACTUALLY, PHYSICALLY DYING," I said, looking up from where I was sprawled on my back on my porch to where Julian was sitting in my Adirondack chair. "I can feel the cells of my body cooking."

"And yet you still have the energy to complain." Julian shoved his damp hair back off his forehead. "You're a medical marvel."

"Make that my epitaph."

"Done," he snorted. "And who shall I notify of your demise?"

I made a face, taking the question a little too seriously. I thought about telling him the name of my accountant, who'd likely be the only person concerned, at least on a practical level, but I was pretty sure Julian wouldn't find it funny. God knew I didn't.

"Alert the national media, obviously," I said instead. "Medical marvel Daniel Michaelson expired from massive heat stroke today—"

"Massive heat stroke? Is that worse than regular-sized?"

"While his friend Julian Ross mocked him and his suffering—"

"Nice of you to mention me."

"To the bitter end."

"Got it." He tapped his temple. "Every word committed to memory."

I sighed. "What idiot thought he wouldn't need air conditioning in Upstate New York?"

"We could go sit in my car, if you're truly that uncomfortable," Julian offered. "Or head up to the lake?"

I shook my head. "Too many people at the lake. Especially today."

Julian's mouth twisted slightly, and I could practically read his mind. He wanted to know why I hated interacting with people, why I'd become a total hermit. But I liked him not knowing. I liked being just Daniel when I was with him. I liked leaving my baggage behind. And although I knew he wondered, he seemed content to let it go.

"There's a smaller place," he said slowly. "A pond where my dad used to take us fishing. The banks are really rocky, so it's hard to sit, which means people don't really hang out there."

I pushed to my feet. "I'll grab you a towel."

We drove down one of the little unmarked turnoffs from the Camden Road, not far from my place at all, and I parked my truck near the water. The pond didn't look very deep, but it looked clean and blessedly wet and completely unoccupied, which was more important.

I shucked off my shirt, tossed it in the front seat, and ran to the water's edge. The bank was rocky, and the tiny pebbles dug into my feet, but holy crap, the water was cold.

"Hurry up!" I told him.

He waded in behind me, grinning.

"You know, my brothers and I used to have handstand contests here," he said. "I had the best form, but Constantine held it the longest."

"That's the middle brother, right?"

He nodded and frowned slightly, like it was weird that I didn't always remember which of his siblings was which. But I didn't ask him questions about his family. It seemed weird when I was hardly about to volunteer information of my own.

"Why does it not surprise me that you had the best form?" I did a quick stroke out to the middle of the little pond, barely thirty feet from the shore. "Competent Julian."

"You know better," he said, following behind me. "More like rambling, awkward Julian. But I watched the most men's gymnastics, so…"

It was my turn to frown. I didn't know why he saw himself that way. He'd never been rambling or awkward in front of me. He was always himself—kind, intelligent, sarcastic, caring.

"Constantine, on the other hand," he continued, "was

able to stay under longest because he didn't worry about trivial things like breathing."

"What?"

He snorted. "He's a daredevil. If you hung out in town for any length of time, you'd know there are three Ross brothers: the quiet one, the hellion, and the troublemaker. Con has very little concept of his own mortality." He shrugged. "That probably explains why he became a police officer."

"The hellion did?"

It was odd to me that O'Leary had pegged people into boxes. Julian wasn't quiet. Not with me. Clearly his brother wasn't much of a hellion anymore, either.

"Yep. You know, I betcha I could still beat you. If you're up for a challenge." His blue eyes shone in the sunlight.

"Bring it. What are we doing?"

"Handstands. Duh."

"Julian, who'll judge our handstands?" Then, because I was twelve, I also added, "Duh."

Julian snickered. "Honor system. I'll rate your attempts honestly, and you'll do the same for… oh, fuck! Shit!"

"What?" I turned and headed for him immediately. "Are you okay? Leg cramp?"

The water wasn't deep, but still, drowning was a real concern.

"No! Worse! I'm being eaten alive by sunfish! Fuck. Gross! Gross, gross, gross. I remember why I stopped coming here." He flailed through the water and up onto the rocky shore. "Oh, god. Ew. There is nothing worse. Nothing!"

I laughed so hard I inhaled nearly a gallon of pond water, and in the end, I was the one who nearly drowned.

Julian helped me out of the water and onto the one

large, flat rock on the shore. I sat there curled on my side, coughing.

"Serves you right," he said primly. "For making fun of me."

I coughed even harder. "And here I thought you loved all animals," I said.

"Not. Sunfish."

I sat up straighter and grinned at him. He'd spread his towel on the stony beach, which could not have been comfortable, but he didn't complain. He hardly ever did.

I was pretty sure I knew why he hadn't sat next to me on my towel. Julian had always been very careful not to do anything too flirtatious or too overtly gay around me, like he didn't want to scare off his poor hetero friend. I could have told him it would take more than that to shake me.

"You okay over there?" he asked, and I realized I'd been staring at him too long.

"Fine," I said. "Perfect." The breeze had kicked up a tiny bit, and it felt amazing against my wet skin.

But Julian frowned and reached for his t-shirt, dragging the thin cotton over his head, like he wondered if his nakedness was making me uncomfortable. Which it absolutely was not.

Ironically, my discomfort began when he put the shirt on.

His chest was still wet, just like mine, and when he pulled the shirt on, it instantly dampened and clung to his shoulders and chest, highlighting every curve and angle. His collarbones, the slim contours of his torso, the strength of his arms.

I felt a little frisson of awareness on the back of my neck, a little electric buzz I'd only ever felt when looking at a woman.

It was so unexpected, I didn't realize it for what it was

at first. It was all tied up in the pleasure of the day, just one more way that Julian was amazing. Of course I wondered what the lake water tasted like on his skin. Wouldn't anyone?

And then my cock stiffened, despite the chill and the dampness of my fucking bathing suit.

Present

"AND THAT's when shit got complicated," I told the cat.

I'd gone back in the water, man-eating-sunfish be damned, and I'd stayed there until my equipment had practically inverted itself into my body in an attempt to find warmth.

Since then, I'd learned that the weirdest things turned me on—the sharpness of a cheekbone in the firelight, the restrained power and affection in a pair of hands as they mussed Honoria's fur, the lean strength in a pair of short but well-formed legs stretched out on my rug, the jut of collarbones peeking out of *that damn sweater.*

But a tiger didn't change his stripes. Not at thirty-three. I wasn't gay. I probably, almost certainly, wasn't even bi. I was *confused.* I was… lonely. This was all a part of my mid-life crisis. *More drama,* I could hear my father saying.

And in this case, he might have a point.

When I'd first met my ex-wife, years ago, I'd fallen in lust with her and confused it with love. We'd had sexual compatibility, so I'd inferred that we were compatible in other things, but we most definitely hadn't been. So wasn't it possible that I was somehow reversing the process here? Imagining sexual attraction because Julian was so very important to me in other ways?

"I'm definitely not imagining this fucking erection," I muttered.

But whatever the hell this attraction was, I wasn't about to experiment with my best and only friend. I willed myself to *calm the fuck down.*

"Daniel?" Julian yelled. "Can we please talk about this?"

"Coming. I was… grabbing a book for you."

I heaved myself off the bed, grabbed a random paperback from the bookshelf, and grimaced. *Mutual Destruction: A Dark Crime Novel* by Chuck Kemper.

Well. That was an erection-killer right there.

I'd read an early version of the book and loved it. Too bad almost nothing of that quirky, honest book with the gay protagonist actually made it to publication. Heather Charles, aka Chuck, had caved to pressure from our publisher and gotten herself a bland, happy bestseller. I'd refused to write to market…

And I'd gotten total failure and a self-imposed exile to a cabin in O'Leary.

I suddenly wondered if honesty was all it was cracked up to be.

I took a deep breath and threw open the door. Julian was waiting outside with his hand raised to knock.

He took a step back and held up his hands, like he wanted to reach for me, but didn't want to scare me off.

"Listen, Daniel. I'm so sorry," he said in a rush. "I fucked up royally, and I don't blame you for being angry. I get that you don't wanna be around me right now, and I'll go away and leave you alone, I promise, but first, please tell me what I can do to fix this. I'm afraid if I tell everyone I lied right now, it'll just fuel the gossips' fire. Maybe you don't care about that, but I don't want them harassing you. So I could say we broke up? Except then they'll still think you're gay. Or maybe I could…" He shook his head. "I'm out of ideas. I'm *so* sorry."

I stared at him for a second—at the sweater with the rolled-up sleeves, at the cowlicks in his dark hair, at the worry that streamed from every pore.

I knew Julian well enough to know that he hated liars. We'd read a thriller together one time that I'd thought was decent but he'd hated because one of the main characters had hidden something from the woman he was protecting. "Honesty is like a *basic expectation* to be a decent person," he'd said. "I expect it from the guy who cuts my hair, for God's sake, so I'd sure as hell expect it from someone who claims to *love* me."

And yet, here he was in my house, telling me he'd lied to protect me—lied to his family and to every person in the town he loved—and he was offering to lie again, if I wanted him to.

Maybe I should have been upset about what he'd done. He certainly seemed like he expected me to be. But all I could think was that it was a really lucky day when I got to be Julian Ross's friend. And the last thing I wanted was for him to go away and leave me alone or to deal with the fallout of his actions by himself.

An idea occurred to me, and it felt so right, I didn't stop to second-guess it or ponder the ramifications.

I stuck out my hand. "Hi. My name is Daniel Michael-son," I said.

He blinked and took a step back. "What?"

"I live out in a cabin off the Camden Road." Another step forward.

"I… Are you having a break with reality right now?" Julian demanded, backing up almost to the couch. "Should I call someone? Oh, Jesus, who would I even call?"

"I have a three-legged dog and a tiny kitten who thinks

she's my therapist." One more step, and then Julian's ass was against the arm of the couch.

"Daniel." Julian shook his head, his eyes panicked. "Babe, sit down. Please."

I grabbed his hand and shook it, even though his was entirely limp from the elbow down. "I'm your new boyfriend."

"You're my…" His blue eyes widened impossibly. "Okay, no." He looked over my shoulder to the bedroom and inhaled deeply. "You don't smell like alcohol. Is it drugs? I promise, I won't tell."

"Baby," I said, clasping our hands to my heart. "Don't deny our love." The way his cheeks flushed was addictive. I was enjoying myself immensely.

But then, I always did with Julian.

"Who even *are* you right now?"

"I'm Daniel Michaelson. I live…"

He grabbed his hand away and pushed my chest with both palms, and I laughed out loud.

"You won't be living here *or anywhere else* if you keep this up."

"Hear that, Honoria? He segues from a lie to an apology to a death threat in thirty seconds." I clapped both hands to my chest. "Is it any wonder I fell for his charms?"

Julian stood and folded his arms. "Should I leave?"

"No! Okay, okay, I'm being serious. I promise." I held my hand out, palm up and crossed my fingers. "See? Pinky swear."

"That is absolutely not how you pinky swear." He rolled his eyes.

"Sit down," I said, pushing him gently onto the arm of the couch again. "Listen to *me* now. I thought about it, and I think you're right. It *wouldn't* be a good idea for you to tell everyone you lied now. And honestly, I don't give a shit about me, Julian. They can think what they want, and I've made that perfectly clear. They don't have to like me."

He shook his head. "Why not confess, then?"

"Because it wouldn't look good for *you*." I gave him a small smile. "Bad enough they know you're friends with the weird guy who lives in the woods, right? But then to say you lied to protect me?" I shook my head. "They're gonna wonder what you're protecting me from. They're gonna harass you night and day."

Julian blew out a breath. "I hadn't considered that."

"I figured."

"So… what do we do?"

"We do nothing."

"Nothing." He blinked.

"Uh-huh. But we do nothing as *boyfriends*."

He pushed the fingers of both hands against his eyes. "Maybe *I* am the one having the break with reality."

"'Fraid not." I grabbed both his wrists and pulled them away from his face, forcing him to look at me. "Here's how this will work. You will go be a veterinarian in O'Leary. I'll stay here and keep throwing wild parties with Honoria and She-Ra. On Saturdays, or any other day you want, you come here and party with us. Okay?"

His lips twitched in a smile. "This… sounds remarkably like what we currently do?"

"Exactly. Because O'Leary has nothing to do with us, Julian. I don't care what they think, and I'm not gonna start now. But you, I care about. So we'll play it this way, at least for a while."

He sighed, but nodded. "You're right."

"And later on, you can break up with me in some kind of incredibly dramatic display, in which you lament my lack of emotional availability, which I imagine is how your past romances ended."

Julian snorted. "Yes, you know me so well."

"There'll be tears, wailing, rending of clothing."

"Wow. Mine or yours?"

"Both?"

He nodded. "Definitely both."

"And then you'll forgive me after a suitable time, and we'll go back to being friends."

"Even after your emotional unavailability and the rending of clothes?" He whistled. "I'm kind of a saint." He licked his bottom lip, and only then did I realize that I was still holding both of his hands in mine—that, in fact, I'd threaded our fingers together in a very boyfriendy sort of way. "But I'm glad we'll still be friends," he said softly.

"Julian, I promise you, we will *always* still be friends."

I'd avoided making promises to anyone for a really long time. No promises, no expectations, no disappointment. One day, I'd tattoo that shit on myself. But *this*? Making a promise to Julian? That was a promise I knew I'd keep.

Chapter Four

JULIAN

"Julian, sweetie, what do you think? Should I get *Laird's Conquest* or *A Dom for the Princess*?"

I stared out the window of the Books and More and watched a swirling cloud of burnt orange leaves fly past, caught on the November breeze like dust motes in a sunbeam.

"I dunno. Either, Mama." I leaned against the window frame. "Get both. It'll save you a trip back next week."

Her answering sigh could have felled a tree, and I looked over my shoulder in amusement as she flipped her long, dark braid over her shoulder, looking more like a teenager than a woman of fifty-something.

My mother was the human embodiment of energy. Vertically challenged as I was, I still managed to tower over the woman by a solid five inches, but it was like the power of a person twice her size had been compacted into her small frame, to the point where she appeared to vibrate, even when she was doing nothing more taxing than frowning down at a pair of romance novels she'd picked up from the sale table.

Meanwhile, I felt more and more like the human embodiment of inertia, letting my life take on a life of its own. It had been five weeks since my announcement at the diner. Five weeks since Daniel and I had officially become fake boyfriends. Five *long* weeks.

I turned back to the window and watched as Daniel strode down the street toward the laundromat, dark jeans clinging to his broad thighs, blond hair catching the sun, capable hands balancing a big duffel bag of clothes. He looked gorgeous, strong, and a little lost, the way he always did when he was in town. It was funny, because I was pretty sure he'd lived in the city for a while, so little O'Leary shouldn't have been overwhelming. Then again, interactions could be pretty anonymous in the city, and O'Leary didn't understand the meaning of the word.

"I just don't know," my mother grumbled. "Myrna says this one is terrific, but I don't think I enjoy the ones with the S-D-B-M."

"Hmmm," I said, still staring out the window, waiting for Daniel to emerge from Spinning Jenny's.

"Do you?"

"Pardon?" I turned around finally and found my mother watching me with small frown on her face.

"Julian, are you even paying attention to me?"

I was still doing penance for my lie-by-omission, as evidenced by my presence in the romance section in the first place, so it was probably best not to test her patience.

"I'm sorry, Mama. I was distracted." I took a deep breath and tried to stop thinking about Daniel, which was a lot like not thinking about elephants. "What were you saying?"

"I *said*, do you like the S-D-B-M books?"

I shook my head. "Pretty sure I don't, since I have no idea what that is."

She sighed, exasperated. "Of course you do. The stories with the whips and chains. *You've been a naughty girl. Or boy, I suppose.*" She tilted her head and looked at me. "Do they have those for guys, too?"

I blinked. Then I coughed. "Do you, um… Do you mean *BDSM*?"

Please, God, let her not mean…

"That's what I said."

It really wasn't, but it also wasn't worth arguing. "I don't… um…" I shook my head. "No."

"No, as in they don't have it for guys? Or no, as in you don't like it?"

"No, as in I don't want to talk about this," I suggested hopefully.

She narrowed her eyes, and I felt vaguely like I had when I was sixteen and worried she'd somehow seen my porn cache, which was ridiculous since my porn cache was now safely out of her house.

I snuck another glance out the window. "Are you almost done here?"

She turned toward me fully, brandishing a book with a scantily clad couple on the cover, like the fire-and-brimstone preacher of a very peculiar church. "You know I always told you that you won't know if you like something until you try it, Julian. Remember when you said you didn't like pumpkin? And now you *love* pumpkin, don't you? And then there was the time I had you read that JD Pritchard book, even though you swore you didn't like mystery thrillers, and what happened?" She paused, but didn't wait for me to reply. "You read all six of his books in a week! So how do you know you won't like this? It might change your life!"

Oh, dear God.

"Mama." My voice was strangled, so I cleared my

throat and tried again. "Remember when I told you that I wouldn't discuss my relationship with you? This… This definitely counts."

"Your relation…" She blinked, then her eyes widened. "I didn't mean… Julian *Ross*! Honestly!" She glanced around the store to see if anyone might have overheard, then lowered her voice to a whisper. "I don't want to know about *that*. I meant the *romance novels*, Julian! How do you know you don't like BDSM *romance* unless you try one?"

"Oh." Was that better? Marginally, I supposed.

She shook her head, but then she opened her eyes wide and grinned at me. "I have the best idea! Let's pick a novel and read it together." Her eyes widened in excitement. "We can be like a book club!"

I laughed out loud, because obviously that was a joke, right? A mother-son romance book club? I wanted to tell her that I was already in an unofficial book club, with Daniel, but I avoided talking about him with her as much as possible.

My mother pursed her lips, clearly *not* seeing the humor.

I sobered, quick as lightning. "No. I mean, that's a cute idea, I'm sure, for some other family," I soothed, though I couldn't imagine who, and I wouldn't wish it on my worst enemy. "Just not for me." The idea of sharing my thoughts on kink with her filled me with horror, and I truly, *viscerally*, needed her to never share her thoughts on kink with me.

"Nonsense! Hot men. Eternal love. What's not to like? Is it the women?" She whispered the last word like it was a dirty secret.

If it was possible to combust from embarrassment, I would have.

"No." Yes. "I'm just not interested in this stuff." If I

wanted to fantasize about hot guys having sex, I'd open a private browser as God intended.

"Because, who cares if you don't have sex with all the same equipment?" she continued mercilessly. "That's not what the books are about, anyway. Or, not entirely. It's more about the feelings they evoke than copying the mechanics. Heck, I've barely dated since your father died, and *I* like reading them."

"Mom! *God*, I really don't want to know this." I ran a hand through my hair, and then it was my turn to glance around the shop, thankful that the only customer besides us was too far away to hear.

My mother made a tsk-ing sound. "Don't be such a prude, Julian. It's not like I'm giving you *details* of my sex life." Blech. I really didn't want to know whether there were details in the first place. Was that immature? Then I was gonna own my immaturity. "I just thought it would be something fun we could do together." She made a sound that was both a sniff and a sigh, hurt and annoyed at once.

Ugh. It was a fucked-up thing when you *knew* you were being manipulated but were helpless to stop it.

"Pick a mystery," I pleaded, feeling myself yielding and desperate to stop it. "Or an urban fantasy. Something with blood and destruction."

She sighed again, more pointedly this time. "Fine. If a simple romance novel threatens your masculinity."

I rolled my eyes. "It doesn't threaten to do anything except bore me. This stuff's not for guys."

I took one of the books from her hand and gazed down at the cover, where a buxom redhead draped in carefully placed plaid lay sprawled atop the muscular thigh of a tan, blond barbarian whose face was contorted with possessive lust.

Wow. The thighs on that guy were… *Ahem*. And the blond hair reminded me of…

"Fine," I heard myself saying, like I was speaking from a great distance away. "Fine. We'll read *Laird's Conquest*. Together."

And that was the moment when I knew out-of-body experiences were real.

"You will?"

My mother's face brightened, and I couldn't back down.

"Yeah," I agreed, even as I wailed internally. "Why not?"

She beamed.

"But let's keep this between us, okay? Marci doesn't need to know, and Karen sure as hell doesn't."

My mother mimed zipping her lips and grabbed the book from my hand along with a second one from the table. "I'll get you your own copy so we can both start *today*!"

Oh. Yay.

She hurried up to the register on the other side of the store, and I turned my attention back out the window in time to watch Daniel emerge from the laundromat and saunter down the street toward Fanaille. His ass, molded by his well-worn jeans, was hotter than anything the dude on the novel cover could be packing under his kilt.

I pressed my cheek against the cold glass, wishing for a cold shower.

For five weeks, Daniel and I had been doing *nothing* as boyfriends. And I swear, I'd never known doing nothing could be so hard.

On the surface, everything was the same as it ever was. We were the same people we'd been last month and for the four months before that. Friends. Bros. But something had changed in *me.*

It was harder and harder to remember that he was *straight for God's sake.* I couldn't count the number of times we'd been sitting on the sofa when some innocent thing—the teasing look in his eyes or the way he swallowed his beer—made my gut clench, and suddenly, I'd be popping wood like a fucking teenager. I'd ended up clutching a pillow to my lap or, worse, moving down to the floor on the pretext of petting Honoria, so I could mentally recite facts about anteaters and wildebeests until I calmed down.

Humiliating? Why, yes, thanks, it was.

I was acutely aware of the fact that I hadn't had sex with anyone in more than half a year. And my hand was *not* an acceptable substitute, though God knew I tried day and night.

But worse than my perpetual need was the way everything felt so fucking complicated now, though I was pretty sure I was the only one who felt it.

There was no need to lie anymore—not that there ever really had been. O'Leary had learned that Shane Goode, of all people, had been behind the disappearances in town, and Daniel had absolutely no need of an alibi anymore, not that he really had in the first place.

It had been a huge blow to O'Leary to learn that the killer had been a local guy—a man a lot of people in town had known and loved, and the rest of us had known and tolerated. It had been especially difficult since he'd been caught only after he'd kidnapped old Frank Lucano, who owned Pickett's Campground, and Everett Maior, Si Sloane's boyfriend. Si had been frantic, and apparently had found them only minutes before Shane killed them both. For weeks, O'Learians had talked of nothing else as we all processed this together.

And while I was as shocked and horrified about Shane as anyone, there was a tiny part of me that was happy O'Leary had moved on to bigger and better topics than my love life. Now, the hottest gossip was whether Hen Lattimer would propose to Diane Perkins before the end of the year since, as Jay Turner had said at the diner last Saturday morning, "God knows neither of 'em's gettin' any younger." It was a sign that O'Leary was bouncing back from the trauma—at least as a whole. I knew some people, like Jamie Burke, whose sister Molly had been Shane's first victim a decade ago, would take much, much longer to heal.

Daniel knew about Shane—I'd told him as soon as I'd heard. He hadn't said anything about staging a breakup or making a heartfelt confession. But the longer the fake relationship dragged on, the harder it would be once it ended.

Daniel paused in front of the bakery door as Rena Cobb and her wife greeted him with smiles. He seemed almost taken aback by the friendly reception; his own smile took a fraction of a second too long to appear, like he hadn't thought he'd need to drag it out today.

My heart squeezed a little at the thought.

I didn't understand why he isolated himself the way he did. I was as introverted as anyone, but even solitary animals needed *some* level of interaction, so I was happy he was chatting with other people and coming out of his shell, finally. It seemed healthy. And maybe it was this fake relationship that was making him more approachable. Giving him a second chance to make some friends in this town. Maybe that was reason enough to keep the lie going.

"And maybe you'd latch onto any excuse," I whispered.

"Two copies of the same book, Angela?" I heard Bill Nickerson ask from the front counter. "Afraid you might lose one?"

"No, this one's for someone else in my book club," my mother said coyly, and I lifted my eyes to the ceiling because I knew almost exactly how the rest of this conversation would turn out. I was glad Bill couldn't see me from where I was standing.

"Oh, yeah? I didn't know you were starting a book club!" Bill said. "My wife's always looking for someone to talk to about her novels. Got room for another?"

"Of course," my mother the traitor said immediately. "I'll give Dhann a call this week. Maybe we could even have meetings here at the store, after-hours!"

Kill me now. I'd give my mother a kidney if she needed it, but there was no way I was coming to a romance book club with Dhann Nickerson… or *anyone*.

"Well, I dunno about having it here," Bill said slowly. "Maybe, I guess, if it's not too big a group?"

"Of course it wouldn't be," my mother said sharply. "But if everyone were here, wouldn't that mean *more* business for you, just in time for the holidays?"

My mother, ever the businesswoman. But Bill still seemed reluctant.

I wandered closer to the front counter, my attention caught.

"I suppose. If everyone were honest," Bill agreed. "But nowadays, who knows?"

"Is this about Shane Goode?" my mother demanded. "Just because he went crazy, that's no reason to mistrust the rest of the people we've known forever."

"S'not that, Angela," Bill said a trifle nervously. "It's the *thefts* that've been going on."

I frowned. O'Leary had always been the most crime-free place in the Western Hemisphere. I refused to believe that somehow in the last month, we'd learned we were harboring both a murderer *and* a thief.

I wandered down the cookbook aisle, the aisle closest to the register, and pretended to inspect titles on pressure cooking so I could catch a glimpse of Bill's face in the gaps between books on the shelves.

Bill Nickerson was an older man, maybe sixty-five, and I could count the number of gray strands combed neatly across the top of his otherwise-bald head. He and his wife, Dhann, had inherited the store from his parents and would likely pass it to their daughters in turn.

"What thefts?" my mother asked. "I've heard nothing." She sounded outraged, and I couldn't tell whether she was more offended by the idea of someone stealing or by the fact that she hadn't heard about it before anyone else.

Bill grimaced. "Started off small, that's why. Lisa Dorian missing clothes from her line, Janice Turner's warm rain boots went missing from her front porch."

"Kids playing pranks," my mother said dismissively. "This is nothing new."

"Yeah, but it's gotten bigger," Bill said, lowering his voice. "Jess and David over at Lyon's Imperial said they're missing a buncha food. Not just a candy bar here or there, but steaks and stuff. Somebody took a radio and a coupla tarps from the hardware store, too. Nobody wants to talk about it, not after…" He dropped his voice further. "After *Shane*. But we all gotta be careful about who comes into our stores and who's walkin' around our yards."

God, I hated that people were becoming suspicious. And more than that, I hated that even after Shane, when Bill said, *we gotta be careful*, he meant careful of people he didn't know. Outsiders. Like Daniel.

"Is it likely that all the missing items were stolen by the same person?" I asked, walking around the bookshelf. "What do the police think? Has anyone asked Mitch Turner or Si Sloane who their suspects are?"

Bill looked up in surprise, then frowned. "Well, now, I'm not sure, Doc Ross. I don't know if anyone's asked them."

Oh, for the love of Dwayne Johnson.

"I'm sure we can take it easy until they let us know there's something to worry about."

"I dunno," Bill said, shaking his head slowly. "Si and Mitch didn't see the truth about Shane Goode until after the fact. Got a lotta people wondering."

Wondering, *what*? I wanted to demand, but I hated to be rude. Instead, I took a deep breath and smiled wider.

"I mean, they're hardly psychic, Bill! But they figured it out pretty fast, didn't they? Especially since lots of people in town were pointing fingers in the wrong direction?" I tilted my head knowingly.

Bill looked chagrined. "Guess you're talking about your young man?"

My young man. Didn't I wish, Bill? Didn't I wish?

I shrugged. "People thought he was involved in the disappearance of those campers and now they know better. You'd think they'd learn that outsiders are no more dangerous than people who've lived here their whole lives."

Bill nodded, still glancing out the window with a slight frown, and I turned my head to follow his gaze. Daniel was still standing on the sidewalk outside the bakery, only now he was talking to Si and Everett.

"T'be fair, your Daniel's not the only one folks are thinking about," Bill said, nodding at Daniel uncomfortably. "There's other folks in this town who're *troubled*."

My mother and I shared a glance. "Who?" I asked.

Bill shrugged. "It's all speculation. But Jamie Burke hasn't been too good the last month or so."

"Oh, but that's not fair," I said reproachfully. "Jamie just found out that the little sister he thought died in a tragic accident a dozen years ago was actually murdered, for God's sake, and by Shane Goode, a guy Jamie considered a friend, no less. How would *you* be doing?"

"'Bout like he is," Bill admitted. "I hear what you're saying, but you can't be too careful. Not everyone's as honest and laid-back as you are, Doc. And Jamie was going off the rails even before anyone found out about Shane." He pursed his lips. "Going into Parker's bar, picking fights. Throwing furniture and causing trouble."

"There's a story between those two," my mother said, nodding her head. "Mark my words. That's what's got him all twisted up."

Privately, I agreed with her. However…

"Jamie Burke is my friend," I reminded her. "Whether he's twisted up or not, he has no more interest in Janice Turner's rain boots than I do in… in…"

"Romance novels?" Bill said, holding up one of the books on the counter, his mouth twisted to the side.

I opened my mouth, then shut it again.

"No, I agree with you, Jules," my mother interrupted, mercifully drawing Bill's attention. "Jamie's a good boy. For that matter, so is Parker." After a moment, she added, "And so is… so is… *Daniel*." She gave Bill a hard look, as though daring him to disagree.

"Well, that may be, and I hope it is. But Jess and David are fit to be tied. That's hundreds of dollars of groceries they're missing. They're gonna press charges for sure, and the thief is gonna end up in *jail*."

"Wow. Happy Holidays," I said softly.

The shop phone rang, and Bill excused himself to get it.

Meanwhile, my gaze was drawn back out the window like a magnet to true north. Daniel was still talking to Ev and Si, but he was hunched in on himself and watching

them avidly, more like a spectator than an active partici-
pant in the conversation. I wished so badly that I could be
standing next to him.

"He's handsome, I'll give you that," my mother said
thoughtfully from beside me. "A tall drink of water."

I laughed softly. "He is."

"Oh, I know!" She slapped my bicep lightly. "You
should introduce me! Right now!"

"What?" My jaw dropped. "No!"

"Why not?" she demanded. "I've been very patient,
Julian. You told me to leave you be, and I have. But it's
been over *a month* since you announced you two were
dating. I don't think it's unreasonable for me to want to
meet him."

"*No*. It's too soon. It's too—" I swallowed and my voice
turned pleading. "Too much pressure, Mama. Daniel
doesn't like crowds."

"What crowd? It's only me." She pressed a hand to her
chest and blinked innocently up at me. "I can be friendly,
Julian. Best behavior, I swear."

I shook my head again. "Not today. Please, Mama. I
want him to be prepared when he meets you, you know?
It's important for him to feel comfortable."

She capitulated with a frown. "When, then? He hardly
ever seems to be in town at all. And if things are getting
serious between you two..."

"Which I never said they were," I reminded her. *Please
don't let anyone start planning our wedding.*

"You haven't said anything at all!" she huffed. "All this
secrecy. I don't know what he does for work, I don't know
where he's from. I think any parent would want to meet
their son's boyfriend. Doesn't Daniel's family want to meet
you?"

I somehow hadn't been prepared for this question, and

it hit me at dead center mass, then bounced around my chest and lit up each of my fears and insecurities like I was a fucking pinball game. I didn't know a thing about Daniel's family. He could have been an orphan, or maybe he talked to his mother twice a day, every day, on the cell phone he hardly ever used.

"I don't know. Maybe Daniel's stronger at standing up to emotional manipulation than I am," I bit off sharply.

The look of hurt that passed over my mother's face had me backing down nearly immediately, furious with myself. Bad enough that I was a lying liar; I didn't need to compound it by being an asshole to my mother, too.

"I'm sorry," I said, dropping my arms to my sides. "I'm very… protective. I care about him."

"And that's why you'll bring him to Thanksgiving dinner."

"Mama…" I shook my head.

"Don't you *Mama* me, Julian. If he's going to be in your life, Daniel's going to need to get to know us." She lifted a hand to pat my cheek gently. "If he cares about you the way you deserve, he'll take it all in stride. Right?"

I couldn't think up an excuse for the life of me. Maybe Daniel *was* leaving town to visit some family he'd never spoken of, and this would all be a non-issue.

Or maybe it was time for me to man up and tell the truth, no matter how humiliating it was. Daniel deserved that. My mother deserved that, too.

"I…" I swallowed. "Listen, when I told everyone that he and I were dating, I…"

She tilted her head encouragingly. "You, what?"

"I…" *Fuck.* I wanted to tell her so badly, but I felt like I owed it to Daniel to tell him first. To not make another fucking decision about this without his input. "Well. I realize I should have told you first," I finished lamely, rubbing my forehead.

"Oh, Julian." My mother threw her arms around my neck and hugged me briefly. "It's okay. I forgive you."

I patted her back. "Gee. Thanks," I said in a strangled voice.

She pulled away and grinned. "And you'll invite him to Thanksgiving." Not a question, an order.

"Yeah." I nodded. "Yeah, I'll invite him." God help me.

My mother's smile widened. "Good. Your aunt and your cousin are coming up from the city, and Theo's inviting his friend Sam, I think."

Oh, joy. My aunt and cousin. "Sam Henderson? What's her family doing?"

"Her mother and stepfather moved out of O'Leary a while back, remember? They're over near Syracuse now. Sam lives with her father. But I guess he doesn't *do* Thanksgiving." The disapproval of people who didn't cook turkey was clear in her voice. "You and Daniel can bring dessert for eight."

She grabbed the books from the counter, tucking one under my arm and the other into her voluminous purse, and waved goodbye to Bill, who was still on the phone.

"I'll let you know about book club!" she called merrily as she sailed out the door.

I could only hope Bill thought she was talking to him, but I was pretty sure he knew better.

Chapter Five

DANIEL

Making small talk was fucking *exhausting*, man. I'd never enjoyed meaningless conversation, but I used to at least be competent at it, the same way I'd never liked running, but I'd put in my five miles three times a week to stay in shape. Pulling open the door to Fanaille, I realized I was nearly breathless from the exertion of being social.

But it felt good, strangely enough. Like chit-chat with Rena, Dana, Si, and Ev had triggered some kind of endorphin rush. I found myself noticing shit I wouldn't otherwise have paid attention to, like fliers for some holiday bazaar at the fairgrounds and the O'Leary Parade of Lights.

It was getting to be *Christmas* for God's sake. A fuck of a lot had changed since last year. And other stuff hadn't changed at all.

"Heya, Daniel." Cal James, the redhead who owned the bakery, nodded in my direction as he filled pastries for the two women standing in front of the register. "Haven't seen you in a bit. How's it going?"

I fought the urge to look down and verify that someone

hadn't slapped a "please talk to me" sign on my chest when I wasn't looking. I'd been coming to town more, it was true. I'd realized O'Leary was important to Julian, so I was making more of an effort to understand the place so he could really talk to me about it. But it still felt odd.

"Good," I said. "Going well."

"Oh, hey, Daniel," Cal's boyfriend said, coming out of the back room. He was carrying a tray of tiny pies— pecan, pumpkin, and apple, each one smaller than my palm. They smelled fucking *amazing*, like edible comfort.

"Those look great."

He set his tray down on the counter, and I saw his name embroidered over his right pec. *Ash.* Duh. Cal and Ash. I'd heard their names spoken together so many times it should have been impossible for me to forget.

Ash's dark eyes were friendly as they met mine. "All the credit goes to the baker," he said, tilting his head in Cal's direction. "I just do the lifting and carrying."

"Lies," Cal said, making it clear that he kept half his concentration on his partner at all times, even when he was helping customers. He turned to one of the women in front of the register. "Poppy, who makes the best key lime tarts in town?"

"Ashley does," the brunette replied obediently. She smiled widely at Ash. "And I'm not just saying that."

Ash grinned and rolled his eyes at me as if to say, *What can you do?* I found myself grinning back.

"So what can I getcha?" Ash asked. "I'm guessing… a tartlet?"

"Two of each, please." I paused. I wasn't likely to get back to town for a while, and Julian *would* be helping to eat them. "Make it three."

Ash chuckled. "Four of each would make it an even dozen," he pointed out.

"Done. And give me a few extra of the pumpkin? They're Julian's favorite."

Ash grabbed a couple of the white cardboard boxes from the back counter and started to fill them for me.

"At this point, it's probably more cost-effective to get whole pies," Cal warned me, finishing up with his customers and moving over to lay a hand on Ash's lower back. "Sure you wouldn't rather do that?"

"Nah. It's not the same," the woman called Poppy said, gathering up her boxes.

"It's not," I agreed.

She grinned. "Hey, I'm Poppy Andrews, by the way. I'm the kindergarten teacher over at the school." She jerked her head toward the front window and the rest of town beyond.

"Oh, right. Daniel Michaelson. Hey."

I offered her a hand and she shifted her boxes to shake it.

"This is my friend Marta. She's from over in Rushton," Poppy said, pushing forward a smaller, dark-haired woman.

Marta bit her lip and blushed shyly as I shook her hand.

"Are you new to town?" she asked in a self-conscious, possibly flirtatious way. Poppy interrupted before I had to answer.

"Mart-*uh*. Of *course* he's new to town! He's Julian Ross's boyfriend. Remember I told you the story about the kitten at the diner?"

"Oh my *God*!" Marta squealed. "That was the cutest, *cutest* story! And I think you two are just the cutest, *cutest* couple!"

I blinked. Even though I'd been coming to town more often in the past few weeks, and people were being marginally friendlier, likely trusting that Julian wasn't dating a serial killer, I'd never encountered someone so… very… aggressively friendly.

I looked at Ash for help, but he just shrugged helplessly.

"Um. Thanks?" I said.

Marta nodded. "Have you thought about an Instagram page? You two could be internet famous!"

"An Instagram page? For what?" I felt my eyes go wide, and I had to swallow against a wave of panic. I'd had an Instagram back in my past life that I'd deleted a long while back. I'd posted shots of my breakfast, my workouts, my novel covers, and whatever outfit of the day Ingrid had chosen for me—making sure everyone had a glimpse of my picture-perfect life, even as it had been unraveling. Was Instagram PTSD a thing? If so, I had it.

"Sure! You know, about you and Julian. As a couple."

I frowned. "An Instagram about us as a couple. Just famous for being a couple?"

Poppy rolled her eyes. "A lot of people do it. And I know, because Marta follows and re-posts all of them."

"And I would totally follow you, too." Marta's grin was radioactive-bright.

"Well. That's. Um." Was there a polite way to say *fuck no?*

"Probably never going to happen, because some of us value privacy and don't need the entire world to know our business," Cal said from behind the counter.

"Oh, Cal," Marta said, grinning. "You're adorable."

"Anyway," Poppy interjected. "We've gotta get these over to the Scarlet Maple. Marta's sister's 'surprise' bridal shower starts in an hour, and she'll have our heads if we're late." Poppy rolled her eyes. "If you get married, do yourself a favor and elope."

I nodded. I'd learned that lesson.

"Tell Julian we say hi!" Marta called over her shoulder as she walked away. "Oh, and tell him I'll be bringing Pansy in for her checkup next week!"

"He's not Julian's receptionist," I heard Poppy hiss, their voices fading as they reached the sidewalk. "I think they have better shit to talk about than your cat, honey."

Huh. "Was that weird?" I demanded, stepping closer to the register as Ash put my boxes on the counter. "I'm not used to small-town people, it's true, but that felt weird."

"Like someone was overly invested in your personal life on the basis of a thirty-second acquaintanceship?" Ash said. His lips turned down in an exaggerated frown and he shook his head. "Nah. Nothing unusual with that, is there, babe?"

"Nope. Welcome to O'Leary," Cal muttered. "'That seemed weird' is practically our town motto."

"Oh, Cal," Ash singsonged, wrapping his arms around Cal from behind. "You're so adorable."

Cal raised an eyebrow and looked over his shoulder at his boyfriend. "Is this you being cute? Are you attempting to be cute right now?"

Ash laughed and squeezed. "Is it working?"

"You're cuter when you don't try." Cal glanced at me. "You look shell-shocked, Daniel. O'Leary's a bit much to get used to."

"You look like a guy who could use some caffeine," Ash said. He stepped away from Cal and pointed me to one of the spindly little tables that lined the front of the bakery. "Grab a seat, and I'll bring you a coffee."

The place was adorably picturesque—the kind of homey look people used professional designers to achieve back in Manhattan, but this place looked authentic. The smells of vanilla and cinnamon seemed baked into the walls. I could see myself writing in here, setting up my laptop on one of the tables by the window.

I could also see someone like Marta standing behind me, reading over my shoulder, with zero sense of personal space or boundaries, so maybe I was better sitting on the sofa at home.

At least I'd been writing again. After months and months where my well of ideas had run dry, and I'd honestly wondered if I'd used up my lifetime's allotment of words by age thirty-three, I'd finally cracked my laptop open a few weeks ago. And it had been Julian, of course, who'd given me the inspiration. Julian… and Shane Goode, the sleeper serial killer.

The story Julian had told me, the picture he'd painted, of Molly Burke and her brother Jamie, of a teenage romance between Molly and Shane, and later of the horrible crimes Shane had committed in the name of love had fascinated the *hell* out of me. The ideas had bubbled up inside me one night until I couldn't sleep until I'd gotten out of bed, dug my laptop out of the closet, and written an entire outline for a book. And the words had freakin' *poured* onto the page, maybe because I knew I'd never be showing them to anyone else and they didn't have to be perfect. In the absence of fear and disappointment, my creativity had re-emerged.

And I'd set my story in O'Leary, of all places.

The bell over the door jangled and a few leaves flew in along with one very wind-blown veterinarian. "Goodness. It's a monsoon out there," he told Ash, smoothing his hair with his hand as he walked to the counter.

He didn't notice me sitting near the windows, and I almost said his name, but hesitated. It occurred to me I'd never seen Julian interacting with anyone else before. It was like the ultimate people-watching experience.

"Morning, Jules," Ash said. "Pumpkin latte?"

Julian nodded. "Extra pumpkin, please."

"You know, I don't think monsoon is the word you mean," Cal said, tilting his head to one side. "Monsoons are wet. Rainy."

"Oh." Julian shrugged. "I was sure it just meant any kind of wind. My bad. A gale, maybe. Either way, *freakin' windy.*"

Cal laughed, but I frowned. Julian was right. Why didn't he stick up for himself?

Ash handed Julian two coffees, and Julian frowned. "Two?"

"One's for your man over there." Ash lifted his chin in my direction with a grin and Julian whirled to face me.

"Oh. Hey!" His cheeks went pink, and he gave me a little wave. "I didn't know you were still here. I mean, I saw you, earlier on the street, but I was with my mom and I figured you'd already be gone, so… ah…"

He looked back at Ash and Cal like he realized we still had an audience. He grabbed the coffees and approached my little table.

Without thinking, I stood up as he approached. It was just good manners or something, not a conscious decision. But that meant we both stood by the table awkwardly when he reached me. Was I supposed to kiss him? The idea made my breath stutter.

"Um. Here." He thrust one of the coffees in my direction.

I smiled because I couldn't help it. He was so adorable —all competent and put-together in his pea coat, jeans, and button-down shirt, but just a little bit nervous, as well.

"Thanks," I said. I leaned forward, telegraphing with my eyes what I was about to do, and gave him a quick peck on the cheek.

That was boyfriendly, right? Casual.

Except he smelled really good—like something dark and spicy. His cheek was just the littlest bit prickly under my lips, like he'd missed a spot shaving. And that close, I found a tiny freckle right at the apex of his cheekbone that I'd never seen before, no matter how many times I'd looked at him. I found my hand tightening on my coffee cup and I didn't back away immediately, even though I knew I should.

In the end, Julian was the one who took a step back, looking flustered and almost fevered, and plunked himself in the chair next to mine. He took off his coat and draped it over the back of his chair.

"At the risk of sounding like Marta," Ash said. "You guys really are a cute couple."

Julian flushed a dark red.

I looked away and took my seat again. Clearly, I sucked at keeping boyfriendly things casual.

"So how've you been, Jules?" Cal asked, cleaning off the countertop with a rag. "We haven't seen you much."

"Ah, yeah," Julian said, taking a sip of his coffee. "I've been busy. At the clinic."

"Uh-huh." Ash came around the counter, a white bakery box clutched in his hand. He set it on the table between Julian and me. "A dozen fresh tartlets. Plenty of pumpkin, since they're *Julian's favorite.*"

Julian glanced at me and blushed even deeper. It was funny, but it wasn't. And what seemed like low-level embarrassment at Ash's teasing, I was pretty sure was actually high-key mortification at the fact that he was lying to everyone. I felt it too, and I barely knew these people.

"Excuse me, Ashley." Cal folded his arms over his chest and watched his partner steadily. "What were you saying not five minutes ago about O'Learians being abnormally involved in other folks' business?"

Ash gave Cal a wink and walked back around the counter.

"Anyway, I think you're doing great at adjusting to O'Leary, Daniel, all things considered," Cal told me. "Not all of us are super-friendly extroverts who like people besides our own boyfriends, even if we've lived here our whole lives."

Ash laughed out loud. "Well, I don't care if you're cranky with the world, boyfriend. At least you admit you like *me*." He grabbed Cal by the hips so they were facing one another.

"Like that was ever in doubt." Cal rested his hands on Ash's chest.

Ash did nothing more than gaze down at his partner with a soft smile—totally G-rated, nothing to see here, folks—and Cal ran a finger over Ash's chin in a simple gesture that was like sealing a promise. But the look they shared was so unbearably intimate, I felt myself go hot, and I had to turn away for a second.

I'd always had an idea of what being in love looked like—characters in books and movies who were willing to take a bullet for the person they loved and all that dramatic shit. But looking at Cal and Ash now, I realized I'd missed the point completely.

Love was *this*. Love was connection. Love was when your rough corners and missing pieces weren't imperfections you needed to correct, they were the tabs and blanks on a jigsaw puzzle piece that perfectly aligned with someone else's and locked you together seamlessly.

I was pretty sure this was the first time I'd ever seen it, and I was positive I'd never experienced it. Ingrid was a decent person, but she'd never been *my* person. We'd sure as hell never exchanged a look like that. The closest I could imagine was…

Julian.

I looked up and saw that he was blushing again—assuming he'd ever stopped—and I wondered what was going through his mind as he watched the pair.

Flustered and a little uncomfortable, I took a sip of my coffee.

"Holy shit!" I said way too loudly.

Cal and Ash startled and broke apart, like they'd almost forgotten I was there, but they turned to look at me in amusement, clearly not ashamed of anything I'd witnessed.

"Sorry. Just… this is the best coffee I've ever tasted."

"You think?" Ash said. "Cool. People around here seem to like them."

"Listen," I said. "When I lived down in the city, my wi—uh. Everyone I knew was addicted to flavored stuff like this. Every weekend we'd have to make a pilgrimage to different coffee places and rate them. Total coffee snobs. I never cared one way or another. This is better than anything I've ever had. By a lot."

Cal laughed and elbowed Ash. "See? I told you. You're good."

Julian watched me with a soft little smile on his lips.

"What?" I demanded.

He shook his head. "Nothing."

"No, tell me. What?"

Julian pursed his lips like he was trying to repress a grin. "Just the idea of you as a coffee snob. It's hard to reconcile."

"What's that supposed to mean?" I demanded, but inside I was grinning. I hadn't ever given a shit about coffee —I legitimately couldn't taste the difference between the stuff at a fast food restaurant and the stuff at a high-end cafe.

"True or false, you currently don't even own an electric coffee maker, let alone some latte machine thing." He waved a hand. "You have a stovetop coffee pot like June Cleaver."

I narrowed my eyes. "Like June Cleaver? I thought it was more… *Bear Grylls*."

Julian laughed. "I mean…"

"No, Julian, this is important. When you look at me, do you see high heels and pearls? Or do you see a rugged outdoorsman who could brew you coffee in the middle of the outback with only a teaspoon and some fishing line?"

"A spoon and fishing—?"

"Don't distract me with trivialities, answer the question!" I poked him in the ribs.

He laughed again. "I um… Did you say pumpkin tartlets?" He pointed at the box.

I shook my head slowly and grabbed the box off the table. "Not for you."

"Okay, okay. You are Bear Grylls," he said. "Never in the history of the outdoors has anyone been as rugged and… what was the other thing?"

"An outdoorsman," I supplied. "A rugged outdoorsman."

He nodded. "That's you. A hundred percent." He batted his eyelashes. "Now can I have a pastry?"

I pretended to think about it, then shook my head sadly. "Nope. I'm not convinced you're sincere."

"You're insane," he said, sitting back in his chair. "You know I could just go buy my own tartlet, right?"

"Not the same." I shook my head. "Everyone knows that pastries purchased for you taste better than ones you buy yourself."

He snorted. "Have you been hanging out with my brother Constantine?"

"No. Maybe *he'd* think I was a rugged outdoorsman."

"Oh, he'd love you," Julian agreed. "Anyone who can give me as much shit as you do would be his best friend forever." He grinned. "Helps that you're not hard on the eyes."

I sighed. "Fine, fine. Your blatant flattery worked." I set the box back down on the table. "You can have one."

Julian grinned and marked an imaginary point on an imaginary scoreboard with his index finger.

"Wow," Cal said. "No, but seriously. You two really *are* adorable. Ash, you think this is what people see when we're around?"

"Nah," Ash said. "We're still worse."

I cleared my throat and sat back. I could feel my *own* face burning.

"Guess we're pretty convincing, huh?" Julian whispered so only I could hear. "Academy Award level?"

I mustered a smile, but the problem was there *hadn't* been anything fake in the way Julian and I were joking around—it was the way we'd always been with each other, or some natural evolution of it, anyway. *Was* it flirtatious? Had Julian read anything into it? My attraction to him was *my* issue to deal with. It was important that I didn't hurt Julian when I had nothing to offer him but friendship.

"So, Julian, Ash and I are thinking of getting a dog in the spring. We wanted to chat with you about the best breeds, at some point."

Ash nodded. "More than likely, he'll have to be alone for a few hours a day and has to be okay in a small apartment most of the time." Ash frowned. "Though some people say we should buy a place outside of town first. Somewhere with a yard."

"When you say people, do you mean Henry Lattimer?" Julian asked.

Ash nodded. "Him. Jay Turner and a couple of others, too."

"They also say we should have a kid first." Cal rolled his eyes. "That's so not happening."

"We're not even married yet," Ash said in mock horror. "What kind of guy do they think I am?"

"Are you two engaged?" I asked.

Cal smiled, and Ash shook his head. "Nah. But it'll happen."

"Inevitable as the snowfall," Cal agreed.

Julian cleared his throat. "Well, don't listen to them. Plenty of breeds are just fine in an apartment, and as long as you take them for regular walks, they'll be good. I can keep an eye out, if you want. People tend to bring me strays for the short-term since the nearest shelter's out in Henrick."

Cal and Ash exchanged a glance, and Ash nodded. "Yeah, do that."

"Julian's good," I told them. "Hooked me up with Honoria and She-Ra."

"Your harem of adoring ladies," Julian snickered.

"Honoria and She-Ra?" Cal repeated.

I shook my head. "Don't look at me. Julian's all about the badass names."

"Mock if you must, but I've never lost an animal once I gave them a warrior name," Julian said.

"That might be more because you're good at what you do," Cal said.

"He's fucking *brilliant*," I corrected. "If you could see him sometimes…" I shook my head and looked at Julian, thinking of the way he'd patched up Trixie and another, sadder time over the summer, when he'd helped me bury a deer who'd been too far gone to save. "I've never met a man—I've never met a *person*—more dedicated or compassionate."

Julian touched a palm to his cheek, clearly uncomfortable with the praise. "So, yeah. Dogs." He cleared his throat. "Dogs are great."

"Bet there'll be more than one person asking you to find them one," Cal said darkly. "Have you heard there's a petty thief on the loose?"

Julian sighed. "I just heard at the bookstore. Honestly, it sounds like a whole bunch of nothing to me."

"Exactly what we said," Ash agreed.

Seeing my confused expression, Cal explained, "A few things have gone missing. Some groceries, a couple of tarps."

"I heard rainboots and a sweater," Julian said. "Not your family heirlooms. Someone's fallen on hard times, or kids are daring each other to steal things."

"Probably. But I guess at this point, after Shane, it doesn't take much to get the town in an uproar." Cal leaned both elbows on the counter. "Never thought I'd be reminiscing about the days when we had a friendlier O'Leary." He mock shuddered. "Most of the time I want people to leave me alone."

The bell over the door jangled again, and a pair of newcomers walked in.

"Hey, guys," Ash said, greeting the pair who walked in. "You looking for Rae?"

The pair were kids—teenagers—both wearing jeans and thick flannel jackets. The shorter one wore her blonde hair pulled back in a tight ponytail and the taller one, a guy, looked like... *damn*. Like a mini-Julian, but with slightly curlier hair and a troubled look in his blue eyes.

"Theo," Julian said. "Everything okay?"

Ah. The youngest Ross brother.

Theo nodded, but it was the girl who answered for both of them.

"We're fine," she said. "We just left Rae over at Hoff's for their shift. It was really cool that Parker had an opening as a bar-back." She pasted on a wide smile. "Which made me wonder if maybe *you* had any openings yet, Cal?" Her voice was wheedling, almost joking, but she rocked back and forth from her heels to her toes with a kind of tension that belied her teasing tone.

Cal and Ash exchanged a look and Cal frowned. "I wish I could, Sam, but I told you I already promised Moira's cousin a job while he's home on winter break. I just don't have need for *two* extra people."

"Nah. It's fine!" Sam waved a hand like she didn't care one way or the other. "Just, you know, thought I'd ask. I could use some cash."

"Everything okay at home?" Julian asked, sounding concerned. "Because I could—"

"No!" Sam looked offended. "Everything's fine. The concert tickets for next summer's festivals go on sale soon, and my dad's '*not spending money on anything that's not a college diploma or a decent dress.*'"

She sounded so bitter it was hard not to laugh, but her father sounded exactly like mine so I felt a strange sort of kinship with the girl.

"Ah, fuck, I'm old. Concert tickets," Cal muttered. He shook his head and grinned. "Maybe Parker needs another person at the bar?"

Sam shook her head. "Nah. I'm not eighteen for another couple months, so that's a no. But thanks anyway. I'll keep looking."

"And I'll keep you in mind, if anything comes up."

"Cool." Sam turned to walk out the door.

"Wait up," Ash called. "Uh. We have a whole bunch of day-old pastries to get rid of. You guys hungry?"

Sam's eyes lit up and Theo grinned, too. "Always," he said.

Ash grabbed a box off the back counter and filled it with the freshly baked tartlets while Cal shook his head indulgently.

Theo wandered over and Julian stood up, so I followed suit. Theo was a few inches taller than Julian, and he smirked at his older brother. "You gonna introduce us? Be rude not to."

Julian rolled his eyes. "Theo, Sam, this is Daniel Michaelson. Daniel, this is my brother Theo and his friend Sam Henderson."

"Hey," I said, stepping forward to shake his hand.

"Bet you already know all about me," Theo said. "Bet Julian can't stop talking about his favorite brother."

"All the time," I agreed. "It's constant. Creepy, really."

Julian elbowed me in the stomach. "So what are you guys up to?" he asked.

Theo shrugged. "Hanging out."

"Where?"

"I dunno." Theo raised his eyebrows. "Wherever."

"Mom know where you are?"

Theo heaved a sigh that nearly rattled the walls. "Not the exact GPS coordinates, *Dad*."

Julian sighed, and I grinned. He really did do a good father impression. I was kinda impressed. Really, Julian hardly talked about his family at all. In the Venn diagram of things we discussed, families were outside the shared loop. But seeing him interact with them, I was starting to think I was missing a big part of who Julian was.

"Have you thought about asking Hen whether Sam can work at the hardware store with you?" Julian asked.

Theo shook his head. "Hen requires parental permission, and Sam's dad…"

"Hardly comes to town," Sam said, stepping into the conversation smoothly, holding a box of pastries. "Ready, Theo?"

"You know, I might have a job for you," I found myself saying.

She narrowed her eyes at me. "You? What kind of job?"

Smart girl.

"The manual labor kind," I said. "There's a huge shed out on my property, and it's got a bunch of stuff the last owner left behind. I wanted to clean it out and repurpose it."

Julian gave me side-eye, and I shrugged. It wasn't a lie. I'd thought about it. Once or twice. And then promptly forgotten. But if Sam needed a job, maybe I could help.

She glanced at Theo, who nodded eagerly. "We can clean it out and I can borrow Fran's truck to haul it away."

Sam turned back to assess me, sucking on a tooth the whole time, like *I* was the one looking for a job. "How much money are we talking?"

I shrugged. "Five hundred bucks?" Seemed a fair, if slightly generous, price. "Half up front, half when you're done."

"No way," she scoffed, backing up a step. "Listen, I'm not into… whatever you're offering. Okay? I want an honest job for honest money."

Julian bit his lip, and Theo said, "Sam, really? He's Jules's *boyfriend*, my dude."

"I have no clue how much shit costs around here," I explained when she glared at me. "I figured that's a decent wage for a dirty job done in the cold. Besides, there was a time when I didn't have much money either, and someone helped me out." I remembered all too well what the last few months before my eighteenth birthday had felt like, and I'd wanted for a lot more than concert tickets. "Let's say I'm paying it forward. Or I can pay you less, if you want."

Something about her face as she looked at me—maybe the way she was half kid and half adult, half pixie and half tough—stirred up a strange feeling of protectiveness in me. I knew what it was to be neither one thing nor the other.

She glanced at Theo, then back to me.

"Fine," she said, tossing her ponytail. "We're in."

"Great. Stop by Monday for the key and I'll show you where the shed is. You can basically set your own hours."

"Okay," she agreed, still reluctant, like she was trying to spot the trap. Her reaction was so unlike the typical O'Leary over-friendliness and so much like my own cautious nature that I had to fight a smile. "Thanks. And thanks again for the snacks, Ash." She gave Ash a bright smile.

"Yeah, nice to meet you, Daniel! See you on Thanksgiving!" Theo called. Then to Sam, he whispered, "My mother is going to lose her mind when she hears I met Daniel before she did."

The teens departed, and Julian turned to me. "You are a softie."

"Nah. It'll be good to get that job done," I said.

"Uh-huh. And you?" He turned to Ash. "Day-old pastries, still warm from the oven?"

Ash winced. "Hopefully they won't notice."

"They'll probably eat them too fast to notice," Cal agreed.

"They looked hungry."

"Teenagers always look hungry, Ash. Look at Rae,"

Cal said. To me, he explained, "Ash's sibling is a caloric black hole. Food goes in, but they never gain an ounce."

"Wait," I said, turning to Julian. "Did Theo say he'd see me on Thanksgiving?"

"Oh. Right." Julian gave me an anemic little smile. "About that."

"Julian."

"Why don't you walk me home, boyfriend," he said. "We can eat a pastry."

He grabbed his coat from the back of his chair and swung it on. A shiny paperback flew out of the pocket and slid across the floor.

"New read?" I said, bending down to retrieve it. "Because if you expect me to go to Thanksgiving, I'm going to require a new book as…" I stopped and looked down at the cover. "Julian. What is this?"

Julian snatched it away from me and jammed it back in his large coat pocket. "It's a book. Obviously."

"It's called *Laird's*…"

"I know what it's called," he said loudly, glancing at Cal and Ash who were watching us with unconcealed amusement. "Um, thanks for the pastries, guys. Great to see you."

"Same," Ash said. "Don't be a stranger. Maybe we could all go out sometime. A double date."

"Oh. Yeah. Maybe," Julian echoed. He grabbed his coffee and strode out of the bakery. I took the box of pastries and followed.

We walked—more of a walk-jog, really—down the street silently for half a minute before Julian turned to me. "Okay, fine, say it."

"Say what?" Honestly, I'd been pondering which topic to broach first, the novel or Thanksgiving. I still hadn't decided.

He sighed. "The book is something I got roped into reading as part of a book club."

"A book club." He'd never mentioned a book club to me before.

"Yes. It's new."

"Right. And your book club is reading…" I pulled the book from his pocket before he could stop me. "*Laird's Conquest.*"

"Yes." He tried to take it back, but I held it out of his grasp.

"*Handsome Maverick Buchanan has taken her father's keep and his title. But can Lady Madelynne MacBryde steal the cold barbarian's heart?*" I glanced at Julian. His face was flaming red and he looked like he wanted to melt into the sidewalk. "Well, can she?"

Julian's nostrils flared as he glared at me. "I don't know, do I? I haven't read it yet."

I considered the book again. To be fair, at least the reader knew exactly what they were getting. And the girl on the cover had significant… attributes.

"Okay. I'll read it when you're done." I handed him the book.

"Oh, fuck off." He stuffed the book back in his pocket and walked on.

"No, I'm serious! I will. Julian!" I grabbed his arm and spun him around. "I should know better than to make fun of anyone for what they love to read. There's a reason there are a billion books in the world."

He ran his tongue over his teeth, like he was trying to gauge if I was serious. Finally, he sighed. "It wasn't my first choice, either. I got… conscripted."

"Drafted into a romance reading book club?" It was really hard to keep a straight face. "By who?"

"By my mother." He sounded so bleak, I nearly

laughed again. "It was supposed to be a secret, but I'm pretty sure she's going to invite half the town now." He sighed.

"That's not cool. Dude, everyone knows the first rule of romance book club is nobody talks about romance book club."

I waited for him to get the reference, and sure enough Julian's lips twitched, seemingly against his will. A full Julian smile bloomed on his face a second later. "You're an ass."

"But a funny one."

"Occasionally. Romance book club," he muttered. Then he snorted. Then he sighed. "She asked and I couldn't say no. I still feel guilty that I lied to her about us, and she knows it."

"Oh. You mean, your mom knows that we—" I gestured back and forth between Julian and me.

"No! No." He looked around like someone might be listening. "Nobody knows *that* except you and me. But I haven't been forthcoming about our friendship. I think she's annoyed that I've known you for so long and haven't introduced you, or at least passed on every bit of information about you."

I frowned. "My life is nobody else's business."

"I know."

"You don't owe your mother or anyone else an explanation."

"I know." His eyes looked weary.

"And you sure as heck don't have to let her press-gang you into reading romance if you'd rather not, just because—"

"Yes, Daniel. I know." He pushed a hand through his hair in frustration. "I need to get home."

He grabbed the book and stuck it back in his pocket,

then turned and continued down the street. Though he was shorter than me, I had to practically jog to keep up with him.

"Are you mad at me?"

"No."

"Really? Because it seems like you're mad at me when all I did was point out that—"

He whirled and faced me. "That I don't need to tell my mother anything about you and that I should have said no. Yes, Daniel. I know, Daniel. Story of my damn life, Daniel. Can we just not talk about this?"

He turned to walk on and I caught his arm.

"Julian," I began, not sure exactly what I wanted to say after that.

He huffed out a breath. "Look, you don't get it. You don't care what anyone thinks of you, you don't care if they're your friends, blah blah blah. That's great. Go, you. I'm not like that. My mother…" He shook his head shortly. "Constantine says I let her get away with too much, and maybe that's true, but I don't like to fight. I don't like arguing. Ever. My dad—" He shook his head again. "Whatever. Suffice it to say, I'm a big, huge pushover, especially where she is concerned. Okay?"

His blue eyes were defiant, like he expected me to give him shit, and I swallowed what I'd been about to say. I'd had my own hard-fought battles with parents who expected me to fall in line, but my scorched-earth style of filial disobedience wasn't necessarily for everyone, and I was hardly an expert on healthy family dynamics.

"Okay," I said.

He blinked. "Okay."

"And Thanksgiving?"

He pushed out a sound that was half-frustration, half-resignation. "My mother would really like to meet *my boyfriend*." He rolled his eyes. "But if that's not your thing, it's fine. I'll… figure something out."

"Find a new fake boyfriend on Craigslist, maybe? I think I saw that in a movie once."

Julian didn't appreciate my attempt at humor if the look on his face was anything to go by.

"It'll be okay," I said, not really sure whether that was true. "If you want me to be there, I'll be there." I shrugged like it didn't really matter much either way, but I wasn't really sure if that was true, either. It felt like it *shouldn't* matter, that it *shouldn't* be a big deal, but a dinner party with Julian's family sounded… fairly torturous.

"You don't mind?"

I shrugged again. "I mean, free turkey…"

He snorted. "There *will* be a ton of food. And we're making dessert."

"*We* are?" I looked at him skeptically. "Are we bringing something from the bakery? Or does your mom enjoy Oreos with spray-whipped-cream on top? Because that's pretty much the only dessert I know how to make."

Julian smirked. "Okay, *I* will make dessert while you help."

"I feel like you're discounting the cookies with whipped cream option."

"I feel like you're right." He chuckled. "How about classic apple pie. Or pumpkin bread pudding. Your choice."

"Well, I'd have to taste them both in advance in order to choose, wouldn't I?"

Julian rolled his eyes. "Is that so?"

I nodded solemnly and widened my eyes. "Maybe one this weekend and one later in the week. So I can make an informed choice."

"An informed choice." He nodded. "This isn't in any way an attempt to get free sweets?"

"Me?" I put a hand over my heart. "Julian, honestly. It's like you don't even know me." I leaned closer and whispered, "Is it working?"

Julian shivered—probably just a result of warm breath against his cold skin, but it gave me a kind of satisfaction I didn't want to think about too much.

"Yeah," he said. "I'm a sucker for those eyes." He sucked in a big breath and let it out. "And you really don't mind coming?"

Julian looked so unsure, it did funny things to my chest. He was so damn strong and competent at most things, and other times, it felt like he was afraid to step a foot out of line. I was shit at offering comfort and all those pesky gentler emotions, but I was stunned by the urge to wrap an arm around him and tell him that everything would be okay. The best I could give him was, "No, Julian. I really don't mind."

"Thanks," he said, biting his lip. "I owe you one."

"Pfft. I feel like family dinners should be at least ten. And a nomination for best fake boyfriend of the year."

Julian rolled his eyes and smiled, which was pretty much payment enough, then he grabbed the box from my hand.

"Give me a damn pastry," he said.

Chapter Six

JULIAN

"Morning," I told Daniel as I arrived at his cabin the next day. "I brought provisions." I hefted the large brown shopping bags I carried in each hand.

Daniel held the screen door open so I could walk past him into the living room and smothered a yawn with his arm. He looked *good*. I mean, he was always sexy as fuck, but it wasn't often I got to see him like this, all sleep-mussed and scruffy, wearing nothing but a pair of flannel sleep pants that hung low on his hips and a faded t-shirt that said *I'm Silently Correcting Your Grammar*.

"It definitely looks like morning," he agreed in a rough, sexy rumble. "But it's not officially morning until I've had coffee."

Shit, I was in a bad way. That voice, combined with the pajamas, had sure as fuck woken *me* up… in all kinds of ways I should not be *up*.

Honoria trotted over to greet me and immediately threw herself down on the floor on her back, presenting her stomach for rubs.

"Wow." I set my bags on the floor and knelt obediently

to ruffle the dog's fur. "Look at you two. This raucous partying has got to stop."

Daniel grinned and stretched, lifting his hands to the ceiling. His t-shirt rode up to expose a few inches of firm abs dusted with golden hair, and I nearly swallowed my tongue. *I wouldn't mind giving* him *stomach rubs, either*, I thought, before forcing my gaze down to the floor, away from all the sexy goodness.

It didn't help, though, because looking down meant I ended up staring at his bare feet and… Okay, look, I swear I'd never had a thing for feet before—like, at all—but his were huge and just a tiny bit hairy and…

Jesus, I really needed to get laid before I managed to talk myself into a foot fetish. *Down, Jules. Bad boy.*

I sucked in a deep breath, like I was about to swim underwater—through a deep pool of lust—and busied myself collecting my bags.

"Yesterday, you said nine o'clock for the Bribery Bakeathon," I reminded him. "If you wanted me to come later, you just had to call." Not that he'd ever called me. I was pretty sure he didn't even carry his phone.

"It's fine." But he yawned again and scratched his chest as he shut the front door and headed for the kitchen. "I got carried away working last night and stayed up too late."

"Oh yeah?" I trailed behind him, and Honoria trotted after me. "Working on what?"

He paused with his hand on the knob of the cabinet where he kept his coffee and shrugged very deliberately. "Just random stuff. Nothing important. So did you bring me breakfast?"

I fought a pang of disappointment at his deliberate subject change as I put my bags on the counter. Yesterday at the bakery, he'd seemed to be opening up a little. He'd lived in the city! He'd had friends who were coffee snobs! It was such trivial information, and it almost felt like he was talking about a different Daniel, one I'd never met before, but I'd hoarded every nugget like dragon treasure, and now I wanted *more*.

"Nope. But you still had half a dozen tartlets when you left my apartment yesterday. Have one of those."

Daniel cleared his throat and turned from the stove, where he was fiddling with his dark-ages manual coffee pot. "About that…"

I blinked at him. "You ate *all* of them?"

"They were in lieu of dinner," he said reasonably.

I shook my head as I unloaded the bags onto the counter—baking dishes, bags of apples, canned pumpkin, flour, sugar, and spices, since I was pretty sure he had *nothing* here. "If there were ever a sign that you're not gay, it would be that. My head explodes just thinking of the carb content."

Daniel turned and his gaze raked me from my fitted, black long-sleeved t-shirt, down over my jeans, and all the way to my hiking boots. His eyes met mine. "You have nothing to worry about."

I felt my cheeks heat. The carb thing had been half-joking. I did know way too much about shit like that, but I'd always been on the skinny side of slender, and I was hardly a fitness nut—not that O'Leary actually boasted a gym anyway, other than a few pieces of ancient equipment in the basement of the rec center attached to the library. But the way Daniel's eyes tracked over me, it felt like he wasn't seeing me as the scrawniest Ross brother, but as…

As a friend, *dumbass. Since he is your* friend. *And he is straight.*

"Uh, thanks," I said.

"And I don't think I need to cut carbs either," he said. He patted his flat stomach. "What do you think, Honoria?"

He looked down at the dog, who was sitting on the rug near the back door and whipped his shirt over his head. "Do I look fine?"

Honoria barked happily, and I very nearly did, too. *Holy fuck.* I'd seen him without a shirt before, but never when I was so far down Lust River. This felt like an extra special level of torture from the universe. His nipples honest-to-God pebbled in the chilly air and I found myself staring at this little constellation of freckles—three brown dots in an acute triangle, pointing the way to his heart. I had the bizarre thought that geometry would have been much more fun if I'd learned it in relation to Daniel.

"She thinks you'd better put your shirt back on before you get a chill," I said waspishly.

Holy fuck. I'd become my mother.

But Daniel just laughed, set his shirt on the counter, and grabbed a pair of mugs from another cabinet.

"So, what are we making here?" He leaned back against the cabinets and stared at my collection of ingredients.

My mouth was dry and I had to swallow before I could answer. "Apple pie. And pumpkin bread pudding. You pick which one for today. And preheat the oven."

He moved to the half-sized oven—which brought him two feet closer to me, because I was a stupid fuck with stupid, stupid ideas—and stared at it dubiously. "Hmm. I don't think it does 'preheat.'"

"Are you joking?" I narrowed my eyes, but he looked innocent enough. "It doesn't *do* preheat, you just turn it on and wait for it to reach temperature."

"Oh."

I rolled my eyes and knocked my hip into his, moving him out of the way so I could set the controls. "You've made me dinner a bunch of times. Dozens. I feel like you're pretending ignorance here."

"I've made you spaghetti, stir-fry, curry, tacos, and steak subs. Know how I know? Because those are the five things I know how to cook." He looked at the ceiling. "Not including sandwiches. And eggs. I know lots of ways to eat eggs."

I laughed. Jesus, he was adorable. "This is good to know." I looked at my assembled ingredients and realized I'd missed one crucial thing. "Shit. Do you have a bowl?"

He tilted his head and gave me an exasperated look. "Of course. How do you think I eat cereal?"

"A mixing bowl. A big bowl to… mix things."

He pursed his lips. "I generally mix them in a pasta pot. Will that work?"

I nodded. "Why not?"

He grabbed a giant pot from a lower cabinet and set it on the counter.

"Okay, we're going with pie today since I need more bowls for the other. I'll bring them whenever you want me to come back for round two."

"You can come anytime, Julian." I darted a look at him, but he was pouring coffee and I couldn't see his face. "I should just give you a key, not that I ever bother locking up. *Mi casa es su casa.*"

I carefully picked up the ingredients I didn't need today and put them back in the bag one by one. *My house is your house*, I wanted to say, except you won't tell me what you've been working on and you won't tell me a single thing about your life before the wind blew you to O'Leary.

But, of course, I didn't say that. I wouldn't. I couldn't.

Instead, I introduced Daniel to the magic and mystery of apple peeling, and I swear to God, it was the most fun and frustrating pie-baking experience of my life. He hung on my every word, he snitched apple pieces nearly as fast as I could cut them, and he stood *right there* next to me, with the heat pouring off his goddamn chest like he was a human furnace, making me so nervous and jittery that it's a wonder I didn't lose a finger to the paring knife.

"Congratulations," I said as I stuck the pie pan in the oven. "We have officially baked the thinnest, most appleless pie in the history of pies."

"But on the upside, I don't need to eat breakfast now." His teasing grin was heart-stopping. "And my hands smell like a fancy candle. I should bottle this. Smell."

He stuck his hand under my nose, so his fingers splayed lightly against my cheek and…

Well, at this point I needed to accept that every breath he took was going to make me hard, didn't I? It wasn't a matter of avoiding compromising situations with him. I was a giant vat of kerosene and Daniel Michaelson was a lit match.

"Yes. Apple pie is the new Axe body spray," I agreed, batting his hand away from my face and angling my body —hopefully inconspicuously—toward the counter as I cleaned it with a rag. "The ladies will love you. Maybe you should go take a shower while this bakes before you get all sticky."

Because thinking of him sticky was totally helpful.

"Don't people have sexual reactions to food smells?" he asked, ignoring my suggestion. "Like, men are supposed find women sexier when they smell like vanilla. I wonder if cinnamon has the same effect."

I could say for sure that it did.

"I have no clue what smell makes women sexy," I told him. "Whatever it is, I'm immune."

"Totally immune?" He grabbed his shirt off the counter and pushed himself up to sit there like it was the most natural thing ever, which it was. I couldn't remember how many times we'd been in this room together over the past few months while something—apparently, one of exactly five things—bubbled on the stove. He'd sit on that counter, near the refrigerator, and I'd sit on this counter near the sink, and it had been easy as breathing.

Now I couldn't breathe without smelling cinnamon, which would ever-after remind me of him.

"I mean, you don't have to talk about this at all," Daniel said. "If it's too personal."

I shook my head to clear it. I'd completely lost track of the conversation.

"I… Sorry, no, it's fine. This isn't hard for me to discuss." I shrugged. "I just don't find women sexually attractive at all. I notice the things that make them attractive, obviously. They're soft and firm in nice places, comfortable to hug. They've got appealing lines." I thought of my mother, who was an unstoppable force and who loved her kids so fiercely. Of Moira, who worked at Fanaille and was the snarkiest person I knew. Of my friend Kara, whose laugh was like sunshine. Of Kathy, my assistant, and the way she'd rest her hand on her pregnant belly. I shrugged. "I *love* women. Just not in a sexual way."

"Not ever? Not even, like, one person?"

Daniel seemed serious, like this was more than just a casual conversation, so I took a deep breath and let it out, thinking about the question.

"Not really, no," I said. "I know lots of guys who identify as gay who have, though. I'm personally pretty far along the Kinsey scale. There wasn't a time when I dated girls or had to figure things out."

He nodded slowly, thoughtfully, and I found myself saying, "What about you?"

Daniel scratched at his nose and frowned. "I honestly

never thought about it growing up." His green eyes met mine. "Me being straight was just… obvious."

I nodded and turned around so my ass rested against the counter. "Sorta like me, but opposite." And wasn't *that* the saddest truth ever?

Daniel held his coffee cup closer with two hands, like maybe he was finally feeling the chill in the air, despite the fact that the kitchen had warmed considerably. "So do you think you ever could… change?"

"Change? You mean, like, fall for a woman? Uh, no. *No.* I can't imagine that at all." It was so far out of the realm of everything I knew about myself, I chuckled. "Definitely not in a sexual way, no."

"Say no a few more times," Daniel suggested. "So I really understand."

I blinked at him in surprise. He sounded almost pissy, and Daniel hardly ever got pissy. I mentally ran through everything I'd said. Had he thought I was saying something negative about being straight or liking women?

"I'm just talking about *my* experiences. I mean, it's awesome that you like women, obviously. I think I've even heard of a couple other people like you," I joked.

Not surprisingly, the joke fell flat.

Daniel jumped down from the counter. "I think I'd better take that shower now."

"Oh. Sure." I felt like he was upset with me, and I couldn't think why. "And then maybe while it cools, we can take a walk?"

He paused in the doorway. "Very Goldilocks," he said. He turned his head and gave me a brief smile. "I approve."

By the time Daniel got out of the shower—dressed in weather-appropriate layers and hiking boots this time—the pie was done baking. Without discussion, we walked out the back door and around the side of his house, past the battered old truck he had parked there, to the little trail we usually walked together. It was basically a three-mile loop with a bunch of smaller, half-broken trails branching off it; a nice easy walk that made conversation easy.

Except today.

Daniel didn't seem overtly angry, but there was a lingering tension in the air, almost like the tangy smell of an approaching lightning storm, and for maybe the first time ever—well, the first time ever *with Daniel*—I wasn't sure how to talk normally. It seemed impossible to avoid stepping on the same conversational landmine when I wasn't sure what had triggered the first one.

"So…" I began.

He held up a hand to shush me and cocked his head as we continued walking, like he was listening to something. The wind was blowing, making the leaves rustle in the canopy above us, and I think I heard a car going past on the Camden Road, but otherwise the woods were silent. And then I heard what he'd been listening for.

"It's a chickadee, right?" he asked.

I nodded and I felt my lips quirk up. "Yeah. Good ear."

"Better be, after all the times you've pointed them out to me. Chickadees, woodpeckers, the red things…"

"Cardinals," I supplied.

"See? You think I'm not paying attention when you give me your *Animal Facts with Julian* talks on these walks, but I am," he assured me.

"Yeah? Sometimes I can't believe I don't bore you to death. I'm always shocked you want me around."

Jesus. Listen to the shit coming out of my mouth. The

equation wasn't a new one: uncertainty plus Julian Ross plus conversation equaled verbal diarrhea of the worst kind. But it was so rarely like this with Daniel. I rambled, sure, but not this way.

"Of course I do. And of course I pay attention to everything about you." He gave me a sideways glance that, thanks to a trick of the light filtering through the trees and my ever-willing libido, almost looked flirtatious.

I cleared my throat and wandered into something that I *knew* would be a minefield, but at least one I was familiar with. "I don't think that's true. If you listened to me, you'd read more JD Pritchard."

Daniel groaned. "This again? Seriously?"

"Seriously, what? I haven't brought him up for months."

"I hoped that meant you'd forgotten he existed."

"He's my favorite author!" I reminded him, outraged. "I know you have some kind of personal hate-on for him because you met him in real life, but if you'd just try to be openminded and actually read one of his books—"

"I told you, I know enough to know I never want to read them. And being friends with you despite your fascination with the guy is about as openminded as I can be."

I folded my arms over my chest, not that he could see me, since he was two steps ahead of me on the trail.

I hurried to catch up.

"Pritchard's last few books were the *best* work he's ever done. It's all personal preference, I know, but…" I hesitated. "I've liked JD Pritchard for a few years now, but I've *loved* him since *Scars*—his second-to-last book. If you haven't read the latest stuff, you're missing out."

"Uh-huh. I'll die having never truly lived. I accept this." Fuck, the things his dry humor did to me. "It's a mystery novel, Julian. He's hardly a superhero."

"I know! I know. But for me, it felt *real*." I turned and walked backward so I could see his face. "There was this tortured main character, right? A detective. He'd lost *every-thing*—money, reputation, friends, livelihood—because he… well, whatever, that's irrelevant."

"Much like JD Pritchard!"

I ignored this. "And the only way he could get his life back was by solving this decades-old murder. And all of the clues pointed toward this woman he was once madly in love with, but who'd dumped him for some other guy years before, but then it turns out… Uh, do you care if I spoil this for you?"

Daniel shook his head, clearly amused. "You won't spoil it."

"Right, okay, so this woman actually *did* commit the murder."

"Jules—"

"Hush! Listen." I laid a hand on his chest lightly. "She committed the murder, but it was to protect her son, so it was all kinds of justified."

Daniel sighed, which I took as a sign that he was deeply invested in the story and begging me to continue.

"And in the end? The detective just *walks away*," I said in a hushed voice. "He doesn't reveal that she's the murderer, he doesn't get the redemption for himself, he just leaves town."

"To go kill himself under a bridge, since he has noth-ing? And you say this *wasn't* a bestseller? I. Am. *Shocked*. Hey, what kind of animal makes tracks like that?" He pointed at the ground.

"God! Can you at least listen politely to my epic re-telling if you can't fucking read the book?" I turned around so we were facing the same direction, specifically so I could hip-check him. "*As I was saying*, the hero realizes that he doesn't need redemption. He doesn't want his job back, or his money back, or an apology from his bosses for doubting him, or whatever. Because he learns that the thing he'd been missing before was *self-respect*."

"Right." Daniel's brow knit. "Sure. Sounds like you and maybe one other person were able to wade through and catch that."

"And so, when he solves the murder," I continued, "he validates his own abilities *to himself*, even if no one else knows it. And then he protects his former lover—who I personally think he was still in love with, though opinions and multiple fanfics might argue this point—without expecting anything from her, and he sorta realizes that he *is* a good person, and he doesn't need anyone else to agree. It was…" I pulled up the sleeve of my shirt and showed him the goosebumps on my arm. "Dude, I can't even *talk* about it without getting all emotional."

Daniel ran a hand over his forehead.

"I'm not kidding when I say, I don't wanna know what the hell this guy did to you in real life. Whether he peed in your cornflakes or stole your girlfriend or whatever, that's between the two of you. If he crashed your car, or called you a shitty name, or took the last everything bagel at your snobby coffee shop." I plowed on, warming to my topic. "Or if he got promoted at your job and you didn't, or stole your work, or kidnapped your parakeet… Wait. He didn't kidnap your parakeet, did he?"

"Poor Bubbles. I miss him so. *Damn you, Pritchard!*" Daniel shook an angry fist at the sky.

"Right. I figured. You don't look like a parakeet kind of guy." Not that I could have explained what a parakeet guy looked like. "Seriously, though… Did he do something terrible?" I supposed that friend-loyalty would compel me to stop buying Pritchard's stuff, whenever the next book came out.

Daniel looked uncomfortable. "No. Nothing terrible."

"Excellent," I said happily. "Then I shall fanboy, no matter what you say."

Daniel smiled. "You're cute, you know?"

Cute. The worst compliment to give a guy who was short and slim. Made me feel like I was one of those tiny collectible stuffed animals. A human Beanie Baby.

"Shit taste in books, though," he continued.

"Thank you." I smirked. "And this is why you can never be in Romance Novel Book Club."

Daniel snorted. "Speaking of, have you started your new book yet?"

"*No.*"

"Because I'm dying to find out if she conquers the barbarian."

"If you're gonna give me shit about this…"

Daniel laughed. "I'm only giving you shit because you're so embarrassed, and I like to see you blush. I really *will* read it after you do."

I'd believe that when I saw it. And what did he mean, he liked to see me blush?

"Oh, hey! I was out here with Honoria the other day and saw something I meant to ask you about."

"Yeah?"

The path wound uphill toward a natural clearing where the trees were a bit sparser and the sunlight gilded the leaves. There was a recently fallen tree right in the center of the path, thickly covered with spindly branches.

"Over there," Daniel said, pointing at the tree. "I saw the weirdest thing. Totally worthy of an *Animal Facts with Julian* episode."

I rolled my eyes, and he steered us in the direction of

the tree, then pointed at a large pile of leaves right beside it, beneath the cover of the hanging branches. He threw an arm around my shoulder and squeezed me to his side.

"So, I was sitting against the tree, pondering life—"

He paused expectantly, and it took me a second to get that I was supposed to laugh at this, since I was too busy having an aneurism from his proximity. We'd never had anything approaching this level of physical closeness before; I'd been very careful to keep my distance, both for his comfort and my own sanity. When I finally did laugh, the sound was like a cross between a donkey braying and a balloon deflating, because I couldn't *not* be awkward.

"Hey, you okay?" He moved his arm from around my shoulder. "My arm too heavy? You know I'm just kidding about the animal facts, right? I could listen to you talk all day."

I sighed. The moment was over and I'd been too busy freaking out to memorize every single second. Story of my damn life. "Yes, I'm fine. No, you weren't… heavy." You demagnetized my brain, but you weren't *heavy.* "I just had something in my throat."

"Oh, good." To my shock, Daniel put his arm over my shoulder again.

For the second time.

Deliberately.

"Anyway," he said, like this was all so normal, like my stomach wasn't churning as I tried to analyze every *possible* meaning and compare it to the most *probable* meanings the way a NASA scientist calculates a moon landing. "I sat *there* and watched a squirrel carry an acorn over *there*. He dug a hole, but then he just covered the hole with leaves and didn't put the acorn inside. And he kept giving me *looks*."

I glanced up, and Daniel looked so genuinely suspi-cious of the squirrel's behavior that I laughed, distracted.

"You think he was a squirrel spy? Maybe had some secret squirrel codes on a secret squirrel thumb drive shaped like an acorn and didn't want you to get them?"

Daniel moved his hand off my shoulder and tickled me right below the ribs. I made a noise that was half growl, half laugh, and jumped a foot in the air, but instead of jumping away like a normal person, I jumped *toward* him, so it was less of a defensive move and more of an attack. We ended up in a pile on the ground, with Daniel flat on his back and me on my back atop him.

"Ow!" He twisted his hips, "I think I may have found the missing acorn."

"Sorry." I rolled off him, trying not to injure him further, and sat up. "Though actually, not really sorry. You tried to tickle me. Uncool."

Daniel remained sprawled on the ground where he lay, staring up at the sky and the tree canopy. He smirked. "I didn't *try* to tickle you, I *did* tickle you. Who knew competent, professional Julian Ross was so ticklish? I'm storing this information away for later."

I shook my head, desperately trying not to think of a future time when he'd put that information to use. The idea of his hands on me was almost worth my hatred of being tickled.

Almost.

"I don't know where you get this idea of me," I told him. "How long have we been friends? I'm, like, ten pounds of awkward in a five-pound bag."

"You're not awkward. You're just… you," Daniel argued, looking up at me. "You ramble a little. You're funny as hell. You're intelligent and calm in a crisis. Maybe you need to change your internal dialogue, *Jules*."

Yeah, that wasn't going to happen.

And also, since when did he call me Jules? And why did I like it so damn much?

"Squirrels are sneaky sometimes," I said. "There was probably another squirrel around, or maybe he thought you were a threat, so he pretended to hide something and didn't. Have fun looking for my acorn, sucker!"

"I didn't know wild animals could be sneaky." He drew his knees up, planting his feet on the ground. I set my back against his leg without invitation and he snorted.

"Of course they can be sneaky. You think your average squirrel has better morals than your average human?"

"Well… yeah? Or more like they don't have morals at all. I mean animals are supposed to be wild and pure and shit, right? No higher reasoning, just instinctive desire to stay alive and procreate. That's why we're so drawn to nature, isn't it? When all the other shit gets to be too much, we can boil things down to their simplest form. It's comforting."

I turned my head to stare at him as he stared at the sky. God, this man fascinated me like no other ever had and, I was very much afraid, no other ever would. Was this what having a soulmate felt like?

"I think it's the opposite," I said honestly, and it struck me that this was shit I couldn't imagine discussing with anyone else in my life, ever. "I don't think nature helps me boil things down to essentials. I think it reminds me that *everything* is possible. Nature is big and wide. There are gay swans and bonobos that have orgies, and crows that randomly try to bring down owls." I tilted my head significantly, thinking of Trixie, and Daniel nodded in acknowledgment. "I think anything can happen out here. And it reminds me that anything can happen anywhere. That's what I find comforting."

Daniel stared at me, his gaze so intense and unwavering, I felt my cheeks heat. "I find *you* comforting," he said softly. And Jesus fuck, how was I supposed to take that?

Platonically, dumbass. Obviously. Clearly. Yes.

Except then, Daniel lifted a hand and traced a finger down my cheek. A muscle in his jaw quivered, and I swear he was looking at me like… like…

"Daniel," I managed to breathe out in a tiny, strangled voice. It was a plea, a poor substitute for all the things I couldn't speak, something that loosely translated to "Please explain to me what's happening here in teeny tiny words I can't misinterpret or overexamine." And Daniel understood, or it felt like he did. His finger traced over my lip.

Oh. My. Actual. Fucking. God. *What was happening?*

No, fuck that. I didn't care as long as it kept happening.

"Anything is possible, huh?" He swallowed. "Because—"

My skin tingled everywhere—the places he touched, the places I wished he would touch, every square centimeter in between. I found it hard to draw breath without wheezing. He watched me still, his gaze worried but hopeful, and the moment was heavy with expectation. This was Christmas morning; this was the silver lining of every Grindr hookup gone awry. It would be life-shatteringly huge and minutely perfect all at once, I could feel it. I wanted him to speak. I wanted to draw it out. No, scratch that, I definitely *needed* him to speak.

I could feel my body canting toward his, almost instinctively leaning in to hear what he was going to say, and it felt like the whole world became silent, except for the rustle of branches overhead.

An acorn hit the ground beside Daniel's head and his fingers twitched against my mouth, but I ignored it.

Come on, I thought. *Come on.*

Another acorn fell, this one on his chest. And then

another, hitting the back of my head. And one more, pinging off Daniel's cheek.

"What the fuck?" Daniel said, sitting up and covering his head. "It's like rain."

Fuck. Moment lost. Again.

I glanced up and saw a gray squirrel perched on a branch above us. "More like sabotage," I snapped. I'd never hated an animal more. "The squirrel is chucking them down at us."

"Oh my God." Daniel jumped to his feet. "You mean squirrels are attacking? Like, with bombs?"

"Pretty much does away with your idea of nature being honest and pure, huh?" I was feeling bitter.

He reached down a hand and dragged me to my feet. "A little bit, yeah."

I was not a happy hiker as we continued along the trail. This morning had been disorienting and disappointing, and I needed a nap, a cold shower, and a drink, in some order or other.

"You okay?" Daniel asked a short time later as we picked our way across a muddy patch of dirt.

"You keep asking me that," I grumbled without looking at him. "I'm fine."

"Maybe you need some pie."

Maybe I needed sex. Maybe I needed to stop fucking fantasizing about a guy who couldn't give me what I wanted.

"Yeah," I agreed, kicking at a leaf on the ground as I passed it. "Pie would be good."

"You worried about Thanksgiving?"

I did look up at that. "Thanksgiving?" I blinked. "That's over a week away." It hadn't made far enough up the list for me to start actively worrying about it.

Daniel shrugged, and now it seemed like he was

actively avoiding looking at *me*. "I was just thinking it might be awkward. With you and me. Pretending to be boyfriends."

"Oh." I nodded. Now that he mentioned it, all the concerns I'd initially had about this little plan—specifically, how shitty I felt about lying to my family—came roaring back. "It's not too late to cancel, if you want. I mean, I told my mom you were coming, but I can tell her you had a change of plans. Or… maybe we could just confess. Maybe it's time." The words were hard to speak, because one part of me was so sure he was going to leap at the chance.

Daniel shook his head. "And open you up to all the questions everyone would ask? No way. Some other time. Maybe we break up after the holidays."

His words felt like a stay of execution.

"I wasn't thinking about calling it off," he continued. "I was thinking about how we could be more convincing. Yesterday at the bakery was a little awkward, wasn't it? The greeting part in particular."

The part where he hadn't been sure whether to kiss me, hug me, bro-slap me, or shake my hand? "Yeah. A little. But we'll arrive together, so that'll make it easier."

"Sure. Yeah. But still, do you think it'll be obvious that we're not together in the way we relate to each other? Physically, I mean."

A low-hanging branch, nearly naked of leaves, hung across the path right near my face, but I didn't see it. I was dimly aware of Daniel reaching out to hold it back so it didn't hit me.

"The way we relate to each other physically," I echoed. "You mean, like, it'll be obvious that there's no chemistry. Or that we… *you*… aren't attracted to me?"

"More like you can tell when people have been physically close. I'm worried that people will know we haven't had sex."

I stopped in the path, my heart thrumming like we'd been walking uphill just because he'd said the word *sex*, because cool, professional me was actually still thirteen, mentally. "I have no idea what you mean."

Daniel stopped, too, and turned to look at me. "Sure you do! You can tell, watching two people interact, whether they've had sex. Guys, girls, whatever. You can see it in the way they move around each other. There's a whole *I've seen you naked* vibe."

I squinted. Pondered. Shrugged. "Okay, allowing for a second that this is a real thing… You're thinking that we won't be able to pull off fake boyfriends because we haven't seen each other naked? Because I've seen you pretty close to naked, up at the pond."

"But you weren't looking at me *sexually*," he explained patiently, and all I could think was, *Oh, Daniel. Sweet, naïve Daniel,* even though he was probably kind of right. I'd still been trying my hardest *not* to notice him sexually over the summer. I might even have convinced myself that I'd succeeded.

I cleared my throat. "Okay. So later on, we can have a couple shots with our pie, you can take off your clothes, and I'll force myself to objectify you." I motioned toward his jeans with one hand. "Go on."

Daniel folded his arms over his chest. "I was thinking more like kissing—" He blinked. "Wait, are you saying it would be hard to think of me that way?"

Oh, things would be hard. Definitely hard.

"Drop them and I'll let you know," I said.

Daniel took a step closer and I had to fight not to retreat. All the flirting, all the banter, all the disappointment, and three fucking *months* of blue balls meant that I was hyper aware of exactly how much he'd invaded my personal space.

"Just kissing," he said.

Just kissing. *Just*.

I focused on his lips, on his tongue darting out to lick them. There would be no *just*.

"As practice, so we can keep our cover," he said, like he was trying to convince me to do something distasteful, and I wondered how well I was hiding my attraction to him, if he thought for a hot second that I wouldn't want to kiss him under any circumstances, ever, even if it was going to amp my unrequited attraction into another stratosphere. I couldn't resist him, and if he thought I could, I deserved an Oscar.

My mind whirled. People say that—hell, I'd said it myself, but I hadn't the first clue what it meant until right then. Fragments of thoughts and warnings swirled inside my head, and my consciousness couldn't grab hold of any of them. I wanted this so fucking much, I was consumed by it.

"Daniel," I began softly, not knowing exactly what I'd say next.

In the end it didn't matter, because he leaned forward and brushed his lips against mine. My stomach lurched and my breathing hitched as I felt myself fall toward him and my lips parted on a tiny puff of air.

My only conscious thought was that there was *no* awkwardness. None. Clearly, we needed to greet each other this way all the time because...

Daniel lifted his hands, framing my face as he slanted his mouth more firmly over mine. I wrapped my arms around his neck and gave myself over to it, to the firm slide of his tongue against mine and the weight of his hands on my face. I wanted to stay like this forever. I wanted to...

Daniel pulled back all at once. One second there, and the next second two feet away. He looked at me and nodded once, and then again several times. "Good," he said. "That was… helpful."

Helpful was not the word I would have used. Life defining. Soul crushing. But I couldn't say any of those things, not unless I wanted to make him uncomfortable around me for the rest of forever.

And it was apparent that I'd already freaked him out with my enthusiasm.

So. Fucking. Awkward, Julian.

"Helpful," I echoed, trying to hide my upset behind a teasing grin. "I'm glad."

Daniel cleared his throat. "Think that the, ah, pie is cool now?"

I nodded. "Definitely. Yes. Pie. Cool."

"Then no more distractions, fake boyfriend," he said, smiling as he ushered me in front of him down the path. "Let's go eat!"

Fake boyfriend. Fake kisses. Fake flirtation. Fake affection.

I was such an idiot.

Chapter Seven

DANIEL

I woke up to the sound of my alarm clock ringing and I knew, in that way you *know things* when you're half-asleep, that I was late for something. I grabbed my phone from the coffee table and hit the button to stop the alarm.

"Goddamn it," I groaned throwing myself back on the couch.

My father's voice came out of the phone.

"Well. Your language leaves much to be desired, Daniel, but it's nice of you to take my call for once."

Oh, fuck. Wasn't that just what this week needed? Wasn't that just what *any* week needed?

"Father dearest!" I said heartily, like my stomach wasn't in free fall just from hearing his condescending voice. "Nice to hear from you."

"Hmm. If that were the case, I'd think you'd have responded to the thirteen messages I've left you since June."

Trust him to know exactly how many times he'd called and exactly how many messages I'd deleted without calling back.

"You're right," I admitted. "I probably would've ignored this call too, except I was half asleep. What did you want?"

It took him a second to recover from my overt rudeness, half a second in which I could practically hear his molars grinding, ruining all those veneers he'd spent a fortune on. I hated myself for sinking to his level, and hated myself more for caring, but this week had been chock full of annoying realizations and I had zero fucks to give about my dad and how many ways I'd managed to disappoint him without trying… again.

"Thanksgiving is this week," he said. "I'm going to assume, based on your attitude, that you won't be making it to dinner?"

I rubbed my forehead with my fingers and looked around the living room. The table was piled high with dirty plates and sandwich crusts, empty cans, and even a discarded pizza box from the delivery I'd gotten Saturday night. My laptop was laying precariously between my knee and the sofa, where it must have gotten wedged last night. I was wearing week-old pajamas, I couldn't remember the last time I'd brushed my teeth, and I hadn't left the cabin in a solid week, except for occasional trots around the yard with the dog, who'd started relying on the doggie door in the kitchen since I was failing her as an owner.

"That's correct," I told him. "I'm busy."

"Busy. Is that so?"

I bristled. "Yes. Yes, it is."

"Alright. Doing what, precisely?"

"Writing," I said, channeling the same no-fucks attitude I'd given him earlier. "Precisely."

He sighed. "Again with this, Daniel? Again with the tortured author schtick, where you obsess over this one thing while the rest of your life burns to ashes? How many times do you have to go down this path before you realize how unhealthy it is?"

Only my father could make my writing career sound like an opioid addiction.

"At least once more," I told him. And then because I couldn't help it, I added, "Given that the rest of my life is *already* in ashes, I don't think there's a whole lot to lose."

Though, even as I spoke the words I knew they weren't quite true. They might have been last spring. Sure as fuck last winter. But not now. Not since Julian.

Julian, who I hadn't seen in over a week.

I winced, and was glad my father couldn't see it.

"And whose fault is that?" my father demanded. "If you would just get yourself a regular job, Daniel. Work in editing, work in education, work at my firm—"

"No, thank you," I said acidly. Yes, there had been an opening at my father's investment firm with my name on it since birth, practically. My inability to get excited about stock dividends had been the first in a long line of disappointments my father had endured. "You were happy enough when I was making good money as a writer," I reminded him. "When my first four books did well, you had no problem bragging to your friends and showing me off."

He sighed so lustily that if the butterfly effect was real, a devastating windstorm was about to hit Southern Europe.

"Your mother and I were proud of your successes, Daniel. Of course we were. We always have been. We love you. But it's been too painful to watch the crash that follows."

Trust my father to find a way to be the victim in every situation.

"I'm not asking you to watch anything. You gave me

my marching orders last Christmas. You're the one who's been calling me. Thirteen times, apparently."

"You insist on painting yourself as a victim," he said, his words so close to my own thoughts about *him* that I clenched the phone painfully tight. "You must understand that your actions have consequences that affect all of us. When things started to go poorly for you…"

"When two books in a row tanked and my publisher cancelled my contract, you mean. Please, don't spare the truth on my account."

Another sigh. "Even after the first book did badly, you became a different person."

"Well, no shit."

"You didn't smile, you didn't want to socialize, you refused to discuss alternate plans for your future."

Alternate plans, like a career in *investments*.

"I wasn't fun anymore," I agreed. And I hadn't wanted to socialize—not when every conversation seemed to revert back to discussing my failure: What was I working on? What would the next stage of my life bring? Why wouldn't I just *try* working for my father? The first two, my so-called friends had asked with undisguised *schadenfreude*. The last, which had been Ingrid's constant refrain, had led to our separation long before my disastrous last book was released.

"When people care about you, they don't want to see you struggling, Daniel."

I clenched my jaw. "It's funny, Dad. I always thought when people who loved you saw you struggling, they'd want to help. To encourage you."

"Which is why I keep offering to help you!" His frustration was nearly palpable. "To give you a position at Michaelson Investments, to get you contacts, to stake you financially if you need it!"

I closed my eyes and leaned back on the sofa.

Round and round and round again. The things he wanted to give me were the very last things I needed, and the only things I wanted from him were somehow impossible for him to provide.

"I don't need money. And I don't want to work for you. I'm happier when I'm writing, and I'm finally back to it after months and months. Now was there another reason for your call?"

"That woman got to you, didn't she?" he demanded angrily. "This is all her fault."

I was confused for a second. *That woman?*

"She called me, you know," he continued. "When she couldn't get ahold of you. Said she'd left you a dozen messages, and you hadn't replied to any. Said she needed to discuss your future, said she had offers for you. I told her to mind her own damn business."

"What? Who?"

"Sabrina, of course. Your *agent*." He spoke the word like it was code for *the leader of your satanic cult* or *your drug dealer*. Or both.

"Sabrina called you? Huh." I couldn't help but smile a little.

Sabrina Sanford was a one-hundred-pound whirling dervish of sarcasm and optimism, a unique combination that was part of the reason I'd signed with her, even though there was a time when I could have found someone with a higher profile. If you fell down one flight of stairs, she'd remind you that at least it wasn't *two*. And when the first negative reviews on my last book had poured in, she'd reminded me that at least I was still tall and no one could take that away from me, which had made me grin for maybe the first and only time last year.

She'd texted me a million times when things had first

gone tits-up, and still contacted me every few weeks. She'd sent me emails, voicemails… pretty much everything but singing telegrams. She had offers to discuss. She believed in me. She knew my next book would be another bestseller and I'd be back in the game. But it was Sabrina's job to say that shit, and I'd been determined not to take her down with me on my shame spiral, so I'd ignored her.

"She called me," he confirmed. "And I told her you weren't interested. She didn't go into detail, but the offers she had weren't from any publishing company I'd ever heard of. And anyway, I told her you were moving on. That this phase was over and done with."

Scale of one to ten, how immature was it that even though I'd killed off the idea of publishing again completely—had shot it, stabbed it, strangled it, and buried it six feet under in my mind—the idea had fresh appeal now that my father had decided I couldn't do it?

There were some people in your life who encouraged you with positivity, and others who encouraged you with criticism, but there were some, like my parents, who encouraged with *discouragement.* Anything they believed I couldn't or shouldn't do became irresistibly tempting.

"Why are you fielding my offers?" I demanded. "Since when is that any of *your* business?"

"I'm not. I'm cleaning up your messes. Sabrina said she'd tried to contact you multiple times, but you hadn't replied. She contacted me to see if I could get in touch with you."

"Wait. Just so I understand," I said patiently. "You want Sabrina to stop calling me, and you *want* me to ignore her, but somehow when I ignore her, this makes you think you have the right to meddle in my affairs."

My father heaved a long-suffering sigh. "I haven't meddled in anything, Daniel. *Honestly.* So much drama.

I've had a couple of conversations. None of the offers she's had sound like anything you'd be interested in."

I counted to ten in my head. "Let me say this clearly, so you can't misunderstand. *Stay out of it. Stay out of my life.*"

He paused, and for a second, I wondered if I'd actually gotten through. But when he spoke, he sounded more bewildered than ever. "Daniel, you've accused your mother and me of not supporting you. But when I get involved, I'm involved too much? I truly don't know how you want me to be. I don't know how to care just enough, but not too much, and only in the right ways." He exhaled harshly. "You make it so difficult to love you, son."

I pushed my head back against the couch cushion and closed my eyes, which were burning just a little. I would not cry over my father like I was a fucking toddler. I would *not*.

"Then maybe stop trying," I choked out. "If it's so difficult."

"I've tried," he said baldly. "But it's like you and your writing. Somehow, I just can't stop."

I said nothing. There was a part of me that craved his love and approval—always had, always would. But I also knew I'd never actually earn either, and that kept me quiet.

"In any case," he said finally. "Thanksgiving."

I took a breath and let it out. "I have plans."

"Where? Alone?"

"No. I'll be with..." *Huh*. Well. There was another issue I'd done my best not to think about for the past week. Friend didn't seem appropriate anymore, friend-I-kissed-occasionally was TMI, and fake-boyfriend was too ridiculous, even if I'd love to hear my father sputter over it. "I'll be staying local. In O'Leary. Thanks anyway."

"Hmm. Then we'll expect to see you at Christmas. This foolishness of you cutting yourself off from the world has got to end. And before you suggest again that we disowned you, we certainly did *not*. We said that it was time for you to find a stable career. To live up to your potential. If you chose to take that in the most dramatic possible way, that's your problem."

Of course it was. "My potential. As a Michaelson."

"Exactly."

"Exactly," I echoed.

I would rather spend Christmas at the bottom of a lake than discussing my potential as a Michaelson.

"And Daniel, consider lightening up, hmm? You hold people to an impossibly high standard," my father the hypocrite said. And then he disconnected.

"Jesus Christ. Jesus *fucking* Christ!" I threw the phone against the sofa cushion and ran both hands through my hair, yanking at the longish strands.

Honoria looked up from her spot on the rug by the fire, and She-Ra darted into the living room from wherever she'd been hiding, like she was afraid of missing some drama.

"The man is going to make me mental," I told them. I paused and considered. "No, scratch that. I'm there already."

She-Ra jumped up on the couch by my legs and sat down primly, staring at me the whole while.

"What?" I demanded. I blew out a breath. "He's ridiculous. 'You hold people to an impossibly high standard. Lighten up.' Can you imagine? What does that even *mean*? I'm light! I'm nothing *but* light. The man doesn't even *know* me. I don't own hundred-dollar shoes anymore, I drive a rusted truck, I don't have cable, and I don't care what anyone thinks of me."

But that last bit was a lie, wasn't it? Because I did still care what he thought of me, or he wouldn't have pissed me off the way he had. And though the trappings of my life had changed completely, in some ways I was still running scared.

Case in point, the way I'd neatly avoided Julian all week.

"Helpful," I mumbled, scrubbing at my cheeks. "I kissed the man, then told him it was *helpful*."

I was definitely crazy because I couldn't think of many things *less* helpful than that kiss. It had been hard enough to avoid thinking of Julian as anything but a friend *before*. Now, it was absolutely impossible.

We'd hiked back here to eat pie, and never in the history of the universe have the simple tasks of walking and eating been so torturous. Every step Julian took I spent either marveling at the miraculousness of the way his body was put together—Just look at all those muscles bunching and flexing as he put one foot in front of the other! How had I never noticed how *hot* walking was before?—or shaking my head at my own idiocy and actively trying to block myself from being aware of him. And then when we'd gotten back here, there'd been pie. Pie that Julian licked off his spoon. Pie that tasted tart and sweet, simple and perfect, just like Julian.

For the first time ever with Julian, I'd cut our conversation short, let out a loud yawn, and told him I was ready for bed. I hadn't protested when he'd offered to leave, either. I was pretty sure he hadn't bought my excuse about an early bedtime, though. Mostly because it had only been 4:00 p.m.

And then I'd doubled down on that awkwardness when I texted him—a rarity in and of itself—to say that I was *busy* and that I'd call him later in the week to get together. That was nearly a week ago.

Running scared? Let me rephrase. More like frozen in terror.

I'd never felt anything like the rightness of that kiss, though. Every bit of it. The tangy, sweet taste of him, the scratch of facial hair under my hands, the spareness of his frame, and the solidity of him. In the half second before our lips touched, I'd been worried I'd hate it and he'd know. I'd been worried I'd hurt his feelings. But by the time I'd been capable of rational thought again, I'd realized I'd gotten everything ass-backwards. Now, I was worried because I'd liked it a lot—too much—and he had to have realized it, but I still didn't know what the heck it meant that I liked it.

There was no way in which I was a good candidate for a—my mind stuttered for a second—*boyfriend*. Not a real one, anyway. I was a failure as a writer, I had a shit track record with relationships, both platonic and romantic, and I hadn't the first clue what the fuck was happening with this sexual awakening *thing* I seemed to be undergoing.

Julian, meanwhile, was a permanent sort of person, a guy who was devoted to his family, his friends, and his career. And he lived in O'Leary, which was about the most permanent, unchanging place west of the Pyramids of Giza… and come to think of it, even Giza had a fucking *Pizza Hut.*

I cared about Julian a lot, and I didn't want him to think I could give him anything *real.* I didn't know if I was even capable of it. And even though I'd been ready to kill the cockblocking squirrel that had interrupted us when I was about to tell Julian it looked like I was maybe, possibly *not-straight*, by now I was glad we'd been interrupted. Better Julian think his fake boyfriend was having a heterosexual freak-out after a practice kiss than for him to know I was a late-blooming, possibly bisexual hot mess who was shit-scared to commit to anything.

I shoved my laptop under the sofa, collected the trash and dirty dishes, and brought them to the sink to wash up. I'd let myself become a goblin this week, focusing on writing so I could tune out everything else around me, but it hadn't worked well. It was hard to be creative when I was expending so much energy not thinking about him, and I felt… ill. Not lovesick or pining, but tired. Restless. Withering. Like Julian was sunlight and I was starving for him.

I leaned against the sink and stared at the cat, who'd followed me into the kitchen and now perched on the counter. "I'm disgusting," I told her. "A total sap."

She didn't disagree.

I picked her up and cradled her against my chest as I walked to the bathroom.

"Okay, first things first: shower, because it's been three days, and that's not a good look for anyone. Then, head for town and see how pissed Jules is." I grimaced. I wouldn't blame him if he was. I wasn't sure if we'd gone a whole week without seeing each other since May, and I couldn't have picked a worse time to have a freak-out.

"He really does deserve better," I told She-Ra, stroking her velvety gray fur, and once again, she had no comment.

———

My stomach growled as I filled a coffee mug before heading out the door, and I wondered if maybe I should stop by the bakery before seeing Julian. Pastries would be a good peace offering, wouldn't they? I hadn't been able to eat the rest of the pie Julian had left behind, since just the sight of it had made me think of kissing him… and then all the things that might follow up the kissing, which had made my heart beat way too fast.

"Bill me later," I told my furry therapists as I grabbed my keys.

I pulled the door closed behind me and stopped short as I spied an ancient blue sedan pulling down my driveway.

"Hey," I said after Theo had pulled up next to my truck and Sam had climbed out of the passenger's side. "You guys working today?"

"Yep." Sam tightened her messy ponytail and frowned at me. "You said that was cool, right? Didn't matter if we worked sporadically since Theo's already got a job and I have some babysitting gigs?"

I fought a smile. Sam and Theo had come by to get the key to the shed last week, as planned, and had spent a couple of hours working on the clean-out since then. Each time they came by, Sam checked in with me before starting. The girl was constantly assuming I'd either change the rules or yank the job away from her entirely. Always looking for the catch. She was like a smaller, cuter me.

"That's what I said when I gave you guys the key," I agreed. "Work as much or as little as you like, whenever you like. I won't be doing anything with that shed all winter, for sure." I actually didn't have any concrete plans for the building at all, but I wouldn't say that.

She nodded as Theo came around the car to stand beside her. "And you don't care what we do with the stuff we haul out?"

"Nope. It's all junk, as far as I know. If you find something fit for *Antiques Roadshow*, it's all yours."

"Fit for *what?*" Theo wrinkled his forehead.

"Is that the show with all the old people?" Sam said pityingly.

I rolled my eyes. "You know, I appreciate how you make sure I never feel too good about myself, Sam," I told her. "I should pay you extra for the ego checks."

She grinned. "I could do that professionally." She slapped Theo lightly in the stomach and he grunted. "Couldn't you see that? After graduation? Professional Ego Management?"

I narrowed my eyes and looked back and forth from her to Theo. "After graduation? I thought you'd already graduated."

Sam's grin died. "Theo did, last spring. I'm a year behind."

"Uh-huh. So shouldn't you be in school, given that this is a Monday?" I paused, fighting the urge to check my phone. I was pretty sure it was Monday.

Theo cocked his head. "Yeah, but it's a professional development day."

"Oh." I shrugged sheepishly. What the hell did I know? "Well, get to work, then, kids."

Sam snickered. "*Get to work, kids*? What's next, grandpa? Don't do drugs, stop listening to that evil rock 'n' roll music?"

"Yes." I narrowed my eyes. "And while you're at it, get off my lawn."

She laughed, then looked around the clearing separating my cabin from the woods, which was basically a carpet of damp, faded foliage and very patchy grass. "I don't think you *have* a lawn, Mr. Michaelson."

"If you're gonna give me shit professionally, you might as well call me Daniel," I told her. I looked at Theo, who'd been mostly quiet. "Right?"

He shrugged. "If you say so," he said sullenly.

I blinked. This was the second time I'd spoken to Theo

after first meeting him at the bakery, and he'd been friendly enough up to now.

"There a problem?"

"I dunno," Theo returned. "Is there?"

I looked questioningly at Sam, who rolled her eyes. "Theo's just pissy because the whole town is wondering what's going on with you and Doc Ross."

I frowned. Had Julian said something about lying? Had he told them we broke up?

Why was I so disappointed?

"What's going on with us?" I hedged, taking a sip of my coffee.

She shrugged. "You haven't been around, and he hasn't been out here."

I blinked. "I hardly ever come to town." And I couldn't believe anyone would notice that I hadn't. "Are people keeping tabs on me now? On him?"

Sam snorted. "Uh, it's not personal. Honestly, you're not that interesting, Daniel." She shrugged. "Just everyone minding everyone else's business, as always."

"Things have gone missing around town," Theo said. "We got a bunch of amateur detectives trying to crack the case." Sam shot him a look, but Theo shrugged expansively. "Sam and I are, like, the only ones who don't give a shit. Ms. Semple from Pearl's Antiques has been peering out the window and writing down times and descriptions for everyone who walks past the store. *Ten o'clock - Theodore Ross walks toward the bakery. Ten thirty - Ross leaves bakery. Must follow up with Caelan James to see why Ross spent half an hour eating.*"

I laughed and Sam smiled reluctantly, too.

"Who's on the suspect list?" I asked.

"Besides you?" Theo asked blandly. "I mean, you are fairly sketchy."

I lifted my chin. "Wow. *Sketchy*. That's a new one."

"Are you and Jules still together?" he demanded.

"Oh, for fuck's sake, Theo! Tone down the caveman. I told you, it's *their* business." Sam shoved Theo's arm.

But Theo's expression didn't change. "I'm looking out for my brother."

Sam sighed. "He's been cranky," she explained to me.

"Who? Theo?"

"Nah. Doc Ross."

Theo pursed his lips and admitted, "He had a run-in with a patient over a bird."

"It was more than that," Sam argued. "You're not telling it right. See, Lina Davenport has this cockatoo she loves more than life itself? Like, this cockatoo eats better than I do."

"Not saying much," Theo muttered.

She elbowed him in the ribs. "Anyway, last week she brought the bird in twice because it's been shedding feathers, and I guess Julian kept explaining to her that it was normal, and when she called a third time, he said he didn't have time to see her. She saw him in Fanaille later and yelled at him. '*If my bird dies, it's on your head, Julian Ross!*'"

"Are you serious?"

Sam and Theo nodded. "And," Sam continued, "Jules told her that her constant yelling was more stressful to the bird than a normal annual molting. She swore she was gonna start taking her bird to the vet in Rushton from now on."

"Sounds like she was being ridiculous," I said, annoyed on Julian's behalf. "Julian's the most dedicated vet I know, and if he thought the bird was sick, he wouldn't hesitate to treat it. The woman needs to chill."

Sam rolled her eyes. "Well, yeah," she agreed. "Obviously. But the point is, it's way out of character. Dr. Ross is always patient. Like, *always* patient."

"No one is *always* patient," I told her. "Just like no one is always having a good day, or always happy. Shit happens."

"Not to Jules." Theo shook his head. "Jules doesn't lose his cool like that. He's *always* polite. Always. I've pretty much only heard of him raising his voice in public twice, and both of them have been since you two started dating." The look he gave me said he blamed *me* for this turn of events. "The first time was when he stood up in the diner and defended you to everyone."

"Ah, that's not the same thing as this at all, though," Sam said. She grinned softly. "That was just classic romantic-movie bullshit. Sappy and sweet at the same time. Defending your honor, right in front of everyone."

My heart squeezed just a little. I'd been a really shitty friend, but I could do better. I *would* do better.

"Well, you can tell everyone that Julian and I are fine. Okay? I've been busy this week, and we haven't gotten to see each other." I smirked. "I've been cranky, too."

Theo narrowed his eyes at me, then nodded slowly. "And you're still coming to Thanksgiving dinner?"

"Of course," I said. "Why wouldn't I? Julian's my boyfriend."

Theo nodded again, once, and his shoulders loosened. "Sorry. I'm just a little protective. He's a really good brother, you know? And it seems like some guys don't appreciate him."

"And you know this how?" Sam's voice dripped with scorn. "Julian doesn't talk to you about his sex life."

"No shit, and thank God." Theo shuddered. "But my mom says he doesn't open up to people very well." He shot an uncomfortable glance in my direction, like he was worried he'd said too much.

Meanwhile, I couldn't imagine who he was talking about. Julian had always been open with me, from day one.

"You can set your minds at rest, young ones," I told them. "I was just on my way to see Julian now."

"Yeah? Cool. That's… cool. He's at the clinic," Theo added. "We drove by there on our way out, and it was *packed*."

"Betcha half of them are just there to make sure Doc Ross hasn't been abducted by aliens and replaced with a pod person," Sam laughed. "An impatient pod person."

Sure enough, when I got to the clinic, the place was more crowded than I'd ever seen it. There were easily a dozen people packed into the tiny waiting room, though only three or four animals, as though every animal required an entire posse of caretakers.

Even Julian's assistant, Kathy, who usually had the air of a perky cheerleader, looked frazzled today. She sat behind the desk rubbing her pregnant belly and barely glanced up when the bell jangled as I opened the door, though every other eye in the place tracked my movement.

"No, Ms. Dorian, I'm afraid we don't have time to see Lexie today. We're booked solid all day long. We could try tomorrow, or… Yes, I understand you're worried, but there's simply not… No, ma'am, he will not let you come in after hours to see her. No, ma'am, I will *not* just go and ask him." She huffed out a breath. "Tomorrow is the soonest we… Okay, yes. Ten o'clock tomorrow. Thank—" She broke off, then pulled the phone away from her ear and stared at it. "So rude!"

At that moment, the door behind the reception desk swung open, and Julian ushered out an older man cradling a poodle.

"I think she'll be fine, Jay. Maybe just some extra water and a little more walking."

Jay nodded. "Yep. Sounds good. Thanks for looking at her, Doc—" He lifted his head and spotted me; then he licked his lips, and his eyes gleamed. He turned to Julian with a coy smile. "Actually, I maybe just had a couple more questions."

But it was too late. Julian's blue gaze had found mine, and he wasn't paying attention to Jay anymore. Instead, he was fixated on me like I was an apparition, and maybe with good cause. I couldn't remember the last time I'd walked into the clinic during operating hours, and maybe he'd worried I'd skipped town after not talking to him for a week. I felt the back of my neck heat as the weight of a dozen stares fell on us.

I moved forward, before anyone else could call his name or claim his attention, wedging myself between him and the poodle-man, and then pushing Julian into the exam room. "We'll just be a minute," I told Kathy. Then I kicked the door shut behind me with my boot.

"Hi," I said, once the latch had clicked into place. The damn door didn't have a lock, but that was fine. I was here to talk.

Except *fuck*, Julian was a sight for sore eyes. He looked good—not objectively good, given the dark circles under his eyes and the pallor of his cheeks, but he was Julian, and he was gorgeous, and I'd missed seeing his face, so I drank in the sight of him like rain after a drought.

Without conscious thought, I took a fraction of a step closer, and closer, and closer again, until I'd eliminated all the space between us. I put my hand on his waist, just to feel his muscles flex under my hand. Part of my brain was whispering *danger, danger*, but the other part was screaming, *Oh, thank God, finally*, so I let it happen.

"Uh, hi?" Julian swallowed convulsively, and his eyes were huge as he stared up at me.

"Jules, I'm sorry," I said.

He blinked. "F-for what?"

"For not being around this week." I shook my head. "It was shitty."

"No, no! God, no. It's fine. It's cool. You were busy. With *things*. I get it." He laughed, and it sounded a little forced. "And I figured I freaked you out with that practice kiss. I, um… got a little too into it, huh?" His cheeks flamed, and he couldn't seem to meet my eyes. "I mean, in my defense, I'm a red-blooded gay man, so kissing an attractive guy is, you know, gonna elicit a certain response. But you were trying to be all PG-rated practice-boyfriendy, and I was all, 'Rawr! I haven't had a Grindr hookup in months!' and basically tried to cannibalize you, which would freak anyone out, right? *Heh heh.* If anything, I owe *you* an apology for pushing things and getting all into it when I know you weren't, really."

"That's not what happened. I… Wait, Grindr hookups?" My mind snagged on that one crucial piece of information.

Julian turned even redder. "Yeah, Grindr is an app that—"

"I know what it *is*, Jules."

"Oh. Did you think we didn't have it out here in the sticks?" He smiled tightly. "I will admit, the pickings are a lot slimmer than you likely had back in the city." His smile fled instantly. "I mean, not *you*-you. Not you specifically. *Obviously.* I mean, gay men. Men who… have sex with other men." His words choked off with a strangled little cough. He took a deep breath and gestured helplessly toward the door and the waiting room beyond. "So, um, I should probably see patients now. Patients would be good."

So *this* was awkward Julian? The one he'd been warning me about for months? *Shit.* Scale of one to ten, how bad was it that this Julian was at least as attractive as cool, competent Julian, and maybe even more?

"I was just surprised you were into Grindr," I said. "I thought that was more one-shot dates and stuff."

"Dates?" He huffed. "I mean, we could call them dates. Basically they were hookups. Booty calls. Scratching an itch. There are definitely some people who find dates that way—Cal and Ash met on an app. Did you know?—but, um, these were not those kinds of dates, no." He pulled at the collar of his blue scrubs. "Is it warm in here? I should have Kathy check the heat."

I lifted a hand to brush the dark hair from his forehead, then trailed my fingers over his cheek to cup his jaw.

"So, what you're saying is that when Dr. Julian Ross needs to scratch an itch, he goes on Grindr?" I teased.

He swallowed hard and tried to back away, but the exam table behind him blocked his retreat. "I haven't lately. Not for months." His lips quirked at the edges in a self-effacing smile. "But maybe I should, huh? For your safety." He paused, then said, "Or maybe it's time for our fake breakup."

I gripped his jaw more tightly. "No."

His eyes lifted to mine, the blue at least a hundred miles deep. "I don't want you to be uncomfortable around me, Daniel. That's… pretty fucking important to me. Okay? And I'm really worried that all this fake boyfriend shit is going to freak you out, if it hasn't already."

I lowered my head until my forehead was just above his. "Do I look freaked out?"

His eyes darted around my face, cataloging my expression. "N-no. But then, we haven't seen each other in a week, so *yes.*"

"I'm not freaked out." My breath ghosted over his lips and he shuddered.

"You're sweet to say that," he said, leaning his head back and putting his hands on my chest like he was thinking about pushing me away. "But the evidence suggests…"

I dragged my thumb over his bottom lip and his eyes heated. "What does it suggest, Jules?" I asked softly.

"E-evidence suggests—"

I leaned in closer, licked my lips. "Mmm hmm?"

"That you're either trying to kiss me, or…"

"Or?"

He shook his head. "Or, I don't know. I can't come up with an alternative." His eyes looked so bewildered, like he was convinced there *had* to be an alternative.

"Julian?"

"Yes?" It was a breath, hardly a full word.

"I'm going to kiss you now. Okay?"

"But what about—" he began worriedly.

"Jules, when I said *okay*, I didn't mean for you to factor all the world's problems in. I just meant '*Do you want me to kiss you, Julian?*'"

"Oh. Then… *yes*," he said like I was the slowest creature in the universe. "Duh."

"Duh," I echoed against his lips. I grinned and wrapped my arms around his waist, bending him backward. He gave a little squeak as he lifted his hands to my shoulders, grabbing on tight. And then I kissed him.

Just like the last time, it was fucking incredible—brand new and familiar all at once. I couldn't get enough; not of his taste, not of his breathy little moans or the way his hands threaded into the back of my hair and held on for dear life.

I straightened and brought him more fully against me, bending my knees to get the angle right. When my cock rubbed against the firm heat of his abs, I moaned at the sheer perfection of it and promptly did it again.

Jules broke the kiss only to duck his face into my neck and breathe, "Oh, *fuck*." I wanted to laugh. I also wanted to push him against the wall and rub against him some more. But the thought of what would happen after that made my brain stutter to a halt.

"That was… I was really… And you were…" Julian's cheeks flamed.

"Great? Hot? Aroused? In any order. Yes," I agreed. "It is. You were. I was. In fact, I *am*."

"But you are straight."

I shrugged. "Nature is big and wide, right? Isn't that what you said?"

Julian frowned. "Well, yeah, but…"

"So what I'm proposing is this. If you have an itch, you scratch it with *me*."

"With you." Julian blinked.

"I'm your fake boyfriend, Jules. It's my job to see to these needs."

He shook his head. "No. No way. No pity… kisses." He flushed. "Or whatever."

"Does this feel like pity?" I ground my erection against his, and he gasped. "You said I was attractive. And I'm 77.4% less likely to kill you than your average Grindr date."

Julian frowned, his blue eyes swimming in confusion. Finally, he said, "I think that data is inaccurate."

"That's because I made it up," I confided in a whisper.

"Oh," he said. But then he lifted himself up on his tiptoes to kiss me, and we were back at it again, kissing and tasting, my hands roaming over his back and pulling up the top of his scrubs to find skin. I pushed him against the exam table and it slid across the floor with a metallic *screech*.

Someone knocked on the door. "Dr. Ross?" Kathy said, sounding mildly panicked. "Are you almost ready for your next patient?"

"Shit," Julian said. Then, louder, "Two minutes, Kathy."

I took a giant step away from him, loving the way he was staring at me like he wanted to pull me against him again, and the fact that he couldn't catch his breath.

I was new to the whole kissing-guys-thing, but I was pretty damn addicted already. And it seemed like I was pretty good at it, too.

"What, um… What are we gonna tell everyone?" Julian panted, waving a hand in the direction of the waiting room.

I smirked. "Not a damn thing. They can think whatever they want. Let them think we were *fucking like bunnies* in here. Because that's what boyfriends do."

"Okay," he said. "Alright. And, um… Us? In private?"

I smiled, wishing the foot of space between us could disappear, along with all the people in the waiting room, so I could kiss him again. The difficulty of my life seemed to grow exponentially with every inch of space between us.

"We can fuck like bunnies in private." I licked my lips as a sudden wave of panic gripped me. "I mean, maybe not literally. There's a, you know, learning curve and all."

He frowned, but then nodded slowly. "So we're basically friends with benefits?"

"I guess, yeah. If you need to define it. We are definitely friends, always." I nodded firmly. "And we'll have benefits for as long as it's… beneficial."

"Benefits as long as it's beneficial," he echoed. "Right. Yeah. Okay. That's good. This is good."

I was thinking it could be very, very good. A chance to figure out what the fuck was happening with me… what the fuck was happening with *me and Julian*… without putting any pressure on the thing. Without any goddamn expectations.

Chapter Eight

JULIAN

Thanksgiving had never been my favorite holiday. Family and feasting and gratitude were all well and good, but I already saw my family plenty, and I just couldn't get excited about a dinner that took twelve hours to prepare and featured turkey, the blandest food in all the land. I was more of a Valentine's Day guy; a day devoted to chocolate, sex, and romance should happen at least twice a year.

This year, though, I was actually getting into the Thanksgiving vibe as I drove down the Camden Road. The sun was shining through the multicolored trees, making the leaf-strewn road look like it was paved in gold, Johnny Mathis Christmas carols—my dad's favorite, to be started right on Thanksgiving Day—were playing on the radio, and I was on my way to fetch Daniel, my fake-ish boyfriend, who'd be sitting next to me at dinner this year and coming home with me tonight.

Now, *that* was something to inspire gratitude, especially given that I'd barely seen the man since he'd found me at the clinic the other day. We were planning to spend the weekend hanging out though, and I'd woken up rock hard just imagining what that might mean, but I'd ignored my aching cock. I was pretty sure any fantasy I conjured wouldn't be as hot as the real thing.

My Monday had already been booked solid, thanks to a peculiar number of mysterious pet illnesses plaguing the town, coincidentally occurring just a couple of days after I'd lost my temper with Lina Davenport. After Daniel had pushed me into the exam room and the entire waiting room had heard us "rearranging the furniture," as Kathy put it, my Tuesday and Wednesday had gotten booked up, too. When I hadn't been working, I'd been making pumpkin bread pudding for Thanksgiving dessert and taking my mom shopping. And while Daniel had stopped by with some pastries for me at lunchtime on Tuesday, it hadn't been nearly enough. I still craved him. I craved the consuming kisses that took me out of my own head, and the free, comfortable conversations we'd always had. And I really, really needed things to be settled between us.

I drummed my fingers on the steering wheel as the trees flashed by.

Friends with benefits. Did that mean fake boyfriends who weren't entirely fake? I got the impression it would definitely involve more kissing. More… itch scratching. But was it scratching an itch for him, too? I didn't want this to be a thing where he gave me what I needed and gained nothing for himself. I *definitely* didn't want this to be a thing where he was thinking of someone else—someone female —while we were… *scratching.*

And now I was officially banning that euphemism from my brain forever.

I pulled up to the cabin and opened my door to the sound of Honoria's barking. Daniel pulled open the front door of the cabin before I'd even reached the top step of the porch. He stood there for a second, framed in the doorway, grinning at me, and my heart stuttered. He was wearing jeans— dark blue ones that molded every inch of his legs and looked like they'd be butter-soft to touch—and he was naked from the waist up but for the towel thrown around his neck. I wanted to lick every inch of his flat belly and broad chest, to rub my face against the sprinkling of hair on his chest.

I cleared my throat.

"Hey. Happy Thanksgiving," I croaked.

"Hey," he said, his eyes raking up from my brown leather shoes, to my own jeans, which were beginning to feel uncomfortably tight in certain areas, and then to my dark purple button-down. "It's definitely a happy Thanksgiving now. How long until we have to be at your mom's?"

Wow. Okay. So this benefits-thing was really happening. I felt my cheeks flush. "Not nearly long enough for you to act on the look you're giving me, so pack it up until later." I waved a hand at him. "She expects us in twenty minutes, and I refuse to show up with…" I waved a hand in the general direction of my dick and felt my face burn hotter.

"An erection?" he said. He licked his lips and the look in his eyes was pure wickedness.

"Yes," I agreed. "That."

"Is 'that' a word you can't say?" He backed further into the house, and Honoria wiggled past him to greet me, so I knelt down to run my hands through her fur, distracting myself. "Three little syllables. Not that hard. Or maybe it is." He snorted at his own joke.

"It's not that I can't say it," I argued. "It's just that talking about it isn't conducive to it going away."

"Interesting," Daniel drawled. "And by *it*, you mean…"

I sighed, giving in. "My *erection*."

His smile was smug. "Okay. Just wanted to make sure

we were on the same page." He backed up a step further and ushered me in with the dog leading the way.

On the same page. I glanced at the front of his jeans because I couldn't help it and sure enough, there was a noticeable bulge there.

This was *definitely* really happening.

Whatever *this* was.

"I… but we… I'm fully dressed," I reminded him, shocked. "And we haven't… done anything."

He shrugged, unconcerned. "Doesn't seem to matter. I've been thinking about it. A lot."

I really, really disliked Thanksgiving. I closed my eyes and groaned. "Eighteen minutes," I reminded him.

He sighed. "You should have come earlier."

Yeah, I really, really should. In every sense of the word.

"I'm almost ready. Just need to shave and throw on my sweater. Come keep me company?"

I opened my eyes and watched him walk into the bathroom, leaving the door open behind him. *Holy fuck.* Was it possible for a guy who was mostly straight until, like, five minutes ago, to be so cool with this? To discuss erections like he'd done it a hundred times?

Apparently, it was. And as I found my feet carrying me toward the bathroom, I told myself I didn't care how it happened. When the universe hands you a gift, you should be polite and accept it, right?

The little bathroom was bathed in light from the window above the toilet and still warm and humid from the shower. Daniel had wiped away a broad circle of condensation from the mirror and now coated his cheeks in shaving cream, which was both adorable and hot at the same time.

Maybe because you think everything he does is hot?

I leaned against the doorframe and just looked at him for a moment, at the big, strong hands that held the razor.

"You were carving something," I said as his movements made me recall something else. "Out on the porch. A couple weeks ago when I came by." I'd been too nervous about confessing my outburst at the diner to ask him about it then, but now I wanted to know.

He paused and smiled ruefully at me in the mirror. "Ah, yes. My attempt at whittling. Seemed like a good hobby. Goes with the whole cabin vibe, right? But maybe it's meant for someone with more delicate hands than mine." He flexed his fingers in front of him.

"Or maybe you just need more practice."

"Hmm. Maybe. It's hard for me to stick with things I'm not good at, though. Personality flaw. When I was young, I took tennis lessons exactly once. Played soccer for two weeks. Switched from French to Italian to Spanish."

I raised my eyebrows at this influx of information, filling a few of the five million mostly missing jigsaw pieces of Daniel's past. "*En serio*? Because you seem to be adapting pretty well to all kinds of new things."

"But I'm good at those things." His grin faltered. "Or at least I felt like I was."

I snorted. "Any better and I'd have detonated," I assured him. "Twice."

My eyes were transfixed by the way the spattering of his chest hair gleamed in the bright sunlight, and I almost wished he wasn't planning to shave his beard off. I wanted to feel it against my cheek when he kissed me later.

Daniel paused again, the hand with the razor hovering over his cheek. "Problem?"

"What? No."

"You're looking at me like you're worried. I promise I've used one of these before."

"No, I just… was wondering what would happen if you grew it out, that's all."

"I can tell you what would happen," he said, making smooth strokes through the lather. "I'd look like a werewolf in about four days."

"You? Nah. You're not the werewolf kind. Maybe more like a lion." I squinted at him and ran through my mental list of animals. Maybe more like a beaver, constantly building dams to wall off uncomfortable topics of…

"Jules. What are you thinking?" His voice was husky and low.

"B-beavers?"

He snorted. "What?"

"Did you know that beavers have more hair in one square inch of fur than a human has on its entire body?" I blurted.

He barked out a shocked laugh, and his hand jostled through the last of the foam. "Shit! Nicked myself."

"Oh, fuck," I cried, rushing forward to grab his chin and inspect the small dot of blood. "Fuck, I'm sorry."

"Stop, Jules. Stop, it's fine. See?" He swiped his cheek with the towel, taking most of the blood with it. "No harm done."

I dropped my hands and shook my head, mortified. No harm done, except proving that I couldn't have a conversation without veering into ridiculous trivia.

"Jules?" His voice was extra-deep and slow.

"Yeah."

"Look at me."

I sighed. "Yeah."

"I really fucking love the way your mind works, you know that?"

I stared at him. "You're making fun of me."

"I swear I'm not!" His hazel eyes were completely sincere. "You are the most fascinating, kind, *good* person I've ever met. And you're hot, too." He bent his head and pressed a swift kiss to my lips. "True fact."

I shook my head. I had no idea how he took my awkward, goofy self and transmuted me into whatever he thought I was. Alchemists had better luck turning lead into gold.

"And here's another truth. You ready?" He didn't wait for me to answer but reached behind me to grab a sweater hanging from a hook behind the door, brushing his chest against mine in the process. "I find your animal facts interesting. And your intelligence is a total fucking turn-on."

"Uh-huh." He was putting me on. He had to be. Even my own family couldn't stand the way I turned simple conversations into an episode of Animal Adventures.

He pulled the sweater over his head and… shit. The dark greenish blue looked really, really good on him. *Insanely* good. It was a little tight across his shoulders and loose around his waist and…

"Need proof?" he asked, stepping close again.

"P-proof?"

He smiled. "I love rattling the calm and collected Dr. Ross."

Rattling me? It felt like he'd done nothing *but* that for weeks.

"But, yeah, animal facts," he repeated. "Toss me one. Watch what happens." He wiggled his eyebrows.

For once, all of my animal trivia deserted me. All I could see were his eyes, which shone greener than usual thanks to his sweater, and…

"Okay," I said, my voice way huskier than usual. "Okay, how about this: When male and female birds look alike, like with doves and finches? It means they mate for life. But when a male gets all fancy in his plumage, like turkeys and cardinals and… others," I said, tugging at the hem of his bright sweater. "That means they like getting around."

Daniel's laughing eyes narrowed. "Wait, are you calling me a turkey or a manwhore?"

I laughed breathlessly. "Eh. Little of column A, little of column B…"

He grabbed me around the middle and dug his fingers into my ribs.

"Hey!" I gasped, squirming away and only managing to back myself into the wall near the door. "No tickling! I told you I hate it! That's… that's…" I broke off, howling with laughter.

Honoria ran in to see what she was missing and skidded to a halt near my feet.

"Payback?" Daniel said, fingers dancing. "Justice?"

"Mean!" I said. "The Geneva Convention—"

"Only applies in times of war."

"Dammit. Fine, I take it back!" I gurgled. "Stop, stop! I take it back!"

His fingers stopped moving and I sucked in a breath, but he didn't step away. Instead, he pressed closer, moving me up against the wall so our bodies were aligned, my chest to his torso, his cock against my abs.

"I want a forfeit," he said, staring at my lips. The temperature in the already warm room ratcheted up several degrees.

"What kind of forfeit?" I asked, confident I knew.

He grinned as he pressed his lips to mine.

And at that exact moment, I swear, the phone in my back pocket began to vibrate, making a hollow, clattering sound against the wall.

Shit. *Shit.*

"Does this mean we're late?" Daniel asked, his mouth hovering over mine.

"Ah… Pretty sure."

"So, text her back." He bit my jaw lightly. "Tell her we'll be even *later*."

My heart was beating hard with a combination of lust and anxiety. I wanted desperately to do exactly what he'd suggested, but I also knew what the fallout would be.

"She's gonna start freaking out momentarily. Calling me. Asking where I am."

Daniel sighed and backed away. "And I guess you can't just tell her you had a change of plans?"

I snorted before the words even fully registered. My mother? A change of plans? "No," I said sadly. "That would not go over well."

Part of me really wanted to give in, though. Really, *really* wanted to.

Daniel tugged at the leg of his jeans, rearranging himself, and I did the same.

"Later?" he said.

"Definitely."

This was going to be the longest dinner ever.

———

THE DRIVE to my childhood home took way longer than usual, mostly because I kept glancing at the man in the passenger seat, unable to look away. My car, which was usually pretty spacious, seemed smaller and oddly free of oxygen, considering how many times I had to focus on my breathing.

"It's going to be fine," Daniel soothed. "I'm, like, ninety percent housebroken, I hardly ever knock over furniture, I eat with a fork, and I can make polite conversation when required."

"I know, I know. They'll love you, and you'll love them. It's just odd," I said. "Having you, with me, with *them*. When you and I are together, it's always been just you and me, and it feels a little bit like worlds colliding." Like *Julians* colliding. I was different when I was with Daniel. Or I felt different, at least.

"It's not too late," he said a moment later. "You could take me back home. Tell your mom I changed my mind."

"What? No. God, of course not. I want you with me. I just hope… you have fun." *I hope you like me when I'm with them.*

"If you're sure," Daniel said.

I laid a hand over his where it rested on his thigh, strangely reassured because he needed reassurance. "About that part, I'm positive."

A second later, we pulled up in front of the immaculate white ranch house with its bright red shutters and detached garage. The lawn was still almost uniformly green, despite the cold weather we'd had, and only the barest sprinkling of leaves dared to dot the surface. No doubt my mother would be out here tomorrow raking again before she put up the Christmas decorations.

Daniel peered through the windshield at the small front porch tucked to one side of the house. "Shit. The *decorations*," he said.

I snorted. There were hay bales flanking the bottom of the stairs to the front door, each with a scarecrow perched on top, surrounded by gourds and pumpkins. The stairs themselves were lined with pots of chrysanthemums and sedums my mother had to have been keeping at the nursery or inside the house until this morning, or else they'd have succumbed to frost.

"The perils of owning a landscaping and floral company," I reminded him. "Ross Landscaping?"

Daniel looked startled. "Oh, right. You mentioned that once when you had to help out."

Different Julians again. I was pretty sure most of O'Leary saw me as an extension of my family. Daniel knew hardly anything about them.

Still, I nodded. "It's rare—like, once a year—that she gets busy enough to ask me, but I don't mind it. I like the work, I could just never do it full time." I gave him a sidelong glance. "My mother's constantly looking for ways to save her garden from the deer, while I'm looking for ways to save the deer from my mother."

Daniel smiled, but his eyes took on a faraway look. "I understand conflicting parental priorities, believe me."

I wondered if he was thinking of his own mother, and I was struck again by how much we didn't know about each other, how much we'd never discussed. And maybe it was true that if none of those things had come up in all our conversations, they just weren't that important. But it felt odd that I couldn't ask him about his family. We'd known each other too long and too well for me to ask him basic information I should have already known. Like when you'd had a long, involved conversation with a stranger at a wedding but couldn't remember their name and were embarrassed to reveal your ignorance.

Theo came loping down the steps before I could get too worked up over it and ambled over to the car. I opened my door and stepped out to greet him, but he surprised me by stopping at Daniel's side of the car instead.

"What's up, man?" Theo asked, offering Daniel his hand.

"Not much, Theo," Daniel said. "You?"

"Thanksgiving madness. Sam's here because her dad

doesn't do the whole turkey thing." Theo hooked a thumb over his shoulder. "We're watching the game. Lions-Bears. You got a favorite?"

Daniel shook his head. "Nope."

"That's good. Be Switzerland. Sam's a Chicago fan, and they're losing, so if you'd said Detroit, I might have had to separate you two."

Daniel grinned. "You may still. It'll be nice to give the sass queen a taste of her own medicine."

Theo grinned and clapped Daniel on the shoulder, leading him toward the house… and leaving me behind.

"Daniel!" I called. "Can you come here, please? I need help with the… *thing*."

"Ah, come on, Jules," Theo said, shaking his head. "You can carry your own shit. Let the man have some fun!"

I sucked in a breath to tell him off, but I didn't have to.

"Theo, do you have a girlfriend or boyfriend?" Daniel said as he jogged back to me.

"No," Theo admitted. "Not… exactly."

"Uh-huh. Well, trust me when I tell you, I like helping Julian. Genuinely."

Theo snickered. "Guess he makes it worth your while, eh?"

"Theodore Antonio Ross," my mother exclaimed from the doorway. "What are you doing?"

"Uh." Theo stood up straighter. "Nothing?"

"Exactly. *Nothing*. Not a single thing. And meanwhile, I specifically asked you if you'd get drinks for your Aunt Teresa and the others."

"But, I…" Theo's face fell. "Sorry, Mama."

Theo shuffled back into the house after my mother as Daniel reached my side of the car and I handed him a brown paper bag from the back seat containing half the components of my dessert.

"So will you?" he teased in a low voice, hefting the bag in his arm.

"What?"

"Will you make it worth my while?" He wiggled his eyebrows.

It was *not* cute.

"Daniel, since when are you and Theo besties?" I demanded.

"Besties." He snorted. "I gave Sam a job cleaning out the shed on my property, remember? They've been by a couple times in the last week or so." He shrugged. "She brings Theo along as, I dunno, moral support or cheap labor or something."

"And you don't think this was a crucial thing for you to mention to me, your *boyfriend*? That you guys chat a lot?"

"You're overthinking things," he said, lifting his free hand to rub at the back of my neck. "Where's calm, collected Dr. Ross?"

I shot him a look. "You know that's not actually me, right? I might look calm, but—"

"Sometimes it's you. I've seen it. When you're in your office or making a plan. And other times..." He grinned. "Other times we end up down a conversational rabbit hole and I end up learning facts about mammals. I like all the versions of Julian equally, but Dr. Ross is the one to channel right now. Okay?"

I blew out a breath. "Yeah, right. Okay. Onward." I hefted the bag containing the other half of dessert, as well as Daniel's bottles of wine.

"You make it sound like we're facing a firing squad," he said.

I paused. "Have I given you any reason to believe we're not?"

"Well, I guarantee I've been through worse holiday dinners." He swept a hand toward the house. "So lead on."

―――――

NOT A FIRING SQUAD, but a whirlwind.

My mother claimed my attention the moment we were inside, needing me to mash potatoes and stir gravy simultaneously, while Daniel was given a polite greeting and directed to the living room where Sam, Theo, and Constantine, along with my Aunt Teresa and cousin Marina, were watching football and chatting.

Once my tasks were done, I escaped the kitchen under the pretense of delivering a new tray of cheese and crackers to the living room and went in search of Daniel.

He was sitting on the end of the brown leather sofa closest to the kitchen, hunched forward on the edge of the seat with his knees on his elbows, staring at the screen like the announcers were giving out winning lottery numbers rather than calling plays. It was odd; I'd never known he was interested in football. He didn't even have a TV.

But as I set down the cheeseboard on the coffee table, I noticed Marina was sitting on the sofa, squashed up right next to him, despite there being plenty of room on her other side, where Sam was sitting. Her hand was laying on the side of her thigh, which meant the backs of her fingers were resting against Daniel's hip.

My boyfriend's hip.

Well, my *fake*-boyfriend's hip, but Marina didn't know that.

Marina had never been close to my brothers or me. She was somewhere between Theo and Constantine in age, meaning she was possibly old enough to purchase the beer she was holding in her left hand, but not by much. I didn't know her very well—I only saw her once a year when she and her mom made the trek up here for Thanksgiving, and she always made it clear that one day a year away from all her friends and the exciting life she claimed to have in the city was plenty.

Looking at her cuddling up to Daniel, I was thinking one day a year might be too much.

I wondered for a second if Daniel was enjoying it. Marina was pretty, all dark eyes and sleek, dark hair curling just beneath the curve of her ample breasts. She was youngish, and her full lips were arranged in a permanent pout, but a straight-until-five-minutes-ago guy still had to be flattered by the attention, right? He had to appreciate the way her boobs were all but smushed against his bicep, like his arm was a magnet and her bra was fucking *lined with iron*. Didn't he?

Outwardly, Daniel didn't seem to notice. He was sitting as close to the arm of the sofa as possible, and his attention was focused firmly on the television, like the buff guy in the black jersey hawking bundled home and car insurance was the most fascinating thing he'd ever seen. At least, until I walked by him.

"Hey," he said, snaking out a hand and pulling me down to sit on the arm of the couch next to him.

"Hey. Exciting game?" I nodded at the television.

"I guess." He shrugged. "Need help in the kitchen?"

His right hand rubbed circles on my back while his left rested on my knee, meaning he was effectively turning his back on Marina, who didn't look particularly pleased to be ignored.

I tried to smother my smile.

"Nope. Mama's got everything mostly under control,

and I'm her assistant. How are you doing?" I tentatively rested a hand on the back of his neck, and he leaned into it. His muscles seemed knotted with tension.

"Better now," he said.

"Let me fill you in, Jules. Bears are up, so the side of truth and justice is winning," Sam said, turning her attention from the TV for two seconds. "Constantine won't stop texting whoever's on the other end of that phone and he blushes when I ask him who it is. Theo's on his fourth beer because he thinks no one has noticed. And Daniel is about to be very sad because he unwisely bet against me and he's going to lose. When's dinner?"

"Julian! The gravy!" my mother called from the kitchen.

"*Tsk*. Your poor mother," Aunt Teresa sighed, grabbing her wineglass from the coffee table and leaning back into one of the side chairs, where she was tucked with her Kindle. "I keep telling her she doesn't need to outdo herself every holiday."

"Next year, you should all come down to the city for the weekend," Marina said, linking her arm with Daniel's excitedly and pulling him back toward her. "I mean, assuming you and Jules are still a *thing* or whatever. We could eat at one of my favorite restaurants and I could show you all the coolest places."

Not fucking likely, I thought. But what I said was, "Thanks, but I doubt that will fly. I think Mama likes having her family under her roof."

"Julian!" she called impatiently.

I sighed and Daniel winked.

"I'm guessing you can't tell her you'd rather take a break and hang out here?" he asked. I sighed and Daniel's mouth twisted wryly. "Didn't think so."

It took an incredible amount of effort to peel myself

away from the couch, and my hand lingered on Daniel's skin until I had to break contact.

"Julian," my mother said, when I'd resumed my place at the stove. "I need your help. You can socialize at dinner."

I bit back a sharp retort. I had zero interest in going to the city for dinner, as Marina suggested, but I could definitely see the attraction of a holiday where I could be the one cuddled up with Daniel on the sofa. I'd never say that to my mother, though. I wasn't sure I had it in me to disappoint her that way. Con, Theo, and I were all she had left.

Still, I poured myself a glass of the wine Teresa had been drinking and gave thanks that this holiday was almost over for another three hundred sixty-five days.

———

"Pass the potatoes?" Con said, speaking through the mound of potatoes already in his mouth.

I fought the urge to roll my eyes. It felt like eight hours had passed since we'd arrived instead of four. My back hurt from standing at the stove mashing the ten pounds of fucking potatoes he was shoveling into his gullet. My mother, who'd insisted on having Daniel come and promised to be on her best behavior, had barely spoken two civil words to him all afternoon. I couldn't recall whether my aunt and cousin had always gotten on my nerves this much or were just particularly bitchy this year. My wineglass had somehow gotten empty *again*, which was weird since I never drank wine. *And* I was seated across the table from Daniel, where I couldn't even touch him, let alone lean into his side and smell his soap-and-Daniel smell, which I really, really wanted to do.

The empty wineglass, at least, I could do something

about. I picked up the bottle from the center of the table and filled my glass halfway. Pacing myself, because Thanksgiving dinner was a marathon, not a sprint.

Aunt Teresa passed Con the bowl of potatoes, but couldn't keep from commenting. "You know, Constantine, if you keep eating like that, you'll be the size of a house. "

Con shrugged, completely unconcerned. "More of me to love," he said, grinning.

"Speaking of which, have you been dating anyone?" She looked at him archly.

I changed my mind and filled my wineglass to the top, then grabbed it like the lifeline it was, ignoring the look Aunt Teresa gave me. I wasn't sure why I didn't drink wine more often. The shit was actually pretty good.

"Mmm. Not really," Con said. He glanced at my mother quickly and then busied himself scooping potatoes. "Nothing serious."

"Now that your brother's settling down, though," Teresa continued, smiling at me from her seat at the end of the table. "Doesn't it make you want to find someone for yourself?"

"Nope. I'll leave that to Jules and Daniel." Con winked at me. "Pass the dressing?"

I lifted the heavy bowl and handed it over.

"Julian and Daniel aren't serious, though," my mother interjected, taking a tiny bite of the turkey she'd slaved over all day. "They've hardly been together a month."

"More like two," Sam said from beside me. She nudged me with her elbow. "Isn't it?"

Uh. Shit. When had I said we'd started dating. *Had* I said? I couldn't remember at all. I stared across the table at Daniel in a panic.

"Well, we were friends for a while first," Daniel said

smoothly, covering my lapse. "So it feels like longer than it's been officially. Right, baby?"

Baby. I swallowed hard and set my glass down. "Right," I agreed. "We've known each other since last spring."

"May," Daniel volunteered. "Right before Memorial Day."

I blinked, stunned that he'd remembered that. I smiled broadly. "Exactly."

"But the dating thing is new," Mama continued. "And Julian is still young."

I turned to her and frowned. "I am?" at the same time Theo, on my left, said, "He is?"

"He's not even thirty," the stranger inhabiting my mother's body said airily. "Plenty of time for playing the field."

"Auntie, didn't you just tell him last Thanksgiving that you wanted him to find a nice boy and settle down?"

My mother gave Marina an icy smile. "Settling down is one thing. Settling down too *fast* is another."

Con's lips twitched like he was finding this very amusing. I was glad one of us was. "That's funny," he said. "You've always told us, 'When you know, you know.' Wasn't that the story with you and Dad? You met in Italy senior year of college knew each other for only three months before he proposed?"

"And Mama and Papa were *not* pleased," Teresa informed us. "That he was moving her away from the city and all her friends."

"John and I were different," my mother said, cutting another minuscule bite of turkey. She didn't elaborate further.

"Or maybe it's exactly the same," I said, taking a fortifying sip of wine. "Maybe we just *know*. Right, Daniel?"

Daniel pursed his lips like he was fighting not to smile.

"Definitely," he said. "Sometimes someone comes along and your life just does a complete one-eighty. You can't fight it."

Mama set her fork down on her plate with a click. "Is that what happened for you, Daniel?"

Daniel grabbed a roll from his plate and split it in half with his thumbs. "With Julian? Absolutely."

"And before Julian? Before you moved here? How did you spend your Thanksgiving last year?" She swept her long hair behind her back and stared at him like she was daring him to answer. Her voice was acerbic, biting.

Best behavior, my ass.

"Mama," I began.

But Daniel cut me off. "Down in the city, as a matter of fact. I ate at Loredo Kitchen in…"

"In Chelsea!" Marina squealed from beside him, grabbing his arm just as she had in the living room. "Omigod, I've been there! We have so much in common, Daniel! I wonder if we know some of the same people!"

Daniel smiled patiently. "I really doubt it," he said. "There's a bit of an age difference."

Marina pouted and sank back in her seat while I cheered silently.

"And who did you spend the day with?" Mama continued. "Your parents? Brothers? Sisters? Surely your family's missing you today."

"I'm an only child," Daniel said, giving her a small smile. "And I don't like to talk about my folks much, if it's all the same to you. We're not all fortunate enough to have such a wonderful family."

Mama blinked. Polite refusal, couched in a compliment? My mother wasn't used to direct opposition and wasn't sure how to handle it. The cheering in my head grew louder.

"And how are you adjusting to life in O'Leary, Daniel?" Teresa asked. "If you lived in the city, this must be a culture shock."

"A bit," he agreed. "O'Leary's different than I'd thought it would be."

"I wouldn't think you'd know *what* it's like, since we hardly ever see you in town," my mother said. She smiled tightly. "You've hardly given any of us a chance to know you."

"Mama," I said again. "This isn't the Spanish Inquisition."

"It's fine, Jules," Daniel said easily enough. He turned to my mother. "I came here as a sort of sabbatical. I wasn't sure how long I'd be here, and I didn't plan to put down roots. I definitely didn't plan to meet Julian." He smiled at me and took a huge bite of his dinner.

Meanwhile, I reached for my wine again.

He hadn't planned to put down roots? I'd never really considered that, though maybe it should have been obvious. He certainly hadn't gone out of his way to meet anyone or establish any ties.

How long did I have before something called him back to the city or to somewhere else entirely? Would he make an effort to keep in touch when he left, or would he be as close-mouthed about his time in O'Leary as he was about his time in New York?

"Can we have dessert early?" Con asked, apparently attempting to change the subject. "Mitch asked if I could do a little patrolling around Weaver Street this evening." He gave us all an apologetic shrug. "Overtime, you know? Can't say no."

My mother's fork hit her plate with a sharp *clink* that suggested he probably should have said no.

"Since when does Mitchell Turner require his auxiliary

officers to patrol the streets of O'Leary on a day when every decent person is at home celebrating a holiday?"

I noticed Sam's eyes were carefully fixed on her plate, and my annoyance with my mother rose. "Cooking a turkey doesn't make you a decent person."

My mother pursed her lips, refusing to debate the matter.

"Hen Lattimer's missing some stuff again. Second time the thief has hit the hardware store."

"The thief?" My aunt reached for her throat like she would have clutched her pearls, had she been wearing any. "What thief?"

"Some petty criminal," I said, waving a hand. "Or some kid who thinks he's funny, looking for attention."

"The kind of thing that wouldn't make the news in the city," Daniel said.

"This time, he stole some kind of cooking grate and some other equipment." Con shook his head. "Our criminal is clearly into the great outdoors."

"It was a coffee pot," Theo said, pouring gravy liberally over his plate. "I know because Mitch and Si Sloane came by to ask Hen about it when I was working. A coffee pot and a frying pan. Like, thirty dollars' worth of stuff Hen woulda had to store in the back room for the winter anyway. Or, more likely, woulda had *me* store. I don't get why everyone is so upset."

"They're upset," my mother said, "because it's a violation to have things taken and most definitely is *not* funny." She gave Theo and Sam a hard look. "The kind of thing I wouldn't want any of my boys involved in."

Theo looked outraged. "I've never stolen anything in my life."

"And it'd be a pretty stupid-assed prank," Sam said.

"Language," my mother said, and Sam mumbled an

apology. "The point is," she continued, "we want this to be the kind of town where people can be open and honest, a place where we can trust one another."

She shot Daniel a look that so clearly stated how ill-suited he was for the town. And with that, I was done keeping my mouth shut.

"Really? Because *I* think we want this to be the kind of town where we give everyone the benefit of the doubt. Where people aren't condemned by unsubstantiated, mean-spirited gossip. Where we let the police do their jobs and mind our own damn business. Where people are friendly and *on their best behavior.* Where they keep their promises. That's the kind of town *I* would prefer to live in."

Mama snapped her mouth shut and looked down at her dinner, not even reprimanding me for my curse word. I felt a mild thrill of victory.

Theo kicked me under the table and winked.

"So, Daniel," Aunt Teresa said, wading into the tense silence that ensued. "What do you do for fun?"

"Um. Well, I like hiking. Reading." He shrugged. "I tried whittling recently, but that didn't go very well. Managed to keep my fingers, though, so it didn't go *badly.*"

Marina laughed like this was the funniest thing she'd ever heard and leaned her head on his arm. Her laughter was like knives in my brain, and I fumed into my wine.

"Reading! That's wonderful." Teresa looked at my mother. "Angela, didn't you say you'd just started a book club in town?"

I could practically hear my mother grinding her teeth, and I was sure I wasn't the only one.

"We did," she said. "But it's full. We're keeping it small." She smiled at me. "At Julian's request. Isn't that right, Julian? You asked me not to invite any of my friends?"

I clenched my molars.

"That's fine. I'm not much into joining clubs," Daniel said. "My tastes are a bit too specific."

"Are you reading one of those Prick-hard books?" Theo joked.

"Pritchard," I snapped. "Like you didn't already know."

"Uh-huh. Does Daniel know what a hard-on you have for the guy?"

"Shut up," I said. "Yes, he knows I'm a fan. Could someone pass the wine?" I motioned toward the fresh bottle in front of Marina, and Daniel reached over to hand it to me.

"He knows you're a *fan*," Theo said. "But does he know you're in love with the guy?"

"Theo, for fuck's sake! I am *not.*"

"Language!" Mama snapped, and I sighed.

Theo laughed. "*JD Pritchard just gets me on a deep, spiritual level. He just, like, gets me,*" he quoted in a stoner voice I was pretty sure I'd never used. Ever.

"Theo, do you enjoy your life?" I demanded, turning my fork and gripping it like a dagger. "Think carefully here."

Con snorted.

"What's this?" Daniel asked, looking back and forth from Con to Theo. "What happened?"

"Don't you dare! Either of you!" I warned, not that anyone listened.

"Jules had his wisdom teeth out," Theo explained, grinning as he got into the story. "You know how some people see giant chipmunks when they get high? Well, when Jules gets high, he starts speaking in tongues about this guy who writes stupid mysteries." He chuckled. "And, like, this guy is no Dan Brown, okay? He's just some… random, not-famous dude."

"Honestly, Theodore," my mother said despairingly.

"You're dead to me. Both of you." I was busy glaring at Con and Theo, which meant I set the wine bottle down on the table a bit harder than I'd intended.

I might have been a bit tipsy.

"Hey! I didn't say anything!" Con defended.

"*Pfft*. You told him, Con! Theo wasn't even there that day!"

"But Jules, how could I not? It was the funniest thing I'd ever seen. You were like, *He's so insightful*. And you practically had heart-eyes going on."

"It was a while ago. Right after I read that book I told you about," I explained to Daniel. My cheeks were *flaming* —I could practically feel them throbbing like Poe's Telltale Heart. "I was… excited."

Daniel was looking at me strangely, which was just *awesome*. Because he needed yet another reason to think I was a completely hopeless, socially awkward idiot.

"This is, like, the most hilarious thing ever!" Marina said. "What else did Jules say while he was coming out of anesthesia? I mean, in my whole life Jules has never been anything but this perfect, boring *adult*. I'm having trouble even picturing him stoned!" Her fingernails dug into Daniel's arm like short, shell-pink talons. "Did you get it on video?"

Teresa looked at me pityingly. "Julian's always been a little grown up. So quiet and serious. But a good boy," she added quickly in an aside to Daniel, like he might be rethinking our relationship.

Wow. I mean who *didn't* love a holiday celebrating family, *am-I-right?*

It struck me that none of these people really knew me at all. They assumed because I was quiet, I had nothing to say. They assumed I didn't argue because I was too weak to speak my mind. They had no idea how much it cost to bite my tongue and smile politely, not a fucking clue.

And of course they didn't, because I'd never let them know.

"That was the whole story," Con said, uncomfortable now. He wasn't smiling anymore. Instead, he gave me an apologetic look. "It was cute. I mean, compared to some of the embarrassing shi—uh, *stuff*—I've done, it was downright dignified."

I drank the rest of my wine in two long swallows and stared at my plate. My stomach burned, and there were tears in my eyes, like the wine was leaking out of me.

Stupid wine.

"Well, I think it's the coolest thing I've ever heard," Daniel said, so firmly that I couldn't help glancing up. His hazel eyes were pure green as he stared at me, but it was clear his words were for everyone else from the angry set of his jaw. "And since I think everything about Jules is fucking awesome, that's saying something, so everyone should leave him alone." He cleared his throat and turned to my mother. "Sorry for the language."

"Oh, come on. We were just having fun," Marina said sullenly.

Daniel tilted his head and looked at her. "Julian has an honest passion for something. Do you know how rare that is? Every author wants a reader like him—someone who reads with an open mind, someone who's not cynical, someone who's not ashamed to love what he loves."

"Someone to stalk them?" Theo chortled.

Sam muttered, "God. Shut up, Theo." Daniel shot him a look that made Theo clear his throat uncomfortably.

"No," Daniel said. "Someone who finds their words meaningful. Someone who derives so much enjoyment from the thing they've poured their heart and soul into. Roald Dahl said, 'Lukewarm is no good.' He said you have to be an enthusiast in life. And frankly, if more people focused on finding the joy in their own lives, they wouldn't spend so much time trying to tear other people down." He looked at me and nodded, like maybe he thought I wasn't sure he was serious.

I swallowed, but the lump in my throat didn't seem to want to move.

"Right." My mother stood up from her place and pushed back her chair. "I think it's about time for dessert. Theodore, Constantine, you two can clear the table."

I stood, too, because I couldn't stay in my seat just then without bursting into tears or crawling over the cranberry sauce to kiss the fuck out of Daniel Michaelson, and I figured that would probably be frowned upon at the dinner table, at least as much as bad language.

Unfortunately, the floor swayed when I stood, and I grabbed at the table for balance.

Shit. Too much wine.

"Jules? You okay?" Daniel asked, his eyes still steady on my face.

"Me? Fine. *Pfft.* I'm always fine!" I snagged my plate and one of the serving bowls and staggered toward the kitchen, where my mother was already scooping leftovers into containers with ruthless efficiency.

I dropped the plate and bowl on the counter with a clatter and pointed at Theo accusingly.

"You!" I hissed. "You have betrayed the sacred bonds of brotherhood."

Theo looked up from the sink he was filling with steaming water and blinked. "What?"

"Whaddya mean, *what*? You told Daniel that embarrassing story about me," I whispered. "That's *what*."

"Jules, I'm sorry. But I swear, it's not a big deal," Constantine said, stacking plates for Theo to rinse. "Daniel thought it was cute."

I shook my head, even though it made the world wobble. "That's beside the point. You are a *betrayer*."

Con and Theo exchanged an amused look. "A betrayer?" Theo said.

"An *oathbreaker*."

Constantine snickered. "I think I like drunk Jules. Tell us more."

"No," I whispered. "And lower your voice. This is *private*."

"Should we tell him he's yelling?" Theo asked out of the corner of his mouth.

"Boys, stop this right now," my mother said. "Leave your brother alone. And Jules, honey, maybe you should go sit down in the living room, hmm? I'll serve your bread pudding."

"I don't want to sit in the living room," I said, enunciating each word clearly. "I want to discuss the treachery that has been perpetrated at our own table."

Mama's eyes widened. "Oh, heavens. How much wine did you—?"

"You were unkind," I told her flatly. "You promised me you wouldn't be."

She pursed her lips. "I was not—"

"Oh, you so were," Theo said, nodding. As the baby of the family, he'd been the one who'd never learned not to talk back. "If any of us had treated a guest that way, you'd be telling us how Dad was *rooooolling* in his grave right now."

"Theodore Antonio!"

"Just sayin'." He held up both palms innocently.

"Shut it, Theo," Con said. "Mom's being overprotective because her chicken's about to fly the coop. *Finally*. But she'll get over it. Right?" He gave my mother a sideways glance, and she went to get more dishes with a huff. "But listen, Julian. Are you listening?" He braced a hand on either side of my face and rolled my head around. Or maybe he was standing still and the world was rolling.

"I'm listening."

"Daniel is so far gone on you there's nothing we could say to stop it even if we wanted to. Okay? He's head over heels, looking at you like you'd look at a brand-new JD-whatshisface novel. You get me?"

I frowned. They had no idea that it was all a lie. A *ruse*. That Daniel was only my fake boyfriend, and he wasn't really *gone* on me at all. That he might even be thinking of leaving town at some point. They didn't know I was already mourning a relationship that would only ever exist in my mind.

Competent, practical Julian.

What a joke.

"He looks at you, you know," Theo said softly. "When you're not looking at him."

I blinked. "That happens sometimes in conversations, Theo," I said patiently. "People look at each other at different times. It's okay."

Theo dropped his head and laughed silently, his stomach rolling with it.

"What Theo means," Con interrupted, leaning in so he was practically whispering in my ear, "is that he looks at you in a way that shows he cares about you. When someone says something funny, he looks at you to make sure you're laughing. And when we were giving you shit, he was ready to throw down to defend you. He *cares* about you, Jules. You don't have to be embarrassed about anything with a guy who looks at you like that."

I pursed my lips and closed one eye. I understood the words he was saying, but they were passing through my mind without sticking.

Con shook his head and his blue eyes—our dad's blue eyes—gleamed. "We'll have this conversation again when you're sober. But in the meantime, just… chill, okay? You don't have to plan for every contingency and anticipate every problem, Dr. Ross. Just go sit with your man and eat some fucking bread pudding."

I nodded. That was doable.

I went back to the dining room and found Aunt Teresa communing with her Kindle again while Marina scrolled through her phone.

Daniel had moved to my seat and had his wallet out to hand Sam some money. "This is to cover my bet, and this is for the rest of the shed project."

"But I'm not done yet," she argued, staring at the cash.

"Yeah, but concert tickets wait for no woman," he said solemnly.

Sam grinned and gave him a quick hug. "You're awesome, Daniel. Thanks."

"Welcome," he said, patting her back.

Sam stood up as soon as she saw me approach and pushed me down into her seat. "You're pretty cool, too, Jules," she said, with no trace of her usual cynicism.

"Oh," I said. "Um. Thanks?"

"So, what's for round two?" Marina asked me, setting down her phone. "More embarrassing stories? Or did you want to whisper-yell some more so we could all hear?"

Daniel stiffened beside me.

I cocked my head to one side and looked at my cousin thoughtfully. "Marina, you're really very pretty."

She snickered. "Thanks. I know I'm not your type, but—"

"And you're not Daniel's type either," I said, wrinkling my nose. "Even when he dated girls, he didn't date girls like you." I turned to him and found his face way closer than I'd thought it would be. "Did you?"

Daniel watched me with cautious amusement in his eyes. "I… actually, I kinda did."

I snorted. "But you've evolved since then."

He smiled. "Yeah, baby. I've definitely evolved."

I nodded, momentarily satisfied. "And now we'll eat some fucking pudding."

"*Language!*" my mother called from the kitchen, though her voice sounded even further away. "Honestly, why do I even bother with you boys?"

"Daniel, I think you might have to drive home," I told him apologetically.

"You think?"

"I might have had one glass too many."

"You might have had one *bottle* too many." His soft laughter in my ear warmed me all the way through. "But I'll take care of you, Julian. Promise."

For tonight, he meant. Or maybe for as long as we were fake boyfriends. Or as long as he stayed in O'Leary.

But for the rest of the day, I wasn't going to think about that. For the rest of the day, I was going to be fucking *grateful*. I leaned across the distance between our chairs and rested my head on Daniel's shoulder.

"So far, I've met competent Julian, adorable animal facts Julian, awkward Julian, and drunk Julian. How many more Julians are there?" he whispered in my ear. "I can't wait to find out."

Chapter Nine

DANIEL

"Tell me again how I'm supposed to see a love story here?" I turned my head against the back of the couch to look at Jules, who was sprawled on the couch beside me, watching my laptop with the same fascinated horror that I felt.

"I'm not sure about love. I mean, you can totally see that there's a chemistry between them." He blinked up at me in the late-afternoon semi-darkness as the credits for *Hannibal* rolled. His hair was sticking straight up in places after his shower this morning, he was wearing my t-shirt and oldest, softest sweatpants with the waistband rolled down and the cuffs rolled up, and something in my chest contracted a little bit at how beautiful he was and how right it felt to have him here next to me.

"Chemistry?" I grimaced. "Between the cannibalistic serial killer and the FBI agent he's gaslighting? Is that what you'd call the basis for a strong, healthy friendship? Because if so, I think that's something we need to discuss—"

"Hush!" Jules smacked me lightly on the arm. "I didn't

say healthy. Pretty sure Hannibal hasn't said a single honest thing in ten episodes. But there's *chemistry*. You can see it. Maybe we just need to keep watching."

"Maybe later." I closed my laptop and set it on the floor, turned on some of my favorite folk music, then leaned back in my seat. "You know, when you suggested hooking up your phone's hotspot to my laptop and spending the day watching Netflix, serial killers weren't what I had in mind."

Jules shifted his body and bent his leg to sit sideways on the sofa, and one corner of his mouth twitched up in a smile. "No, you suggested the ever-uplifting *Game of Thrones*. A rollicking good time, right up there with *Titanic*."

"*Titanic*," I grunted. "Stupid movie. They both could have fit on the door."

"They *so* could have fit on the door."

"But then there wouldn't have been a story, right?" I sighed and scratched absently at my stomach, my eyes to the ceiling. "Not a good one anyway. Imagine if he'd lived. Instead of Rose becoming some kind of artist, skydiver, horseback-rider, cool-as-fuck grandmother, she and Leonardo DiCaprio would've ended up married way too young. They'd probably be living in some shitty tenement since her mom would've cut her off. Leo would've kept playing poker and gambling away the money from whatever possessions she managed to pawn, since homeboy's skill of drawing naked ladies was never gonna pan out. She'd've popped out a couple kids, since birth control wasn't a thing, and the whole time she'd be thinking that if she wanted to be trapped in a loveless relationship, she could have married the prick with the gun, because at least then she would've been *rich* and miserable, which I can tell you from experience is better than poor and miserable."

Julian said nothing for a second and I shifted my head

again to find him squinting at me like he was trying to read my brain through my skull.

"Who hurt you?" he demanded.

I licked my lips uncomfortably. "No one hurt—"

"No, seriously," he continued, leaning forward to grab my hand in both of his. "Who hurt you? Were you dropped on your head a lot? Did bullies stuff you in a locker? Did JD Pritchard steal your girlfriend?" He paused. "No, never mind, I still don't wanna know if he was involved."

"Since you've got a *crush* on him?"

Julian's face flamed, and he pushed my hands away. "I'm still a little bit hungover. It's not okay to tease me yet about things you might have heard yesterday."

"Apologies," I said. "When does teasing season open, so I can mark it on my calendar?"

"I'll let you know," he said primly.

I ran my tongue over my front teeth to hide my smile. Was it weird that I loved these random conversations we lapsed into? Was it weird that I loved him giving me shit?

It was probably weird.

"*You* said you were too hungover for that much bloodshed," I reminded him. "So in your wisdom, you picked the cannibal show instead."

"Hey! People on Facebook said it was amazing. And it was!" He hesitated. "In a very dark sort of way. That makes me never want to eat meat again."

"The perfect way to keep that Thanksgiving feeling going all year long!"

"Well, considering what yesterday was like, that might not be inaccurate."

I laughed and stretched my arm out on the couch behind him. "It wasn't that bad."

"Are you joking?" He peered at me closely. "It was a

shit show. My mother was in rare form, my brothers can't keep their mouths shut, and I got *drunk*. At my *mother's house*. In front of *my family*. Just thinking about it is making me nauseated."

"You sure that's not the hangover?" I asked. "Or the serial killer show?"

He threw himself back to lay flat on the seat cushion, covered his eyes with his forearm, and groaned. Honoria, who'd been lying on the floor in front of the fire, lifted her head so she could groan in sympathy, and Julian chuckled half-heartedly.

"Calm down! You didn't do anything crazy." I shrugged. "And if you're gonna get drunk, that's the best place for it to happen, right?"

"Wrong!" His voice was muffled. He moved his arm to look at me. "You're not taking this seriously."

"Or possibly you're taking it too seriously. You don't have to please them or answer to them, Jules." I was living proof of that. I lived life on my own terms now.

"Easy for you to say," he sighed.

I frowned, considering. It didn't feel easy. It felt like a hard-won thing. I'd spent a really long time trying to please people who refused to be pleased—parents, critics, readers. I'd had to reshape my whole life in order to break free of it. But now that I'd done it, I couldn't imagine going back. I didn't even like to think about the guy I'd been before.

"What?" Jules said, blue eyes watching me in concern. "What are you thinking about?"

I sighed. "I'm thinking that your family loves you. Your mother, Con, and Theo, at least. Marina's more in awe of you."

"Awe. Yes, I felt the awe."

I chuckled. "It was there. She's just at an age where the awe pisses her off."

He made a hmphing noise. "I think you're categorically wrong, but okay."

"Your family is really protective of you, Julian. It's not a bad thing."

"My family is…" Julian shook his head. "The way my mother treated you was…"

"Protective?" I supplied. "I mean, I get why you weren't happy, and she went about it wrong, but I'm not mad at her."

Julian sighed. "I'll never live this down. I didn't charge my phone last night, but I'm guessing when I turn it back on there'll be four missed calls from my mother, three emails from concerned O'Learians my mother turned to for sympathy, and at least two texts each from my brothers, giving me shit."

"And a partridge in a pear tree?"

"Stop being cheerful," Julian grumbled. He heaved himself off the sofa and walked to the charger he'd plugged into the wall this morning. The line of his back when he bent over was…

Distracting.

"I'm rarely accused of being too cheerful," I told him. "This is novel." I bit my lip. "Speaking of novels, how goes the plight of Lady… what's her name?"

Julian glanced up from his phone. "Madelynne. Madelynne McBride *Buchanan.* The laird married her."

"Color me shocked. So she tamed his heart after all?"

He sank down onto the cushion and quirked an eyebrow. Coupled with the hair, the shirt, the pants, and the memory of the kiss that had been seared into my brain, it was a fucking compelling sight. "No. They're married, but it's a marriage of convenience so he can take over her father's land. Their fathers have been feuding for twenty years or something. His father was an asshole."

"Of course." I shifted onto my hip so I could see him better.

"But Buchanan's first wife hated and betrayed him, then ran off while pregnant and died of exposure."

"Gasp."

"So he can't bring himself to trust Madelynne, and he's all dominant and controlling and whatnot. The marriage isn't a happily ever after guarantee here. It's only a catalyst for trouble, really." He waggled his eyebrows. "Stay tuned."

I forced a smile, thinking of my own marriage and debating whether it was something I should mention to Julian or not. There was a point where keeping certain things from him felt a little like lying. But we weren't in a romantic relationship, right? So there was no reason for me to recount my sexual history.

And I would rather attend one of Hannibal's dinner parties than open this door with Julian. He saw me as a whole, complete person, rather than as the bits of ash and paper left behind after failure upon failure upon failure had burned me down. I knew him well enough now to know he wouldn't look down on me like some people had, but he might just pity me… and that might just be worse.

"Hey, think we can get pizza tonight?" he asked. "We could do half pepperoni, half broccoli, or… What?" he said when I'd stared at him a bit too long. "Will the vegetables contaminate the whole thing? What's going on in that inscrutable mind now?"

"Inscrutable? Hmm." I trailed my hand up his bent leg, from his knee to mid-thigh. "Well, I'm thinking a lot of things, Jules. For example, I'm thinking about how I hoped Netflix meant something that didn't involve Netflix at all. I'm thinking of how you looked this morning when you woke up in my bed."

Julian's blush was visible even in the fading light. "That's *not* what you were thinking about."

Well, he was right. Partly. But the image *had* been simmering in the back of my brain all day long.

It had been pretty obvious even before we left dinner at Julian's mom's house that we'd have to postpone our plans for "*later*" last night. Jules had been adorably tipsy—not nearly as out of control as he seemed to think, but way more than I figured he should be for anything more than sleep.

When we got back to the cabin, he'd nearly fallen over Honoria in his haste to get to the bedroom. He'd needed to lay down to get his pants off, which had led to him giggling for a solid minute while I'd stood in the doorway and watched him struggle.

In my defense, he'd been hilarious, and I'd kinda felt half-drunk myself, watching him make himself comfortable in my space.

Once he'd finished kicking off his pants and peeling off his sweater—both of which he'd thrown on the floor, as he'd been horrified to discover this morning—he'd lain like a starfish in the center of my bed, blinking at the ceiling like the fight with his clothing had sapped the last bits of his energy. It had taken way more effort not to crawl on the bed and kiss him than I'd imagined possible. Instead, I'd forced him to sit up long enough to take some Tylenol and drink a full bottle of water before tucking him under the covers. He'd fallen asleep with a little smile on his face, and after feeding the animals and brushing my teeth, I'd fallen asleep watching him.

"I woke up with you half-naked in my bed," I told him now, shifting my hand higher up his leg. "Your face was buried in my armpit like you enjoyed it there."

"Huh." He wrinkled his nose and cleared his throat. "Well. That, uh, doesn't actually surprise me too much."

"Really?" I raised my eyebrows and shifted my hand down onto the cushion near his waist so I was leaning over him slightly. "You have a thing for armpits? Armpits and facial hair?"

"You don't have to make it sound so weird. Facial hair is undeniably sexy. And a lot of guys think armpits are sexy, too." He shrugged, but his eyes were hot.

"Hmm. Well, I definitely didn't miss the part where you were gay." I twisted to put a knee on the couch and braced my hands on the cushions at either side of his waist so I almost hovered over him. "But you know I'm new to this whole thing."

"I know," he said softly. There were a thousand swirling questions in his eyes, and I knew he'd never ask them.

"Nature is big and wide, right?" I dipped my head and rested my chin on his chest. "You said the other day that you couldn't imagine ever falling for a woman. But…" I hesitated. "I don't know. Things don't seem to be that static for me."

"That was *my* experience, Daniel. Lots of people…"

I put a finger to his lips. "I know. I'm not looking for validation, Julian. I'm just explaining. In my whole life, I've never found guys hot. And it's not that I've been closed off to it, it's just that it's never occurred to me. But I find *you* hot."

He frowned. "Me?"

"You sound so surprised." I laughed. "Were you not there for those kisses?"

"I was. I just mean, if there was a guy who was gonna trigger a gay… awakening, for lack of a better word… the chances of it being *me* are so slim. Like, infinitesimally tiny. Chris Hemsworth, Daniel. The Rock. Idris

Elba. Any of them, I could see. But me?" He shook his head.

I snorted. "I don't know if you triggered it," I lied. "Maybe a person just awakens when they're supposed to awaken. Maybe I've always had this capacity to be bisexual or pansexual or demisexual… some other kind of sexual I'm about to invent for the first time. I don't need to pin it down with a vocabulary word. That's…" That's what my parents would have done. They loved to categorize shit. "I'm not going to label it. I'm just gonna enjoy it."

"Okay," he said dubiously.

"So, as I was saying, I find you insanely hot." I bent my head and kissed his chest through his t-shirt—*my* t-shirt. "I've spent hours thinking about what your skin would feel like under my fingers. I've jerked off to the memory of you fully clothed at the pond that day last summer."

"Last summer? At the pond? You were… already, even then?"

"Even then," I agreed.

He touched my hair tentatively. "That's… wow."

I snorted. "But I feel like I'm late to the game. I feel like I'm missing a lot of beginner information."

I was teasing, but partly serious, too. This attraction to Jules was new and consuming, and I was doing my best to just accept it and go with it, to figure it out as I went along. But I was also thirty-three years old. It had been half a life-time since I'd felt this clueless about sex. I didn't know how to touch him the right way. I had no practiced moves. Hell, I didn't even know what turned a guy on, since I'd never considered the possibility that armpits were sexy.

"*Wellllll.* You could always try a scientific approach," Julian suggested. "Come up with a hypothesis and then test it out, gather some data and make some conclusions?"

I nodded. "I suppose I could do that. Where should I

begin?" I leaned down so my chin was just grazing the t-shirt over his stomach, my eyes fixed on his.

He swallowed. "Um. You could maybe think of something you've always enjoyed having *done* to you and see if you enjoy doing it to someone else? Or you could think of something you've heard about and try it, to see if you find it interesting?"

"Those things help me figure out what *I* like," I said, nudging his shirt up with my mouth until a few inches of skin above his navel was exposed. "But what if I want to find out what might drive someone else crazy?"

"Crazy?" his voice was high-pitched and breathy.

"Uh-huh," I breathed against his bare skin. "For that, I think I'll need a subject matter expert. Someone who could give me advice and kinda talk me through what he wants. Someone who's gorgeous and sexy as fuck, but with a scientific mind. Someone like… *you.*"

Julian shivered from head to toe and his eyes went half-lidded, a reaction that seemed completely out of proportion to what we were doing.

Well, well, well. *Interesting.* Did Julian get off on the words? How lucky that I seemed to have an endless supply.

"Like for example, right now, I'm having the strongest *urge* to take your shirt off. You have the most beautiful skin and I want to see it all spread out in front of me. What would your expert opinion on that be, Doctor?"

"I…Yes. Good," he agreed.

I leaned back onto my knees and pushed his shirt up over his abs; then he took over, arching and shimmying until it was over his head, but I stopped him when the oversized material was still wrapped around his arms.

"Stay like that," I said. "Just like that."

He nodded.

God, but he was gorgeous. His skin glowed like gold in

the light from the fire, all lean muscles and wide shoulders and small, flat, brown nipples. I swept my fingertips from his shoulders down to his waist, just to see if he was as smooth as he appeared, and he was. *Holy shit*, he was.

"I'm not sure I'm getting enough information with this observation," I told him. His eyes had been tracking every movement of my hands, and now they flew to my face as I leaned over him once again. "I'm going to have to use alternative methods."

I dipped my head closer to his chest and ran the tip of my tongue over one of those nipples, never breaking eye contact, and then drew it more firmly into my mouth.

"Oh, fuck," he said, arching his chest up against me and closing his eyes. "*Fuck*."

Jesus. The tendons in his neck stood out as he threw his head back on the cushion. I wanted to taste those, too, so I gave in to the impulse, licking at the salty skin there, loving the way the day's growth of beard felt against my cheek. Once again, I was rock hard for this man before he'd even laid a hand on me, and I knew without a doubt that whatever my "official" orientation might be, I was one hundred percent oriented toward Julian Ross.

"You taste good, Julian," I said. "Really good. I could do this all day long. Does that sound alright?"

He released a breath that was half sigh, half moan, all agreement, and I let my tongue explore his skin for what felt like hours, mapping a path back down his neck, stopping to play with his nipples again, exploring every ridge of his ribs and the smooth plane of his stomach, before dipping into his belly button.

"Oh, God," he panted, squirming beneath me. "I think that's enough data."

"Barely getting started," I said. My voice was more like a growl.

I dipped my nose into his exposed armpit and inhaled. *Well, fuck.* It smelled *good*, as in *really* good. Musky and salty, like concentrated Jules mixed with a little of the soap from my shower. I nuzzled into the hollow and gave an experimental lick that made Jules's hips kick up.

"In my expert opinion, you should let my hands go now," he moaned.

"Should I?" The truth was, I craved his hands on me, but I wanted to take things slowly, and I was sure—as in, rock-hard-certain—that if he started touching me, I wasn't going to last long.

"Yes!" His eyes were wild and his lips were bright red from biting them. "Seriously, right now. I'm dying. Dead. Right here. On this sofa. My death will be on your conscience," he babbled.

"Soon," I whispered, and I stopped his words with a kiss.

But if I'd been hoping to slow things down, tasting his mouth was a definite tactical error. He poured himself into the kiss, sliding his tongue against mine and conveying every ounce of his need and frustration. If he was hoping to drive me crazy, he succeeded.

I pulled back, breathing hard, and pushed to my feet next to the sofa. I pulled the shirt off Julian's wrists, and half a second later, he was pushing down his sweatpants, clearly *done* with my controlled experiment. I paused to admire the hard length that laid against his belly with a weirdly proud, possessive sort of feeling. I'd done that to him. *Me.*

I stripped off my own shirt and sleep pants like the fate of the world depended on my speed. I grabbed my own cock by the base and squeezed because *holy shit*, things were reaching a critical point.

Had I ever been this turned on in my life?

"Come here," Julian said, leaning up to grab my hands so he could pull me down on top of him. "Come here, come here, come here."

There was a second, maybe less, when I hovered above him—my hands holding his wrists to the cushions, and my knee between his spread thighs—where I felt like I was almost standing outside of myself, contemplating what would happen next. I was naked. He was naked. Cocks were about to touch.

And then I thought, *Fuck, yes! Finally!* and lowered myself down on top of him.

He made a sound that was a cross between a laugh and a relieved sob as his hands trailed up and down my back. "Oh, damn. I think there's a problem with your experiment, Daniel."

"Yeah? What's that?" I could barely concentrate on his words. I was too busy staring down at the picture we made and trying to process the sensations. Who knew the scratch of his leg hair against my thighs could be so unbearably exciting? Who knew that the length of his cock against mine could make my mind short-circuit?

"Uh-huh. There is literally nothing you could do to me right now that I wouldn't want."

His eyes were burning blue, and I bent down to bite the curve of his shoulder as a reward, just because it looked so bitable. His eyes slammed shut and he arched his whole body against me with a groan.

"Julian!" The shock in my voice was almost laughable, but seriously, *who the fuck knew* that sex could feel like this?

Julian laughed up at me, and I realized I'd spoken this thought aloud.

"We haven't even gotten to the best part yet," he said. "Welcome to the joys of frottage."

He pulled me against him harder, setting up a rhythm.

"Motherfucker." I planted a foot on the floor and rutted against him. Both of us groaned. "I think frottage Julian might be my favorite Julian of all," I breathed.

Julian laughed again, threading his hands through my hair, and then leaned up to kiss me, which required a bit of finagling thanks to our height difference and the limitations of the sofa, but that was okay too. Every gasp, and groan, and awkward, desperate fumble ratcheted up the intensity and connection.

Twin ripples of joy and satisfaction ran through my bloodstream. For the first time in maybe forever, I felt totally in tune with my partner. His pleasure was my pleasure. His every exhale and sigh were mine, and mine were his. It was the simplest, most profound thing I'd ever experienced. I didn't want it to end, but also had never needed to come so badly. I could feel my balls drawing up and precum—his and mine—leaving damp trails on our bellies.

"I'm close," he said, his hand coming down to grasp at my lower back.

"Oh, thank God. Me too."

But even as I said it, I was coming, lightning shooting down my spine as my legs stiffened and I shot all over him. He followed right after me.

I slumped sideways toward the cushions so I wouldn't crush him, he shifted toward the edge slightly to accommodate me. I dragged the thin blanket from the back of the couch over us, and we lay like that for a long time after, pressed up against each other in all our messy, sweaty glory, without saying a thing.

The light from the fire made rippling shadows up and down the bare length of him, and the room was utterly silent, but for the sound of breathing—ours and the dog's —and the crack of a log in the grate.

There were a lot of things I could have said then,

maybe even things I should have said, like how perfect that had been, how amazing he was, but he already knew the former and wouldn't believe the latter. I wanted to tell him how much I cared for him and wanted him to be happy, how badly I wanted not to hurt him, but the first felt too much like a promise and the second too much like I was jinxing myself.

I'd once made a living conveying emotion with words, but I was starting to realize that the most important emotions didn't require any words at all.

So, instead, I pressed a kiss to the top of his head and felt him relax even further against me, taking this moment of peace and silence for the gift it was.

Chapter Ten

JULIAN

TUESDAY MORNING SUNSHINE poured in the window of my apartment, and somewhere out on Weaver Street, someone was ringing bells for Christmas donations, but here in my apartment, the only signs of life were my racing heart and the rasp of Daniel's breath in my ear.

"You know… silly me… when you said you wanted to take me out for coffee—" I paused for air and lolled my head against the refrigerator door, shivering when my naked back met chilly metal. "—I sort of expected actual coffee."

"Did you?" Daniel licked at the side of my neck and splayed his big hands against the small of my back, pulling our messy stomachs more firmly together. "I thought this would be a more effective pick-me-up. Caffeine'll kill ya, you know?"

I shivered again, feeling my scrub pants slip another notch further down my thighs. "I definitely feel perkier."

"Me too." He sighed, a content sort of sound. "I've gotten used to starting the day this way."

"Three days and it's a habit?" I said lightly, trailing my hands down his back and ignoring the way my quieting pulse wanted to kick back up at his words. I *wanted* it to be a habit. I wanted him to get so addicted to me he'd never want to stop. "I would've come over last night, but *someone* said he was busy."

That was the wrong thing to say, apparently, no matter how teasingly I'd tried to say it. Daniel pulled away without looking at me and reached for the jeans and underwear bunched around his ankles.

"Can I use your bathroom?" he asked.

A snarky retort was on the tip of my tongue. *No way*, I wanted to tell him. *You can rush me up the stairs, push me against the refrigerator, and rub me off, but using my restroom is a hard no.* But for the first time ever with Daniel, I held back. I had no idea how he'd respond.

"Yes. Sure. Of course," I said instead.

"Great. Thanks."

Weren't we polite?

When I heard my bathroom door close, I leaned back against the refrigerator and rubbed my hands over my face. I was standing in my kitchen with drying cum stuck to my stomach. I still had my sneakers on.

What the hell had been wrong with what I said?

I grabbed a paper towel and dampened it in the sink to clean myself off, then straightened my clothes, grabbing my shirts off the floor where one of us had thrown them. I picked up Daniel's sweatshirt, too, and folded it neatly on the counter. Then I made tea for both of us.

"So what's on the agenda for the rest of your day?" Daniel said, coming back into the room wearing a smile so bright I had to blink to clear my vision. His chest was still naked, and the sunlight made the hair on his chest glow like he was some kind of Thor fantasy come to life.

I cleared my throat and picked up my mug, blowing on the hot liquid.

"Oh, so much excitement. I'm booked solid for the rest of the day, actually."

"Because of the holiday?"

"Partly," I agreed. "Partly because people want to stare at me like an animal in the zoo. Partly because they're hoping you'll show up and we'll start kissing in the waiting area." The looky-loos were starting to piss me off, and it showed in my voice.

Daniel grabbed his sweatshirt from the counter and threw it on. When his head emerged, he quirked an eyebrow at me. "You think they're ready to see that?"

I snorted. "Wanna go downstairs and find out?"

"Nope. Not even a little," he said. And while there was nothing particularly insulting about that—I mean, he was joking, right? And I was, too. I wasn't fourteen. I had no need to get all PDA-happy in front of the town—it stung anyway. Much like the stilted phone conversation I'd had with my mother over the weekend, where she'd apologized for her behavior at Thanksgiving, but claimed she'd only been looking out for me. Making sure I wasn't making a mistake.

I'd assured her I wasn't. But I wasn't sure of anything anymore. Daniel and I were physically closer than ever, but I couldn't help feeling like he was pulling away.

"Well," I said, turning away and dumping my tea down the drain untouched, "sadly, *I* do have to get back downstairs."

"Yeah, of course." Daniel nodded. "See you tonight?"

I turned on the water to wash out my cup and hesitated. "There's a planning meeting tonight. For the Light Parade."

"The Light Parade."

"You might have seen the fliers up around town." Unless you were blind, you couldn't miss them. "The name's a little misleading, though. The lights don't parade, the people parade to see the lights. All the shops in O'Leary set up displays. A bunch of businesses that don't have storefronts on Weaver Street set up booths in the church parking lot." I shrugged. "My mother's on the committee, so I usually run the booth for the landscaping business while she runs around handling minor catastrophes." I darted a glance behind me.

"Oh." Daniel licked his lips. "And when is that?"

I turned back to the sink, apparently determined to take the top two layers of glaze off my mug through overwashing. "This weekend. Saturday. But there's a meeting for the vendors tonight."

"Right. You guys sure love your town meetings, huh?"

Us guys.

"Oh yeah. You know me," I joked. "Nothing I love more."

He laughed, and it seemed to break whatever weird tension I'd caused between us. He came up behind me and wrapped his arms around my waist, pressing himself against me.

"And after the meeting? You could come out to the cabin. The animals miss you."

"Honoria and She-Ra, huh?" I shut off the water and relaxed against him. He took my weight easily. "Not you?"

"Don't be ridiculous. You know I love having you there."

I sighed. The truth was, I loved being there. "Okay," I said. "I'll come."

———

THE PLANNING MEETING was every bit as awkward as I'd expected it to be. Someone—my brothers, or maybe my mother, or possibly all three—had told one or two people *in strictest confidence* about what happened on Thanksgiving, and that person had told another, and so forth. By the time I got to Goode's Diner shortly after sundown that evening, it had already made the rounds. As I took my coat off, Lisa Dorian greeted me with, "Looking a little peaky, Doc Ross," and then added in a whisper loud enough to be heard in Rushton, "You know, we have pamphlets about binge drinking over at the library."

Old Jay Turner, who was standing nearby, burst into laughter that devolved into wheezing. I gave them both a chilly smile and walked away to try to find a drink.

Non-alcoholic, obviously.

It was still early, and Jamie, who managed the place, hadn't set out the food yet, nor did I see him in the restaurant chatting with any of the other early birds, so I headed for the swinging doors that led to the kitchen. But when I pushed the door open, I quickly saw that he wasn't alone.

"You can't be serious, Jamie." Parker Hoffstraeder was standing in the center of the kitchen, arms folded across his chest, glaring at Jamie. His short hair gleamed like a gold coin in the overhead light, and he was still wearing a thick green vest over his sweater, like he'd recently come in from outside. "I refuse to let you do this. You hear me? I won't let you."

Jamie was busy doing something at the counter, which was completely covered with half-filled dishes, pans, and trays. He didn't turn around or in any way indicate that he'd heard Parker speak, but from where I stood, I could see that his jaw was clenched.

"That's great," Parker said, when it was clear Jamie wouldn't reply. "That's just wonderful. Typical James

Burke, right there, ladies and gentlemen. Silent and stoic to the bitter end."

Jamie whirled around, whacking what looked like a tray of sandwiches with his hand. The tray hit a saucepan, and the saucepan hit the floor with a resounding crash, spraying viscous, dark fluid all over the floor… and all over Jamie.

Jamie's face turned a violent shade of red and his entire body expanded like a puffer fish. Given that he was six foot something and barrel-chested to begin with, the sight was impressive.

Jamie Burke was one of the sweetest, gentlest men I knew, but he also had a temper to match his red hair, and right now he was looking at Parker with murder in his eyes.

I stepped forward, like somehow *I* was gonna be able to avert this fight physically, but neither of them even noticed me. They were locked in some kind of staring contest that could only end in death or hard fucking.

I cleared my throat, and Parker's eyes darted to me for half a second, breaking the tension. Jamie clenched his eyes shut.

"My life is none of your goddamn business, Parker," he bit out. "You don't get an opinion."

Parker shook his head. "That's bullshit. You're not gonna fuck everything up just because you've got your panties in a twist over—"

"You have no say in the matter! You *left* O'Leary, and now you think you can just come back and everything will be like it was? Fuck that. One of us has got to go. And if you do one goddamn thing to make this harder than it has to be, I'll—"

"Yeah?" Parker taunted, taking a step closer. "You'll what. Tell me, Jamie. What will you do?"

Jamie's brown eyes popped open and he glared daggers at the other man. Parker smirked.

"That's what I thought. All talk. No action." He pointed a warning finger at Jamie. "You're not getting out of this, understand? I'm not leaving, and we're gonna figure our shit out, one way or another."

Parker looked at me and nodded once, a greeting and a goodbye. Then he turned and walked out the back door.

When he was gone, Jamie just… deflated. He braced both hands on the edge of the counter and took a deep breath, letting his head hang down.

"Jamie?" I said softly. "You okay?"

Jamie shook his head.

I took a step forward and placed a hand between his shoulder blades. "You wanna talk?"

He shook his head again. But this time he took a deep breath and straightened. He grabbed a rag and started cleaning up the mess on the floor.

"Let me help," I said, picking up the spilled pan and dumping it in the dishwashing sink.

"I'm good, Jules. Sorry you had to see that," he said, not meeting my eyes. "I'll, ah… I'll have the food ready in a few."

"Nobody gives a shit about the food, Jamie." I grabbed the rag from his hand. "What's going on?"

"Just the usual. Contemplating murder. *God*, that man makes me fucking *insane*." He slammed his hand down on the countertop with bruising force. "One of these days, he's gonna make me lose my mind, Jules. Mark my words. Which is why—" He shook his head. "Never mind." He took a deep breath. "What's going on with you?"

"Who cares? Jamie, babe, do you want to…"

He shook his head again. "Just… give me a minute, okay? Alone?"

I hesitated, but he raised his big brown eyes to mine. "Please."

I nodded. "If you need me…"

"I know. Thanks." He smiled tightly and turned back to his cleaning while I walked back out the door.

I was still distracted, though, which probably explained why I didn't see my mother standing there waiting for me.

I'd spoken to her only the one time since Thanksgiving and hadn't seen her at all, which was probably a healthy amount of interaction for a nearly thirty-year-old man and his mother, but unusual for *us*.

"Mama. Hey."

"Julian." My mother knotted and unknotted her hands in front of her, looking uncharacteristically nervous.

"Is everything okay?" I demanded, unreasonably panicked by her nervousness. My mother didn't *get* nervous, and the last time I'd seen her truly uncertain was when she'd had to tell me about my dad's heart attack.

She frowned. "Yes, of course."

"You're alright? And Con and Theo?" I hadn't seen either of them in days.

"They're fine." Her eyes softened. "Theodore's right over in the corner with Sam and Rae, and I just talked to Constantine this morning."

I nodded, finally convinced. "How's work?"

"Good. Way more business than I'd anticipated. Looks like Micah's Blooms is downsizing for the holiday." She shook her head like she was mildly troubled.

"Isn't that a good thing? More business for Ross Landscaping?"

"Oh, yes. Good for us, but bad for him. I thought the man had better business sense. I hope everything's alright with him. He's not a young man."

I blinked. Micah Bloom had opened his nearly eponymous shop just three doors down from my clinic and I saw him every day. He was maybe forty; hardly ancient.

I pressed my lips together. "I thought he was your biggest competitor. I thought he pissed you off when he opened his shop here in O'Leary."

She shrugged. "Well, yes, but I don't dislike the man, Julian."

I nodded. Contrary as it seemed, I knew she meant exactly what she said. She disliked what Micah Bloom represented.

The conversation halted for a second and I looked around the room at the various groups of O'Learians making polite chit-chat.

"How's Daniel?" she finally asked, drawing my attention back.

"He's good. Busy." With something he'd never specified and I didn't feel comfortable asking him about.

For once, I had no desire to talk or think about Daniel. I felt like I'd done nothing all afternoon but spin my wheels mentally, wondering what I'd said that made things so awkward in the kitchen this morning, and then questioning whether things *had* been awkward or if I'd imagined the feeling entirely.

"That's nice." She toyed with the end of her long, dark braid, and I noticed a few more lines of grey running through it. "I know I didn't make a very good impression on him last week."

I snorted.

"I'm sorry," she continued. "I know I told you that the other day on the phone."

"You said, 'I'm sorry, *but*,'" I reminded her. "'I'm sorry, *but* I don't want to see you make a mistake, Julian.' An apology doesn't contain a but."

"You're right." She looked at me steadily. "I was wrong

about that, too." She blew out a breath. "I talked to Constantine earlier today, I told you. He gave me a lecture."

"Con? Lectured you?" I couldn't imagine him doing that. I couldn't imagine her taking it.

She smiled ruefully. "It was unexpected. But then, maybe I don't know my sons as well as I think I do. I still think of Constantine as the same angry boy he used to be. I think of you as the same quiet boy you used to be, the same young man who needed to apologize to the world for a few words you spoke to your father in anger."

I held up a hand. "I don't want to talk about that."

She nodded slowly. "Alright. The point is, Constantine isn't the same boy. He's a thoughtful young man now. One with a good heart. Still a little wild at times, of course." She smiled briefly. "But he reminded me that you're not a boy anymore either. Whatever choices you make, they're yours now. I can't… shield you from things anymore. And if I try, I'm not going to protect you, I'll end up holding you back."

"Constantine said that? My brother Constantine?"

"Not exactly that," she allowed. "I think his exact words were, 'Stop giving Julian shit about Daniel. He's a grown man, and he knows what the fuck he's doing.'"

I blinked. "And what did *you* say?"

"I told him to stop using filthy language," she said, like this was the most obvious thing, and I supposed it was. "And then I told him he was right. I need to stop pressuring you to live life the way I want you to."

"Huh."

"So if you don't want to finish the romance novel, you don't have to."

I smirked. "I don't mind reading the romance novel," I admitted.

"Really?"

"I need to find out how Lady Madelynne gets on with her barbarian, don't I?"

"You can be sure she earns herself a happy ending, Julian." She cupped my cheek gently with her palm. "And I'm sure you'll earn one for yourself, too."

I swallowed hard. Last week, I would have found that a lot more inspiring. Right now, I felt like every move I made—standing up in a crowded diner and announcing I had a boyfriend, agreeing to this fucked-up friends-with-benefits thing, constantly saying the wrong thing with Daniel—was the wrong one, and I didn't even know what a happy ending would look like anymore.

"So," she said briskly, patting my chest. "To that end, I'd like to apologize to Daniel in person."

"You don't have to. Honestly. Daniel's said from the beginning that he knows you're overprotective because you care."

"Did he? Good." She nodded once. "I think I really *will* like him once I get to know him better. I'd like you to bring him to the Parade this weekend. Maybe he can stand at the Ross Landscaping table with you. Kind of a welcome to the family thing."

"But we're not getting married," I told her. "It's not that serious. We're just… It's not…" I threw up my hands. How the fuck to explain that we were fake boyfriends who'd likely be staging a fake breakup, if I didn't manage to *really* break up our friendship first?

"I know. It'll work out or it won't," she said, throwing her braid over her shoulder. "And he can come this weekend or not. But I want you… and *him*… to know he's welcome. Alright?"

"Yeah. Alright." I wrapped my arms around her. "Thank you, Mama. That's very nice of you."

She patted my back and sniffed gently. "You don't have to sound so surprised, Julian. I'm a very nice person. Ordinarily."

"I love you."

"I know. And I love you." She hesitated. "And for what it's worth, your father knew you loved him too, Julian. He never doubted it for a minute."

Chapter Eleven

DANIEL

"You're sure you don't mind?"

I turned my head on the seat to look at Julian's profile. The cut of his jaw made me want to lean in and kiss him, as it always did these days, and the tiny patch of hair near the apex of his chin did funny things to my chest.

Trust Julian to shave the tricky back area perfectly, but to miss the most obvious spot right near the front. Trust *me* to find such a weird thing adorable.

"For the third time, Jules: no, I don't mind going to the Light Parade. Do you want me to tattoo it somewhere?"

Julian darted a glance at me and then turned back to the road that led to the center of town. "You didn't seem particularly excited when I mentioned it to you, that's all."

I sighed. My feelings about the parade were similar to my feelings about my divorce from Ingrid: fifty percent acceptance, forty percent annoyance, ten percent non-specific dread. But Julian had asked me with that cute little lip-bite he sometimes did, and his blue eyes had shone with vulnerability, like he was expecting me to say no and had already prepared himself for it, and what the hell could I say but yes?

"I didn't say I was *excited*. Not about the lights, anyway. Can't say I'm excited about the crowd, either. But you said there'll be free food." I grinned. "And my fake boyfriend will be there to defend me from any irate villagers with pitchforks. Or any crows that want to harass me out of my nest."

Julian rolled his eyes. "You won't need defending. And yeah, there'll be a ton of free food. Cal and Ash will be there with pastries. I think Goode's is passing out cocoa. Burger Geek has some kind of burger things." He hesitated. "I do need to run the table for my mom for most of the event, though. So, you can either stay with me or walk around on your own, if you think you'll be bored."

"Yep. You said that. Do you have a preference? Want me to stand by your side like a good fake boyfriend? Or wander around so I'm not distracting you?"

"Either," Julian said quickly. "Whichever. Your call. *Totally* your call."

"Oookay." I narrowed my eyes. "Guess we'll play it by ear, then."

Julian nodded, and we lapsed into silence broken only by some old-fashioned Christmas carols playing softly on the radio. The silence itself was nothing new—one of the things that had made our friendship so remarkable was the way we'd always shared easy silences, and neither of us felt the need to smooth over the awkwardness with meaningless conversation. But this silence felt fraught—the sugar coating over something bitter, the smooth layer of dirt over a grave.

I turned my head again, this time letting it lean against the cold glass of the passenger's window, and tried to figure out exactly when shit with Julian had started to go so spectacularly wrong. Was it the moment I kissed him? Was it the second we agreed to be friends with benefits? Was it the minute after we'd first come together on my couch two weeks ago, when I'd felt the tug to make this situation permanent, even though I knew Julian could do so much better? Or was the whole thing doomed from the moment I met him, since I was shit at relationships?

Lose one friend, maybe it's no one's fault. Lose your wife, all your friends, your career, and the respect of your parents, though, and you can't help but notice the common thread.

"We'll park around back, in the alley behind the clinic," Julian said as he glided the car through the crowded streets. "Most of Weaver is blocked off for the parade already, and I'd bet all the on-street parking is taken."

"Sure."

He pulled into an open spot just a couple doors down from the rear door to the clinic, a door I was very familiar with, since I used it more often than not when Julian and I spent time together in town. But today, when he got out of the SUV, he took a second to pat the roof of the tarp-covered car that rested on cement blocks beside it.

"What's that?" I asked when Julian walked away. "Is it yours?"

"Oh." Julian's cheeks were pink, and I didn't think it was from the cold. "Yeah. It's my old car. My first car." He strode down the alleyway like we were late, though if anything we were early. "I think it's better if we walk back here all the way down to the church. It's only a block down, but I can hear how crowded it is already, and—"

I leaned down and lifted the corner of the tarp to reveal a bright red exterior. "Oh my God! What kind of car is it?"

Julian stopped and turned but didn't walk back. "A 1990 Toyota Celica. We should really get going."

"Oh." Not exactly a Ferrari, but still. "Is it a convertible? Why's it up on blocks? How did I not know you had this?"

Julian sighed and braced his hands on his hips. "Yes, it's a convertible. It's up on blocks because it's not registered anymore. And you didn't know I had it because it never came up. Sometimes I even forget it's there." He licked his lips. "You know my mom's going to start texting any minute, right?"

"Jules, we're way early." I pulled the tarp up further. "This thing is in great shape! Why not put it on the road?" I loved the sleek lines of the car—it was cute and a little unexpected, just like Julian.

"It's over a quarter century old, Daniel. It needs work. It'd be… expensive."

I made a face but nodded. I was clueless about cars except when it came to driving them or riding in them. "Maybe sell it, then. Some collector would love it and could…"

"I'm not selling it." Jules stalked forward and snatched the edge of the cover from my grip, smoothing it back into place. "I'm not registering it, I'm not fixing it, I'm not driving it. I like this car exactly where it is. Now can we go to the fucking parade?"

I looked at him in shock, my hand still outstretched. "What's your problem, Julian?"

"I don't have a problem, *Daniel*. I just want to get to the place we said we were going. Or, you know what? You don't really want to go anyway, so why don't you just take my car and go home?"

Something cold and slimy slithered in my gut. "I was just asking a question."

"Right. Sorry. My bad. I didn't realize this was question time." Julian folded his arms across his chest, angrier than I'd ever seen him. "How about we discuss *your* first car, Daniel. Or where you lived when you got it. Or how you got the money for it. Or who you were dating when you did. They're just *questions*, right?"

I stared at him, stunned. "You know I don't like to…" I closed my eyes and rubbed my forehead as the irony of what I was about to say struck.

"Sorry," I said softly. "I didn't realize this was something off-limits. That's all you had to say."

He huffed out a breath and cocked one hip to the side, his posture relaxed just slightly. "No, *I'm* sorry. It's not off-limits, I'm just not used to having to explain it. It's about my dad, and…" He shook his head. "It's hard. So another time, okay?"

I nodded. "Sure."

Julian managed to smile. "Okay. Let's do this, then." He beckoned me closer, and when I reached him, I held out a hand for his, wanting to ground myself in him. Julian threaded our fingers together and tugged me gently down the alley.

We emerged at the church parking lot, where it looked like Times Square had exploded and the shards had landed in O'Leary. There were dozens and dozens of small wooden booths, all painted blue, green, and white, and each strung with an insane number of fairy lights. There were tinsel Christmas ornaments, a huge inflatable dreidel, and a dance area in one corner that was covered in fake snow where a DJ was setting up a booth.

"This is…" I began, then paused, unsure how to finish.

"Extra?" Julian suggested. "Garish? Kitschy? Cute?"

"All of those things," I agreed. But there were pink-cheeked kids chasing each other up and down the street, the air smelled of chocolate and pine, and people were *laughing*, genuinely enjoying this time with their neighbors as they set up these little displays, so really, it was mostly *cute*.

Julian led me to the back, where his mom was setting up a gorgeous display beneath a white and gold Ross Landscaping banner.

"Oh, I'm so glad you boys are here," she greeted us. She pulled Julian into a fierce hug, then stood on tiptoe to press a warm, maternal kiss to my cheek. "I need some help."

Julian had said his mother was determined to apologize to me for her behavior at Thanksgiving, but as far as I was concerned, that kiss balanced the scales. I couldn't help but contrast it to my own mother's chilly perfection. It seemed like Jules and I both had parents who liked to get their own way, but where his mom was overprotectively involved in his life, my parents had all but written me off when I didn't meet their expectations.

Though maybe that wasn't entirely fair. My father had called me twice in the last two weeks, leaving messages each time to confirm that I was expected home for Christmas. He'd somehow even gotten Sabrina in on his act, getting my former agent to text me repeatedly, making all kinds of threats about coming to get me if I didn't come home. I didn't actually think anything would be fundamentally different if I went home—I imagined the same crown roast, the same cocktails, the same professionally decorated Christmas tree, the same expressions of disapproval on my parents' faces—so I had no plans to leave the cabin, but I'd give them points for trying.

"What's going on?" Julian asked his mom.

"Theo and Sam were supposed to be here to help me set up all of these centerpieces." She gestured at a huge flat of greenery. "There's a bunch more in the truck." She jerked a thumb over her shoulder at the area where the vendors had parked. "Margo Martin can't get her overhead lights to work, and she swears up and down it's an issue with the power and not her lights, which I seriously doubt. And apparently, I'm the only one around who can go and troubleshoot it for her."

"Where's Theo?" Julian asked, shooing his mother to one side as he jumped in to fix up her display.

"I have no idea! Sam needed to move some things." She sighed impatiently. "I couldn't tell you why she needed to move them today, or where she was moving them to or from. All I can tell you is that neither of them are here, and now I'm four hands short."

"And here Jules and I are, with four hands between us," I said. "What can I do?"

She smiled, wide and genuine. "You picked a good one," she told Julian, nudging him in the ribs. "If you and Julian can just finish setting up this display, I'm going to go see what Margo's talking about. Then maybe you two can help me get some of the pre-decorated miniature trees out of the truck?"

I glanced at Julian, and both of us nodded.

"No problem," I said.

She winked at me and squeezed Julian's shoulder, and she ran off.

"Okay, you've clearly got an artistic vision here," I said, watching Julian work. "How about I hand you the centerpieces, and you arrange them."

"My artistic vision is basically not to crowd things on top of each other," Julian said, rearranging a basket filled with pinecones and greenery. He smiled at me. "Also known as *don't make it look shitty*."

I grinned, handing him a long piece of greenery interspersed with berries. "Exactly my style as well."

"Yeah, I kinda…" Jules paused and clapped a hand to his front pocket, which was buzzing slightly. "Shit. That might be a text from Theo." We swapped places, and he yanked the phone out.

He blinked for a second, swallowed, and slipped the phone back in his pocket without replying.

"What'd he say?" I demanded. "Everything okay? Do they need a ride?"

"No. That wasn't Theo." He bumped me out of the way and resumed his spot without looking at me.

"Oh." I waited to see if he'd volunteer anything further, but he didn't. A minute later, I could hear the phone faintly buzzing again. "You gonna get that?"

Julian glanced at me briefly and, I swear, guiltily, then grabbed his phone again. This time, he turned away from me slightly and typed out a quick reply. This time, I also caught a glimpse of the earlier message.

Hey, Jules. Curtis again.

Curtis… *again.*

Something unpleasant settled in my stomach, curdling the sandwich I'd thrown together for lunch. I'd never heard of anyone in town named *Curtis.*

There were a hundred explanations, of course—college buddy, old friend, professional acquaintance—but he would have told me if it was any of those people. No, this was a boyfriend… a former boyfriend.

Who was contacting Julian… *again.*

My brain stuttered for a second, and the first emotion to surface when it rebooted was *hurt*… which scared the fuck out of me, naturally. There was no reason whatsoever why Julian couldn't have a male friend. A hundred male friends. Hell, even a hundred guys he… you know… hooked up with when he wasn't with me.

I made an involuntary choking noise and tried to cover it as a cough.

We weren't exclusive. I mean, not that I had any desire to hook up with anyone else, but Julian could. If he wanted to.

Julian gave me a half-smile and slid the phone away again. "You wanna go grab some more stuff from the truck?"

I nodded shortly and followed him around the back of the little booth and then over to the truck that bore the Ross logo. A dozen small fresh pine trees—each about three feet tall, flocked with fake snow, and festooned with ribbon—were standing in the bed. Julian clambered up and passed four down to me before jumping back down.

"I think we'll arrange these in front," he said, grabbing two of the trees. "Since they're nearly the height of the…"

The high-pitched buzzing of his phone interrupted him.

Jules tried to ignore it.

"Something important?" I asked.

Julian shook his head, but he still set down the trees and reached for his phone. "Old friend is in the area. Wanted to get together. I told him I was busy."

"Oh." I felt stupid. "That's cool. We could all go out, if you want."

A little smile twisted the corners of Julian's mouth. "You want to go out with me and an old friend? When I practically had to pry you into the car to come today—"

"Hey! Not true."

"Oh, yeah? Name one time you've *hung out* with anyone

besides me, not including Thanksgiving, since you've lived here."

I spread my hands wide. "Uh, *now*! Look at me hanging out with all of O'Leary."

"Right." Julian rolled his eyes and tucked the phone back in his pocket. "If I didn't know better, I'd think you were jealous."

"Jealous. *Pfft.* No." *Yes! Oh, motherfucker. Yes, I was.* Holy shit. That was the last thing I needed, because if I was jealous, that would mean I really cared, far beyond friends with benefits, and if I really cared…

Julian's lips twitched again, like he was somehow finding humor in this incredibly terrifying turn of events. He took a step toward me and slid his palms up my chest.

Despite the two layers of cotton and the thick fleece jacket I wore, his touch made me shiver.

"You weren't jealous?" he asked coyly.

"No."

"Not even a little?"

"Julian, no. Honestly, why would I be?" I scoffed. "Fake boyfriends don't get jealous." I took a step back and his hands dropped away. His face fell, too.

"I was kidding," he said, turning away and grabbing those poor trees, which were steadily losing their flocking. "Jesus, Daniel. It was just a joke." He stomped away through the parked cars toward the tent, so I picked up the remaining trees and followed him.

When he reached the edge of the parking area, he whirled to face me. His blue eyes sparked in the setting sun, and he could almost have passed for some kind of avenging angel… one who wielded a pair of flocked trees in place of swords.

"And you don't have to keep reminding me that this is fake," he hissed in a furious whisper.

"What?"

"Every time you say boyfriend, Daniel—every *fucking* time—you have to say *fake* in front of it. Like, do you think I'm going to forget? Do you think I'd ever actually believe that any of this was real? Me? With *you*?" He laughed, but it was a miserable, scathing sound that didn't sound like Julian at all. "Not fucking likely. The wonder is that anyone believed it could happen in the first place."

I ground my teeth together. I knew how wrong we were for each other. Of course I did.

"And you know what? If it eases your mind in some way, the guy texting me isn't an old friend, he's a Grindr hookup I had last spring wanting to hook up again. I was gonna say no, since I figured I'd be busy with you tonight, but maybe I'm kinda sick of your fucking attitude. Maybe I should—"

I had no recollection of how the kiss happened. I mean, it was all me. No doubt about *that*. Jules was just standing there holding a couple gaudy twigs, looking at me like I was what happened when the devil and his wife had a baby, telling me about how he was basically gonna go fuck some other guy while I went home, and the next thing I knew, I'd thrown down the trees I carried and I… Well, I grabbed his jaw with both hands and attacked his face with all the finesse of an octopus in a cartoon latching his suckers into some poor unsuspecting victim.

At least, that's how it started.

But then Jules let his trees fall to the ground also. He lifted himself up on his tiptoes, and I bent down so I could wrap my arms around his waist and haul him against me, spreading my feet for balance as I lifted him up.

He was so warm. God, so warm and vital and *alive*. He was *everything.* He smelled a little like pine sap and a little like something citrusy and musky and delicious. My fingers slid up his back beneath his jacket, cold fingers unintentionally coasting along his smooth skin, and he pushed himself more fully against me. Christ, it was like it hadn't been hours since I'd kissed him, but years.

I set him back down on the ground, but only so I could lean into him, practically bending him back with the force of my kiss. And he gave as good as he got, his breath coming in furious pants against my lips.

Fuck.

How long would it take us to get back to Julian's place?

A high-pitched whistle rent the air, along with teasing laughter. "Kiss him, Doc!"

Julian and I broke apart instantly, and the laughter only got louder.

"Aw, I didn't mean to spoil your fun," an old man in a Santa Claus costume said, wagging his eyebrows. "I was just encouraging you."

"He had a rum toddy before we left the house," a woman dressed as an elf said apologetically, wrapping an arm around the man's shoulders. "Come on, Jay. Time to go get ready for the parade."

Jay chuckled and let himself be led away. Meanwhile, Julian watched me cautiously, like he wasn't sure how I was going to react.

I wasn't sure either.

Holy *fuck* I wanted him. But obviously, it wasn't as easy as wanting. I wanted a hell of a lot of things. A successful career and a decent family and world peace and… I couldn't *have* any of those. I didn't have the ability to acquire or maintain them. And I didn't have the ability to keep Julian, either. I fucked up every relationship I had, or it fucked *me* up, or both. I couldn't stand watching it happen again. I couldn't stand having it happen with Julian.

I cleared my throat loudly. "You go ahead and take those to the booth. I'll get the rest of the shit from the truck and leave it here."

Julian gave me a derisive look that called me a coward. Then he picked up the decorated trees and disappeared into the line of booths.

I tried not to think as I made trip after trip to fetch more decorations and lay them on the lawn. I tried really hard not to recall the hurt expression on Julian's face, or the sinking feeling in my stomach when I thought about him and *Curtis.*

I brought the final batch of decorations to the booth when I couldn't avoid it any longer. Julian's mother had returned and greeted me with a warm smile, while her son made a very obvious effort to ignore me completely. I caught her looking between us, like she was wondering what had happened in the fifteen minutes she was gone.

Tons, Mrs. Ross. *Metric shit-tons of revelation, and none of it good.*

I needed space. I needed to draw breath without smelling Julian.

I debated the best way to extricate myself from this situation and deeply regretted that my truck was all the way back at my place. It wasn't an impossible walk—maybe two or three miles—but it was getting dark, and the Camden Road was unlit.

"Daniel," she said, interrupting my deep contemplation of the dried grass and the toe of my boot. "I wasn't able to fix Margo's issue. Do you think you could come with me and take a look?"

I hesitated. I probably had even less electrical knowledge than your average person. But the alternative was standing here with Julian, pretending he wasn't angry and I wasn't hopeless.

"Oh, Daniel would love to," Julian said acidly. "He's kind of a renaissance man, you know? Go get 'em, Bear Grylls."

I ground my teeth together. "Yeah," I told Angela. "Happy to."

Julian didn't even look up when we left the booth.

The sky was nearly dark now, even though it was still early, with a turquoise sunset on the horizon that reminded me of waterfalls in places way warmer than here. I jammed my hands in my pockets and tried to match my steps to Julian's mother's.

"You can call me Angela," she said out of nowhere, and for a second I blinked, wondering if she could read my mind. "I mean, I'd say call me Mama, like my other boys do, but it's likely early days for that yet. No pressure."

"I…" I swallowed. *Shit.* No wonder Julian hated lying to her. I barely knew her and I could hardly get the words out. "I really appreciate you being so kind to me."

She made a noise that could either have been agreement or disagreement. "We didn't get off on the right foot. My fault."

"You love Julian. I get that. You want what's best for him."

She nodded. "I definitely do."

"Well, hey, Angela!" A youngish woman in the *ugliest* ugly sweater I'd ever seen laid a hand on Angela's arm and flipped her blonde ponytail over her shoulder. She was visibly pregnant.

"Karen." Angela kissed her on the cheek. "How's the baby?"

"Ex*haus*ting. *God.* You have *no idea*," the blonde said to the woman who had three grown sons.

"You should sit!" Angela said sympathetically. "Maybe over at Fanaille!"

"Cal gives me dirty looks," the blonde sighed. "He's the *worst* brother-in-law. I think it's because I told him he couldn't be a godparent unless he and Ashley were married. But it's not *real* unless they're married, is it? They could break up whenever they wanted, and then what would happen to Blakely?" She patted her stomach protectively.

Meanwhile, I rubbed a hand over my mouth to keep from inadvertently speaking.

"Caelan's a curmudgeon just like his grandmother before she retired," Angela said. "He's a good man, and I guarantee he only wants what's best for the baby, godparent or not."

Karen made a noise like she wasn't convinced. She darted a look at me from under her lashes, then stuck out her hand. "I'm Karen Mitchener-Martin."

"Uh. Hi. Daniel Michaelson."

Her fingernails were bright red with little green decorations, and they dug into my skin as we shook hands. She smiled broadly. "Where are you from, Daniel?"

"Oh, I live out on the Camden Road," I told her, pretending that's what she meant.

Angela pursed her lips like she was fighting a smile.

"Well, you've certainly made waves in our little town," Karen said. "You and Julian."

"Have we? We've almost entirely minded our business, as far as I know."

"But Doc Ross is such a dark horse! If you'd asked me to pick a man in this town who was most likely to run off and fall for someone *nobody knew*, it wouldn't have been him. Right, Angela? Always rock-steady and reliable."

"He hasn't run off," I tried to say, but Karen talked over me.

"I didn't know him when he was in school, but Janice

Turner said that he was the *quietest* child. Like, unnaturally silent and cheerful. But suddenly— *Ow!*" Karen grabbed at her back dramatically.

Angela frowned in concern. "Oh, honey. Go find somewhere to rest, why don't you? Mackie will be worried if he finds you've overdone it."

Karen nodded pathetically. "It's these shoes." She lifted one slim red-soled stiletto off the frozen grass. "They're the worst for trekking around like this. But I refuse to yield, you know? I refuse to be one of those women who just lets herself go once she gets pregnant."

"No one could accuse you of that," Angela said. "But remember what's most important now. Little Blakely."

Karen patted Angela's shoulder as she walked away.

"She's, um…" I struggled to think of a word to describe Karen that could be accurate and inoffensive.

"She's a good person but supremely self-centered and often misguided. Karen hasn't the first clue about human nature."

I blinked and stared at Angela. "I sort of assumed you were friends?"

"We are." Angela shrugged and tossed her long, dark braid over her shoulder. "I've been alive for more than fifty years, Daniel. I started out very much like Karen at one point, so I have plenty of sympathy for her. I just don't take her shit."

"Ah."

"But she's wrong about Julian," she said softly.

Oh, shit. This was about to be one of those mother-to-son-in-law talks, I could tell, and I was so not worthy of it. I could feel my jaw lock against the need to tell her the truth.

But she didn't say anything else. She led me to the one dark booth right near the dance floor and the frazzled-looking woman staring at the nonfunctional lights like she could fix them with the power of her concentration.

"Got reinforcements, Margo," Angela said. "Margo, this is Daniel. Daniel, Margo Martin. She's Ash Martin's mother and Karen's mother-in-law."

Margo seemed relieved to have us there, even though this was most definitely the blind leading the blind. She happily left the booth to us and went off to grab some coffee.

Meanwhile, Angela and I ended up using flashlights and checking the light bulbs one by one to see if any were burnt out, which was absolutely mind-numbing and not nearly the distraction I needed. I started to maybe see the practicality of having a professionally decorated Christmas tree, like my parents did.

"What did you mean before?" I finally asked. "When you said Karen was wrong about Julian?"

Angela looked almost surprised. "Well, that she thinks he's quiet, for one thing, when you and I both know the boy won't stop talking once he gets started."

I laughed. "He's so smart, though. I could listen to him talk all day."

"Even the animal facts?"

"Especially the animal facts."

Angela smiled. "And then that she assumes being quiet means Julian's cold, when that's the furthest thing from the truth. He keeps quiet because he feels too much. He worries too much. Julian's like an iceberg popping out of the water, you know? You only see the very top bit. Oh, look at that! We got half the string working. These bulbs must be *ancient*. Start from the other side now."

I moved down the line and busied myself checking bulbs again, but my mind was caught up with thoughts of Julian. I was thinking of the conversation we'd had about

Titanic and how outraged he'd be to learn that he wasn't Rose or Jack but the iceberg.

I supposed that made me the boat. Once unsinkable, ripped to shreds, doomed.

"Did Julian ever tell you about his dad?"

"That he died when Julian was in college? Yeah."

"Did he tell you how?"

I paused and looked up. "Heart attack, I thought."

Angela nodded. "It was so, so sudden. He was perfectly fine one minute and then… gone. At forty-four."

"I'm sorry."

"Thank you." She hesitated. "Did Julian tell you what happened just before he died? About their fight?"

"No." Julian had fought with his dad right before he died? "But it's probably better if I hear about it from him, right?"

"You're sweet, Daniel, but this is common knowledge around here. Not exactly a secret. You see, Julian wanted this car…"

I stopped working and turned to look at her. Angela's face was barely visible in the glow of the lights from the nearby booths.

"It was a convertible. A 1990…"

"Toyota Celica. I've seen it."

She nodded approvingly. "Well, the car first belonged to Francis Goode. You know him?"

"Goode, like the diner?"

"Exactly like. He owns the place now, inherited it from his father. It was his cousin Shane who… Well, you know."

Was a murderer. Yeah, I knew. Heck, I'd written a book about it that was currently sitting on my hard drive.

"Anyway. Fran was a nice boy. Drove this little car around town like he was hot stuff. And Jules—he must've been maybe thirteen or fourteen at the time—he would just go starry-eyed over that car. And more likely than not, the man driving it." She tossed me a wink, then she sobered. "But Fran joined the Army after that, and when he came home, he wasn't the same. He didn't want anything to do with the car anymore. He put it up for sale."

She sighed and faced me, making no effort to look at the lights anymore. "Now, Jules had wanted that car for *years* by that point. He'd saved every dollar he earned after school and on weekends, every birthday check from his nonna. The car was safe, it was reliable, and Julian was an adult who had the right to buy a car if he wanted to. But John, Julian's father, absolutely hated the idea of the car. Convertibles were terrible in the snow, he'd seen one too many accidents in his time, Julian should be saving his money for school."

I nodded. "Conflicting priorities."

"A dumb argument, really," she said. "So stupid. And it went on for months, since both of them were partially right and neither would admit the other had a point. And then one day, Julian went out and bought the car."

I could see where this was headed and it made my stomach hurt for Julian.

"He took me for a ride in it," she said with a grin. "It was beautiful. But when his father got home? Oh, the shit hit the fan." She cleared her throat. "Pardon my language."

I gave her a half-smile.

"Mostly, at that point, John just wanted to win," she said softly. "It's a hard thing for a man to know his son's grown and can make decisions on his own. He was hurt that Julian didn't take his advice in the end. He forgot, I think, how many times *he* hadn't taken his own father's advice, when he was nineteen. He called Julian *ungrateful* and *immature*. And Julian told his father he was old and didn't understand anything. Said he didn't need a father anymore."

"Oh, God."

"Julian stormed out of the house, and John died that night."

"Angela—" I didn't even know where to begin.

"It was so terrible," she said, tears in her voice. "Julian blamed himself for the stress causing the heart attack, even though John's doctor told us later that John's blockages had been growing for years. And to this day, no matter how illogical he knows it is, I don't think Julian's forgiven himself for the things he told his father in anger. He doesn't let himself get angry much anymore. He doesn't speak up."

I scratched a hand through my hair. "Except with me. He gets angry with me. Clearly."

"Yes," Angela said simply. "I can see that he does. You make him feel things, Daniel. You make him feel safe. You *reach* him, even the parts of himself that he's guarded for a long while."

I stared down at my hands. The sounds of the parade were all around us—the DJ was belting out a rollicking version of Frosty the Snowman, people nearby were laughing and chatting—but it all seemed far away. Angela was talking about Julian, but she might as well have been talking about me.

"But be careful, Daniel." She scooted closer and squeezed my hand. "Remember that iceberg? What you see is only the smallest part of what there is. And he shows you more of himself than he shows most people—maybe *anyone*—but at his core, I think there are insecurities and worries he's scared to show even you. And the closer you two get, the more of him you see, the more you mean to him, the harder he'll try to keep you from seeing those things. Deep down, Julian is afraid."

Well, that made fucking two of us.

"So what do I do?" I asked. "How do I... make him not afraid?"

Angela chuckled. "You can't, honey," she said gently. "We all have things we're afraid of, and no one else can take those fears away. You just show him that it's okay to be afraid. That you accept his fears and his anger and all the other parts of him he doesn't like to show, the same way you accept all the good things about him. You stick by him. You let yourself be vulnerable and open. You love him scared. And then *he'll* realize he doesn't have to be."

I nodded but didn't say anything because I was afraid if I opened my mouth I might let out a great, big, snotty, totally un-manly sob. God, I couldn't imagine letting someone see all of me—all my failures, all the stupid shit I'd gained and lost. How terrifying would that be?

But Julian... Julian was different.

From the beginning, he'd seen and accepted me. He'd accepted my flaws and my boundaries. He'd understood things without me articulating them.

I knew he had flaws and insecurities—a hundred different Julians' worth—but I felt almost protective over them. He was perfect as he was, even when he was angry, even when he wouldn't speak, even when he confused the fuck out of me. There was no part of him I didn't want to know. There was no part of him I didn't care about, didn't *love*.

So Julian and I needed to have a talk, for damn sure. One where I explained to him that I didn't want there to be any more Curtises, or strained silences, or arguments between us. One where I was gonna have to be honest and vulnerable, to give him all my mistakes and failures, and hope he could dust them off and find the glimmer of good intention behind each one.

I wanted him to be happy, whatever that entailed. And whether we ended up friends or something more—and Jesus, didn't *that* thought make my stomach flip?—I just really, really hoped there would be a place for me in that happiness.

Chapter Twelve

JULIAN

"No one else?" I asked Kathy, emerging from the exam room after tidying up from my last patient Monday morning. "Are we clear?"

Kathy twirled in her chair and gave me a grin. "Yep. That was the last one, and then we're done until tomorrow."

"Thank you, Jesus," I said, leaning back against the doorframe. "I need a nap."

"Same." Kathy rubbed her enormous belly and wiggled in the chair, trying to get comfortable. "Judging by the kicking going on all night long, I feel like I'm carrying a litter of babies, though Dr. Morgan assures me there's just one very active fetus."

"Little Julio is excited to meet us, that's all."

"Julio?"

"Named in honor of his or her favorite Uncle Julian, obviously."

"Ah. Obviously." Kathy grinned. "There you go. *Decided*. Julio Chang, boy or girl. Rick's parents will love that."

I smiled tiredly, and Kathy's grin slipped.

"So we know why *I* haven't been sleeping. What's your excuse?" she asked. "You *floated* into this place at the beginning of last week, practically leaving a trail of glitter and rainbows behind you. I didn't even have to *ask* how your Thanksgiving weekend was—"

"Because you heard the whole story of Thanksgiving through the gossip mill."

"Not about anything that would have caused the glittery floating," she shot back. "But here you are today, after the Light Parade, the jolliest nondenominational holiday gathering in the *entire* greater O'Leary/Camden area…"

I snorted.

"…and you need walls to prop you up. What gives?"

I straightened from my slouch. "Nothing gives."

"So you're fine."

"Obviously."

"And things with you and Daniel are fine."

"Of course." This was true, in the sense that we hadn't spoken in almost two days, so they hadn't had a chance to become un-fine. I was pretty sure Daniel was massively pissed at me, but if I didn't give him a chance to tell me so, then it was almost like things were fine.

Right?

I moved to the file cabinet to file away a stack of charts from each of the patients I'd seen that morning.

"And the rumors that you argued at the parade? That Daniel ended up going out with Cal and Ash and a bunch of others while you went home with a *headache?*"

"Are greatly exaggerated. I did have a headache." Also, true. By the end of the parade, I'd worked myself into a huge fucking *throbbing* headache.

"Hmm."

"*Hmm?*" I turned my head to glance at her. "What's that mean?"

"It means I had those files stacked there so I could take care of the billing before I refiled them, which is the process we've had for like three years now."

"Oh. Right."

"It means," she said gently, "that not everything has to be okay all the time. You know that, right?"

I sighed and started pulling out the charts I'd tucked away.

"Don't try to psychoanalyze me, Chang. Oh, hey, did you follow up with Mary Muldoon? I saw her in the bakery this morning, and she said she was thinking about adopting a Russian blue. She wanted me to examine it."

Kathy ignored this redirect. "Julian, not everything goes right in a relationship, especially in the early days. When Rick and I got together, I was—" She shook her head. "Well, you know better than anyone what a mess I was."

When Kathy and Rick got together, they'd been explosive. Every second day, Kathy would come in fuming about some Neanderthal behavior Rick had exhibited or crying over something he'd said. The next day, there'd be flowers on her desk, and a few days after that, fresh hickeys on her neck. Lather, rinse, repeat. I remembered because I used to tease her about it relentlessly.

Now, I envied her. At least her drama had led to something *real*. Meanwhile, I was steadily losing my mind, and in the end, I was pretty sure I was going to lose my best friend as well.

My cock had gotten more action in the last week than it had in years. So much action, it started to get hard every time Daniel Michaelson spoke, moved, or existed in its vicinity, like he was Pavlov and it was the dog. Daniel was insatiable, and I'd let myself believe that meant things were *progressing* somehow.

But it was like every time we were together that way, every time we got physically close, he pulled back from me in other ways. I'd tried to tell myself I was imagining things, but I knew better. The fighting and kissing and fighting again at the parade had been the last straw. I was not down to ride this roller coaster, not when I worried that every dip could lead to total derailment.

"You want the truth? Here goes: I don't know if Daniel and I are going to work." I slammed the file drawer shut and turned to lean against it. "We're very different people, and we want different things." As in, I wanted a relationship and he wanted… Well, actually, I had no clue what he wanted.

Kathy was silent for a minute. "Well, I'm sorry to hear it. But Jules, it doesn't have to be all or nothing, right? Perfection doesn't exist in relationships. It's okay to fight, and mess up, and be dense and oversensitive at the same time. It's okay to be bad at it at first, even if you were really good at the friendship thing before. The rules are different now. You have to figure out how to talk to each other. You have to ask the questions you think you already know the answers to." She looked pensive for a minute. "Remember when Hen Lattimer came in here a while back with Daphne?"

I sighed. I did *not* want to talk about this. At all. "Which time? The man was in here weekly last month, convinced that Daph was dying."

"Right. Because she wasn't eating the way she ate when Everett took care of her, and she was sleeping too much, and she sometimes ignored him. Remember what you told him?"

"I told him Daphne was a cat, and that's what cats do."

Kathy smiled. "You told him to be patient and not to give up. That they'd get used to each other." She raised one eyebrow pointedly.

I sighed. "You suck at extended metaphors."

"I know!" she said cheerily, turning back to her computer screen. "Poor Julio. But I'm a mom now, so I have that mom-voodoo thing going on. Leeesten to me, Julian. Don't give up."

———

Don't give up.

Right.

I was pretty sure that only worked when there was a real thing to give up. Cautious retreat wasn't giving up, it was the only way to save a doomed operation, which is what was happening here.

I stalked the length of Weaver Street with my head ducked down. The bitter wind stung my eyes and whipped random papers and hapless holiday decorations into a miniature tornado around my ankles, but I couldn't stay indoors. I was filled with frantic energy that had no outlet; the knowledge that something had to change, and no clue how to change it.

For the sake of our friendship, this fake-boyfriend-benefit-fuckery had to stop. I wanted too much from him. I wanted the real thing. And all that wanting was like a giant vacuum, sucking everything good from our relationship.

I'd joked in the past about the many kinds of Julian I sometimes was—awkward-Julian, professional-Julian, family-Julian—but I'd never been more totally and completely *me* than I was with Daniel. With him, I'd always been my true self, and he'd *liked* it. I'd never doubted that he liked it. Though it had rankled, a little, that he didn't talk about his past, we'd had this little make-believe fanta-syland where none of it mattered. His cabin in the woods had been our clubhouse, and we'd never let the real world intrude. Families were contentious subjects? Well, we simply didn't discuss them. O'Leary was only mentioned in passing, and mostly as the butt of a joke.

Then suddenly, our clubhouse had been re-districted; now, we were firmly, incontrovertibly grounded in reality, and all those topics we'd been able to ignore before had become conversational landmines that would explode with the lightest footsteps. I didn't know how to talk to him anymore without triggering an uncomfortable silence. I didn't know how to *be* with him anymore, except for the moments when we were kissing and frotting and coming our brains out. I was becoming this meek, silent little crea-ture, this *Daniel*-Julian, and you know what? I fucking *hated* Daniel-Julian.

The worst part was, I could see so clearly in my mind what it would look like if we could just be together for real with none of these barriers in place. Daniel was everything I wanted in a guy. He made me laugh when no one else could, he took me seriously when no one else would, he let me talk with endless patience, and he gave me a fresh perspective on the world time and time again.

I loved being around him. I loved who I was when I was with him. I… loved him. That was the long and short of it.

Plus, let's be honest, he was the hottest thing on two legs. By far the hottest guy to ever grace the… how had Kathy put it? The *entire* greater O'Leary-Camden area. And the way we came together physically was powerful enough to birth tiny stars.

It wasn't enough. It wasn't enough for me to feel these things in isolation—that was like trading one fantasy world for another. But at the same time, how the fuck was I going to give it up? Even if we could somehow rewind and become friends with no benefits again, how could I make myself stop loving him?

I was so lost in my head, I crashed, full-tilt, into someone walking in the other direction.

"Oh, shit! *Shit*," I said, as bags of groceries fell to the sidewalk, along with the person I'd bumped into. "Shit, I'm so sorry!"

Parker Hoffstraeder looked up from where he'd sprawled on the sidewalk, shaking his head like he was trying to clear it. "Jesus, Jules. Is there a veterinary emergency at the Imperial I don't know about?"

I glanced up and saw that I'd walked nearly the entire length of Weaver Street, almost all the way to the fairgrounds. I was standing in front of Parker's bar, Hoff's, which was across the street from Lyon's Imperial Market.

"I totally wasn't watching where I was going," I said. "Obviously."

I reached out a hand to haul him to his feet, then helped him pick up his bags. "You know, most other animals don't have issues like this. Birds never crash in mid-flight. They've evolved to avoid it using these complex strategies. They did a test on male budgies and found that… um." I flushed. "Never mind."

Parker looked down at me in concern, his pale cheeks pink from cold and his blond hair ruffling in the wind. "Everything okay?"

"Oh, yeah!" I waved a hand. "You know, the usual." I was horrified to find tears forming in my eyes. "Just out for a walk." I sniffed. "Clearing my head." Figuring out how to dismantle my life and re-mantle it.

Was re-mantling a thing?

"Uh-huh." He tilted his head to one side and studied

me. "I have an idea for clearing your head. Have you had lunch yet?" He jiggled his groceries.

"No, but I couldn't—"

"Sure you could! I could use a distraction, and I like having someone to cook for. Come on."

He unlocked the door to the bar and held it open so I could lead the way, then locked it behind him and led me past the rows of tables and stacked chairs to the back, where the kitchen was.

"I've never been back here before," I said, taking in the long stainless-steel workbench, the giant grill, and the industrial refrigerator.

"Not a surprise," he said, "considering this place was a window factory until a few months ago." He nodded at a stool set near one of the benches. "Have a seat."

"More like the *ruins* of a window factory," I said, watching him lay down his bags and grab a bottle from one of the shelves as I took off my coat and gloves. "I remember walking past this building when I was a kid. I always figured there'd be ghosts here."

He snorted. "In this factory? Not that I've seen." He paused. "Now, if you mean the town of O'Leary, on the other hand, the place is chock full of 'em."

Parker sounded sad or maybe just resigned. I wasn't able to get a read on him. We'd never been close, even before he moved to Boston for college with his friend Ethan Scott, and I hadn't done anything to change that since he moved back a few months ago. There was history between him and Jamie Burke—bad history, if the scene I'd walked in on the other night was any indication—and Jamie and I were friends. I hadn't consciously taken sides, but I was beginning to realize that in the time-honored O'Leary tradition, I'd closed ranks against an outsider... even though Parker wasn't technically an outsider.

Parker arranged a pair of shot glasses on the table in front of me, and I looked up at him in surprise.

"Is that Fireball?"

"That's what it says on the bottle," he agreed, pouring a liberal amount into each glass. "Guaranteed to clear your mind."

My eyes widened, and I shook my head. "Eh. It's only lunchtime."

"So? Live a little, Julian. Get out of your head."

I sighed. That was exactly what I needed—to get out of my head, even if it was just for a minute. I downed the shot, coughing at the cinnamon burn.

"That's the spirit," he said, tossing me a wink as he downed his own shot. "Now, how do you like your burger?"

"Medium." I watched him unpack ingredients from the grocery bags and stack them on the counter. "But Parker, don't you already have the ingredients for burgers here? I've had them myself." And they were pretty good, too, though I'd never say so in front of Jamie.

"Yeah." He shrugged. "But here I make gourmet burgers on brioche buns with aioli and fried eggs on top. Every once in a while, I just want something sloppy and fried like my mom used to make, on a bun that tastes like white bread, where the cheese-to-meat ratio is way too high. You know?"

I scratched my head. "No. But I'm willing to let you convince me."

He laughed again, but his gray-green eyes were sad. "You don't know how much I appreciate that, Julian. Way too few people around here trust me anymore."

I frowned.

Just then, a *crash* came from upstairs, loud enough that

I jumped off my seat, convinced the ceiling was caving in. Parker just shook his head.

"Welcome to the construction zone life. It's been five days, and I'm already thinking his job cannot be done soon enough."

"Construction?" I took my seat again, keeping a careful eye on the ceiling.

"Yeah, didn't you notice the trucks in the parking lot when we walked in?"

I shook my head. "I wasn't really noticing anything, which is why I bumped into you."

"Ran into me like a getaway car fleeing a jewel heist, more like." He rubbed the seat of his jeans ruefully.

Heat climbed my cheeks. "I'm so sorry. Again."

"Nah, it's fine. Just giving you shit," he said. "Anyway, yeah, I'm having the second floor finished out. Upgrading the electrical, adding some walls and plumbing fixtures. Turning it into some industrial-loft-style apartments." He began mixing meat and some spices in a bowl with his hands. "Think O'Leary's ready for that?"

"An apartment for you?"

"Yeah. Plus one other. The back one will look out over the fairgrounds, and the front one—the one I'm taking—faces the street."

"So you'll have a view of the grocery store and the parking lot?"

"Uh-huh. I plan to invest in binoculars so I can scrutinize everyone's purchases when they walk out of the Imperial, and make inappropriate comments later on." Parker started forming the meat into disks, his fingers swift and sure. "'*Hey, Ms. Dorian, do David and Jess give you a discount on whipped cream when you buy it in bulk like that?*' Or, '*Hey, Mitch! I see you bought a big container of peanut butter. Funny enough, Marci just bought a giant jar of jelly. Anything you two would like to tell us?"* It'll be great."

I snorted. "Those two have definitely got something going on," I said, referring to Marci, the dispatcher at the police station, and Mitch, who was technically her boss.

"I wouldn't be surprised." He set the finished burger patties on a tray and washed his hands. "But I'm just kidding. Town gossip might be the one thing I *didn't* miss about O'Leary."

"Oh, yeah? You missed us? I sort of remember hearing you couldn't wait to leave? Ethan, too."

He turned away to set the burgers on the griddle and didn't reply, so I bit my lip and changed the subject.

"I'm sure it'll be convenient, living upstairs. Not sure I'd want to live over a bar, though. I've seen it get pretty rowdy in here." Mostly when Jamie had come by to hassle Parker on football Sundays, though I didn't say that out loud.

"Oh, yeah. I know how bad it can get. The first apartment Ethan and I had back in college was over a bar in Allston. When the football game was on downstairs, I couldn't hear myself think. This time, I'm taking precautions. Soundproof insulation," he said, pointing a spatula at the ceiling. "They've already got it installed over the bar area since I wanted my space done first, and they're working on this side today. Won't be able to hear a damn thing, even when the place is packed and the music is loud."

"Good idea."

Parker turned back to me and lined up the shot glasses again to refill them. This time, I didn't protest.

"Makes the whole upstairs toasty warm, too. Hottest place in O'Leary, even when it's fucking cold out like it is now." Parker wiggled his eyebrows. "Wanna come up and see?"

He was so obviously joking, I grinned. "Actually, yeah." Another *thunk* resounded through the building as something fell upstairs, followed by a call of, "*I'm good!*"

I laughed. "Maybe when the work's done, though. Might give me some ideas about how to fix up my place over the clinic."

"Fair enough." Parker took a couple of burger buns—the thin kind in the value pack—and put them on the griddle next to the burgers. "Now. Let's stop talking about the war zone upstairs and talk about what's got you running around O'Leary, mowing down innocent pedestrians."

I rubbed at a spot over my eye. "Could we… maybe… not?"

"Not the chatty kind, huh?" Parker's mouth twisted to the side, and he nodded, folding his arms over his chest, spatula and all. "That's okay. I bartended for a lotta years, you know. Managed a bar, too. I've got tricks."

"Tricks?"

Parker poured out two more shots. "Let's play a game."

"Uh." I laughed uncomfortably. "Isn't that a movie quote?"

Parker cocked his head. "No, that's '*I want to play a game.*' *Saw*, right?"

I made a face. "No! I meant the one from the '80s. With the computer!"

"*War Games?*" Parker laughed. "God! That movie's older than we are!"

"Barely," I grumbled.

"Fine, then in honor of your silver status, old man, you can go first. The game is Truth or Dare."

"Oh. No." I shook my head vehemently. "There's not

enough Fireball in all the land for me to play Truth or Dare. Nothing personal," I assured him. "I'm not a very daring person."

"Wow." He gave an exaggerated frown like I'd impressed him somehow. "Well, then it looks like we're playing Truth or Truth, Julian. The game where you can either answer my question or volunteer another uncomfortable fact. Pretty ballsy choice, but I'm down."

I scrubbed a hand through my hair. "At any point, have you interrogated prisoners? Because, if not, you missed your calling."

"You're up first 'cause I'm a nice guy," he said, turning away to flip the burgers. "Ask me anything. Make it good."

"Okay, then. Tell me what's going on with you and Jamie."

"Heh." He shook his head. "Should've expected that, after the little scene you witnessed the other day. But that's not a question."

"Hey, if you're already uncomfortable, we don't have to play this game," I said, like that hadn't been my intention in the first place.

"Not at all, my man. Just rephrase."

I blew out a breath. "Fine. What are your feelings for Jamie Burke?"

"I love him," Parker said easily. "Always have, always will."

"Love? Or *love*-love?"

"Are we twelve?" he mocked. "Love. More than anyone. Even when he stopped talking to me."

"Why did…"

"My turn," he said, pointing at me with his spatula. "Take your shot."

I had no idea what the rules of this game were, and I

was pretty confident he was making them up as he went along, but I did as instructed.

"Okay, what's the deal with you and Daniel?"

"Hey." I scowled. "That's the same broad question. Rephrase."

"Nope, answer."

"What? How come you get to…"

"Have you ever played this before? No? Then I'm in charge. Answer, or volunteer."

"You suck," I said without heat. I rested my elbow on the countertop and grabbed a chunk of my own hair in frustration. The urge to confide the whole mess in someone was strong, and really, what did I have to lose? "This stays between us?"

"Bartender's code."

"Fine. When I stood up in the diner last month and… you know…"

Parker put cheese on the burgers and snorted. "Did the *Romeo and Juliet*? Yeah, I know."

"Well, we weren't actually together. We were just friends. And I, um. Made it up. Daniel is… was… straight."

Parker turned away from the stove. "Bull*shit* he's straight. You two have been all over town acting couple-y."

"An act. Well, initially."

"Okay, now you've intrigued me," he said. "Spill."

"Isn't it my turn to ask a question?"

"Sure. But I'm gonna get to the bottom of this story, so just how much alcohol do you want to drink today, Julian?"

A fair point. "Okay, well, I lied, like I said. But Daniel was cool about it. He agreed to maintain the fiction, at least through Thanksgiving, so I wouldn't get grilled by my family about being an asshole. But, uh, things evolved."

"Evolved. Sure. As things tend to do. And did you

mean *this* Thanksgiving or next? Because I'm pretty sure that ship sailed two weeks ago."

My cheeks heated. "Well. Like I said. Things *evolved*. It... we..." I cleared my throat. "You're sure this is between us?"

"Pinky swear," he said, holding up his hand palm-out like he was pledging an oath. It was so reminiscent of Daniel's misguided efforts at pinky swears, I felt tears come to my eyes. I was just that sappy.

"Well, it turns out that Daniel's interested in me. Physically. He's never been with a guy before."

"He's attracted to you."

I sighed. "It... would seem so. Yeah."

Parker snorted. "You sound apologetic about it. Who are you apologizing to?"

"I don't know. To Daniel, I guess." Was the alcohol hitting me already?

"Apologizing for being too attractive." Parker nodded. "Logical."

"What? That's not what I said!"

Parker smirked. "So you're apologizing because you *coerced* him into being your fake boyfriend, you sly dog."

"No!" I sat up straighter, faintly outraged. "I would never. It was his idea, not mine!"

"Oh. So you coerced him into hooking up with you. Say no more." Parker mimed zipping his lips.

"Parker, for fuck's sake! You know I didn't. I didn't do *any* of those things. I'm not apologetic in the first place!"

He nodded slowly, grinning. "Right. Because whatever his sexuality is, was, or becomes, it's nothing to be sorry about. And whatever happened was his choice as much as yours."

I scowled. "I... I guess that's true." It felt weird to think about it that way. On some level, I guess I did feel like this was my fault. I'd been the idiot who stood up in Goode's Diner and proclaimed us *together*, after all. But I'd offered to rectify that. I'd offered to stage a breakup time and time again. Everything *after* the diner had really been kind of a dual effort.

Or a dual clusterfuck, depending on how you looked at it.

"So!" Parker's eyes gleamed. "You're both attracted, you hang out, you're friends. You *evolved*. Does that mean you have sex?"

I hesitated. We hadn't technically gone beyond frottage, but…

"In some form or another?"

I nodded.

"So, you're together."

"We're friends with benefits," I said miserably.

"Oh, Jesus fucking Christ." Parker rolled his eyes. I shot him a look, and he explained, "If there were ever a term to be stricken from the collective vocabulary of the world, it's that one. Friends aren't attracted to each other, Julian. Not consistently, anyway. Not to the point where you have sex multiple times. If you're hooking up with someone who's your friend, it means one or both of you lack the balls to say what you're really feeling."

I trailed my finger on the countertop. "Yeah, well."

"Sorry," Parker said, blowing out a breath. "I get overexcited. This is a subject that's near and dear to my heart."

"Don't be sorry. What you said was sadly accurate."

Parker poured me another drink, and I took it without hesitation.

"And Daniel's got secrets," I said, setting the glass back down. "He doesn't talk about where he's from, he doesn't talk about what he does for a living, he doesn't talk about the future." I ticked these crimes off on my fingers. "We talk about all kinds of stuff—we can argue and be silly, I can ramble about shit and he thinks it's cute. But he won't volunteer about his past at *all*."

"He's a mystery wrapped in an enigma, hmm? What does he say when you ask him?"

"Ask him?" The alcohol was definitely hitting me now. "What do you mean?"

Parker blinked and said with exaggerated patience, "I mean *ask him*. Like, 'Hey, Daniel, is there a reason you don't like to talk about your life before O'Leary?' Or, 'Hey, dickwad, I need a little validation, so could you maybe explain what this relationship is to you?' Or however you do it. What does he say when you ask those questions?"

"I…" I lifted my hands and then lowered them again. "I haven't. I can't say shit like that. It would ruin everything."

He snorted. "Oh, my God. I'm about to change your life. You ready? Because there's this amazing new way of obtaining information that people don't volunteer. It's called *asking*."

"Does it involve Fireball?" I asked sourly.

He laughed. "Only in the really hard cases. But seriously, why won't you just open your mouth and ask the question?"

"Because! What if he feels pressured? What if he feels like I'm forcing him to make something official when it's not, or define something he's not ready to define? What if it's mortifying, because he can tell from my questions that *I* have feelings beyond friendship with benefits, and he *doesn't*? It would ruin our friendship."

"Well, maybe." He shrugged. "I mean, that's a risk you run. But it's okay that you have needs too. So maybe Daniel will say, 'Well, I'm not ready to define our relationship yet, Julian, but I do like you rather a lot.' And you'll say, 'Jolly good! I'd appreciate if you'd keep me in the loop as your feelings *evolve*, old chap.' And then you'll offer him tea, and it'll be great."

"*Or*, maybe he'll decide I'm not worth the effort and just move on."

I bit my lip. That was the crux of the issue, right there. There was no one who'd ever seen the real me before, all the various Julians rolled into one, and everyone who'd caught a glimpse had backed away. If prior experience was anything to go by, this quasi-relationship with Daniel was doomed when I opened my mouth.

I reached for the whiskey again, voluntarily this time, but Parker moved the bottle out of my grasp and turned to grab a soda from the fridge instead. He cracked it open and set it in front of me.

"That's rough, Julian. You're in a really shitty situation."

"Yeah." The confirmation wasn't particularly helpful.

Parker turned back to the griddle and assembled the burgers and buns into sandwiches, then cut them in half and handed me a plate.

"But the solution to the problem is undeniable. *Ask. Him.*"

"Parker, did you miss the part a minute ago where I told you I'm incapable?"

"You're not incapable, Julian, you're scared shitless. That's different. Incapable, I can help you with. Scared shitless, though, you're gonna have to overcome on your own."

"You're just a big warm hug, aren't you?" I grabbed half of the burger with both hands. It smelled amazing.

Parker snorted. "It's kind of selfish, when you think about it."

"What?" I paused with the burger halfway to my lips. "What's selfish?"

"Your behavior. I mean, you're probably feeling like you're pushing down your own needs so you don't rock the boat, being a martyr and blah blah blah. *Look at how nice Julian is!* But meanwhile, you're getting pissy and resentful, analyzing every conversation from ten different angles, inferring things he never meant, and getting angry over petty bullshit. Am I right?"

I said nothing.

"And he's sitting there thinking he's just a terrible human, because obviously you're miserable and constantly annoyed, when really he can't do a damn thing to help fix the issues in this relationship because he doesn't *know what they are.* If you want him to read your mind, Julian, you're fucked. You're worried about ruining something by speaking up, and you'll end up ruining it anyway by staying silent."

Parker pushed his own plate away without taking a bite. "One day soon, if you're not there already, you're gonna reach critical mass because you can't push your own needs down anymore, and you'll explode all over him like an atomic weapon. The fallout will change the landscape of your entire lives forever. Nuclear fucking winter."

"Um. I don't... That was..." I set my own burger down, untouched.

Parker sighed. "I may be projecting slightly." He sucked on a tooth. "Did you know Jamie has a new boyfriend?"

I blinked, slightly dizzy from the conversational whiplash. Or maybe the alcohol.

"No, I didn't know. Who? And since when?"

"Some guy named Brian Carr from over in Camden."

He slid the plate back and forth along the counter. *"Brian Carr.* Fucking stupid name."

"Brian. Isn't that the guy Jamie dated a couple years ago? I thought they broke up. No, I *know* they did."

"Well, everyone loves a second chance romance, right?" Parker said brightly. "Seems like they're back together, and now Jamie's got all kinds of *plans.*" He scratched his chin. "I'm happy for him."

I'd never heard anyone express happiness in that tone of voice before, but I refrained from commenting on it.

"Well, when they dated before, Brian pissed him off to no end," I volunteered, carefully not looking at Parker. "He was all over Jamie, all the time, and not in a cute way."

"Yeah?"

"Mmm. The final straw was on Valentine's Day, when he sent Jamie a gorilla-gram at the diner. That's a singing telegram delivered by a man in a gorilla suit," I explained when Parker looked at me blankly.

"A what?"

"You heard me." I laughed. "And let me be clear: this was a very, very not-safe-for-work singing telegram, in which he rhymed *food* with *lube.*"

"But those words don't even——"

"I *know.* And the best-worst part? It was Brian himself in the costume. So, like, everyone was just sitting there trying not to vomit their lunch, and Brian, Captain Oblivious of America, took the head off his costume and got down on one knee to ask Jamie to move in with him, or something." I winced. "The relationship was over in seconds."

"That…" Parker snorted and clapped a hand over his mouth. "Oh, fuck. That made my day." He laughed again. "I didn't think it was possible for me to feel better about this, but I do. So, thank you."

"Eh. Just cranking the O'Leary gossip mill." I winked.

"Now back to your problem." He picked up his burger with renewed enthusiasm.

"Oh. *No*. Thanks anyway. I've had about as much real talk as I can take."

"No," he insisted around a bite of meat. "No, Julian, don't do that. Please, listen." He grabbed a napkin from the counter and wiped off his hands. "If you never listen to another thing I say, listen to this. You need to talk to him. I know it's hard. People like me tell you to just man up, but it's not that easy when you feel like you're risking something you care about, right?"

"Yes! Exactly!" I threw my hands up. "Sometimes the stakes are too high. It's easier to just… I dunno, keep moving forward. Let things… coast."

"Down the path of least resistance?" He raised one eyebrow. "Putting off the inevitable?"

I sighed.

"What you have right now with Daniel, or what you *think* you have… it's not real, my friend. A relationship built on doubts and fears can't be."

He took a bite of burger and chewed thoughtfully while I silently choked on my own ruined dreams. Not to be too dramatic or anything.

"It *could* be, though," he continued. "You just have to put in the work to get there. You're worried about rocking the boat, but you don't know if you're even *on* a boat or just sitting in your own damn bathtub. And take it from me —you're not doing him any favors by not speaking up, because you're letting *him* believe something is real when it isn't."

"I hadn't thought of it that way before," I whispered.

Parker nodded. "Nobody wants a yes-man, Julian. It might seem fun on the surface, but when push comes to shove, all those yeses are gonna collapse like a house of cards, and Daniel's gonna realize the Julian he thought he knew was just a role you were playing." His mouth twisted sympathetically. "And that will hurt him way worse than any words you could possibly say. Trust me."

"So what do I do?" I said, massaging my forehead with my fingers. "How do I fix it?"

"You do the work. Take the risk. Start the conversation. Up your standards. Know in your heart that you deserve more, and believe that he does, too. After all, don't we all want someone who thinks we're worth fighting for, even if it's hard? Even if it pokes at all our tender places?" He rubbed a hand over his own chest and gave me a small smile. "And don't give up, okay? Even if he gets angry and pushes back. Even if he stops talking to you for a week… or ten fucking years. Don't let anyone or anything, including your own fear, force you into maintaining the status quo if it's making you miserable. If you can't say a wholehearted yes to something, Julian, you've got to say *no*."

Chapter Thirteen

DANIEL

THE TOWN of MacBryde was full of surprises. Its bucolic appearance and unhurried pace made it seem idyllic, but beneath that calm facade, it hid a wealth of stories just like anyplace else. Stories of tragedy and inspiration and redemption, stories of love earned and twisted and broken, stories of—

I stopped typing at the sound of Honoria's eager barking and pushed the keyboard off my lap so I could run to the door, managing to trip over my laptop's charging cord along the way.

I forced myself to pause and take a deep breath.

Jesus fucking Christ, this had been the longest two days since… well, since I'd gotten to O'Leary, for damn sure. Julian had promised in a text yesterday that he'd come by today, and he couldn't come soon enough.

I was finally ready to talk. Past ready, really.

I'd rushed back to the booth Saturday after my conversation with his mom, eager to smooth things over, but Julian had made it clear he wanted no part of my apologies. He'd ignored me for most of the evening, and when I'd asked him to come back to the cabin with me, he'd pleaded a headache. So instead of a quiet evening of explanations with the man I was belatedly realizing was far more than just a friend, I'd ended up at Parker Hoffstraeder's bar, drinking beer with Cal, Ash, Constantine, Silas Sloane, Everett Maior, and a couple of women I'd never met before, Moira and Mari. It should have been fun—would have been fun, because every single one of them was smart-mouthed, good-natured, and accepting—but despite the endless flow of old stories and fresh laughter, I'd felt Julian's absence like a sore tooth. In the end, Constantine had driven me home with a commiserating smile and left me with the comforting words, "The best thing about Jules is he never holds a grudge with people he cares about."

But then two entire days had passed with no contact whatsoever, leading me to believe that either Julian had secretly been training in Olympic-level grudge holding or that I was too late. He'd had enough of this tilt-a-whirl friends-with-benefits thing.

Honoria kept barking, and I made myself move toward the door again, at a normal pace this time. Julian was here now, and we would talk shit out. I would tell him how important he was to me, so there'd be no doubt. I'd tell him we—our relationship—could be whatever he needed.

I ran a hand through my hair as I opened the heavy wood door and made myself smile… but it wasn't Julian standing there, it was Sam.

"Oh," I said, pushing open the glass storm door. "It's you."

"Wow. One of the less enthusiastic greetings I've received recently," she said, tightening her perpetual ponytail. Her cheeks were pink and her hands were chapped red from the cold. "Were you expecting a certain *doctor* to make a house call?" She wiggled her eyebrows.

"Are you old enough to make jokes like that?" I demanded, backing up so she could step into the warmth of the living room, where Honoria immediately attacked her.

"What, you didn't play like that with *your* Barbies?" Sam sank to her knees on the carpet in front of the fire and let Honoria flop on top of her. "My Malibu Barbie and Astronaut Barbie had a passionate love affair going on. They came from such different worlds, but they were meant to be together," she said in a fake-breathless voice.

I sat on the sofa and grinned. "Sounds like the back of Julian's romance novel. I mean, Julian's *mom's* romance novel," I corrected. I was pretty sure he didn't need that information getting out there.

Sam waved this away. "Who gives a shit? Why pretend like it's this shameful thing? Romance is awesome. If you're gonna read it, own it."

"Not always that easy to own things, Sam." I sighed.

Sam rolled her eyes. "I swear to God, you just achieved a perfect, *'You'll understand when you're older, Samantha'* voice. My father would be super impressed."

"Sorry." I winced. "I didn't mean it like that. Just… you know… there are things you *do* understand more when you're older."

"Uh-huh. Definitely. I mean, I wouldn't know the first thing about standing up for what you like, and who you love, and who you are, or anything important like that. I'm only a queer kid growing up in a tiny town with a best friend, Rae, who's non-binary and a dad who was determined that I'm gonna be the first kid in my family to go away to college, even though I have zero interest." She shrugged. "I'm sure I'll understand really important stuff once I get older."

I squeezed my eyes shut. "Yeah, okay. Point made. I'm not just channeling *your* dad, I'm channeling mine. Sorry."

She snickered. "Dude, you're fine. At least you admit you're doing it. Unlike my dad."

"Does he give you shit?" I asked. "About being queer?"

Sam's hands toyed with Honoria's fur and she gave the question some thought. "Not so much for that. I think he'd rather that I was into wearing dresses and looking like some 1950s finishing school graduate. But he's obsessed with me not getting tied down, that's for sure. And God forbid anything get in the way of my education at some fancy college." She looked at me and raised one eyebrow. "Which is total bullshit."

I hesitated, then said, "At the risk of sounding like your dad again, is it really bullshit that he wants you to get an education?"

"*He* never got one. He and my mom got pregnant with me right out of high school. Got married. Dad got a job at a factory and worked there for like sixteen years, until they closed down last spring. Now he's unemployed," she added, like this was common knowledge. Knowing O'Leary, it probably was. "And he and my mom broke up about three years ago. She got remarried and they moved to Syracuse last year."

"So…" I was hesitant again to say all the standard grown-up shit, but really, didn't it just make sense? "I mean, if your dad's struggling with unemployment because he didn't get an education, doesn't it make sense that he wants you to? And he doesn't want you to get married young so you won't have to be divorced later. He wants you to learn from his mistakes so you won't have to deal with the stuff he's dealing with."

Sam looked at me like I had three heads. "He's miserable because he got forced to do shit when he was a teenager—getting married, having me, getting a job he didn't like in a town he never wanted to stay in. Forcing me to live his dream just perpetuates the cycle."

I thought of my own father, of his absolute certainty that he knew the right path for me in my career, in my relationships. It was maddening because he'd been so quick to give up on me when I didn't meet his terms.

"Do you have something you'd rather do instead?"

She sighed. "I wanted to stay in O'Leary. I like it here. I wanted to do what Jules did and commute to school. I wanted to be a teacher. I'd be a damn good one."

"And that's not good enough?"

She sighed again. "We had a big fight. I told him I wanted to go live with my mom in Syracuse. He said if I left, I shouldn't bother coming back."

"So what happened?"

Sam spread her arms as if to say, *Here I am*. "My situation's fucked. But we'll see what happens when I turn eighteen."

"I've kinda been where you are," I found myself saying slowly. I didn't really plan to say it because, *fuck*, I hated talking about my shit, but Sam looked so lost and I wanted her to know she wasn't alone. "I actually ended up leaving home when I was about your age, because my dad told me if I wasn't gonna study business and join the family firm, I wasn't welcome under his roof. I don't think he believed I'd actually do it until I was gone."

Sam grinned. "No shit? You just left? Fuck you, peace out?"

"I did." I grinned back at her, but my smile died quickly. The memories were painful. "I worked at a movie theater and couch surfed for a while. It was… Okay, if I'm being honest it was the worst time ever. It sucked. I was cold and hungry, and thank God it only lasted a couple months. If you're considering trying to survive on your own, I don't recommend it."

"No shit." Sam's eyes were bleak and she rubbed a hand over her nose. "What happened then?"

"I had a trust fund from my grandfather and I inherited it when I was eighteen. So for me, it was a temporary thing, a power play against my dad, and I knew it." I shrugged. "It was still stupid. Makes me cringe to think of the shit I said. But I ended up going to college and studying creative writing."

"And your parents?" she whispered. "Did they ever speak to you again?"

"They did. Eventually. And then they didn't again the next time I disappointed them. They care about me, but it's like they only know one way to show it." I frowned, staring at the fire. "But then again, I guess I only know one way to react to them, too. We're like the grooves in a record; we always play the same damn songs, one after another."

"So… if you changed your song, would they change theirs?" she asked. "If you reacted in a different way, would it change things?"

I blinked, transferring my stare to her. "I… I don't know. Maybe your dad would, too."

Sam looked doubtful, but before she could respond, Honoria jumped off her lap and began barking again. My heart started to pound crazily almost before I realized what was happening. I stood up, but then stared at Sam without moving for a long moment, paralyzed, thinking over what she'd just said.

"I'm guessing that's Jules?" Sam looked faintly amused. "Are you going to puke or something?"

"No." Maybe.

She pushed herself up. "Well, I'm gonna get going.

You're either gonna vomit or kiss the hell out of him, and I don't need to see either one."

But I was still frozen in place when she passed me, and she reached out to punch my arm. "Dude, are you cool? You want me to tell him you're sick?"

I shook my head. I definitely didn't want her to do that. "I fucked up with him, I think, Sam. I think… I think I've been playing the same songs with Julian," I whispered.

Her lips twitched. "Jesus. And they say teenagers are dramatic. Just tell him you fucked up, Daniel. *Apologize.*"

"It's probably too late for that. Julian deserves so much better," I said desperately. I could hear Julian's boots on the porch stairs, and while a few minutes ago I'd been literally tripping over things in my excitement to see him again, now I was fucking petrified.

I was realizing—right then, because my timing was perfect as always—I'd always sort of taken for granted that certain things were fixed and immutable. My father was overbearing and disliked everything about me that didn't fit his own narrative of what a son should be, so there was nothing I could do to change that relationship. My writing was either critically acclaimed or it wasn't, and I couldn't change anything about it without becoming inauthentic. My friends and my ex-wife had turned away when I needed them, so clearly I was unlovable, and there was nothing I could have done to change those outcomes.

I was shitty at relationships.

I was doomed to failure.

Pitiful and forever alone, woe is me.

But what if… and I know it sounds ridiculously simple, but I cannot express how revolutionary this idea was to me in that moment… what if I could stop reacting to things the way I always had, like the world was out to get me, and just maybe trust that someone could see me beneath my failures and disappointments. I knew I could do that for Julian. Maybe Julian could do that for me?

"Daniel." Sam stood on her tiptoes and gripped me roughly by the shoulders like some kind of tough-love pixie. "If you think Julian deserves someone better, then *be* someone better, because you're who he wants. Okay?"

"Sam," I said as Jules knocked on the door. "You're the smartest person in the room. Fuck anyone who treats you like a toddler."

Sam laughed and shook her head, pushing me away. "You're so weird."

She pushed open the storm door and I turned as Julian walked in and greeted the dog.

"Hey, Sam." He darted a wary glance at me. "How's everything?"

"Eh. Same shit, different day," she said. "Your boyfriend here just let me get warm. I came by to say that I'm making progress with the shed, but I've left a bunch of stuff there to get carted off next week. I'll get back to it." Her gaze swung back and forth between Jules and me. "And I'll let you two get on with your… record playing." She wiggled her eyebrows at me.

Jules squinted at her. "Our what?"

But Sam sashayed out the door without replying.

"Is that, like, a euphemism for sex? Do teenagers even know what record players are?" He went to the door to watch Sam walk away. "Does she have a car? Is someone giving her a ride? Isn't it cold out in the shed?"

I backed Julian against the door. "Hi."

"Oh. Um." He swallowed. His blue eyes were huge and uncertain. "Hey."

"I'm going to kiss you," I said. "Is that alright?"

"Yeah," he breathed. Then he shook his head. "Or no. *No.* Actually, we should talk first."

"We definitely need to talk," I agreed. "But first—"

I kissed him with everything I had—with all the longing and the fear that had built up over two days without speaking to him, with all the aftershocks of the revelations I'd just had still running through me. At first, he didn't respond, but then he did, relaxing into the kiss, relaxing into me. And that was when I thought maybe, possibly, everything was going to work out alright.

I eased back before I could lose myself in it completely, brushing one last chaste kiss across his lips before trailing my hands down from his neck to his arms.

Julian lifted a hand and rubbed his fingers across his mouth, staring at me like he wasn't quite sure whether he wanted to talk or just keep kissing. But the kissing wasn't the issue between us—it never really had been. He needed words, and I wanted to give them to him.

At least, I was pretty sure I did.

"I have questions," Julian said. "Things I need to ask you." His voice was husky and a little uncertain.

"I know. You can ask me anything."

He blinked and then took a step back, like my easy acceptance had made him skeptical. "Really?" He was so fucking cute.

"Yes. Really." I couldn't help grimacing. This was not going to be fun. At all. "Ask anything and I'll try to answer."

"Okay." He licked his lips and I could practically see the wheels turning behind his eyes. He hadn't expected me to agree. He didn't know how to begin. "First, how are you okay with *this*?"

He motioned between us, to the bare inches separating my t-shirt-covered chest and his heavy coat.

"Why are you still wearing your jacket?" I asked.

He shook his head impatiently. "Because you didn't let

me get in the door properly before you started kissing me?" He unzipped his coat and removed it, throwing it over the sofa. "Happy now?"

I was, mostly because I was still really nervous, and anything that delayed him leaving was a good thing.

"Now. Tell me, please," he said. "How are you feeling about this, us? *Is* it freaking you out? Does it feel right? Because I do know you're attracted to me," he said, holding up a hand like he wanted to forestall my protests about *proving* my attraction. "But how do you *feel* about that?"

I nodded. Okay, this was a fair question. An easy one, really. And it was a sign of just how oblivious I'd been and how badly I'd screwed up with Julian if he was really questioning stuff like this.

It was fucked up that we used to talk about *everything*, and all of a sudden, once sex was thrown into the mix, neither of us had spoken about anything important.

I grabbed his hand and towed him to the sofa, relaxing into the middle seat while he plopped on the end, close enough to touch but not so close that we couldn't have a conversation.

Probably.

"It's not fucking me up or freaking me out. It confused the hell out of me for a minute," I admitted. "And there was a time when I wondered if it was real, not because it wasn't powerful but because it *was*. I'd never felt anything like this before, ever. And I still don't know how to label it, or even if I want to. But so much has changed this year, Julian, and I've redefined myself in so many ways, this is the most minor way. And the very best way, too, because of you. "

"And you're okay with the whole world knowing you're… with me?"

"O'Leary has known we were together for a long while now," I reminded him. "And that was my idea. I'm *happy* for everyone to know we're together. Especially if it means no more texts from Curtis," I added sourly.

"Right." Julian narrowed his eyes. "Okay, since you bring that up… What the hell happened the other night?"

I stretched my neck against the sudden tension. "What happened was that I was jealous. Totally, sickeningly jealous. You called it right."

"But you said—"

"I know what I said." I ran a hand through my hair. "I have a terrible track record with relationships, Julian. Terrible. Abysmal. Worse than I am at whittling."

"Not that I've seen that to judge," he said wryly.

"I'm scared of what a real relationship with you would mean. I'm scared I'll fuck something up again."

"You're scared?"

"Uh, *yeah*." I snorted. "Jesus. You have no idea how much."

"I might have some." His lips tipped up a tiny bit.

"You're my best friend. And I can't go ten minutes without wanting you. Not just for sex, though… I mean, yeah, that too." Julian's smile widened. "I just want to be with you, to talk to you. Do you know that listening to you talk is a huge turn-on for me?"

"You've mentioned it," he whispered, wonder in his tone. It sounded like he was still having trouble believing it, and *fuck* did I want to show him the truth of it *right now*.

But no. This was talking time.

Though it would be followed quickly by other stuff if I had my way.

"You have *no idea*," I repeated.

"So what does that mean in terms of us being in a… relationship?" he asked in a strangled voice.

And okay, the questions were getting progressively harder now, because I had no idea what *he* wanted, and admitting what I wanted felt like walking on a tightrope.

Over a canyon.

In the wind.

But this was Julian, and if there was anyone I could do this for, it was him.

"You're my best friend," I said again. "And I'm attracted to you. And I'd prefer to keep the physical side of this. And I'm not great with labels. So we can call it whatever you want, whatever you're comfortable with," I hedged.

"I'm not comfortable being friends with benefits anymore," Julian said flatly. "That's for people who… who lack the balls to admit they have feelings for each other."

I blinked. "Okay."

"I'd like us to be dating. I'd like us to be boyfriends for real," he said confidently, like he was laying down terms for surrender. But his breathing was just a little fast, his eyes just a little too wide. I'd bet anything that his pulse was running a mile a minute.

"Yeah, I'd like that too," I agreed. "It hasn't felt fake since… well, ever."

"Holy shit." Julian ran his palm over his forehead. "It worked."

"What worked?" I asked, pulling his hand away and holding onto it.

He shook his head and one corner of his mouth twitched as he looked up at me. He squeezed my hand. "*Asking.* I, um, talked to Parker Hoffstraeder yesterday. About us. About how I could fix things between us. He said it'd be as easy as asking you."

"Nah, it's not easy to talk about this stuff." I brought up my other hand and clasped the nape of his neck. He shifted on the sofa to face me. "Shit, Julian. There's nothing harder. You might have noticed I'm allergic to it."

"Yeah, kinda. We're a pair, huh?"

"We *are* a pair. But maybe now instead of being a pair of dumbasses who are scared shitless, we can be a pair of…" I trailed off because Julian put his hand on my thigh and metaphors failed me.

"Dumbasses who laugh in the face of fear?" he suggested, grinning.

I laughed. "Just as long as we're a pair, baby. The rest is all details."

This time, it was Julian who kissed me, pushing up so he was kneeling on the seat, wrapping his fists around my hair like he wanted to make sure I was real and couldn't get away. But there was nowhere else in the world I wanted to be.

"We don't have to talk about everything right now, right?" Julian said, breaking away from the kiss with a gasp. "We can discuss things as they come up?"

"Yeah," I breathed. "As they come up. Good plan." I put my hands on his waist and slid up under his sweater—that oversized sweater I fucking loved—on a path to his chest.

"Oh, fuck," he said. "Yes. *That* right there."

"It's tricky when I can't see what I'm doing," I teased, moving my mouth to nip at his jaw, inhaling the fragrance of citrus and soap and *Julian*. "You're gonna have to guide me." I scratched his nipples lightly with my fingernails.

"Oh, motherfucker. I think you're doing *just* fine."

"*Language*, Julian," I teased, and Julian's hands in my hair tightened when I laughed.

"Don't you *dare*," he said. He let go of my hair and tore the sweater over his head, then let out another harsh string of expletives when I replaced my fingers with my mouth.

"Oh, fuck, that feels good. Daniel, Jesus…"

"Yeah?" I said, my voice coming out as a harsh rasp. "You think I'm doing okay with all these new skills?" I pulled Julian over to straddle my lap and shifted my hips to rub my cock against his. "*Oh, fuck.*"

"You're a fucking prodigy," he breathed. Then, "More."

I laughed, because I couldn't help it. "It has *never* been like this for me before, Julian. Never. Not with anyone. Maybe all this time I've been waiting for you."

"Daniel—" he said helplessly, tucking his face into my neck.

But now that the words were flowing, it seemed like I couldn't shut them off. "I worried at first that this wasn't real. Like I was confusing friendship for sexual attraction." I groaned at the feel of him moving against me. "I'm such an idiot, Julian. Does this feel like friendship?"

"*Ngh.*"

I took that as a no.

"I actually said to myself, *maybe this is loneliness.* Maybe this is just because Julian is the only person I care about anymore. But then I went out with those guys the other night, after the parade. And all I could think about was how much I missed you. *You*, Julian. Not people. Not friends. *You.* You're what I want."

I pushed Julian the other way on the couch, planning to crawl over him. But I'd forgotten the stupid laptop I'd left there until Julian's elbow slapped the keyboard and the machine elicited a shrill, outraged noise at the abuse.

"*Shit!* What did I just land on?" Julian did an ab roll that would have been impressive under other circumstances and twisted to look behind him, like he was worried he might have landed on something *living.*

"It's nothing. Just my computer." I grabbed for the

machine to move it aside—at that moment I would have happily thrown the fucking thing out the window so we could get back to what we were doing—but Julian stopped me with a hand on my arm.

"What the heck is this?"

Oh. *Shit.*

I sat back on my heels and blew out a breath as he read the words on the screen.

"MacBryde?" His blue eyes searched mine curiously.

Shit. Damn. Fuck. Was it still talking time? Because my dick was so not on board.

I had the feeling that if I deflected or promised to tell Julian all about it later, he'd have agreed. After all, his eyes were still dark with lust and his cock was straining at the fly of his jeans. But postponing important discussions was a bad habit, so I told my dick to calm down.

"It's a fictional town in a story I'm writing based on O'Leary," I told him. "That's what I do… *did*, I mean. Before. Back when I lived in the city. I was a writer."

"Holy shit," he breathed. "Daniel, how could you not tell me? Can I read what you've written? Have you ever tried publishing?"

"I have. Not this." I pointed at the computer. "This is just for me. But in the past, I've published six books."

"No fucking way!" He grabbed me by the shoulders and shook me excitedly. "Have I heard of them? Did anyone buy them? Fuck. Can I buy them online right now?"

"Yes, a couple sold well, and fuck *no*, Julian. If you're thinking of reading right now, I'm doing something wrong." This time I did take the laptop away and set it on the floor. "You can read it later."

He let it go with a pout that turned to a grin when I

pushed him back down on the seat and came down on top of him, bracing my weight on my forearms.

Still, though, he hesitated.

"Is this one of those things you'd rather not talk about?" he asked seriously. His hands reached up to cup my face.

I thought about it. He was giving me an out, if I wanted it. But I was shocked to find that I didn't, really. Still, I bent down and set my forehead to his chin, addressing my words to his chest so I wouldn't have to look at him.

"It's painful. The last couple of books were… shit, Julian. God. Critics slammed them. They didn't sell well at all. I thought I was going to be a writer forever, like I'd found my calling. And then I failed." I took a deep breath and focused on the feeling of his fingers carding through my hair. "That's when everything else fell apart, more or less. I got depressed, and ended up depressing all of my friends. My parents were disappointed."

His hands stilled. "And so, you moved here? Left everything behind?"

I nodded against his skin. "A fresh start."

"I wish you'd told me." The words weren't an accusation but a simple statement of fact.

"I didn't want you to know. I liked the way you saw me. Not Daniel-the-failure, but *me*."

"I get it. I mean, I like the way you see me, too. But…" Laughter bubbled out of him. "God, you're wrong."

I lifted my head in shock. "Excuse me?"

"Sorry, but I mean, rarely in the history of the world have people been as wrong, baby," Julian said solemnly. "You had one book that didn't sell well—"

"Two."

"Fine, *two* books that didn't sell well. That's not a failed career." He yanked at my hair now, making sure he had my attention. "That's not the sum total of what you have to offer the world as a writer."

"I don't know. The thought of trying to publish anything again is terrifying."

His eyes softened. "But we laugh in the face of fear, right?"

I snorted and bit gently at his chest, loving the feel of his muscles contracting as he squirmed. I licked at the spot I'd bitten, and Julian gave a gratifying gasp.

"No sidetracking me right now," he said sternly. "This is important."

I sighed.

"One time when we were hiking, you told me I needed to change my internal dialogue. Do you remember?"

I grunted a negative. "Sounds like some shit I'd say, though."

"Well, I think you need to change yours. Because—no, lift your head! Look at me for a second. Because even if you never wrote again, Daniel Michaelson, *you* would not be a failure. Your career doesn't define you. A failed book doesn't mean a failed career, and baby, a career setback doesn't mean a failed *life*."

Staring into his eyes, I couldn't doubt his sincerity. And I don't know what kind of strange magic he was working, but when he said it, I swear I felt the truth of it, too, deep in my gut. I hadn't known I needed to hear the words until that second—maybe I wouldn't have been ready to hear them until right then—but it was like a key turning in a lock, a weight lifting from my shoulders.

I didn't say anything for a moment. I couldn't.

Julian must have mistaken my silence for disbelief because he continued, punctuating each sentence with a gentle shake of my head. "I think you're amazing, you know that? You make me laugh. You make me *think*. You make things seem possible. You make me a better person. You make me..." His grip on my hair loosened, and he shook his head like he couldn't summon any more words.

But that was fine. Because I was *done* talking.

"Do I make you want?" I asked.

"What?"

I shifted down and pushed his knees apart with my own so I could lay between his thighs. I held his gaze and licked one hard brown nipple.

"Do I made you hard?"

"Daniel," he whispered. I felt his hands fluttering over my shoulders, like he wanted to stop me and also very much didn't want to stop me, which was good since I had no plan to stop.

I kissed a path down his chest, over the flat plane of his abs, nuzzling my nose into the fine trail of hair that began right above his waistband, then sat back further so I could undo the button.

"What are you doing?" His voice sounded drugged.

"Julian, once again, if it's not clear what I'm doing..."

"No! I meant... We haven't done that."

"You mean *I* haven't done this." I pulled down his jeans and underwear, and after a brief fumble with his boots I managed to get him completely, gloriously naked. "But I'm a prodigy, remember? And I think I understand the general idea."

"Are you sure?"

"Julian, I'm positive."

I'd never experienced a blowjob from this side of the equation, but I was ready to. I was fucking *eager* to.

The first time we'd done more than kiss felt like a life-time ago. Julian's body laid out before me was familiar now, but no less exciting. The hardness of his chest, the width of his shoulders, the hair on his thighs, and—*fuck, yes*—the hardness of his cock made my mouth water. I'd wanted to do this for a while now, but Julian had never suggested it, and I'd never pushed the issue. It had seemed a bit too revealing, a bit too *real.*

Now I resumed my position at his waist, dipping my tongue into his navel, soaking up his cries, memorizing the way he bit his lip, and loving every minute of the realness.

I moved lower, kissing a zigzag path over his hip, holding his gaze the entire time. I licked at the juncture of his hip and thigh, and he shifted his legs open further, like he wanted to make sure I wasn't missing the rock-hard cock begging for my attention. I grinned smugly.

"I'm getting there," I promised.

"There's a certain etiquette to these things," he informed me breathlessly, jutting his hips into the air. "Teasing is very rude."

"Is it?" I licked up his other thigh, loving the rasp of hair against my cheek.

"*Very,*" he insisted. "As in, there will be payback."

"Interesting." I nuzzled his balls with my nose, and the scent of him was heady. "I was thinking maybe you could give me some animal facts. You know, as inspiration?"

Without giving him a chance to respond—because I really don't think he could have—I licked a long, wet stripe up across his skin.

"Oh my fucking God." Julian threw a hand over his eyes. "Daniel, *please.*"

But I had no mercy, mostly because I was really, really invested in what I was doing.

I sucked one ball and then the other into my mouth, mapping the texture with my tongue. It was salty and strange, but the effect on Julian was *incendiary.* His legs flexed out straight like he'd been electrocuted, his back bowed, and he let out a string of nearly incoherent pleading that sounded like *Oh fuck oh fuck oh fuck please please please.*

Jesus.

My own cock was hard enough to slice through my jeans and into the sofa, but I didn't care. Watching Julian like this was… fucking incredible. He was so responsive, so completely given over to what I was giving him.

I eased back and touched the hard length of him, which was bobbing against his stomach, begging for attention.

His hand came away from his face and his eyes met mine, fever-bright.

"You ready?" I asked.

"I needed to see this part," he croaked.

And I could have told him that this wasn't going to be the only time, that I would gladly do this every evening and mornings, too, but instead, I laid my hands flat on his stomach and took him in my mouth in one swift movement. No more teasing, no more experimenting. Nothing but total commitment.

And then I choked.

Oral sex *seemed* like it should be an easy thing—open mouth, insert dick, right? Yeah, no. It wasn't that simple. This was no porn flick, and apparently, I had a well-developed gag reflex.

"Daniel! *Shit*," Julian cried. "Are you okay?"

I nodded. My eyes were watering a little.

"Do you want to wait, or—?"

I absolutely did not want to wait *or*. I eased back a little and recalculated. I held the base of him in my hand and concentrated on his head, lapping at the salty liquid that pooled there, and then sank down again, taking as much of him as I could manage.

"Jesus Christ!" Julian wailed. "Please. Again!"

I did as he commanded, slurping him down eagerly over and over, and it got easier. The rhythm came naturally after a minute, and I was able to take more of him than before.

He moaned, and his hips made little bucking motions like he wanted so badly to fuck my face, but he was trying to hold himself back. One day, I promised myself, he'd be able to do it without restraint.

"Oh, fuck. You're so fucking good at this," he said.

I was?

"Did I say prodigy? I meant... God, I don't know. What's better than a prodigy? *Hngh*." He stuffed a hand in his mouth and squeezed his eyes shut. "Shit. I wanted this to last and I... *Fuck*. I'm going to come."

I pulled away with a *pop*. I wanted him to come, I did... but I wanted to try something else.

"Fuck me, Julian," I begged.

His dick twitched, and his eyes popped open, liquid blue and dazed.

"Yes! Yeah, I... Wait, what?"

"Fuck me. I want you to. If you're into that, I mean." We hadn't talked about this, like *at all* over the weeks of frottage and hand jobs. We hadn't even alluded to doing anything more. But it felt... *right*. I wanted to connect with him in every possible way, to cement this connection.

"I am. I am into that. But... I..." His eyes whirled around the living room like he was looking for something that wasn't there. "I don't have... anything. Supplies. Condoms. Lube."

Oh. Right. Shit. I really was an idiot. I hadn't even thought.

"I have lube," I volunteered. "And condoms." Somewhere.

His eyes widened further. "*You* have lube? Really?"

"Uh, *yeah*. Gay men haven't cornered the market on personal lubricant, Julian Ross."

His surprise gave way to a bright smile, and when he grabbed my face to kiss me, he tasted like laughter.

"I apologize," he said solemnly, though his eyes were bright. "Bedroom?"

I nodded.

Somehow he managed to get off the couch even faster than I did and ran into my room. It was cooler in there, and I could see the sun setting out the window, giving the little room a private, otherworldly glow.

Julian threw himself on his back in the center of my bed, fanned out like a starfish on the faded quilt. He grinned up at me. "What are you waiting for?"

Shit, right.

I yanked the side table drawer open, nearly dropping it on the floor in my haste, and found what I needed. Exactly two condoms and a half-used bottle of lube, which I threw on the bed.

"What happens first?" I asked eagerly.

Julian bit his lip. "Well, first you take off all your clothes. That's kind of important."

I huffed out a laugh and pulled my t-shirt off. "I swear I've had sex before. I have. It's just…" I shrugged as I shed my jeans and climbed on the bed to lay on my side next to him.

"Nerves?" Julian trailed a hand through the hair on my chest and *fuck* that felt good. My stomach *trembled* with need.

"Partly, yeah. Mostly, I'm feeling like a sixteen-year-old who's trying very hard to lose his virginity. Very excited and not at all sure what to do."

"Sixteen? You really were a prodigy." He let his hand

drift down to the waistband of my briefs, already tented with my erection, and lightly snapped the elastic. "These need to go too."

I snorted. "Yeah. I just… I need a minute." Because all this needed was for me to come all over myself before he even touched me, and it was very possible that I was going to explode the second air hit me.

"Take your time," Julian said lazily. "I'll amuse myself." He started stroking his own dick with long, slow pulls—up and down, then around the crown—and that was *not* helping.

"You're going to kill me," I groaned, burying my head in his arm. "This is the way I'll die."

Julian grinned. "Better than heatstroke," he said, and I had no idea what the hell he was talking about because I was too busy watching his fingers as they wrapped around his shaft. This was familiar, too—I'd seen him do it before—but everything was different now.

My hand was moving before I thought better of it, knocking his out of the way and taking over his task. He was hot and perfect under my hand and *fuck* I wanted him.

"Daniel? Can we make a quick change to the agenda?" Julian asked breathlessly.

"Yeah. Sure. Anything you want."

"I think this time, our first time… I think it'd be better if *you* fuck *me* instead."

I met his eyes in the dim light. "Really?"

He nodded. "I like it both ways, but for today…"

"Yeah. Okay." I wasn't sure if he really meant he'd prefer it this way, or that he thought I would. It was like Julian to be thinking of *me* and what would be easiest for me. But it didn't matter. There'd be time later to try out everything.

He grabbed the bottle of lube and squirted some on his fingers, then drew his legs up to his chest.

I quickly slid my underwear down and off, then gripped the base of my shaft *tight*, because holy shit, the sight was incredible. His fingers slid into his opening—first one, then two, stretching himself for me—while he moaned and his eyes ran up and down my body like he couldn't believe this was really happening.

Neither could I.

I wasn't having any kind of sexuality freak-out—I hadn't lied to Julian when I said that I was fine with this. How could I not be? But it felt momentous, still, to be doing this for the first time. To be doing this with *Julian* for the first time.

"Shit," he breathed. "I really, really want my mouth on you."

"I want that too, but not now. Not unless you want this to end very differently."

Julian smirked. "I can't lie. I have never felt sexier in my entire life than I do right now."

"*I* can't lie. You're the sexiest thing I've ever seen in my life."

His smirk softened into a bright smile. Then he picked up the condom packet and ripped it open with his teeth. He shifted onto his side, pushing me onto my back, and rolled it down my length before coating me with extra lube. And then he straddled my thighs.

My surprise must've shown on my face because he chuckled softly. "This wasn't what you wanted?" His fingers trailed up and down my cock.

"If there is one thing I've learned with you, Julian Ross, it's that just because I don't expect something doesn't mean I don't want it. Or need it. Now hurry up and kiss me."

He did, leaning over to press a quick kiss to my lips

before kneeling again and lining me up at his entrance. I grabbed his ass with both hands and helped to open him. The long slow slide into the heat of his body was something I would never, ever forget, and I hoped the look on his face as he took me—pure, orgasmic bliss—was seared into my retinas, because I wanted to see it every night before I fell asleep.

"Holy fucking hell, Julian!" The sensory overload was nearly too much. Jesus *fuck* it was tight and hot.

He gasped a little bit and bit his lip—I didn't think I'd ever be able to see him do that again without thinking of sex—then braced one hand on my thigh and the other on my chest. He started to ride me with undulating motions that made his cock bob against my stomach over and over. I hadn't known a body could move that way. I sure as fuck hadn't known Julian could. Christ, it was perfect.

But it wasn't going to last long.

I slid one hand up his flank so I could feel his muscles tense and release and my other hand went to his cock, desperate to make him come before I did, to make this good for him too. I knew by now how Julian liked it—how hard he liked to be gripped, how much he loved it when I rubbed my thumb over his glans. Right then, I used every single piece of knowledge I'd acquired, trying to show him without words how fucking *thankful* I was for him, trying to press my commitment into his skin.

"Daniel!" Julian threw his head back and came with a cry, coating my hand and chest.

I rocked my hips up into him, keeping our rhythm when he faltered. I could feel the orgasm coming, but I still gasped when it hit. Tiny pinpricks of light exploded behind my eyes, and my hearing turned to static. For a second I thought, *Holy shit, I actually* did *die.* And the thought didn't bother me nearly as much as it should.

It took a long minute for me to crack open my eyes. The room was completely engulfed in shadows, and it felt like I'd passed out for a really long time, but Julian was still balanced above me, panting, his eyes steady on my face.

"Hey," he croaked, and my spent cock twitched. "That was, um…"

His voice trailed off, and I got it, because even the purplest prose couldn't describe what that had been.

"We should have these talks more often," I said. "They're very… *cathartic*."

Julian chuckled, choked, hiccupped, then broke into wild laughter, clapping one hand over his mouth and smacking my chest with the other. "Have you never heard of afterglow?"

"Maybe you can teach me." I waggled my eyebrows suggestively.

"Oh, I'll teach you alright." He leaned down and kissed me. "There's an appropriate time for everything."

But later, after we'd showered and eaten sandwiches, after I'd tucked a yawning Julian, who confessed he hadn't slept well in days, into my bed, after I'd curled up beside him and started drifting off, Julian's eyes popped open.

"Holy shit. Did you name your fictional town after the heroine in my romance?"

Which just went to show that Julian had a few things to learn, too.

Chapter Fourteen

JULIAN

I WALKED down Weaver Street Saturday morning thinking what a shame it was that winter was such an under-appreciated time of year. I usually liked to hibernate from late November until the last snowfall was melted, and the mud had mostly dried—which around here could mean May or June—but that was so misguided of me. December was gorgeous! The air was perfectly crisp and cold, the nearly bare tree branches had a sort of sparkly beauty to them. Plus, I was fucking *loving* these holiday decorations. If the whole world had burst into song and started dancing in the streets with their dry-cleaning, like in that one episode of *Buffy*, I probably would have joined right in.

"Morning, Doc Ross! Morning, Daniel!" Dana Cobb called out from high atop a ladder in front of the Crabapple Bed and Breakfast. The woman was what my Nonna Betinelli would have called "abundant"—curved and well-padded from her legs up to her pale, round face. Though she was well over fifty, she still wore her hair in a high, cheerleader ponytail, and she smiled *constantly*, like she was determined to put as much perkiness into the world as her wife Rena did sass. "What's a pair of handsome gents up to this morning?"

"Morning, Dana," Daniel said. "We're heading to the diner for breakfast. Julian has a craving for pancakes."

More like Julian was going to be rewarded with pancakes after an extremely athletic round of sex last night and possibly the best blowjob I'd ever delivered, if I did say so myself, this morning.

I had to bite my lip to keep the shit-eating grin off my face.

"You need any help up there?" Daniel offered.

"Well now. You offerin' your services, stud? I wouldn't mind spotting *your* ladder." She waggled her eyebrows suggestively, then giggled at Daniel's flustered blush. "Nah, I'm fine. Just securing the garland. Supposed to be a hell of a weekend, tonight and tomorrow."

"Snow?" Daniel said eagerly. "How much?"

"Nah. No white stuff this time." She sounded a little disappointed. "Just wind and dangerously cold temperatures, to quote the weatherman."

"Oh." Daniel *definitely* sounded disappointed. The guy loved snow more than any kid. I made a mental note to tease him about it later. "I could do without the cold."

Dana tsked. "You sound like my Rena. Some of us see it as a good excuse for cuddling. Isn't that right, Doc?" She shot me a wink as she climbed up two more rungs.

Now *I* was the one blushing. But Daniel wrapped his arm more firmly around my shoulder and I found that I didn't mind the teasing much at all. Everything was a lot better when your favorite person in the world was wrapped around you.

"What do you say, Doc?" Daniel whispered in my ear. "That sound like a decent way to spend the weekend?"

"I suppose you could convince me," I agreed. "But we're gonna need a lot more pancakes."

"Happy, carb-loving Julian is my new favorite Julian," Daniel said. He made a thoughtful noise. "So far."

"Are there any Julians you dislike?" I asked, amused.

"Well, I will say there's one I like *less*," Daniel said sadly. "Like vegetable pizza Julian. So misguided. Poor guy. But other than that, I think—"

"Ah, fuck a duck!" Dana shouted half a second before a giant plastic snowflake came crashing down on the sidewalk. "Sorry, gents! Maybe you should watch out for falling snow after all." She laughed uproariously at her own joke, and the ladder swayed.

Daniel and I exchanged a wide-eyed look.

Daniel bent down to pick up the decoration and held it up to her. "You sure you don't need help? I'm a little taller than you, and I might be faster."

Dana sighed. "I suppose I ought to give my pride the day off and let you help, otherwise I'll be out here all day. You sure you don't mind?"

"Nope." He leaned down and pressed a kiss to my lips. "Wanna go get a table and I'll be there in five minutes?"

I nodded. "I'll get you coffee, too."

"Best boyfriend ever," Daniel said softly. And it was funny that no one else in this town would realize just how meaningful those words were, because now they were real.

I bravely resisted the urge to perv on Daniel as he climbed the ladder, mostly because it *was* really cold out here without Daniel beside me, and hurried down the street.

It was hard to believe we were so deep into winter already. It felt like I'd spent most of the fall involuntarily strapped to an emotional thrill ride—*Did Daniel like me? Could he like me-like me? Could I handle it if he didn't? Could I handle it if he did?*—where every alternate week brought a higher peak and then a lower valley. I used think I liked rollercoasters. Now I'd be perfectly happy to never ride one again. I wanted peace and calm and *Daniel*, and this life we were building together.

The past couple of weeks had been good. Insanely good. So good, there were moments where I wondered if I'd wandered into someone else's life by accident, or I'd been handed a gift meant for someone else. But every time I looked in the mirror, I saw my own widely grinning face. And I was starting to believe that maybe this kind of happiness had been out there waiting for me all along, I just had to believe I could get it.

Daniel spent hours every day on his laptop. Now that I knew how he was spending his time, I could understand how draining it was. But he was nearly finished with his revisions, and he said he'd let me read it when he was done. I promised myself that I'd be honest but not too honest with my feedback. The world had enough negativity in it. And although I hadn't asked him about it specifically, I was pretty sure I understood why Daniel had such a hate-on for JD Pritchard: my favorite author must have been one of the assholes who turned on Daniel after his books flopped. I'd resolved that I was never going to buy another Pritchard mystery…

I mean, I might read one from the library, or whatever, because the books were fucking good even if the guy was an asshole. But I definitely wouldn't *purchase* it.

Daniel had opened up about his family, too—his privileged childhood where he struggled to please his parents, his time living on his own, the way his parents had welcomed him back into the fold once he was successful, and how it seemed like they'd turned away from him just like everyone else when shit went bad. But he'd also been honest about the fact that he'd never tried to change the patterns of behavior they'd fallen into.

It was a lesson I needed to learn, too.

"Do my eyes deceive me, or did I see Jules Ross strolling arm in arm with his man just a minute ago?" I whipped my head around to see Parker jogging up behind me, bundled in a plaid jacket. "Did you cowboy up and have a conversation, or did you punk out and plan to ignore it forever?"

I sighed and turned back around. Parker kept pace beside me. "There's nothing more annoying that someone who gives good advice and rubs your face in it."

"Sure there are. Like, people who give *shitty* advice and rub your face in it," he said cheerfully. "So? Update?"

I sighed again, more loudly this time, but I couldn't help the smug grin that tipped my lips. "I talked to him."

"And?"

"And he talked back."

"Revolutionary!"

"Uh-huh. And now things are good." I felt my smile widen involuntarily. "Great, actually."

"Yeah? I'm glad, Jules." Parker stuffed his hands in his pockets.

"And how about you?" I turned to look at him. "Things with you and—"

I broke off when the sound of laughter further down the street distracted me. A familiar-looking guy was standing outside the bakery talking to Jamie, whose coppery hair glinted in the sunlight. As we watched, the guy stood on tiptoe and pressed a kiss to Jamie's cheek, then linked his arm with Jamie's and towed him down the street away from us.

Brian, I realized. Jamie's former and apparently *current* boyfriend.

"Don't you just love a visual illustration?" Parker said wryly. "There's no me *and*… It's just me. And I'm fine. I'm focusing on my business. My family's coming back to O'Leary for the holidays to see the new place, which'll be interesting. "

"But have you talked to Jamie? Have you gotten past whatever your issues were? Because if you followed your own advice and told him—"

"Nothing to tell, Jules," he said with false cheer. His smile slipped for a second. "Listen, when you care about someone, when you love them, you want them to be happy, right? Even if it kills you in the short term? Self-sacrifice and all that shit? Sometimes it just makes sense to keep your mouth shut. But I appreciate your concern. You ever need another burger and advice session, you know where to find me, yeah?" He hooked his thumb toward Hoff's.

I nodded slowly. "Yeah. Okay."

"And congrats, man. It's good to see someone figure their shit out." He clapped me on the shoulder and walked off toward his bar.

The diner was packed with the typical Saturday morning crowd, and so hot I was already roasting by the time I found a table in the back and waved to let Diane know I was going to take it.

Kelly Dwyer called out a greeting and her daughter waved at me cheerily. Old Abe Connor nodded hello. Moira Keller, who was sitting with a guy I'd never met before—I would have remembered that gorgeous mocha skin, high cheekbones, and green eyes—winked and grinned as I passed her table. I couldn't remember why I'd ever gotten impatient with my overly friendly town.

"Hey, Jules!" Si Sloane said as I took off my coat and slid onto the padded bench that ran behind the line of tables.

Everett Maior, his boyfriend, turned to smile at me.

"Morning! God, I'm starving. What's the special today?" I asked. "Something holiday-ish?"

"Would you call piña colada pancakes holiday-ish?" Everett asked. "Because if so, then yes."

"Piña colada?" I blinked. "I was thinking something cinnamon."

Si laughed. "That's because you hadn't realized that Diane is running the show this morning and she's trying to make a point."

"About… pineapple?"

"About the fact that Christmas is only a couple days away," Ev corrected. "Which is just enough time for my grandfather to book her that Caribbean vacation she's been hinting at for weeks."

"Ohhhh." I grimaced. "Well, I hope it works."

"Yeah, hope it works better than these pancakes, at least," Si said, picking listlessly at the pancakes on his plate, which seemed to be covered in tropical fruit. "Or I'm gonna boycott this place until the gift-giving holidays are over."

"Right," Ev snickered. "Or you could just tell Diane *no*, like some of us did, baby."

"But she was so excited, Ev." Si shrugged helplessly. "I couldn't say no. Besides, I was thinking my *boyfriend* could share some of his omelet with me."

"This is what love looks like," Ev said with a sigh, pushing his plate to the center of the table.

"Worth it!" Si said happily, digging into the omelet.

"Yeah," Ev said, watching his boyfriend. "It really is."

And yeah, I smiled cheesily enough to make any lactose-intolerant person in the vicinity ill, because I knew exactly what he was talking about.

But before I could slide too fully into the warm, gooey

love vibe, Theo slid into the chair across from me, ducking his head like he was trying not to be noticed, and Sam crowded onto the bench between my table and Silas's table.

"Julian," Theo said anxiously. "We have a problem."

"Theo, I haven't had coffee yet," I informed him. "You can give me your Jason Bourne routine after I'm caffeinated."

"No, I'm serious! There's a woman over there, and she's asking about Daniel." He nodded toward the far side of the diner. "The one with her hair up in a bun-thing—"

"A French twist," Sam interjected. "Which, like, is either way out of style or coming back into style and we haven't heard about it yet."

"She's wearing a fancy suit like she doesn't know she's in O'Leary," Theo hissed, like this was tantamount to wearing the sign of the antichrist.

I sat up straight and tried to look around Theo's bulk.

"Jesus! Don't *look*," he whispered furiously, while Sam yanked at my shoulder to pull me down.

"Well, do you know who she is? Do you know what she wants?" I demanded. "Maybe she's a friend."

"If she was a friend, she'd know where he lived and wouldn't be asking Diane if she knew Daniel," Sam said reasonably.

"Maybe. Or maybe she just knew the name of the town and came to surprise him." Though as I said it, it sounded less and less plausible. "What did Diane say?"

"Just that he lived out on the Camden Road. And I know Jay Turner overheard, too, but he didn't say anything either. You know how people here are with outsiders."

I almost laughed. Suddenly Daniel was now an insider and the lady looking for him was the stranger. It made my heart squeeze in a good way and reminded me why, for all its faults, O'Leary was the only place I'd ever considered home.

"Well, she's gonna see him in a minute," I warned them. "Daniel stopped to help Dana Cobb, but he's coming to meet me. In fact, you're in his seat."

"Then you need to go over there and find out what she wants before Daniel walks into something," Sam said. "Do you know about his family? They sound exactly like the kind of people who'd put a private investigator on his tail."

"On his tail? Are we in a cop show now? Can I be Cagney?"

Sam gave me a scathing look. "Is that some outdated pop-culture reference? Because if so, you and Daniel deserve each other."

"Is that an insult? Because if so, you really need to work on your shade game."

Sam groaned. "Never mind. It's worse when you try to talk like you're my age."

"Hello!" Theo said. "Hi. Sorry to interrupt, but the woman is still over there."

Ev leaned over from the other table. "Hey. I really fucking hate it when people butt in on conversations, but uh… I'm butting in on your conversation. Need Silas or me to go talk to the lady?"

"Ev, honey, I can't go over there and grill the woman for coming into a public place and eating… Oh. *Damn*. Looks like Diane just brought her the pineapple pancakes. I guess I could go over and try to avert a public health disaster."

"No one needs to go over there," I said. But because Theo looked like he was going to argue, I held up a hand. "But fine. I'll go anyway and see who she is, okay? Will that make you happy?"

Theo nodded. "I'm only looking out for Daniel, bro. He's a good guy, and he likes his privacy."

And so the wackadoodle stranger who lived in the woods became a good guy who valued his privacy. Only in O'Leary.

"All I wanted were the fucking pancakes I earned," I muttered to myself as I crossed the restaurant. "Pancakes and coffee and no more rollercoasters. Apparently, this was too much to ask."

The woman was pretty. Really pretty. And I'd peg her as a little older than Daniel, but not by much. Forty or something. Her dark hair was smoothed back in the twist thing Sam named, but instead of looking harsh, it just highlighted her high cheekbones and big brown eyes. She was wearing what looked like a pantsuit, which on a Saturday morning around here *did* make her stick out like a sore thumb, but which fitted her perfectly, showing off her petite frame and what even *I* had to admit was an impressive chest, so I was pretty sure Daniel would appreciate the view. All in all, this looked like the kind of woman Daniel might have dated... before.

But that was then, right? He'd left that life behind. He lived in O'Leary now. He had a boyfriend.

I swallowed hard as I approached the table. "Hey," I said. "I'm Julian Ross."

She blinked at me expectantly, volunteering nothing, so I continued, "I heard you were looking for Daniel Michaelson."

"You know him?" She tilted her head to the side. "Because no one around here seems to know much about him at all." Her eyes scanned the room, and I saw Jay Turner at the next table carefully pretending he wasn't overhearing us.

"I do. I'm, ah..." I balked at introducing myself as his

boyfriend. Claiming the man in front of the entire diner once was plenty, and it wasn't my place to out Daniel, in any case. "We're close. Who are you?"

She studied me for a second, then shrugged. "I'm Sabrina Sanford." She dropped the name like a pebble into a lake, expecting it to make a ripple, but the name meant nothing to me.

"Sabrina Sanford," she repeated. "His agent? Honestly, if you guys are that close, I'm surprised you haven't heard of me, if only because I harass him twice a week." She grinned.

"His agent," I repeated blankly. Some corner of my brain told me I should be glad that this wasn't a former flame, but I couldn't quite get there. Weren't agents for, like, *big-name* authors?

"His agent. For his books." She mimed typing in the air in front of her, like I was a kindergartener who might not understand her otherwise. "His dad said he's writing again and I want first dibs on whatever he's got. I've got offers he would not *believe*."

"Oh. Yeah. Of course." I rubbed at the back of my neck. "His new book."

"Have you read it?" Her eyes narrowed. "Is it as good as his other stuff?"

I shook my head wordlessly. I hadn't bugged him about reading it or any of his other stuff. I'd been too busy enjoying the way we fit together like puzzle pieces once more, now that all our cards were on the table.

"Well, I'm gonna make sure he sends you a copy after we get this baby published," she said. "One for everyone in the whole town. I've been trying to get him to write again for months. No, *years*! Shit." She chuckled. "Time flies when you're chasing after Daniel Michaelson."

Yeah, it sure did.

Jay Turner leaned over, like he just couldn't stay silent anymore. "Pretty sure Jules won't need your help getting anything from Daniel, miss. Man's gotta expect somethin' for being Daniel's boyfriend." He gave me an encouraging wink.

I rubbed at my eyebrow. So much for subtlety.

"Boyfriend?" Sabrina looked me up and down, and all at once I became aware of the ratty boots I was wearing, the sweatshirt I'd borrowed from Daniel's closet that morning which hung on me, and the fact that I didn't have an ounce of styling product in my hair. "Well. That's an interesting development." She shrugged. "You're cute, honey, I'll give you that, though you're no Norwegian supermodel. But you're a damn sight friendlier than Ingrid ever was." She leaned across the table and widened her eyes. "I'm pretty glad she's his *ex*-wife, to be frank," she confided.

I found myself nodding woodenly, the muscle memory of an appropriate response. But inside, a sound not unlike the torpedo warning on a submarine echoed through my ears. *Battle stations, men!*

Just because Daniel hadn't mentioned an ex-wife didn't mean he wasn't going to tell me about it. I knew that. I knew he'd dated women—dozens, thousands, millions— and it stood to reason that some of them would have been serious relationships, too. This shouldn't have been such a big deal. But I'd been so sure I'd laid all our issues to rest when Daniel and I started talking openly, and this woman with her scientific appraisal of me had just pulled back the covers and showed me that they were very much still awake and alive.

"Daniel is, um… He's helping a friend," I said, trying to smile though my cheeks were numb. "He'll be coming in —*oh*." I glanced out the window and saw Daniel walking past the diner window, listening to a stocky guy I recognized as Bob Henderson, Sam's father, and Paul Fine who ran the movie theater.

God, he looked good. Tall, blond, perfect. Even though he wasn't dressed much differently than I was—old jeans, bed head, sweatshirt—he wore it confidently, making the messy look deliberate and cool.

For as long as I'd known Daniel, I'd looked at him and thought, *He belongs with me.* Even when *he* didn't know I was thinking it, even when *I* didn't want to acknowledge I was thinking it, it rested at the back of my brain. And yeah, part of the reason I'd never pushed him to talk about things before was because I didn't want to rock the boat, but that wasn't the only reason. There was also a part of me that didn't want to think about where he'd been before or *who* he'd been before. Here in O'Leary, he was *my Daniel.*

But now, I looked at him and thought, *Holy shit. He could have so much more.* So much more than this shabby diner and the neighbors who inserted themselves into your conversations. So much more than piña colada pancakes and a tiny cabin in the woods. So much more than a derpy dog with three legs and fresh town drama every ten minutes. So much more than… me.

He'd been married to a Norwegian supermodel for God's sake.

He opened the door and strolled inside and paused to look around the room. He seemed a little uncomfortable and my heart clenched with the knowledge that he was looking for me.

But the second after his eyes lit on mine, they scanned past me to Sabrina, who waved at him animatedly. Studying him closely, I saw his expression go from pleasure, to surprise, then to worry as his eyes flicked back to me.

Yeah, Daniel. I know about the supermodel.

Though, Ingrid, or whoever she was, was incidental at the moment.

Daniel walked forward slowly and maybe a little cautiously. It was almost funny. It *would* have been funny if it was happening to anyone but me. I wondered for a second if he'd pretend we were just friends, but that was unkind. Daniel might have been afraid, but he'd never denied me that way. He was loyal.

He came up right beside me and laid his hand at the small of my back, giving me a quick kiss. And then he turned to Sabrina and his face broke out in a grin.

"Holy shit. How the hell did you get here?"

She rolled her eyes. "One rental car, four hours, and a very twisty road. Come here and give me a hug, you ingrate!" She slid out of her seat and Daniel bent down to embrace her. It was a hug of long friendship, nothing more, but it killed me a little anyway.

He had a whole life out there. How had I never really *gotten* that before?

He let her go and stood back, putting his arm around me again. "You met Julian?"

"Yes. Your boyfriend." Her emphasis on the word suggested they'd be discussing that later.

Daniel nodded, then shook his head in disbelief. "Shit. I just can't believe you're here!"

"I threatened to come and find you," she said, settling back into her seat. "Did you think I was bluffing?"

"Yeah." Daniel ran a hand through his hair. "I absolutely did. This is pretty far from Manhattan."

"Amen, and not just in miles. I asked the lady at the bed and breakfast where I could find a Starbucks, and she laughed and sent me here."

Daniel shrugged. "You get used to it."

"So I see." She laughed and it made her look even prettier. "Sit down. I have so much shit to tell you about."

"Oh." Daniel looked at the two-person table and then at me. "Jules and I were going to eat, but you could join us. We could find a bigger table and—"

"No way!" I blurted. "Don't be ridiculous! You two talk!"

Daniel frowned like he might argue.

"I'm serious," I said, stepping away from his hand. "Your, um, agent came all this way to see you. You can eat pancakes with me… any old time." The words stuck in my mouth because ten minutes ago that would have been true, and now I wasn't sure at all. Either way, I would *not* be something Daniel had to worry about.

"You sure?" Daniel looked at me suspiciously, like he knew I wasn't as okay as I sounded, like he could see the chaos inside my head. Ironically, *that* made it possible for me to smile more naturally, at least for a second.

"I'm positive. We'll talk later."

"Tonight," Daniel insisted. "You can come out to the cabin."

"Sure," I agreed easily. "We'll figure something out lat—"

"Samantha?" someone yelled. "Samantha Louise Henderson! What the hell are you doing here?"

All eyes in the room, including mine, turned around to see Sam's dad, red-faced and stunned, staring at Sam like she was a ghost, and not the friendly kind.

Sam bolted up from the table where I'd left her and gave her dad approximately the same look, with maybe a little fear thrown in the mix. Then she ran around the far side of the diner, ducking around tables, nearly plowing into Diane, who was carrying a tray of breakfast plates that fell to the floor in an enormous clatter, and out the front door.

Theo ran out a half second behind her, and Samantha's father ran out a few seconds after that.

"Well. I guess you do have your own brand of excitement here, hmm?" Sabrina looked distinctly unimpressed.

"Welcome to O'Leary," I told her. And with a quick squeeze of Daniel's hand, I ran out to find my brother.

Chapter Fifteen

DANIEL

"Hey, Jules. Me again. I, uh, texted you earlier. Just wanted to make sure everything was okay with Theo and Sam." I lowered my voice. "And to make sure you were still coming out here tonight. Don't make me hunt you down, baby. Remember, I know you're ticklish. Call me back." I hung up and tossed the phone on the kitchen counter with a clatter, pushing away the nagging sense of worry at the back of my mind.

Sabrina wandered in from the living room. She'd shed her high heels, but was still wearing a tailored suit that probably cost as much as a month's rent for someone here in O'Leary.

She looked about the same as ever, but the incongruity of seeing her here in O'Leary was off-putting. I remembered Julian at Thanksgiving, worrying about his worlds colliding, and all of a sudden, I realized exactly how he felt. The Daniel I'd been the last time I saw Sabrina wasn't the man I was now. This place had changed me. Julian had changed me.

"Everything okay?" Sabrina nodded at the phone.

"Yeah. I think so." I opened a cabinet at random and found coffee mugs, so I decided to brew a pot of coffee for lack of anything else to do.

"You know, I'd like to believe you're distracted because you're so happy to see me," Sabrina said. "Or because you're anxiously awaiting my opinion on the chapters you just let me read. Or because you're overwhelmed with delight at the fact that Copperlane is offering you a deal, sight unseen, that could make both of us a tidy amount of money."

"I *am* happy to see you. And I *am* delighted by the offer. After everything that happened last year, it's amazing." Almost too good to be true.

"I seem to recall telling you last year, before you entered your own personal witness protection program, that it would all be fine. Patience, I told you. These things happen, I told you." She leaned both forearms onto the counter next to the stove, sliding into my field of vision.

I flashed her a small smile before turning the burner on under the coffee pot. "I do remember that. Vaguely."

"But you insisted that you were done with writing. Your muses had all deserted you. Didn't even have the urge to pen a short story, as I recall."

I scowled. *Muses.* I'd never talked about muses in my life.

"I didn't have the urge. Until recently."

"Mmm hmm." She turned to lean her ass against the counter, folding her arms over her chest in a way that showcased her cleavage. I noticed—I mean, how could I help but notice? But it was a distant hum of awareness. Not even a fraction of what I felt when Julian was in the room, even before we'd added benefits to our friendship.

"So what changed?" she asked, and it took me a second

to realize that she was asking about the writing, not my sexual fantasies.

"I did," I said without thinking, but it was true.

"Right." I could feel the weight of her stare as I took down coffee mugs and rifled through the fridge for milk. "Speaking of changes. Are we gonna talk about the cute gay elephant in the room?"

"You think I'm cute?" I said innocently. "I'm touched."

"I meant your boyfriend, though I suppose it could go for either of you. I'm all for love is love, honey, but since when do you play for that team?"

I shrugged. "Since now." Since Julian.

"And how long after he found out about your best-selling books and your trust fund did he manage to convince you that you were gay?"

I threw my head back and laughed. "Are you serious?"

She shook her head. "Look at it from my perspective. You feel like a failure, you wind up depressed. Instead of going into therapy like a normal person, you decide to take a sabbatical or whatever the hell all this is." She circled a hand in the air, like *all this* could indicate the ancient kitchen, the rough cabin with its menagerie of pets, the woods surrounding us, little O'Leary, or all of the above. "You won't return calls or texts, so I have to drag my ass out here to confirm you're still alive, and then I find you've been indoctrinated into some kind of country cult, where the members won't even confirm they know you, and some dude you've known for less than a year has conned you into rethinking your sexual orientation and now he won't even answer your texts." She nodded at the phone on the counter. "What the hell am I supposed to think?"

"Have you ever thought of writing fiction yourself?" I asked. "You kind of have a knack for it."

She tilted her head to the side and stared at me.

"You want to know what made me decide to start writing again? Jules did. Not because he conned me into it, but because he inspired me. As a *friend*. For a year, I didn't even want to *look* at my laptop because all I could see when I did was failure. He helped me remember why I loved writing in the first place. And he sure as hell didn't brainwash me into falling for him." I smirked. "I did that all by myself."

Sabrina looked thoughtful, but she stayed quiet, so I continued.

"You know when I told Julian about my books? *Two weeks ago*. Maybe a little less." She narrowed her eyes, but I nodded firmly. "It's true. I came here as no one, Sabrina. As some dude named Daniel, with no family or friends or connections, no trust fund. I was an asshole to everyone I met—I didn't want friends or connections. I was sick of people. Hell, I was fucking sick of *myself*."

"And Julian worked this miracle?" she asked skeptically. "You don't need therapy, you just needed the love of a good man?"

I felt my face heat. "I could probably still use therapy. But yes. Having a good man like Julian in my life definitely helped. And frankly, so did this place. I don't think I could have changed anything in the city. Hell, I *know* I couldn't. I needed a perspective shift. I needed to realize that the shit I was so worried about—being successful, having a multitude of friends, getting my parents' approval—that's not all I'm good for. A couple of flops don't make a failed career, and a failed career doesn't make a failed life," I paraphrased.

Sabrina sighed and dropped her arms to her sides. "I guess I understand that. This was your *Eat, Pray, Love* period."

"My what?"

She shook her head. "Never mind. It was your sabbatical. A break from the ordinary that helped get you out of your head. I get it now."

I took the coffee off the burner and poured it into mugs without saying anything. I'd called this a sabbatical before, but that didn't feel right anymore. Sabbaticals were temporary—a short stop before you resumed your regularly scheduled life or moved on to something new. This was more like a tectonic shift.

"Well, lots of people are going to be glad to see you back, anyway. Rick Marules asked me just the other day what you were up to. Anna. Heather. Little Carly, the redhead at my office." She ticked off the names on her fingers, counting out a handful of the dozens of people I'd once considered friends. "They all heard I was coming here to get you, and they were *thrilled*. And your father. God. You know, the man actually came by my office this week? *My office*." She snorted. "After being Mr. Butter-wouldn't-melt all fucking summer, telling me to never contact you again, like the villain in some opera, and now he wants *me* to be the missionary who brings you the good news." She rolled her eyes. "But whatever. I guess we all start rethinking our priorities once we—"

"Sabrina, I'm not going back to Manhattan."

I held out her coffee mug, but she didn't take it, so I set it on the counter by her elbow.

"What are you talking about? Of course you are. Now that I've found you and told you about—"

I took a sip of my coffee and shrugged. "I haven't been stranded on a desert island. I have a truck and I know where Manhattan is. I always have. And don't get me wrong, I'm really glad to see you, but you're acting like I've been a face on a milk carton. I chose to come here. Now I'm choosing to stay."

"But Daniel, you can't just duck out on your life! You have people back in the city who care about you. You have opportunities there you'll never get here. That?" She motioned toward the living room. "That stuff you just let me read is your best work in ages. In fact, I'm stealing your laptop so I can finish."

I grinned. "Or I could email it to you." I didn't *want* to care whether she liked it or not, but apparently, it was impossible for me not to. Even now, I still wanted to know someone else was moved or entertained by what I wrote.

"Or you could bring it to me when you come back home, where you belong."

"Home," I repeated. "You know, you and my father are the only people who've attempted to contact me since the day I left. Him, because he feels like I owe him something. You, because you're hoping I'll sign on the dotted line." I tempered the words with a smile.

"Hey!" Sabrina pushed herself off the counter. "That's not fair! I care about you. I wouldn't go traipsing into the fucking Forbidden Forest here for just anyone."

"I know." I grinned. "And I hope you'll come back to visit. Because *this* is my home now. I'm happier here than I ever was back there."

She hesitated. "Daniel, there's something you should know before you make any decisions either way."

Out in the living room, Honoria started barking like she'd spotted a squirrel encroaching on her territory.

"Chill out!" I yelled to the dog. "You're safe!" To Sabrina, I said, "Is it about the offer? Because if me moving back is a requirement, that's gonna be a deal breaker."

"Not that," she said. "It's your father."

Honoria barked again, but I ignored her.

"What about him?"

"Your father hasn't been the same since what happened in August." She sighed. "I'm sure he told you he was fully recovered, but he's not."

I frowned. "Recovered from what?"

Sabrina blinked. "From his collapse." When I stared at her blankly, she added, "At the Sun Party in East Hampton? To benefit the children's hospital?" She shook her head in despair when I remained clueless. "Anyway. It was this big to-do because your dad fainted. They thought it was heat stroke, but they did some tests after the fact and found he'd had an undiagnosed heart attack sometime before and… How the hell do you not know all this, Daniel? It was all over the internet. Well, I mean, if you read the social pages. He ended up giving a huge donation to the hospital where he was taken."

I stared at the hardwood floor, not quite sure how to feel. My father pissed me off like no one else, but he was my *father*. His constant, annoying presence was a given in my life.

"So you're saying he's… what? Sick? Dying?"

"No." She shook her head. "I mean, not that I know of, Daniel, but jeez. I have no clue! He doesn't exactly report his checkups on Snapchat. But he doesn't look…" She broke off and screwed up her mouth. "He doesn't look *right*, I guess. Not like he used to. He looks old."

There was a noise in the doorway to the living room, and I looked up to find Julian there. His mouth was slack, and his eyes were troubled. I didn't have to ask if he'd heard what we'd been talking about.

"Hey," he said. "Sorry, I didn't even think to knock."

"Of course not. Why would you?" I motioned for him to come to me and after a quick glance at Sabrina, he did. He wrapped his arms around my waist and tucked himself into my side. I took a deep breath, feeling my body relax now that he was beside me. "Everything okay with Theo and Sam?"

Julian shrugged. "I guess. They got in Theo's car and drove off this morning, but Theo finally texted me back to say Sam had been grounded and there was a *mix-up* with her dad." He snorted. "Pretty sure the mix-up was that she was grounded and snuck out."

"And you never got your pancakes," I said sadly.

Julian looked up at me in shock and his cheeks turned red, like he was remembering I'd promised them as a reward.

"I could make you some here," I offered.

"*Aaaand* that's my cue to get going."

I frowned at Sabrina. "You don't have to leave."

"To be honest," she said, "I'm dying to get back to your book. Besides, you guys have a lot to talk about." Her mouth scrunched up in a sympathetic grimace. "I'll be staying at the bed and breakfast in town. The, uh, big Victorian one across from the drug store."

It was cute that she assumed there was more than one hotel in O'Leary. As far as I knew, there was the Crabapple Bed and Breakfast and the campground out near the Camden Road, and Sabrina didn't strike me as the type to camp.

"I'll see you tomorrow?" I asked.

She gave me a sly grin. "You will if you want your laptop back. You have no internet and the signal's too shitty for me to email it to myself." Her smile softened when she looked at Julian. "It was nice to meet you."

"Same," Julian said. "Oh, and if you're looking for something different for dinner, the bar across the street and a block down from the Crabapple is great. It's called Hoff's."

Sabrina nodded. "Alright. I'll give it a whirl." She

knocked her knuckles against the kitchen doorframe as she left the room, rustled around for a second collecting her stuff, then the front door slammed behind her.

"I'm sorry for interrupting," Julian said. "I didn't mean to make her feel unwelcome. Honestly, I should have just stayed in town."

"You should be exactly right here where you are." I pulled him against me more fully so we were chest to chest. "How much did you hear?"

"The part about your father." Julian still sounded faintly apologetic.

"I would have told you all about it anyway," I said. "We don't do secrets now, right?"

He laughed shortly. "Right."

"Speaking of which. Ingrid. I swear that wasn't something I consciously held back, Julian. It just never came up and I… I know it sounds like a cop out, but I don't think of her anymore. Ever, really."

"I know you didn't mean it intentionally. I don't care. I mean, *much*. I'll need a minute to work through my mortal jealousy over the fact that you were *married* to the woman, because I'm petty like that. But logically speaking, I don't care."

I rested my lips against the top of his hair, hiding my grin. "I was married to her for a year. And we were together for a year before that. And you know how often I thought about her after the divorce was finalized? Only when someone else brought her up."

He snorted. "Yeah, right."

"Yeah," I repeated. "Right. And we've been dating how long?"

Julian shrugged, his face still buried in my chest. "Jesus, who the hell knows? Do we count it from the day we started being fake boyfriends? Or the day we started, you know, hooking up? Or from almost two weeks ago, when we made it official?"

"Hmm. Or from the lake last summer, since it's basically all been foreplay for me since then," I mused. "I see what you mean."

Julian's head came up. "All foreplay since then, huh?"

"Yep."

"All the deep, meaningful conversations. Foreplay?"

"So much foreplay. But anyway, my *point* was, even after however long it's been, I miss you after *hours*. I don't stop thinking about you anymore. All the different Julians you are… are perfect. Perfect for *me*."

Julian snorted. Then he sighed. "Tell me everything I missed from Sabrina. She has an offer for you?"

"Yeah. It's a good offer. I mean, it's a great offer. I'd be a fool to turn it down."

Julian nodded. "So you're gonna do it?"

"No. I don't think so. I don't need the money and I don't need the drama of publishing again. I like writing just for myself." I brushed the hair off his forehead. "You have no idea how stressful publishing can be."

Julian tilted his head and studied me. "But you gave Sabrina your book to read."

"I…" I blew out a breath. *Caught.* "Yeah."

"Uh-huh. So you might be scared that people won't like it, but you want it to be read. Right?"

"Maybe."

"And we laugh in the face of fear now, right?"

I snorted. "Do we?"

Julian smiled softly. "We do. *You* do. This is a shot at redemption, baby. And you deserve that."

I shrugged. "It's all hypothetical now anyway. Let's see what Sabrina thinks once she reads it."

"And the other thing?" Julian prompted. "Your dad?"

"I don't know, Jules." I chafed his outer arms absently. "I know what I *should* do, but…"

"You'll regret it if you don't," he said solemnly. "Even if it's terrible? Even if it escalates into, like, a fistfight on top of the Empire State Building—"

"Wow. That… would be a hell of an escalation."

"Even if it all goes totally wrong and nothing gets resolved, you'll know you tried. That's a really huge deal. When my dad died—" He hesitated.

"Your mom told me," I said, brushing my thumb over his cheekbone. "The basic facts anyway."

"Did she?" Julian huffed out a laugh. "She must really like you."

"I think she really loves *you*, and she wanted me to know why it's not easy for you to talk about things sometimes."

He nodded. "Yeah. Well. It was *such* a stupid fight we had, Daniel. Looking back—" He shook his head, and his blue eyes went hazy. "It plays out like some kind of teen drama. Not a very good one. And that was such a shitty way for us to leave things, you know? That wasn't *us*. That wasn't *me*. I know he knew that I loved him, and I was just angry." He tapped his temple. "But I don't *know it*." He tapped his chest above his heart. "If I had a chance to talk to him one more time? You'd better believe I'd take it."

I nodded slowly. Julian was right and I knew it, but…

He splayed his palms over my cheeks. "I see you'll need convincing," he teased.

My lips twitched. "You can try."

Julian lifted up on his tiptoes and pressed his lips to mine… and then his phone rang out in the living room.

"Shit. Left it in my coat pocket," he said, stepping back from our embrace and holding up a restraining hand. "Hold that thought. Don't move a muscle."

I grinned and relaxed back against the refrigerator, thinking maybe I could get Julian to move his *convincing* to the bedroom.

But out in the living room, Julian had answered the phone, and I knew immediately that my plans were going to be put on hold.

"Calm down, Theo! I can barely understand you. What do you mean missing? I thought you told me earlier that everything was fine?" Julian huffed out a breath. "How long has she been gone?"

Chapter Sixteen

JULIAN

"Sam's been gone most of the day," Theo said in a frantic whisper. "We left the diner and I took her back to our house, but she was freaking out and afraid her dad would figure out she was here. *Which he did.* He's downstairs right now demanding answers from Mama, and I told them I was gonna try to track her down, but she's not answering her damn phone."

"Theo, start at the beginning. Why is Sam running from her dad?" I looked up as Daniel came into the living room, already frowning in worry.

"Speaker," Daniel mouthed, and then I clicked the button that let Theo's voice play out for us both to hear.

"Jules, it's complicated, okay? I lied earlier about her being grounded. Sam and her dad just don't get along, so she moved out a few months ago. She tried living with her mom and stepdad in Syracuse for a hot minute, but that was even worse. So she told her mom she was coming back to O'Leary, she just didn't… officially come back. Not to her dad's house. Her dad assumed she was with her mom, and her mom thought she was with her dad, until Mr.

Henderson saw her at the diner this morning and realized something was up. He called Sam's mom, and now it's all a huge clusterfuck."

"I had no idea." I looked at Daniel and he shook his head. "Daniel didn't either."

"Is he there?" Theo's voice had a new tension. "Is Daniel with you?"

"Yeah. We're at Daniel's place right now."

"Oh, thank fuck," Theo whispered. "Okay, listen, you need to go out and check the shed."

"The shed?" I asked.

"The one out back that Sam was cleaning out for me." Daniel was already grabbing his jacket from the hook and shrugging it on. "Why, Theo? You think she's hiding there?"

"Shit." Theo sighed. "I might as well tell you because you're gonna see for yourself, but…" He lowered his voice another notch. "Sam's been staying there for a while. Sleeping there. At night."

"What?" Daniel and I chorused in a two-part harmony of outrage.

"In a rickety shed in the woods? What the hell?" I demanded. "It's literally freezing outside. That's incredibly dangerous."

"It's not rickety, it's structurally sound, but it's *cold*. If she needed a place to stay, why wouldn't she just come sleep on my couch?" Daniel asked. "Jesus, Theo. What the hell were you two thinking?"

Daniel held the phone while I grabbed my own coat and tugged it on, along with a pair of gloves. I beckoned Daniel to lean down so I could throw a hat on his head and he smiled at me distractedly.

"It wasn't me, okay? I wanted her to come stay at our house. Mama would have let her. But Mama would have insisted on telling Mr. Henderson, and Sam didn't want her dad to know where she was. So what the hell was I gonna do, Daniel? I could either support a plan I hated, or turn my back on a friend when things got shitty. What kind of choice is that?"

"No kind," Daniel said.

"I don't get why she couldn't let her dad know where she was." I took the phone back as Daniel threw open the door.

"Because he would have made her go back home, Jules. Duh." Theo's voice suggested I was an idiot.

"He would have made her wear a dress and go to an ivy league school or something," Daniel said wryly. "There was constant tension there, it sounded like."

"She told you?" Theo demanded

"A little." But then Daniel looked at me and added, "Not a damn thing about her living in the fucking shed though."

It was really cold out—*dangerously* cold, as Dana Cobb had warned us it would be—and windy, too. With the sun nearly ready to slip below the horizon, it was only going to get colder.

"She knew if she got anyone involved, they would have told her father or gotten the state involved, or something like that, and she just wanted to be left alone. She's gonna be eighteen soon. I was gonna help her get a place after that. She could've stayed here with me, like in your old room, Jules."

I followed Daniel around the side of the house and down an overgrown path I'd never used before to a free-standing shed maybe a hundred feet from the cabin, but hidden from view by a thick stand of trees. It was a windowless wooden structure with a thick metal roof designed to withstand tons of ice and snow, built in roughly the same style as the cabin itself, but with no windows and only one padlocked door large enough to drive a four-wheeler or snowmobile through.

"The last owner used to keep a small tractor here for plowing the driveway," Daniel said. "Along with a pile of junk that's older than anything else on this property. Lamps, furniture, gardening equipment."

"We cleaned all that out," Theo said. "Well, most of it."

"She's not here," Daniel said as we got closer. He made a frustrated noise and ripped the hat off his head. "Where else could she be Theo?"

"Wait, how do you know?" I demanded. "We haven't even been inside yet."

"Padlock on the door, babe." Daniel grabbed a small key from his pocket, and went to work on the lock. "Sam and I both have keys, but she could hardly have locked herself in."

Daniel threw open the door, and we stepped inside.

Hardly any light penetrated the space, so I turned on my phone's flashlight. One side of the shed was still full of junk—what appeared to be an iron bed frame, a couple of metal lockers that might be used to store tools or supplies, lamps, car parts, tarps, and even an old pair of boots.

On the other side of the shed, though, it was clear someone had tried to make themselves at home. Another heavy tarp was spread along the dirt floor to create a kind of makeshift floor. Several sleeping bags were stacked to form a sleeping pallet, with a stuffed backpack for a pillow. There was even a large blue cooler with a frying pan and a coffee pot like Daniel's perched on top.

"Was she *cooking* out here?" I demanded.

Theo was silent.

"Theo, it's done, okay? She's not staying out here

anymore. She shouldn't have been out here in the first place, and you're just lucky nothing bad happened."

"She ate over here a lot, or just ate granola bars. But she'd cook occasionally," he admitted. "If she was able to grab some groceries from the Imperial."

I frowned. "Why wouldn't she be able to grab groceries?"

"No, Jules," Daniel said softly. "He doesn't mean *purchase* groceries. He means to literally grab them."

"It's not her fault!" Theo defended. "She didn't have any money, and she wouldn't let me give her any. She tried to find a job every damn *day*, but everyone wanted permission from her dad, and…" He sighed. "She was gonna pay everyone back once she was eighteen and got work."

"Jesus," I said, as the light finally dawned. "*Sam* is the one who's been going around stealing stuff?" The thief terrorizing O'Leary was a scared seventeen-year-old?

"She only took what she needed," Theo said. "It seriously wasn't even that much. And she didn't take anything expensive, or try to sell any of it. And she stopped completely after Daniel, um…"

"Paid her," Daniel said, rubbing a hand over his forehead. "On Thanksgiving."

"Yeah," Theo said miserably.

"Theo, what has she been doing all this time? Just hanging out here at the cabin?"

"No! She goes to school. She gets good grades. She hangs out in town, with me and with Rae. You've seen her! Her dad never leaves the fucking house. Like, ever. He's unemployed and now his entire day is watching game shows and reruns, and he's taking his bitterness out on her."

"And that sounds terrible," I agreed. "But has he been hurting her, or abusing her psychologically? Because it's hard for me to see how *this* situation is better." I kicked ineffectively at the stuffed backpack.

"Sometimes it seems like it'd be better to live life on your own terms," Daniel said. "And once you realize you might have made a hasty decision, it's hard to find your way back. Things that seem simple from the outside are not fucking simple." He lifted both eyebrows at me.

I nodded slowly. "Okay, well, we need some more ideas, Theo."

"I'm fresh out, bro. She's not here, she's not with Rae because Rae's at work, she's not at Daniel's… Before the shed, she was camping out in a little tent, but I *know* she's not doing that tonight."

Daniel and I exchanged a look, and Daniel shrugged. "You *sure* she wouldn't, Theo? Even if she was that freaked out today?"

Theo hesitated.

"Do you know something else?" I tried to use my best older brother voice, the kind that hopefully compelled him to speak. "Theodore, if you have information—"

"She texted me. Maybe an hour ago. Said she'd found a place to crash tonight and it was warm. I wondered if she'd found a way to heat the shed, but now I think it must be somebody's house."

"So she's safe?"

Theo hesitated, then admitted in a rush, "I don't *know*! And her dad's calling the police, or maybe he already has by now. I need to find her before they do, or else—"

"Or else *what?* Theo, what terrible thing is going to happen if her dad finds her? He's going to make her wear a dress and go to college? Or is he being abusive?" I asked again. "Because those are two very different situations, to me."

"No," Theo admitted. "He's never hurt her. She would

have told me. This is just about him being a controlling asshole."

"Okay. So wouldn't it be better for her to be safe for the next couple months, even if it's with a controlling asshole, than for her to be out on her own? Wouldn't it be even better if we could get Mr. Henderson to agree to let her live at the house with you and Mama?"

"Speaking as someone who's been in this position, Theo, I'm gonna say it would," Daniel volunteered.

"Fine," Theo said, caving. "I'll tell her dad about the text, and he can let the police know. Not that it'll help much. Unless someone actually knows the warmest spot in O'Leary."

"What did you say?" I braced a hand against the side of the shed.

"That's the text she sent me earlier. 'Safe and sound in the literal warmest place in O'Leary. Good for tonight and maybe tomorrow too. No specifics in case they confiscate your phone.' And then a laugh-cry emoji."

"Maybe the police can trace her texts? Isn't that a thing they do on television?" Daniel asked. "Do they even look for runaways Sam's age? Especially if she texted that she'd found a warm place to stay?"

"I guess we need to see," I said, but my mind was caught on the words of Sam's text. The "warmest place in O'Leary" sounded familiar, but I couldn't think why. It might have just been a thought I had about Daniel's cabin, or maybe something that occurred to me at the diner.

"I think she's fine. I was mostly trying to get to her before anyone else did, but maybe that's not such a big deal anymore, because now that her dad knows she's been around, she's not gonna be able to do what she's been doing anyway." Theo sighed. "Sam's good at taking care of herself."

Daniel snorted. "That's debatable. Running away when shit gets hard might seem like the best thing to do. It's really tempting to say *fuck it* and just leave things behind. But you're just delaying the inevitable. Her dad's gonna need to be dealt with eventually." He gave me a rueful glance, and I knew he was thinking about his own father and maybe the other things he'd run away from.

All afternoon, I'd basically been hiding. Technically, I'd been shopping, wrapping, cleaning my apartment, and even organizing my tax receipts when nothing else presented itself. My refrigerator and office were never cleaner than when there was something I wanted to actively avoid thinking about. It hadn't worked very well, though. In between bouts of scrubbing out already-clean crisper bins and scouring the bottom of my bathtub, I'd remember the look on Daniel's face when he saw Sabrina, I'd think about all the opportunities waiting for him in the city, and I'd feel a sick sense of horror that staying here in O'Leary—staying with *me*—could only hold him back.

And I'd realized, while this anxiety was churning in my stomach, that it wasn't *my* decision to make, it was Daniel's. I wasn't gonna be like the dumbass hero of some romantic comedy who proactively breaks up with the love of his life so he won't hold them back. *Gag.* But I was resigning myself to the idea that Daniel would definitely be going back to the city at some point, even before I heard about his father being ill. And once he was there, who knew whether he'd ever decide to come back to O'Leary? Once people left this place, they didn't tend to come back. Though Parker had, so...

"Julian?" Daniel said, stepping closer so I had to tilt my head to look up at him. "What's up?"

I shook my head, thinking of Parker. "The hottest spot in O'Leary, he called it."

"What?"

"Parker's bar. Hoff's. I was with him the other day and he was telling me about all these renovations he's doing."

"Oh, shit!" Theo said excitedly. "That's right. Park's making apartments upstairs. Rae said the back rooms are a mess, and the other day they were cleaning for hours because the workers sprayed in insulation and it kept flying out of tiny cracks in the ceiling like it was snowing in the bar!"

"And did you say Rae was working today, Theo?" Daniel asked.

"Yeah. They were working a day shift, so they're probably getting out right now, or maybe a couple minutes ago."

"And if Sam asked Rae for help?" I prompted.

"Rae would have gotten her upstairs through the back entrance. I'm going to call them," Theo said. "I'll call you back and let you know what they say."

"We should go check anyway," I said. "Even if Rae didn't help her get in, Sam might be there. If she is, we can talk to her. Offer to be there when she sees her dad. Maybe suggest that she contact him to let him know she's okay."

Daniel nodded. Without speaking a word, we both walked out of the shed, he locked the door, and we moved toward the cabin.

"You think I should tell her dad?" Theo asked dubiously. "That it's a possibility?"

"Yeah, I do. We're jumping in my car now, so maybe give us five minutes head start so we can be there to support Sam before her dad shows up. And I'll give Constantine a call and let him know what we're thinking, too, just in case Mr. Henderson's already called the police."

"I'll drive so you can make phone calls," Daniel said, and I nodded.

But when I called Con, I got his voicemail.

"Call Silas," Daniel suggested, driving far too fast down his rutted gravel driveway. "Or call Parker to check if she's upstairs."

But Parker and Silas didn't answer their phones either.

"Where the hell is everyone in O'Leary tonight?" I demanded, hitting the button to call Everett.

Ev answered on the third ring. "Jules! What's up? Saw you run out of the diner this morning and I thought—"

"Ev," I interrupted. "Is Silas there?"

"No." Everett's voice went serious in an instant. "He got called out. Is there a problem? Call dispatch and they can get you through."

"It's not an emergency," I said. "Sam Henderson ran away from home and I have an idea where she might be."

"Oh, that's great! Si and I saw her at the diner this morning, and later her dad called Mitch to see if the police could help find her. I guess the poor guy's a wreck. The guys were looking into it, but then O'Leary Fire called and asked for help working crowd control at a scene, so Mitch, Si, Carmen, and Con all got called in."

"Well, Daniel and I are on our way to check it out. I'll be in touch."

"If you could find her, that'd be really helpful," Ev said. I swear I could hear the clanking of dishes in the background. "Looks like the firefighters are having a bitch of a time getting the fire under control in this weather, so who knows how long it'll be before Si and the others can look for Sam again. I'm bringing them thermoses of soup."

I chuckled. "Best boyfriend ever?"

"You know it," Ev said. "More like buying their good-will since I plan to take Si on a nice long vacation next month. Somewhere warm."

"Damn, doesn't that sound nice? Listen, if you see him, just mention we're heading to Hoff's."

There was a loud, metallic clang, like Ev had dropped his soup pot. "*Shit.* Wait, what?"

"Hoff's bar," I repeated. "That's where I think Sam might be. Upstairs in the new apartment."

"But Jules," Ev said slowly. "Hoff's is where the fire is."

I didn't even have to ask if Daniel had heard. His eyes met mine across the darkness of the car and he began to drive faster.

We ended up parking a fair distance down the street, since most of Weaver was blocked off by barricades, and running the rest of the way on foot. Smoke filled the air, even blocks away, and reflected the glow of the fire, so the entire town was glowed an eerie orange-gold.

There was a crowd of people standing in front of the bar—dozens and dozens of O'Learians, some in coats and hats, others with nothing but t-shirts and jeans like they'd rushed from the bar without their belongings—staring at the fire with horrified, shell-shocked expressions.

"It just happened so fast," someone said.

"There wasn't even an alarm," someone else was saying. "Everything was fine, and then suddenly there was smoke, like something was burning in the kitchen, and the next thing you know…"

We pushed our way to the front of the crowd, which was pressing against the blue barrier that blocked off the street just before the bar. "You guys've gotta step back," Constantine called from the other side of the barricade. "Let the firefighters do their jobs." But the man directly in front of the barrier, Parker Hoffstraeder, stared at the building with a terrible grief written all over his face, and seemed not even to hear Con speaking.

Beyond him, a group of firefighters in their gear were

talking with Mitch and Si, shaking their heads worriedly. Beyond that, more firefighters were up on a ladder, uselessly spraying water from a hose in an attempt to battle the flames.

"Con," I said, jostling my way over to him. "Listen—"

"Jules! Stay back, man. This is the worst fire I've ever *seen*."

"Con, we think there may be someone inside."

Con shook his head. "Nah. One good thing is that Parker saw the smoke coming from the basement and got everyone out before it really started going. Place is gonna be a total loss though. Wouldn't surprise me if it burns to the ground."

With a sickening *pop*, one of the windows on the first floor shattered and fire began to lick up the outside of the building.

"Doesn't help that it's so fucking cold and windy. The second the guys spray water, it basically turns to ice."

"Constantine, listen. Sam Henderson might be upstairs in that building."

Con frowned at me and then at the building. "Impossible. What the fuck would she be doing there?"

"Hiding. In one of the unfinished units upstairs. She was avoiding her dad and it's *possible* she might have gone there to get out of the cold. Rae might have helped her get in."

"Silas! Gideon!" Con called over his shoulder. "Com'ere."

Silas jogged over settling his knit hat on his head, and Gideon Mason in his yellow protective gear followed more slowly behind. "What's up?"

"Jules says Sam Henderson was upstairs."

Si and Gideon exchanged looks and Gideon ran a hand over his face.

"How sure are you, Jules?"

I swallowed. "Fifty fifty? We might know more if we can find Rae Martin. They might have helped her get upstairs through a rear entrance."

"*Fuck*. I can't send my guys in there, Si. It's too fucking hot, the sprinklers aren't fucking working, and I'm concerned about the structural integrity of the fucking place."

I was hardly one to fault a guy for swearing, but Gideon was a little much even for me.

"I'll go," Daniel said. "Give me a coat or whatever. I'll run in."

"Cute," Gideon said. "So heroic. No."

"But—"

"Let me rephrase," Gideon said, more loudly. "Not just no, but no fucking way! It's not a question of willing-ness, it's a question of safety. The building is nearly consumed."

From nearby, Parker gave an agonized gasp.

"The stairs to the apartments are in the back," Silas told Gideon. "And if the upstairs is well-insulated, there's a chance she hasn't been overwhelmed."

"Assuming she's even up there," Gideon reminded us.

"Who's up there?" Bob Henderson demanded. I wasn't sure when he'd arrived or how much he'd heard, but frantic didn't even begin to describe his appearance. Unkempt was pretty much his default appearance, but right now he looked haunted. "Are you talking about Sam? Is she still inside?"

"We don't know, sir," Gideon said, taking control of the situation. "We need to ascertain whether she even—"

"Nothing to ascertain!" he said. "Theo Ross talked to Rae. Sam was upstairs."

"Fuck," Gideon said, and under other circumstances it

would almost have been amusing. Did the man know any other words?

He stepped away to confer with the other firefighters, and Si and Con went with him.

"Are they gonna help her?" Bob said, looking at Daniel and me in panic. "Who's rescuing her?"

I looked at Daniel and he shook his head. The fire was climbing the side of the building faster now, greedy flames licking at the wood-shingle exterior.

"Oh, for God's sake," Bob cried, jamming a hand through his hair. "I'll get her myself."

He pushed his way through the barricade before I even understood what was happening. Daniel tried to grab at his coat to hold him back, but Bob was moving too fast.

I yelled for Con again, but he didn't hear me.

Bob ran past the firefighters, nearly slipping on the icy ground, but he was able to get to the far side of the building unchallenged. One of the firefighters manning a hose yelled for him to stop, but Bob had already disappeared into the roiling smoke.

"Jesus fucking Christ," Gideon said, responding to the other firefighter's alarm. "What's that idiot doing? Chris, Michael, Patrick, go after him. And when you get him out, *sit on him* if you have to!"

The remaining crew members scrambled to follow orders.

"Holy *shit*," I breathed, staring at the building numbly. "Holy shit."

I felt Daniel's arms come around me from behind, and I let myself relax into his embrace for a second.

"She didn't think he loved her," Daniel whispered in my ear.

I turned my head to look at him. "What?"

"They were fighting. He told her if she left his house,

she shouldn't come back." One side of his mouth tipped up in a grim smile. "But he loves her."

"Parker? Parks!" Jamie Burke pushed through the crowd, making his way to Parker. "Jesus Christ. Are you alright?" He grabbed Parker's face with two hands. "Are you okay, baby?"

Parker's face crumpled, and he tipped forward toward Jamie's chest. Jamie's arms swallowed him up, and I could hear Jamie whispering something in Parker's ear as they stood and watched the building burn.

Someone in the crowd behind the barricade on the far side of the street let out a cheer. "They're bringing someone out!

A siren sounded a short alarm as an ambulance arrived on the scene, and the officers moved the barricade so it could get through. Paramedics rushed toward the far side of the building with a stretcher.

It was a long while before we could see anything on our side of the building, and I held on to Daniel's forearm with both hands as I waited to see *which* someone had been brought out. It was a shitty, shitty thought, but I couldn't help being grateful that Daniel was standing with me, and that the people I loved best were safely away from the building.

Eventually, the paramedics rolled the gurney back, and we could see Bob Henderson laying there, his forehead grimy and bleeding, his face covered with an oxygen mask.

"Shit," I breathed. "Sam."

Daniel's arms tightened.

Tears stung my eyes. Theo was going to lose his mind.

But a second later, another giant lump emerged from the smoke, and as it came closer, I could see it was Gideon… with Sam cradled in his arms. She was coughing in rough, chest-racking barks, and her arm was clenched tightly to her chest, but she was conscious. She was *alive*.

"Thank God," Daniel whispered. "*Jesus*."

Constantine walked around the building with a group of firefighters, assessing the burning building stoically. I waved him over, and after finishing his conversation he walked over to us.

"Two more minutes," he said, his voice rough from the smoke in the air. "She would've been gone, Jules."

"What happened?"

"You saw her dad run in after her. He got about two feet in the door, as far as the stairs, before debris fell and knocked him on the head. Fortunately, it's a damn hard head." Con shook his head. "They needed to drag him out before they could go after her. And this is why you don't run into burning buildings."

"And Sam?"

"She managed to get herself out as far as the landing on the second floor, and they brought her down. Looks like she banged up her arm, and she's suffering from smoke inhalation, but she should be okay." He shook his head. "God, she was lucky. Gideon says the fire went fast—too fast."

"Too fast? What's that mean?" I demanded.

"Arson?" Daniel stared at Con. "They think it was deliberate?"

Con shrugged. "Nobody's saying anything official until the investigation is done. But I will say, there were supposed to be sprinklers in the building and they're clearly not working. That, plus possible use of an accelerant? If it were me, I'd start making a list of people who might have a grudge against me."

Parker made a noise like a wounded animal and took a step away from Jamie, toward us. "Someone set the building on fire? Someone… someone destroyed my business?"

Con looked instantly contrite. "*Shit*. I didn't see you there, Parks. Don't mind me. I'm just running my mouth. You know how I am. The fire marshal will do a whole investigation of everything. Speculating doesn't do any—"

But Parker already rounded on Jamie. "Do you really hate me this much, Jamie?"

Jamie's eyes widened. "What?"

"Because I knew you were pissed that I came back." Parker's voice was wrecked with smoke and tight with tears. "I knew you didn't want me in O'Leary. You made that perfectly clear. But I thought you'd come around eventually. I thought if I stuck around long enough, you'd remember you used to love me before you hated me." His nostrils flared and his throat worked. "Guess I lost that bet, huh?"

He pushed his way through the crowd and disappeared.

Chapter Seventeen

DANIEL

"No! It's too early," Julian complained as I rolled over to silence the alarm on my phone. "It's still dark, Daniel."

"I know, baby. Go back to sleep. You don't have to be up for hours yet."

But instead of rolling back to his own spot, he kept rolling until he was tucked against my back with his arm slung over my torso. I smirked, though he couldn't see it.

"Remind me why you have to wake up at the ass-crack of dawn again?" he mumbled into the skin of my back, making me shiver.

"Because I have a good four hour drive even if the traffic's not bad, which it will be since this is Christmas Eve. And because I have some shopping to do for my parents before I leave town. And because I wanted to stop by Sam's house and see her before I get on the road."

Julian grunted. We'd spent the previous morning eating breakfast with Sabrina before she drove back to Manhattan, and almost the entire previous afternoon with Sam, whose father had been discharged from the hospital after a single night of observation. Sam had looked surprisingly fragile, all tucked up on the couch with her arm in a cast and sling, like the fire and the ensuing investigation had knocked all the sass out of her. I figured that might have something to do with the fact that she was back under her dad's roof, too. She and her father had talked for hours, she said yesterday, and they were figuring out how to get along. I knew from experience it wouldn't be easy. They'd lobbed words at each other like grenades, and it would take time and effort to set things right. But after the fire, nothing seemed quite so insurmountable.

"Wait, shopping?" Julian said lifting his head slightly. "*Before* you leave town? Wouldn't you rather wait until you hit civilization, where they have Nieman Marcus?"

"Nope. I've decided I'm getting my mom one of the I-Heart-O'Leary mugs they sell at Hardison Drug."

He snickered. "Oh, I'm sure she'll love it. And your dad? Does he get an O'Leary themed gift too?"

"You know it. I already got his yesterday at the Books and More," I said, turning so I was laying on my back and Julian's head was cradled on my chest. "I got him a picture frame that says *A Gift from O'Leary*."

"Wow. Inspirational."

"I think you mean *simple* and *fitting*." I pinched his side and he yelped gratifyingly. Out in the living room, I heard dog tags jingle.

"You're waking Honoria," I warned him. "Are you gonna get up and feed her?"

"You tickled me!"

"You deserved it. As I was saying, I got him that picture frame, and when I get to the city I'm going to print off a copy of that picture you and I took up on Jane's Peak. Remember?"

"Yeah." His voice was soft. "Was that the second or third time you dragged me up that mountain?"

"Hill. And third, I think. It was after you'd introduced me to the wonder and majesty of Bear Grylls."

I ran my fingers up and down his back, while his fingers traced patterns onto my chest.

"So, you're saying you got your dad a picture of you and me, in a frame from O'Leary."

"I mean, I'll get him a bottle of his favorite scotch, too."

Julian was silent.

"What?" I prompted, squeezing him against me.

"Nothing, really." He shrugged. "Just trying to imagine how your father's going to react to you presenting him with a picture of you and your boyfriend, that's all."

It was my turn to shrug. "I don't know if he'll care all that much. For all his sins, he's not homophobic. I think he'll be startled, and I get that."

Julian nodded minutely.

"But Julian, if he doesn't like it, I don't care. You know that right?" I tilted my head so I could look down at him and tipped his chin toward me with my forefinger, drawing his blue gaze to mine. "I'm going there to talk to them, and hopefully, my father and I will be able to figure out a way to move forward like Sam and her dad are doing. But I'm not there to try to please him, babe. If he likes my choices, great. If he doesn't, I hope he can keep that to himself, or express it in a way that doesn't sound like disapproval, because otherwise, I'm done. And either way, I'll be back in O'Leary in no time. This is my home now."

Julian nodded, but I could see doubt in those eyes, and it killed me that there was no easy way to reassure him. We hadn't been together long enough to trust in our own stability—it had been only two weeks since we'd talked openly for the first time, less than two weeks since we'd had sex. And in that time, Sabrina had come to town, Sam had gone missing, and Parker's bar had burned to the ground. Stability wasn't even on our horizon.

I held him more tightly and let him bury his face in my chest.

"It should take about a week. Maybe a couple extra days, if people have time off over the holiday." I repeated what I'd told him yesterday, and again last night, hoping this time he'd believe me. "I'm going to spend Christmas with my parents in the Hamptons. I promised Sabrina I'd go to her company's holiday party. And I need to make an appointment with my accountant. Then I'll be home."

"Okay. I'll be here when you get back."

"And you're gonna stay here at the cabin?"

"Yes, I told you I would, as long as the weather's not awful. It'll be easier to take care of Honoria and She-Ra out here."

"And after I get back?"

Julian lifted his head to look at me, a frown on his face. "What?"

"After I get back. Will you stay here then, too?" I swallowed. "I mean, we could move to your apartment. But there's more room for the animals here. Or we could just alternate, I guess. Or maybe it's too soon and you want to table this for a little while. I'm fine with that, if you need more time to—"

"Daniel?"

"Yeah?"

"You're rambling."

"Oh." I ran a hand over my face. "Guess I was. Sorry."

"It was very cute," Julian said, prying my hand down so he could press a kiss into the center of my palm. He pushed his toes into the mattress and pushed himself further up the bed, so his lips hovered over mine. "I like to think I've rubbed off on you."

I snorted. "You've rubbed off on me *plenty* of times, baby."

Julian bit my lower lip, then released it quickly. "That was a terrible joke."

"And that was a terrible punishment, if that's what you intended," I said breathlessly. "It's not exactly a behavior deterrent if you—"

"Daniel."

"Yeah?"

"Shut up."

Julian kissed me, rubbing his half-hard dick against my hip, knotting his fingers into the hair on either side of my head.

With a moan, I skimmed my hand down his back and over the curve of his ass. He sucked in a breath that was not quite pain, not quite pleasure.

"Tender?" I asked.

Jules shrugged. "Not too bad," he said, but I was pretty sure he was underselling it. "Besides, you'll be gone tomorrow. I want to still feel you tomorrow night when I'm in this bed alone."

My heart lurched a little at the strain in his voice that he tried to hide, even as my cock jumped at the imagery.

"What about me?" I countered, holding him firmly against me.

"Huh?"

"What about me, tomorrow night? You'll have the animals to keep you warm, but I'll be in bed at my *parents'* house, for God's sake. All alone. Cold..."

"Your parents' house in the Hamptons isn't heated?" he asked dryly. "Did you want to borrow a blanket?"

"Cold in a spiritual, emotional sense, Julian," I said, rolling my hips just a little, so Julian's cock rubbed against my stomach and he hissed.

"Oh." His voice was syrupy thick now. "Not sure how I can fix that for you, unless you want me to come to Long Island with you."

It was tempting. *God* was it tempting. Having Julian beside me would be like donning a Kevlar vest, making me impervious to anything my parents had to say. But then, I was going there partly to make myself vulnerable, to try to set things right. Showing up with my boyfriend in tow would only distract from that purpose. They'd be rude to him—far, far ruder than Angela had been to me on Thanksgiving—just to needle me, and I wouldn't be able to handle it.

Sadly, this was something I had to tackle on my own, just this once.

"I had another idea," I told him. "You could fuck me this time."

We hadn't tried it this way after the first time I'd suggested it, because I fucking loved topping him, and Jules had been perfectly content to bottom. But now, after Julian's earlier words, I wanted it—I wanted to take him inside me, I wanted to feel the lingering sensation even as I drove out of O'Leary. And what's more, I wanted to give this to him. Just one more tiny piece of evidence he could turn over in his mind over this next week, to reassure himself that this was real and that I truly wanted him.

Maybe Julian felt all of that already because he kissed me again, more fervently, bracing himself on my shoulders. He pulled back and stared down at me for a second, panting, like he was trying to memorize my face, and I reached up a hand to cup his cheek. "I'm going to miss you," he said.

He kissed his way down my body, placing a kiss on my chin, then one in the center of my chest, one just below my navel, and one just above my cock. He took me in his mouth—calm, competent Julian, but with eyes that glowed blue fire and told me exactly how much he loved every second.

His fingers toyed with my balls as he sucked, then moved further back brushing across my taint and skimming lightly over my hole. I had to press myself back against the pillow and close my eyes tight so I didn't come from sensory overload.

Jules released my dick with a soft *pop* and laughed lightly, letting his breath ghost over the flesh. "You're so fun. *God.* Half angel, half devil. You suck my cock like you're planning an invasion of Europe or practicing for the Olympics, all strategy and focus, and then the second I touch you, your mind melts down."

"Are you complaining?" I asked in a strangled voice.

"Not even a little. Best of both worlds," he said happily. "Now, lift your knees."

Shit. Okay, that… made this real. But I wanted it. I did. So I complied.

"Oh, *fuck*," Julian breathed. "Baby, I'm not sure if I've ever mentioned this before, but you're really, really hot."

"Yeah?"

"Mmm." He licked a stripe across my hole. "Like, *seriously* hot." And then he repeated the action again and again until I was a quivering bundle of nerves that could do nothing but moan, whine, and beg.

"Julian, please."

"Please what?" He replaced his tongue with one cool, slicked finger and pushed it inside me. "Is this what you need?"

I don't know if it was because I was so relaxed or because I'd magnified the thing in my mind, but the burning sensation was… barely there. Even when he added a second finger and began stretching me open, the quick bite of pain only added to the pleasure.

Maybe I'd been born to do this.

Maybe I'd been born to be with Julian.

"Enough," I said, opening my eyes to see him watching me with abject lust and affection and *need* stamped across his features. "Please, Jules? Fuck me."

Julian swallowed. He leaned over to grab a condom from the table, then sat back on his heels so he could roll it down his length.

The sight made my breathing hitch. *That* was going in *me*. And I wanted it more than I wanted to breathe. "Now," I told him. "Hurry, Jules."

He hesitated for only a second before pushing himself inside me.

Okay. Okay, this was… harder. I sucked in a breath and blew it out, willing the burn to subside. I was so *full*.

"You okay?" Julian pushed the hair back off my forehead, which was so similar to the affectionate gesture I used on him that I couldn't help but smile. "We're gonna go as slow as you want right now, okay?" he soothed. "We can be here all day. Like, did you know that rattlesnake sex can literally last all day? Hours and hours. And I, um, definitely cannot last *that* long. But we can—*Fuck*!"

He shifted and I gasped in pleasure, which he mistook for pain if the frown on his face was anything to go by. Meanwhile, his arms and legs were starting to quiver.

I knew from personal experience just how hard it was to hold back and whatever little tiny part of my heart that wasn't already his took flight from my body and entrusted itself to his keeping.

"Jules, baby, do that again."

His brow wrinkled adorably. "Do what? Do you want me to pull out?"

"Move, *please*. Don't hold back."

"Oh."

He didn't need any further encouragement. He thrust inside me, hard and primal, and Jesus Christ, I felt *claimed*. Owned. Wanted. Accepted. Understood. I'd had a ring on my finger for a year and hadn't understood what commitment was supposed to feel like until now. Until Jules.

The knowledge shook me to my core, and after that it took about ten seconds for me to be on the edge of coming. I grabbed my cock and stroked it once, twice, three times, and then I was coming all over my stomach, all over Julian's stomach, gluing us together in yet another way.

Julian came not long after and I swear I could *feel* the hot pulse of him filling the condom inside me, branding me.

"I'm yours, Julian," I panted, after he'd eased himself out of me, but before I let him leave the bed. "And you are mine."

———

"So." We stood outside in the driveway next to my car and I was attempting, somehow, to say goodbye. It was even harder than I'd imagined. "Call you tonight?"

Julian nodded. "Or text me. Let me know you got there safe."

"I'll call. I'll want to hear your voice," I told him. "And I'll want to say goodnight."

Julian's mouth twitched up at one corner, but his eyes were unrelentingly blank. He was wearing my favorite baggy, gray sweater, and his arms were wrapped around himself like he was trying to protect himself from the wind, or maybe trying to hold himself together.

He was giving me calm, resigned Julian like he thought I'd buy that shit, like I couldn't see the sadness and the fear festering just below the stoic surface, like I hadn't already seen all the Julians and fallen for each and every one.

"And I'll be back in ten days. Two weeks, tops."

Julian nodded. "Sure. Take as long as you need."

"But I don't *want* it to take longer. I want to get back here as soon as possible. You know that, right?"

"Of course I know it." But the look on his face said something different.

"Julian, believe me."

"Daniel, I believe you mean it," he insisted. But I knew believing I *intended* to come back wasn't the same as believing I'd actually be back.

I sighed. The only way to prove it, really, was to do it. To show him that Manhattan couldn't hold me when it lacked the one thing I truly wanted—him.

I pressed a soft kiss to his lips. "Two weeks," I said. "And I'm texting you every day."

"Go months without a text from a guy, and now all of a sudden, he's gonna be texting every day? I used to think you didn't *have* a phone."

"That was back when there was no one I needed to talk to that I couldn't see in person," I reminded him. "Now I do."

Julian smiled at that, a genuine one, and I savored it.

"Oh!" he said. "Hang on. I have a present for you."

He ran to his car and removed a shiny green bag from the trunk. "Open it tomorrow morning."

"Can't I open it now?"

"Is it Christmas now?" he retorted. "No way. Open it tomorrow."

"Okay," I agreed, smiling. "I left yours in the top drawer of my dresser. It's not much. I'll bring you back something better." I'd gotten him a little Christmas orna-ment shaped like a squirrel, just in case we ever forgot the cockblocking assholes that helped bring us together.

"I'm sure it's perfect and I'll treasure whatever it is," he said solemnly. His eyes filled with tears, but he blinked them away. "Okay, goodbyes *suck*. So just give me a kiss and leave fast." He hesitated, then added, "And come home fast."

I swallowed and did exactly as he asked, pressing my lips to his and then getting in the car without another word. It was one of the harder things I'd ever had to do.

I made it about an hour before I pulled over at a rest area, grabbed the foil bag I'd thrown on the passenger's seat, and reached inside. I pulled out a hand-written note in Julian's tidy block print and… a whittling kit.

Dear Daniel —

Just because you're not good at something immediately doesn't mean you won't be.

Keep trying. I believe in you. And I love you.

—Julian

Two weeks, I reminded myself, tracing my thumb over the word *love*. Maybe less.

Chapter Eighteen

JULIAN

"SOMEONE NEEDS to explain to me what the fuck that movie was about," Caelan James demanded as we walked out of the Fine Theater into a lightly falling January snow. The temperature was almost mild and the air was perfectly still, our voices absorbed by the swirling flakes like we were in a sound-proofed chamber.

"Well, there was a lot of symbolism," Ev began. "Lots of love and redemption themes."

"I don't mean *literally*, Ev." Cal's voice was bitter. "I mean, why do people pay good money to have their fucking hearts ripped out, ground up, flame broiled, and stuffed back in their chests?"

Ash wrapped an arm around Cal's shoulders and pulled the man against his side and pressed a kiss to his temple. "Sorry, baby."

"I think it was beautiful," I offered. "That woman sacrificed everything so that he could be happy. That's what love is, right? Wanting the best for someone even when it hurts?"

"It was beautiful," Silas agreed, "but not particularly uplifting."

"Well, I think it was terrible." Constantine finished buttoning his coat and stuffed his hands in his pocket. "Wasteful. Too bad the woman didn't know it was all going to end that way, or she would have run a mile in the other direction."

"Oh, I don't know," Ash argued. "Think of all the important things we'd miss out on, if we knew in advance they'd end badly. Would you really exchange love for safety, even if you knew it would end eventually?"

Cal made a strangled noise. "God, you're so damn cute. Just… disgustingly cute, Ashley Martin. How the hell did I end up with you?"

"Karmic backlash?" Ash suggested. "And now you're stuck with me?"

"Can't be karma," Cal said solemnly. "I haven't done anything that good."

Ash laughed good-naturedly. Si and Ev exchanged a glance and clasped hands. Con sounded like he was choking.

Walking alone at the back of our little group, I rolled my eyes, confident that no one could see me.

Come with us! they'd said. *It'll be good for you to get out of the house*, they'd said.

Uh-huh.

And then Cal and Ash *and* Si and Everett, had proceeded to act like the happy couples they were the whole time we were at the movie, laughing softly to each other, holding hands, sharing those significant little glances the way people in love so often did. It was a little bit like torture. If it weren't for my brother, who was at least as grumpy as me for reasons I couldn't fathom, I'd have been one very miserable fifth wheel. As it was, I couldn't wait to get back to my apartment, put on my comfiest pajamas, and…

And what? I asked myself for the seven-hundredth time in the past twenty days. *What the hell should I do?*

I pulled my phone from my pocket to check the time and saw a pair of texts from Daniel.

Daniel: Hey, baby. Any big plans for tonight?
Daniel: Are you going to be home at the cabin? Or staying in town?

My thumb hovered over the screen as I considered my reply, which I'd started doing more and more often over the weeks since Daniel left.

Initially, our texts and phone calls had been casual and constant. Daniel had told me about all the things he did for the holiday, and how he was getting along with his parents. His dad had aged a lot in the last year, he said, and finally seemed to understand that Daniel was never going to take over the family business. They'd had actual discussions about things that weren't Daniel's future. His parents wanted to meet me at some point.

But as time wore on and days turned to weeks, conversations between Daniel and me became a little more stilted and a lot less frequent. Daniel sounded frustrated every time I spoke to him, and I knew logically that a lot of it was the endless cycle of delays that had turned his ten-day trip into a three-week odyssey—new tax forms to sign, new business arrangements that needed to be made, more meetings he couldn't miss, and since he was delayed already, more dinner parties and galas his parents begged him to attend, now that they were on better terms.

But the seeds of doubt planted in my head by my brief conversation with Sabrina were insidious, tenacious little fuckers that had grown and swelled into giant doubt *monsters*, rampaging across my brain like Godzilla across Tokyo. The pictures Daniel sent only fed them—the winter beach near his parents' house; him in a tuxedo at a party on New Year's Eve; the view from a window high above all the traffic and bustle of the city. *What would he want back here?* the monsters whispered. *Why would he come back to you now that he's remembered he can have all of that beauty and luxury and opportunity?*

It was pathetic and illogical, and I was a self-sabotaging idiot, but recognizing this didn't seem to matter because there we still were.

So I sent him pictures in return. Pictures of the giant pile of snow Mother Nature had dumped on us last week. A picture of myself on the sofa at Daniel's cabin, curled up under a blanket with the dog and the cat on New Year's Eve. A short video Con had taken of me on Christmas, rambling at the dinner table about the differing origins and social practices of geese and swans. A recap of an email conversation I'd had about finally, *finally* selling my old car.

Funny things.

True things.

Things that showed him I was doing okay, handling my life, so he wouldn't feel guilty for leaving just because I was in love with him.

Things that would remind him of exactly what he'd be getting in exchange for that luxurious life in the city, if he came back here for good someda—

I stopped in the middle of the street in a sudden moment of clarity.

Wow. Wow, I really *was* a self-sabotaging idiot.

Daniel had showed me he cared about me in a hundred tiny ways over the past few weeks. He'd communicated with me. He'd shown me what he was doing and what he was seeing so that I could be with him vicariously. He'd communicated. He'd said he missed me. And what had I done?

I'd reverted to my default settings.

Don't make waves. Don't make him feel guilty. Don't be needy. Don't show him how badly you want him.

But why? Why was it so fucking hard to tell Daniel what *I* needed and wanted? *If you expect him to read your mind, you're fucked*, Parker had said, and things with Daniel had only proven he was right. So what on earth did I have to lose by calling Daniel right this very minute and telling him to get his ass back to O'Leary ASAP? What the hell would it cost me to tell him — out loud, for once — that I loved him?

The group ahead of me had gotten to the corner of Weaver Street and paused, looking right and then left, and I could hear them talking about which way to head for dinner—left to Burger Geek, right to the diner? Neither one really fit the bill anymore. People had quickly become used to Hoff's, and its absence left a void. I'd heard whispers that Parker was thinking about leaving town again and heading back to Boston.

Con noticed I'd stopped and turned to face me. "Hurry up! If you're crying over that fucking movie, Jules, I'm leaving you here."

I shook my head, grinning, and caught up. "Guys, listen, this has been really fun, but I have to get home."

"Exciting plans with your electric blanket and *The Great British Bake Off*?" Con scoffed. "You *have* to come eat with us so I'm not the one lonely loser."

I tilted my head. "No, what I *have* to do is call Daniel." Ideally, so I wouldn't *be* a lonely loser anymore. "If he can't come back this weekend, maybe I can go visit him."

Con nodded approvingly. "Finally pulling your fucking head out of your ass, eh?"

"*Language*, Constantine."

He smirked. "Go get your happy ending, brother."

I pulled him into an impulsive hug and he laughed out loud. "Wow. Somebody spiked your popcorn tonight, Julian Ross, but I like it."

As the guys headed off for burgers, I stood on the corner with my phone in my hand and my heart in my throat. Taking a deep breath, I dialed Daniel's number.

He answered on the first ring.

"Jules! I was just about to call you. Where—"

"No, wait," I interrupted, stalking down the street toward the clinic and home. "Please just wait and listen, because I have to get this out." I swallowed. "I did it again. I stopped telling you how I feel and asking for what I need. And I'm sorry about that. Because the truth is, I miss you so fucking much, Daniel, it's unreal. I miss you kissing me, I miss you teasing me about Romance Novel Book Club, I miss you pushing my hair out of my face all the time, I miss you kissing me, I miss the way you listen, I miss the way you make pie-baking erotic, I miss you every time I see a fucking squirrel, which is really ridiculous, I miss you kissing me—"

"You said that one three times," Daniel laughed.

"Well, yeah, because they're all different kinds of kisses." I slowed my steps as I got to the laundromat right next to the clinic and explained. "There are morning kisses, kisses when I'm standing at the counter in the kitchen and you come up behind me, kisses when we're on the sofa, and those kisses when we're walking out to the car and have to get in separate doors, so you kiss me goodbye before we're separated like you're gonna miss me for the twelve seconds until we're buckled in our seats." I blew out a breath and kicked at the slippery layer of snow that coated the ground. It was really coming down now, and by tomorrow we'd have a foot or more to contend with.

"Anyway, listen, I know you have important shit that you're doing right now, and I do *not* want to distract you, I swear. But maybe I could come down. Like, for a visit. At some point. Or you could come here. Or we could meet halfway, even, because I really—"

"Jules."

"Yeah?"

"Look up."

"Holy shit," I said into the phone as a person who looked an awful lot like Daniel and talked an awful lot like Daniel stepped out of the alcove in front of my bright red door.

I ran at him and jumped, and Daniel caught me with a smile and a soft *oof* sound that made us both laugh.

"You're here," I said, peppering his face with kisses. "You're here, you're here, you're here."

His arms tightened under my ass. "Of course I'm here. I told you I'd be back." He set me down, then bent his head to kiss me as the snow fell around us.

"Come inside," I said, towing him to the door. "Come in and... *oh*."

On the stoop were a suitcase and a medium-sized box, brightly wrapped in blue paper.

"I'm a little late," he said. "But I did tell you I had another present for you."

I bit my lip and pushed open the door, my stomach churning with happiness and nervous anticipation. Was it possible for a stomach to churn with only *good* things? I led him upstairs and busied myself making coffee while he greeted Honoria and She-Ra, hoping the mundane task would help my hands stop shaking.

Didn't work, though. I handed him the coffee with trembling fingers.

He immediately set it on the coffee table and drew me down to his lap. "Why are you shaky?" he demanded, grinning up at me. "Cold?"

I shook my head. "I just can't believe you're here."

He pushed my hair back with his fingers and his eyes were green-gold even in the low light from the lamp. "I missed you, Julian Ross."

"Me too." My face heated. "If you didn't get that from my rambling a minute ago. And I really am sorry that I clammed up when I should have been open."

Daniel shrugged. "How many calm weeks have we had together? Two? It's gonna take time to change our... what's the word again?"

"Internal dialogue?"

"Exactly." He rubbed his thumb over my bottom lip. "But we'll get there. I know it." He hesitated. "And speaking of things we should discuss. Grab your present."

I raised one eyebrow, but leaned over from where I was straddling him to grab the box he'd left next to the couch.

"What is it?" I demanded.

"Don't tell me you're one of *those* people—the kind who want you to tell them what's in the box before they open it."

I grinned and shrugged. "Maybe?"

"Open it, baby."

I pulled off the ribbon and tore at the wrapping, opened the heavy white box and found...

"Papers?"

"A manuscript," he corrected.

"Oh my God. Your book! Or... no... A new JD Pritchard book?" I stared at him in stunned disbelief. "You managed to get me a copy of the new Pritchard when I didn't even know there *was* a new Pritchard? Jesus. I could get used to having connections, you know."

Daniel pursed his lips. "Read it."

"Uh. Okay? *Love Song* by JD Pritchard." I looked up at him. "Thank you so much, really. This is—"

"Keep reading."

I dutifully removed the first page and read the second. "Copyright…"

"Next page."

"*To the love of my life… Julian?*" I looked up at him and down at the book, then up at him, and down again.

Long story short, it took an embarrassingly long time for the penny to drop, while Daniel sat there staring at me with a patient, wary sort of smile on his face, like he wasn't sure if I was going to kill him or kiss him.

I wasn't sure either.

"You are JD… *You* are…? But how could you not tell me? How could…"

Biting his lip and wrapping an arm around the back of my neck, Daniel said, "I told you I wasn't particularly insightful, baby."

"Holy fuck," I breathed, as so many things settled into place. Of course, I'd felt like Daniel and I had known each other for years since the first day we met—in a way, I had.

"You mad?"

I shook my head. Shock was still the predominant emotion, but amusement was following quickly.

I smacked his arm, *hard*. "You know I haven't read Pritchard in *weeks* because I thought you hated him or he'd done something personally awful to you?" I accused.

Daniel chuckled. "Aw. That's really kinda cute."

I narrowed my eyes. "Come to think of it, maybe I am mad."

"Keep reading," Daniel prompted, nudging the box against my stomach.

"*To the love of my life, Julian,*" I repeated, and this time it wasn't my name that tripped me up, but what came before it. "Love of your life?"

He nodded firmly. "The only one."

I took a deep breath and tried to keep reading, even though my blood was fizzing through my veins, making me light-headed.

"*I once thought solitude was perfection when really it was stasis. You taught me that creativity can't blossom in isolation, that sometimes we see each other more clearly than we see ourselves, and that the greatest gift we can ever receive is someone who accepts us just as we are.*

But I still won't eat broccoli on pizza."

I sniffled. "Shut *up.*" I shoved ineffectively at his shoulder.

"You still surprised I came back?" he asked, cradling my face in his big hands.

I shook my head. "No. You came back for the pets, obviously." I took a shuddering breath as I pointed to the dog and cat curled up together on the rug by the radiator.

"Obviously. And?"

"And you really liked those tarts at the bakery."

"Uh-huh. And?"

"And because you love me," I admitted. "Because O'Leary is your home."

"Exactly." He tilted my head down until my lips hovered just above his. "And also because I was fucking *dying* to know if Lady Madelynne ever won that barbarian's heart."

I laughed and leaned down to kiss him, not giving a good goddamn about Lady Madelynne's happily ever after, because I knew that I'd found mine.

———

Want more O'Leary? Julian's brother Con finds love in *The Secret*, the third book in the Love in O'Leary series. Grab your copy here → https://readerlinks.com/l/1570171

And don't miss *The Note*, a Love in O'Leary novella, available here → https://readerlinks.com/l/1570176

About May Archer

May is an M/M author who lives in Boston. She spends her days planning vacations, mainlining diet soda, avoiding the gym, reading M/M romance, and when all other forms of procrastination fail, writing it.

Visit her website at mayarcher.com to sign up for her newsletter to hear about sales and upcoming releases, freebies and behind the scenes info and more! Or join her Facebook group, Club May!

facebook.com/may.archer.author

instagram.com/mayarcherauthor

amazon.com/May-Archer/e/B075JQVGLX

bookbub.com/authors/may-archer

Also by May Archer

Love in O'Leary Series

Whispering Key Series

The Sunday Brothers Series

Copper County Series

The Way Home Series

Licking Thicket Series

(cowritten with Lucy Lennox)

Champion Security Series

(cowritten with Lucy Lennox)

Honeybridge Series

(cowritten with Lucy Lennox)